By Jonathan Kellerman

FICTION

ALEX DELAWARE NOVELS

Serpentine (2021)
The Museum of Desire (2020)
The Wedding Guest (2019)
Night Moves (2018)
Heartbreak Hotel (2017)
Breakdown (2016)
Motive (2015)
Killer (2014)
Guilt (2013)
Victims (2012)
Mystery (2011)
Deception (2010)
Evidence (2009)
Bones (2008)
Compulsion (2008)
Obsession (2007)
Gone (2006)
Rage (2005)

Therapy (2004)
A Cold Heart (2003)
The Murder Book (2002)
Flesh and Blood (2001)
Dr. Death (2000)
Monster (1999)
Survival of the Fittest (1997)
The Clinic (1997)
The Web (1996)
Self-Defense (1995)
Bad Love (1994)
Devil's Waltz (1993)
Private Eyes (1992)
Time Bomb (1990)
Silent Partner (1989)
Over the Edge (1987)
Blood Test (1986)
When the Bough Breaks (1985)

BY JONATHAN KELLERMAN AND JESSE KELLERMAN

Half Moon Bay (2020)
A Measure of Darkness (2018)
Crime Scene (2017)

The Golem of Paris (2015)
The Golem of Hollywood (2014)

OTHER NOVELS

The Murderer's Daughter (2015)
True Detectives (2009)
Capital Crimes (with Faye
Kellerman, 2006)
Twisted (2004)

Double Homicide (with Faye
Kellerman, 2004)
The Conspiracy Club (2003)
Billy Straight (1998)
The Butcher's Theater (1988)

GRAPHIC NOVELS

Silent Partner (2012)

The Web (2012)

NONFICTION

*With Strings Attached: The Art and
Beauty of Vintage Guitars* (2008)
*Savage Spawn: Reflections on Violent
Children* (1999)

Helping the Fearful Child (1981)
*Psychological Aspects of Childhood
Cancer* (1980)

FOR CHILDREN, WRITTEN AND ILLUSTRATED

Jonathan Kellerman's ABC of Weird Creatures (1995)
Daddy, Daddy, Can You Touch the Sky? (1994)

SERPENTINE

JONATHAN KELLERMAN

SERPENTINE

AN ALEX DELAWARE NOVEL

BALLANTINE BOOKS

NEW YORK

Copyright © 2021 by Jonathan Kellerman

Published in the United States by Ballantine Books, an imprint of
Random House, a division of Penguin Random House LLC, New York.

BALLANTINE and the HOUSE colophon are registered trademarks
of Penguin Random House LLC.

ISBN 9780525618553

To Faye

Special thanks to
Clea Koff and Joy Viray

SERPENTINE

CHAPTER

1

My best friend, a seasoned homicide detective, is a master of discontent.

Some say Milo Sturgis *enjoys* the cold comfort of a sour mood.

Grumbling, grimacing, and mumbled curses peak during the muddled middle of murder investigations, when promising leads break their promises. He always gets past it; his solve rate is near-perfect. Which is why his bosses tolerate the biliousness, messages ignored, memos tossed in the trash unread.

I've come to think of Milo as allergic to obedience, wonder if it's rooted in his rookie days when gay cops didn't "exist" in the department and he had to look over his shoulder and write his own rulebook.

But I could be wrong. Temperament's a strong factor in determining personality so it could just be the way he is. I wonder what his baby pictures look like. Imagine him as one of those infants who look as though they've been weaned on sour pickles.

Like a lot of things, we don't talk about it.

◆

He doesn't call me in on all of his cases, just the ones he terms "different" once he's gotten his bearings. This time, he didn't wait.

I picked up his phone message when I returned from an eight a.m. run up Beverly Glen. *"Misery lusts for company, I'm coming over. If it's a problem, text me."*

I left the door unlocked and headed for the shower. Before I took two steps, the bell rang.

He'd called from the road.

"Open."

He barreled through, convex gut leading the way, head lowered, bulky shoulders piled up around his neck like a muscular shawl.

A charging bull if a bull could find an aloha shirt that fit.

He took a moment to stoop and pat the head of my little French bulldog, Blanche, murmured, "At least someone's smiling," and continued toward the kitchen.

Blanche cocked her head and looked up at me, expecting clarification. When I shrugged and followed him in, she gave a world-weary sigh and padded along.

Milo's usual thing is to raid the fridge and assemble snacks worthy of construction permits. This time he filled a coffee cup, sat down heavily at the table, and tugged at the aloha shirt as if aerating his torso. The shirt was sky-blue polyester patterned inexplicably with cellos and bagels. He wore it tucked into baggy khaki cargo pants that puddled over scuffed desert boots.

My true love is a master artisan. She'd designed the kitchen to be sunlit from the south, and this morning's glow was kind to Milo's pallid, pockmarked face. But nothing could mask the cherry-sized lumps rolling up and down his jawline.

I filled a mug and settled across from him. "Now I'm scared."

"By what?"

I pointed to his cup. "No food."

"Sorry for defying your expectations." His lips curled but the end product wasn't a smile. "Maybe I had a big breakfast? Maybe I'm showing discretion?"

"Okay."

"That was a shrink okay if I've ever heard one—which is fine, I need therapy."

I said nothing.

He said, "There it is, the old strategic-silence bit . . . sorry, I'll dial it down." He breathed in and out. Pressed mitt-like palms together. "Namaste or whatever. Glad I caught you." Sip. "Hoping you're free today." Sip. "Are you?"

"Appointments from two to five."

"That'll work." He picked up his cup, put it down. "I plead guilty to acute petulance. But it's called for."

"Tough case."

"It should be so simple." Sausage fingers drummed the table. Another long inhale–exhale. "Okay, here's the deal. Just got a mega-loser shoved in my face like I'm a goddamn rookie. Thirty-six-year-old unsolved. We're talking freezer burn."

"There's a new cold-case campaign?"

"No, there's just *this*. Listen to the chain of command, Alex. An equally rich buddy of Andrea Bauer—remember her?—sits next to a relative of the victim at a rich persons' thing. Bauer butts in, she's connected to the cops, can help. Instead of calling me directly, Bauer contacts a state assemblyman. *He* hands off to the mayor who can't even clear the goddamn sidewalks of garbage, couple of cops downtown just got *typhus* at a homeless encampment."

He pushed his cup to the side. Lowered a fist to the table but stopped short of contact.

"City's returning to the Dark Ages but Handsome Jack's got time to *personally* contact the chief who punts to Deputy Chief Veronique Martz who calls me yesterday just as I'm about to go off-shift. Important meeting, her office, can't be handled over the phone. I drive eighty-six minutes downtown, cool my heels in her waiting room for another twenty, finally get ushered into her sanctum for the ninety seconds it takes for her to give me the victim's name and the basics and warn me not to argue."

I said, "Thin file?"

"She didn't *have* the goddamn file, locating it is part of my assignment. I asked where the basics came from. She said there's a coroner's summary, I should ask for that, too. I called Bauer to ahem thank her. She's in Europe."

Andrea Bauer was the widow of a developer who'd left her a couple hundred million bucks' worth of real estate. Her home base was an estate in Montecito but she owned board-and-care facilities for mentally challenged adults in several states. Last year one of her charges had been murdered along with five other human victims and two dogs. A week after closing the case, Milo had received a Rolex from Bauer. Against the rules. He'd groused, "Steel, not gold?" and sent it back.

I said, "Maybe you should've kept the watch."

He stared at me. Cracked up. Brought the cup back to arm's reach and drank.

As he ingested caffeine, his shoulders lowered a bit. Running his hand over his face, he shot up, went to the fridge and pulled out an apple, sat back down and chomped. "Don't say a thing. This is for the pepsin. Good for digestion."

One bite later: "Thirty-six years."

I said, "Look at it this way: You're the A-student who got rewarded with extra homework."

"The bright side, huh?"

"You said you wanted therapy. Who's the victim?"

"Woman named Dorothy Swoboda, all Martz could tell me is she was found shot to death on Mulholland east of Coldwater. Which isn't even my shop, it's Hollywood Division. Which I noted to Martz. Only to be ignored. Google gives up nothing on it, only thing I've found is in the *Times* archives. Twenty-four years old, found in her car over the side of a cliff, everything burned up. Nothing in the article about murder, the implication was a one-vehicle accident."

I said, "Maybe a bullet was found at autopsy and the paper didn't follow up."

"That would be par for the course," he said. "Even back then, you're not Natalie Wood or O.J. or Baretta, who cares?"

"Who's the relative?"

"Swoboda's daughter, woman named Ellie Barker. Her, Google likes. She made a fortune from exercise wear, sold out a couple years ago for gazillions."

"How old is she?"

His eyebrows arched. "Thirty-nine."

"Three at the time," I said. "She probably has no memories of Mommy."

"Exactly, Alex. This isn't a police thing, it's a psych thing, that's one reason I'd like you along when I talk to her. Maybe you can slide some insight her way and she'll realize she needs you more than me." His smile was an off-center crescent. "Think of it as a potential high-end referral, we both come out ahead."

"What are the other reasons you want me there?"

"Just one," he said. "Turn on the laser, give me your impression of her, so I know who I'm dealing with. Ultra-rich folk expect the world to spin around them. If she's unbalanced on top of that, it could get nasty when I fail."

"When not if."

"I'm being realistic. You know what usually solves the oldies: DNA, bad guy's in CODIS. Thirty-six-year-old homicide, the body burned to a crisp? What's the chance any bio-material was there in the first place, let alone collected. This is a woman who can activate politicians with a phone call. I don't give her what she wants, she's not gonna be charitable."

"A woman who lost her mother at three might be more humbled than you think."

He finished the apple. "You've made a new friend without meeting her?"

"Just pointing out possibilities."

He got up, tossed the core in the trash. "Fine. I'll give her a chance. But the case may not give me one."

"When are you due to meet her?"

"Forty-five minutes, Los Feliz."

"If we leave now, barely enough time to get there."

"So she'll wait," he said. "Good moral training."

2

We took Milo's latest unmarked, an Impala the color of brussels sprouts reeking of pine disinfectant and refried beans. He generally drives with a heavy foot. This time he was ballet-light and a stickler for amber lights. That and traffic clogs from Bel Air into Beverly Hills, the Strip, and Hollywood ate up fifty-five minutes. He savored the red light at Western and Sunset before turning left and climbing the loop that begins Los Feliz Boulevard.

Los Feliz is an interesting district. Unlike the high-end homogeneity of the Westside, it's a kernel of affluence set between the urban grit and enthusiastic crime rate of East Hollywood to the south and the Eden that's Griffith Park to the north. One section, Laughlin Park, is gated, filled with mammoth estates, and boasts a roster of film-biz residents dating back to Cecil B. DeMille, Charlie Chaplin, W. C. Fields, and Rudolph Valentino.

Ellie Barker's address was on Curley Court, a street neither of us knew.

Milo said, "Probably Laughlin, I'll have to get past some rent-a-guard." But GPS proved him wrong and we reached our goal after making an untrammeled right and cruising through a roundabout followed by four brief, open streets.

The Curley Court street sign was nearly obscured by the shaggy branches of a monumental deodar cedar, one of a score that lined the block.

Like its neighbors, the house we were looking for was generous but no mansion: two-story cream-colored Spanish from the twenties with a flat lawn leading to a low-walled courtyard.

The grass had been tended but not coddled; dandelions sprouted like stubble on a carelessly shaved face. Hugging the wall, two forty-foot coconut palms shared space with a pair of equally towering Italian cypresses. Close to an unlocked iron-scroll gate, doddering birds-of-paradise coexisted with spatulate clumps of blue agapanthus.

Old-school landscaping. It would be easy to assume a resident with a traditionalist view, maybe one preoccupied with the past. But my training's led me to run from easy answers. For all I knew, Ellie Barker rented the place.

The courtyard was gravel-floored and empty. The front door had a Gothic peak and was equipped with a rectangular peep-window and a tarnished brass loop for a knocker.

He stood back. "Go for it."

"What do I say, psychologist on duty?"

"Hmph, no sense of adventure." Stepping past me, he lifted the loop and let it fall hard.

From inside the house, a woman's voice trilled, "One second!"

"Cheerful," he said. "Why the hell not when the universe is your toy."

Rapid footsteps followed by a flash of pale eyes in the window, then the door swung wide.

A smiling strawberry blonde held out a hand. "Lieutenant? I'm Ellie."

Milo pretended to not see her fingers. Ellie Barker's smile shrank to something tentative and anxious as she dropped her hand.

Pleasant-looking woman, medium height, medium build, the hair wavy, worn to her shoulders and parted in the middle. Her clothing revealed nothing about socioeconomic status: short-sleeved white jersey top, straight-leg blue jeans, white canvas slip-ons. No jewelry other than an Apple Watch around her left wrist.

Eyes, now doubtful, were gray-green, the skin surrounding them lightly tanned and sporadically freckled. Thirty-nine and showing the advent of laugh lines and forehead furrows.

She looked at me.

Milo said, "This is Dr. Delaware, our consulting psychologist."

I shook her hand and her smile managed to stretch but lose wattage. "Someone thinks I need help? I do but I wasn't thinking psychotherapy."

"Dr. Delaware helps us with unusual cases."

"I see," she said without conviction. "Sorry, please come in."

She led us through a domed Mexican-tiled entry hall and into a step-down living room with a high, wood-beam ceiling. Across the hall, a smaller dining room was brightened by lead-mullioned windows. Cutting through both spaces, a Mexican-tiled staircase climbed to the second floor.

The furniture in the living room was beige and brown and sparse. Bare white walls, unused fireplace lacking tools or a screen. The rental hypothesis gained traction.

"Please, guys." Indicating a three-seat sofa facing a bare oak coffee table. "Can I get you something to drink—Coke, tea, water? I can make some coffee?"

"Water's fine," said Milo, sitting near the left arm of the sofa. I took the opposite end.

"Flat or fizzy?"

"Flat."

Ellie Barker looked at him, hoping for thaw. He studied the ceiling.

She said, "Sure, water coming up," and hurried off past the dining room into a kitchen doorway.

I said, "Looks like the butler's on vacation."

"So she's doing the regular-gal thing for our benefit."

Ellie Barker returned with two bottles of Dasani that she handed to us before settling in a facing love seat. "Thanks so much for doing this, guys. I hope it's not a giant hassle."

Milo checked himself midway through an eye roll.

Not soon enough. Ellie Barker flinched.

Thrown off for the second time, she coped the same way and turned to me. "A psychologist . . . part of me does think it's crazy, trying to find out after all this time. I can't exactly pump myself up with hope. But if I don't ever try . . ." She looked at the floor.

I said, "Is this the first time you've tried?"

"No, it's the third time but to my mind the first two don't count."

"Nothing came of them?"

"Less than nothing," she said. "Private investigators. I think they were taking advantage of me."

"Because . . ."

"It was too quick. Like going through the motions. They were corporate security types, maybe that was my mistake, I don't know." Daring a look at Milo.

He uncapped his water bottle, took a long swig. "Was one of them Sapient Investigations?"

Green-gray eyes widened. "They were the first. How did you—do they have a reputation for taking advantage?"

"They're among the biggest and they concentrate on California. Mostly Northern California where you're originally from. Their emphasis is on computer fraud, industrial espionage, tax cases."

"You researched me."

"Just the basics."

"I see." One slender freckled hand tugged at the fingers of the other. "I got the referral through my executive board—my former board, I had a company that I sold." Small smile. "You probably know that, too."

Milo said, "What was the second outfit?"

"Cortez and Talbott. They're down here. Costa Mesa."

"That's Orange County," said Milo.

"Does that make them a poor choice?" said Ellie Barker.

"Don't know their work, ma'am, but generally it's best to keep things local."

"I guess I figured with the internet, geography wasn't relevant." Color spread around delicate ears. "A friend of mine—an engineer at Google—recommended them, I thought they'd be close enough."

"Did either of them give you written reports?"

"They both gave me one-page letters basically informing me nothing could be done. Plus bills for way more hours than seemed reasonable. I paid them and gave up. Or thought I had. But it kept gnawing at me—wanting to know anything."

She stared into her lap. "I read a story in college titled 'Man Without a Country.' I'm a woman without a past. I have no idea who my biological father is or where I was born. My first birth certificate was when my stepfather adopted me. My mother was already dead and he put down his own mother's birthday as mine. I'll be forty in a few months and I realized I'd probably lived the majority of my life. If that doesn't sound coherent and rational, I can't help it."

She twisted her hair. "At this point, you're probably thinking, Oh boy, a sad case, what a waste of my time."

Gray eyes glistened with moisture. Ellie Barker wiped them hurriedly.

Milo said, "I'll be frank, ma'am. You may be walking up a dead-end road, I don't know enough to say. But if the doctor and I limited ourselves to what was obviously rational, we'd both be out of work."

Ellie Barker's smile was immediate, grateful, pathetic. Needy kid finally getting something from surrogate dad.

"Well," she said, "I just hope you don't think I'm some kind of flake. I majored in business, I like to think I'm practical. I thought I was doing pretty well suppressing the whole thing. Then something weird happened. I was at the Palace of Fine Arts in San Francisco for a fundraiser and they sat me next to a woman and she was really friendly, asking me about myself, how I'd ended up with all the old-folk donors. I was feeling pretty low because I'd just gotten Cortez and Talbott's report so I told her about looking for my mother. She seemed sympathetic, and then the woman on the other side of her must've overheard because she said she had police connections. So I switched seats and talked to her—Dr. Bauer—and she said she'd see what she could do and took my number. The next day she called and said she'd contacted my state assemblyperson, Darrel Hernandez. I didn't even know his name, politics isn't my thing. A few days later, one of Hernandez's assistants phoned and said *she'd* called your mayor and then . . . do you know all this?"

Milo nodded. "The wheels of justice grinding at warp speed."

Ellie Barker flinched. "You think it was tacky? Using an advantage someone else wouldn't have? I considered that, Lieutenant. But it's not like everyone loses their mom at three so I rationalized it as some sort of karmic leveling-out."

"No need to justify, ma'am. I was just commenting on . . . an atypical situation."

Ellie Barker leveled her gaze at him. "You're telling me you were pressured. I guess I should've figured. Does that mean *we're* just going through the motions?"

No anger, just the habitual resignation of an abandoned pup.

"Ms. Barker," said Milo, "I never just go through the motions." He'd sat up straight, put some steel in his voice.

"So you'll try?" said Ellie Barker. "I'd be so grateful. Even if it goes nowhere."

He pulled out his pad. "Tell me about your mother, ma'am. Start from the beginning and tell me everything you know."

"Sure. I do want to say thanks so much—but could you do me one *teensy* favor, Lieutenant?"

"What's that?"

"I'm not used to being called ma'am."

3

E llie Barker opened her mouth to speak, froze, and began fiddling with her fingers.

"Sorry, I'm trying to sort out my thoughts." A tongue-tip raced between her lips. "I could use some water myself, just a second."

She was gone longer than it took to fetch the Dasani dangling from her hand. After sitting, she set about working the cap. It resisted, plastic quivering. She put the bottle down, defeated by shaky fingers.

Her right hand rose to her throat.

Touching a necklace of dark-green speckled beads that she hadn't been wearing when we entered. Fingering orbs like a rosary. Her eyes soared to the ceiling and stayed there.

Milo said, "Take your time."

She shook her head. "Every time I go through this I'm confronted by how little I know. Not that the other guys really cared. They said anything relevant would be found on the internet, they had access to bases I didn't. Is that true?"

"The internet's a tool, no more, no less."

"One of many in your toolbox, I hope."

"We do the best we can, ma'a—Ms. Barker."

"Ellie's fine."

He leaned forward. "Ellie, whatever you think you do or don't know, we have to start somewhere."

"Sure. Of course. Sorry." Another lip-lick. Both hands squeezed the bottle. Bubbles floated and descended. "Okay, here goes. My mother's maiden name was Dorothy Swoboda. When she was with my father— technically he was my stepfather but he's the only dad I ever knew— I assumed she took his name. Barker. Stanley Barker. I found out later they'd never actually married. I don't know who my biological father was because my stepdad had no idea and there's no record of my birth."

"Nowhere?"

"Not as Eleanor Swoboda, not as Eleanor Barker. That one thing Sapient and Cortez looked into and agreed upon. After my dad filed the certificate he got me a Social Security number and that's the extent of it. I never knew about any of this. Why would a kid be concerned with paperwork? And I was happy with my birthday, he always got me a cake."

I said, "When did he tell you he was your stepdad?"

"When I was a teenager."

"How old?" said Milo.

"Fifteen. I wanted to know more about Mom. Up till then I'd never asked. Maybe I was in denial, but it had never been an issue, Dad and me was what I was used to. Then I started being a teenager—questioning everything—and demanded he tell me what he knew. He got a funny look on his face, like he'd been waiting for this moment but dreaded it."

She gave the bottle another try. Frowned. I loosened the cap for her.

"Thank you, where was I . . . okay, I demanded. Dad left the room and returned a few moments later with a glass of whiskey in his hand. He said, 'Sit down, Ellie,' and then he told me there was going to be a lot to handle, was I sure. I said something like 'Fuck, yeah.' Charming, huh?"

Milo said, "Goes with the teen territory."

"And not liking it went with the dad territory," she said. "He was pretty cut-and-dried. When he met Mom she had me, he knew nothing beyond that. I didn't push the bio-dad issue because he already looked pretty stricken and I didn't want to hurt him. Besides, he *was* my real father, I had no interest in some guy who'd abandoned me."

She took a long swallow of water. "The truth was I went from being obnoxious to feeling bad for him. He looked like he was going to cry. I *felt* like I was going to cry. Then he said, 'Let's go out for ice cream,' so we went to Baskin-Robbins."

Small smile. "I remember what I had. Jamoca Almond Fudge in a sugar cone. At first I could barely get it down, like there was a lump here." Tapping a spot above the green necklace. "In retrospect, should I have pushed for more information? Maybe. But he was my dad. It just didn't seem right."

Milo took out his pad and pen. "His full name . . ."

"Stanley Richard Barker. *Doctor* Stanley R. Barker, he was an optometrist."

"How old were you when he and your mom met?"

"Not sure. Dad said a baby."

"And when she died?"

"Not even three, thirty-three months."

"Is Dr. Barker still alive?"

"I wish, Lieutenant. He passed a while back."

"How long ago?"

"When I was in college . . . nineteen years ago."

"Where was college?"

"Stanford. I did my undergrad there and was planning to enroll in the MBA program. When Dad passed, I was in my sophomore year and spending the summer doing research for a professor. European economic history, bone-dry. After Dad passed, I dropped out and got myself what I thought would be a mindless job, working for a clothing manufacturer in Oakland. The funny thing is, it led to some interesting things."

"You started your own company."

She shrugged. "I was lucky."

I said, "You had a good relationship with your dad and didn't want to rock the boat. After he died you didn't need to worry about that."

Her head bobbed and she winced. As if I'd embedded a hook.

"He wasn't a whoop-it-up dad," she said, "but he was a great dad. Quiet, reserved, and incredibly smart. Earned a B.S. in physics from Cornell, came out to California to work for the government then went to optometry school at Berkeley. He was really into optics—not the political cliché, the real thing. He opened up an office in Danville, this upper-crusty place where we ended up living, then a second down in Oakland just so he could service poor people. He probably could've been Pearle Vision or LensCrafters but big business didn't interest him, he just liked helping people see better and made a good living at it. The money he left me helped me bankroll Beterkraft."

She finished her water. "When I was home, we'd play Scrabble or Trivial Pursuit, watch goofy old movies."

Her mouth twitched. Holding something back.

I said, "When you were home from college?"

Another flash of color spread at the edges of her face, this one intense enough to turn her earlobes scarlet. "Before that. I went to boarding school when I was fifteen. Dad had a lot of patience but I turned incredibly difficult—no need to get into the details, let's just say I was a pain and he tried his best and when he finally suggested I try living away, I said sure. Actually, I didn't say it very politely. On one hand, I was thrilled to get away from rules. On the other . . ." Shrug. "But obviously none of that's the issue."

I said, "You asked about your mother when you came home from boarding school."

She stared at me. "No getting around the emotional probing, huh?

Yes. Exactly. Things changed when I was at Milbrook—Milbrook Preparatory Academy for Girls, it's in Palo Alto, a feeder for Stanford. For all my behavioral issues, my grades had always been good. But now I was living with seventy other girls, and girls can get pushy and nosy. Everyone talking about their family, bragging, wanting to know about yours. I knew so little, obviously I didn't want to talk about it. But a few of them pushed and pushed and then they started making fun of me—my parents were spies or criminals. Or worse, welfare cheats. I tried to ignore it but eventually it got to me and I struck out. Literally. I ended up smacking one particularly obnoxious little bitch in the nose and got into major trouble."

She passed the empty bottle from hand to hand. "Two months in and poor Dad has to come and beg the dean to keep me. He convinced her but I saw how much it stressed him, so I promised to keep it together. But by then I'd been tagged as a weirdo loner and everyone avoided me. Which on one hand was good, the questions stopped. But then with the pressure off, I realized the questions were *valid*. Who *was* she and how had she died? Who was *I*? So on Christmas, the next time I was home, I brought it up. Dad told me she'd died, had been cremated, and he'd scattered the ashes in a park somewhere they used to go."

The bottle wobbled and nearly fell out of her hands. She managed to hold on to it, placed it gingerly on the table. "I don't want to tell you how to do your job but, again, is all this really necessary?"

Milo said, "The more we know, the better chance we have."

"Sure but I don't see why—all right, fine, you're here to help me, I won't be obstructive."

"What happened next?"

"Nothing until Dad passed and I broke down, just went numb, the feeling of *aloneness*."

Biting her lip, she looked away. When she spoke next, her voice was weak, tinged with the vibrato of suffering.

"Stanford assigned a nurse to look after me. They suggested I see a counselor but I blew that off. Eventually, I told myself life sucked, I just had to be strong, didn't need a babysitter. I know I was privileged—no money worries because Dad's executor was taking care of me on that level."

"Who was that?"

"Dad's lawyer, Lawrence Kagan. I'd known him as a customer—Larry with the Coke-bottle glasses. I knew Dad liked him but had no idea he trusted him that much."

I said, "Was the trust justified?"

"Totally. Mr. K was honest and lovely to me." She breathed in deeply. "It's when he drove down to Palo Alto to read me the will that I saw the adoption form. Dad had decided to do it after Mom died because I was technically attached to no one. That kind of brought everything back—who was I, where had I come from. Larry had no idea—don't bother contacting him, he's also gone."

She smiled. "That day in his office. He put on one of the Coke-bottles Dad had made for him and shuffled papers like someone out of Dickens. When he showed me the adoption form, it choked me up. That Dad had always cared. Then I noticed Mom's name. Dorothy Swoboda, not Barker, and he explained about no marriage. Which seemed pretty daring for Dad, but maybe it was her idea? Meanwhile, Larry's reading the will, I'm Dad's sole heir and there's a lot of money. It took a while to settle down emotionally. A year or so. That's when I first began looking for information about her using her actual name. I had no idea where to start but figured California was logical. I learned that a lot of personal documents are county forms so I worked my way down from Contra Costa to Alameda, et cetera, et cetera. It was tedious but strangely exciting. Finally I found the coroner's report from L.A. County and then an article in the L.A. *Times*. Confusing because the paper made it sound like a car accident but the report said homicide. That freaked me out. I put the whole thing aside for a long, long time."

I said, "Your family was living in Danville but your mother died in L.A."

"I thought it was weird. Dad certainly never mentioned it. Maybe she was down here on some sort of trip. Or visiting someone?" A beat. "Or they'd separated. I really have no idea. That's part of what I'd like to know."

"Did your dad give any indication of marital problems?"

"Never. But he wouldn't have. He was private. He never talked about her, period."

That sounded more hostile than private. I said nothing.

Milo said, "Did he leave you any photographs of her?"

She held up an index finger, stood and hurried up the stairs. Returned with a folio-sized brown leather album that she thrust at Milo.

Twenty or so oversized pages, each blank but for the first, where a trio of mementos was lodged under horizontal plastic strips.

At the top, a copy of the *Times* piece. Bottom of the page, two brief paragraphs.

Below that was a faded color snapshot with crenellated edges and lowermost, dead center, a negative photostat—white lettering on a black background—of a thirty-six-year-old L.A. County Coroner's death certificate for Dorothy Swoboda, white female, twenties, precise age unknown.

Cause: bullet wound.

Manner: homicide.

Milo tapped the album. "Can I take this?"

Ellie Barker hesitated.

"If it's a problem, you can make copies and send them to me."

"No, it's fine . . . but if you could return it when you're through—"

"I'll make copies and get it back to you." He looked at the photo. "These are your parents?"

She nodded. "There's a date stamp on the back. It was taken when I was two, I have no idea where."

Milo and I studied the shot. Man and woman standing next to each other, a foot of space between them. The setting somewhere outdoors; diamonds of milk-colored sky speckling the gaps in a green-black curtain of trees. Stout trunks, the ground littered with needles.

Some sort of conifer forest. Maybe the place where Stanley Barker had scattered Dorothy's ashes.

He stood on the right. Midforties, average height, pear-shaped, with sparse dark hair and an owlish face made more so by black-framed eyeglasses. Despite the outdoor setting, he wore a light-blue suit with broad lapels, a white shirt buttoned to the neck, and black, bubble-toed shoes.

Hands pressed to his sides, forcing a half smile. Not a natural poser.

The woman was young enough to be his daughter—early to mid-twenties. Long-stemmed and taller than Barker courtesy white spike-heeled sandals and bright-red hair assembled in a sprayed, wavy updo that showed off a pale swan neck.

The face perched on the neck was lean, oval, symmetrical. The right structure for beauty but blocked from beauty by hard eyes and a brittle smile.

Still, a markedly attractive woman, wasp-waisted and full-busted, with curvy contours emphasized by a maroon dress cinched corset-tight by a broad silver belt.

This one liked to pose. She'd placed her hands on her hips, cocked her left haunch slightly higher, and positioned her feet at a forty-five-degree angle from each other.

No jewelry but for a green band worn low around her neck and resting in the hollow above her sternum.

Neither of them dressed for a forest. Neither of them happy.

I said, "Looks like the same necklace you're wearing."

Ellie Barker's fingers climbed to the beads and rested atop them protectively.

"It's the only thing I have of hers. Dad gave it to me after we got back."

"Back from?"

"Ice cream. He'd had it in his pocket and when we were back home, he put it on me. He said everything else of hers had been clothing that he'd given to Goodwill. He said he'd bought the necklace for her at an art fair. She didn't really like it but would wear it when he asked."

"Malachite?"

"Serpentine. Nothing precious, just a rock with minerals— hydrogen magnesium iron phyllosilicate." She smiled. "I memorized that."

Milo took the album, closed it, placed it in his lap.

Ellie Barker said, "I tried to get the details from the coroner but they said something that far back they don't keep full files, I was lucky they had that. I said I'd like to know who killed her and they said that's a police matter. So I went back to the article and it said Mulholland Drive off Coldwater Canyon. I google-mapped and found out one side of Mulholland was Beverly Hills, the other the Hollywood Hills. I tried both police departments, did a lot of waiting while I was on hold. The people I finally spoke to said they'd get back to me but never did. So, again, I gave up. I tend to do that . . . then I went to that fundraiser."

I said, "What was the cause?"

"Children," said Ellie Barker. "Kids whose parents had died."

Milo said, "Any questions before we get going?"

Ellie Barker continued to play with the green beads. "Do you think there's a chance?"

"These old cases are tough unless biological evidence has been preserved. Even then, sometimes all we get is victim DNA. Or there's offender DNA but it can't be matched to any database. But let's see."

"What about familial DNA? All those public-access genealogy files you hear about? Like what they use now to catch killers."

"If we have something to match, we'll use every possible method," said Milo.

"Thanks. I have to say this is the first time I feel I'm being taken seriously. You have my contacts—phone, email."

"Got them from Deputy Chief Martz."

"No idea who that is but thank him for me."

"Her. Sure."

"I'm down here for as long as you need me."

"Where's your home base?"

"I own a house in Napa that I'm renting out. I have a one-year lease on this place."

I said, "Why Los Feliz? Any personal connection?"

"I wanted somewhere reasonably close to where . . . it happened. There were no vacancies up on Mulholland, and this place cropped up for a reasonable rent. I'm not even sure where exactly it happened. If you find out, could you tell me?"

Milo said, "Okay. I should tell you this is a safe neighborhood but a few blocks south it can get rough."

"Oh. Thanks, I'll bear that in mind."

We stood. Ellie Barker pressed forward to shake Milo's hand. Making sure she got hold of it.

"Whatever happens, Lieutenant, thank you so much. At least I'll know I had a professional working for me—no, that came out wrong. You're not my employee."

Milo smiled.

"At least I hope you don't feel that way," she said. "I want you to do your job unobstructed by me or anyone else. You'll be working to discover the truth and I'm sure that's important to you, why else would you choose your career?"

A glance at me. "You, too, of course."

Before we got to the door, a latch turned and it swung open. A man in blue shorts and a white sweat-soaked T-shirt surged in wiping his face with a purple cooling cloth. Fitness watch around his wrist, water bottle clipped to his waistband, earbuds running to a phone that sagged a pocket.

Breathing audibly. He saw us, stopped short, clamped his lips and flared his nostrils.

Out came the earbuds.

Ellie Barker said, "Hon, this is Lieutenant Sturgis and he brought a consulting psychologist. Guys, Brannon Twohy, my still-significant other."

The man said, "Still?"

She pecked Twohy's cheek. He bore it without response. She massaged his biceps. "I'm giving you props for endurance, hon. My doing the quest and all that."

Twohy shrugged. "Is what it is." He draped an arm over her shoulders but left his hand floating in the air, an odd detachment.

Ellie said, "Brannon's been super-supportive but I'm sure he's more realistic than me."

Twohy didn't argue.

He was younger than her, maybe thirty. Tan and rock-jawed with close-set dark eyes uncluttered by curiosity. Deep tan, black and wavy shoulder-length hair.

"I reek, gotta shower."

Ellie said, "How'd it go?"

"Seven point eight miles, record speed."

"Good for you."

Twohy said, "Once I get to eight, I'll be cool."

He headed for the stairs, taking two at a time.

"Brannon gave up his job to come down here with me."

I said, "What kind of work does he do?"

"Marketing. He was working for a consortium of organic vintners in St. Helena, is looking for something here." She eyed the staircase. "I'd better get up there. He'll need an Advil for his muscle aches and unless I suggest it, he won't bother. Thanks, guys."

Milo drove back toward Los Feliz Boulevard, speeding and alarming squirrels.

I said, "What now?"

"Lunch enhanced by finely distilled spirits."

"You can drink on this job?"

"Seeing as it's not a normal gig? Till I hear different," he said. "Which I won't. Who's gonna rat me out?"

◆

He managed a dubious left across three lanes of Los Feliz, descended south to Franklin Avenue, continued west toward the core of commercial Hollywood. Turning left on Cherokee, he pulled into the rear lot of Musso & Frank.

Hundred-year-old restaurant managing to thrive in a city that despises longevity.

The lot's smaller than it used to be, and good slots are at a premium. Milo's badge impressed the lot attendant and he eased between a red Ferrari and a silver Porsche turbo.

He tucked the album under his arm and we entered through the back, the way most people do at Musso. Catching eyefuls of the mammoth stainless-steel kitchen filled with hardworking staff and savory steam.

A red-jacketed waiter nearly as old as the establishment trudged us to a red leather booth. John F. Kennedy had killed the men's hat industry because of an oversized cranium too hard to fit, but this place still featured brass hat racks. The clientele was people old enough to remember the restaurant when it was middle-aged and twenty-somethings yearning for something they couldn't quite figure out.

The waiter looked at us as if sizing up a bin of produce. "Need menus?"

"God forbid," said Milo. "Coupla Martinis, one big unstuffed olive in each, yes to vermouth."

"Without vermoot it's gin. Food to wash it down?"

"Two orders of sand dabs."

"Good." He left at an even slower pace.

I said, "Nothing like a pal who takes charge."

"You'da picked something better?"

"Nope."

"Besides."

"Besides what?"

"I'm paying."

The drinks came quickly.

Milo rolled his olive around, creating glassy swirls in the crystalline liquid before taking an uncharacteristically modest sip. He sat back, smiling. "Nectar of the gods."

I said, "I heard the gods preferred Old-Fashioneds."

"Only the ones in charge of Hades."

I laughed and drank. Crisp as a perfect morning.

He said, "You are now fortified. Proceed with wisdom."

"Give me another look at the photo."

He placed the album on the table, flipped it open, and rotated it facing me.

I said, "Don't want to read too much into one image but these two don't look thrilled to be with each other. Combine that with her not taking his name and ending up four hundred miles from home, a trial separation or a complete breakup at the time of her death should be considered."

"My thoughts exactly," he said, tapping the photo. "This is not a lovey-dovey situation. Toss in no marriage and the commitment level's questionable."

"Barker was committed to Ellie."

"Like she said, good dad. Maybe because he'd come to love Ellie and Dottie *wasn't* a great mom. Cutting out and leaving a three-year-old behind? Or maybe she didn't leave voluntarily."

I said, "Your basic domestic homicide."

"Like you said, no love lost in the photo," he said. "And just playing the odds, who kills women? Guys who supposedly once loved them. Right off the bat, I can see two possibilities: Dottie runs away from Stan out of fear, he tracks her to L.A. and kills her. Or he kills her at home, drives her body far enough to where it's not gonna be connected to him, and sets her on fire."

I said, "And Ellie wouldn't have been a problem witness, given her age. He could've left her with a sitter or a friend. Or he even took her along, sedated, and stashed her in a hotel room while he took care of business."

"Poor kid rides with Daddy unaware Mommy's body is in the trunk? Nasty. However it went down, it worked. Barker was never busted and Ellie's got no memory of anything."

He extracted the olive and ate it. "Just thought of something. According to the *Times* article, Dottie died on a Saturday night. The guy wouldn't even have missed work."

A basket of sourdough French bread arrived. He buttered two substantial chunks and polished them off. "If we're right, Ellie's gonna be *real* thrilled about the outcome. Then again, that assumes I can prove anything."

"Hey," I said, "the quest is what matters, seeing as you're out for truth and justice and kindness toward all living things."

"God, I hate that."

"High expectations?"

"High-level delusions," he said. "Like I was anointed after pulling Excalibur out of a rock without throwing my back out."

His eyes shifted back to the photo. "She's cute but kind of brassy-looking, no? Like she knew how to take care of herself."

I said, "Check out the pose. Like she'd done some modeling. Or wanted to."

He nodded. "Older guy, cute young thing. Maybe she never settled down to blissful pseudo-matrimony and cheated on the Stanster one time too many—hell, maybe she had a boyfriend *with* her in L.A. and that's what brought her down here."

He took a longer swallow of Martini. "Listen to me, getting all hypothetical."

I studied the picture some more. "Not only don't they look romantic, they don't seem to fit together."

He peered. "Dr. Scrabble and Ms. Cocktail Lounge?" His thumbnail pinged the Martini glass. "For her one of these is a nightcap, for him it's warm cocoa?"

"She was a single mother before she met him, unmarried or escaping Ellie's bio-dad. She could've believed she was out for stability but then it got boring and she looked for some excitement."

"She parties, Stanley finds out, and boom."

"Or," I said, "Mr. Excitement turned out to be a bad bet."

"The boyfriend did her?" he said. "Interesting . . . some gigolo rips her money and jewels. Which supposedly she didn't have but are you buying that all she had was that necklace? She looks like a woman who'd go for bling."

I said, "Maybe Barker told Ellie there was no bling to avoid uncomfortable questions. As in he killed her and cashed everything in except for the piece he'd bought her."

"That she didn't like. And he bestows upon the kid. That's a little creepy, no? Putting it on her like some sort of ceremony."

I said, "Ellie doesn't see it that way. The necklace means a lot to her. She wasn't wearing it when we came in but put it on while fetching herself water. Maybe her own ceremony."

"That so?" he said. "Didn't notice." He frowned. "*Shoulda* noticed. Damn—that's why I wanted you there. You're like a laser, lighting up corners."

I shook my head.

He said, "What?"

"Sword, rock, delusions."

"Hey," he said, "you can handle it—and here's the grub. Time to step into reality."

We tucked into sand dabs, potatoes, and green beans, topped the meal with lemon meringue pie. It's not my usual lunch and when we stood, I was fighting torpor.

Milo looked invigorated. He threw cash on the table and we left.

Twelve thirty. Enough time to get me home for my appointments. I said so.

He said, "Oh, that—yeah, sure."

As we got in the car, he said, "Maybe this is irrelevant but Ellie also seems to have found herself an odd fit with Runner Boy."

"She's cheerful, he's borderline grim?"

"That, too, but I was thinking socioeconomic status. All that money she's got. I know, a male tycoon with a hard-body girlfriend, I might not notice. So yeah, I'm caught up in convention, but she is serious rich. I found a reference to the sale of her company in *Forbes.* Quote unquote, 'less than three hundred million.' And she's apologizing about taking Mr. Fitbit away from his nine-to-five. What's that mean? Low self-esteem?"

"No accounting for love."

"Yeah, yeah, insufficient data. But the way she plays herself down—working hard not to come across mega-loaded. Couldn't that mean she feels she doesn't deserve her good fortune?"

I said, "Or she's unpretentious."

"Huh. Okay, I'm meandering into irrelevant stuff." He started up the Impala and sped out of the lot.

"Something else about her bugs me," he said.

"What?"

"I don't hate her."

He tuned the radio to citywide police calls and ignored traffic rules. Free of regular police work he had no reason to absorb the never-ending tide of mostly petty crimes other than to block out conversation. Which was fine with me. I was slipping in and out of caloric drowse.

The dominant calls were 415s. Meaning anything the department viewed as a disturbance. Most frittered out to nothing. Two miles in, I turned down the volume. "What's next?"

"You'll be in your office healing young minds and I'll be fruitlessly looking for information on the late Ms. Swoboda. Seeing as it's Hollywood, I already asked Petra to take a look and see if there're any records. So far zilch. I was hoping that guy at the archive—Jake Lev—could help, but he left the force and, get this, went back to Harvard where he'd dropped out years ago. Go know, huh? Unfortunately the genius they put in his place isn't Ivy League material. If nothing shows up by tomorrow, I'm going down myself."

Checking his Timex. "I'll get you back easily. Custody cases?"

"Two," I said.

"Pays the bills," he said. "But I'm still hoping Ellie'll come through for you as a patient. Less than three hundred mill?"

"Not going to happen," I said. "She's focused on you."

"Huh. Yeah, I'm feeling that." He reached up and touched his shoulder. "Like a pile of boulders right here."

◆

He got me back with time to spare so I walked to the service porch door, descended to the garden, stopped by the pond to feed the fish and net out some leaves, continued to the casita that serves as Robin's studio.

She was working on two projects: rescuing a 1789 Vinaccia mandolin abused by a faculty committee at the U. that had failed to safeguard a donated collection, and tweaking a 1937 Martin D-45 guitar worth 300K for a former folksinger turned property mogul in Connecticut.

The mandolin was all squinty handwork, the guitar past the power-tool stage, so the studio was quiet as she sat assembling specks of inlay.

Painstaking work. I stood back until she put down her tweezers, lifted her magnifying specs, and flashed me a gorgeous smile. Her auburn curls were tied back loosely. Today's bib overalls were red, over a black tee and jeans. She's five-two on a good day and special-orders them at a safety-clothes place in Idaho. They're tough and functional and relent when confronted by her curves.

Blanche remained in place. Long a shop companion, she also knows enough to kick back when the work gets delicate. Once Robin walked toward me, she padded along. The two of them reached me the same time.

"Hi, girls."

Blanche stood on her hind legs and hugged my knees.

Robin said, "Make your choice and live with the consequences."

I swooped Blanche into my arms and let her lick my face as I kissed Robin full and long.

When we unclenched, Robin laughed. "Playing both ends, very devious, darling. Ever consider the diplomatic corps?"

"I prefer honest labor."

"Good point, I prefer you honest. Coffee? It's half-caf."

I touched my gut. "No room for anything."

"How come?"

"Lunched with Big Guy. *À la* Big Guy."

"You gave in to temporary loss of control? I like that. Where'd this gluttony go down?"

"Musso." I gave her the details.

"Sand dabs, I'm jealous. Does that mean a decent dinner's out of the question? I was planning something nice."

"Sure, where do you want to go?"

"There." Pointing at the house. "You cooking."

"No prob, I'll put something together."

"No need to be theoretical," she said. "I read your mind and bought two steelhead fillets."

"Mentalism," I said. "That explains the vibrations here." Tapping my forehead.

"Does it? What about the throbbing here? And here? And *here*?"

I looked over her curls at the shop clock on the far wall. "Appointment in forty-five minutes."

"That won't be a problem," she said. "I'll see to it."

6

By eight thirty p.m., I'd finished two court reports and begun charts on the two kids I'd seen in the afternoon. Robin was back in the studio checking out the mandolin's progress, Blanche was snoring in her open-door crate. I returned to my computer.

Neither Ellie Barker nor Milo had found a thing on Dorothy Swoboda but I looked anyway. Google pulled up one woman by that name, dead since 1895, gravestone in Missouri.

I switched to a broad-based Nexis periodicals search, found only the *Times* squib. Switched the subject to *Stanley Richard Barker* and got three hits.

Two were puff pieces from the *East Bay Times*. Forty-two years ago, "Dr. Stan" had been lauded for donating eye exams and glasses to underprivileged schoolkids. Not in Danville, the paper was quick to point out. In "less affluent neighboring communities."

One year later, Barker had attracted similar praise for opening up a second branch of his SEE-RITE optometric shop in Oakland.

The third reference was a nineteen-year-old obituary in *The San Francisco Examiner:* The body of a Danville man had been discovered by hikers in a gully below a trail in the Las Trampas Regional Wilderness. Stanley R. Barker, sixty-four, a Danville ophthalmologist (*sic*) had been reported missing a week before by an unnamed receptionist.

I looked up the locale, found descriptions on several travel sites specializing in outdoor recreation: five-thousand-plus acres of regional park consisting of two ridges sprawling across Contra Costa and Alameda counties, the nearest city, Danville. Sections had been left wild, others featured marked trails.

Beautiful place according to every source but, with drops approaching a thousand feet, best suited for "highly athletic, experienced hikers under favorable meteorological conditions."

I rechecked the *Examiner* piece. July 15, so probably mild weather, unless Barker had gotten lost and ended up stranded in the dark.

In the photo I'd just seen, Barker was soft-looking. Wearing a suit outdoors. I supposed he could've embraced fitness at an advanced age, but his death-site seemed curious.

What I also found curious was that Ellie Barker hadn't mentioned his unnatural death.

Maybe when balanced against her mother's murder, a fatal accident seemed benign. Or there was just so much bad karma she could tolerate at one time.

Mom in a car, shot and burned and rolled over into a ravine.

Dad found, decaying, in a gully.

There was a certain confluence.

I looked up Wikipedia's description of the park, stopped short at the end of the first paragraph.

Trampas was Spanish for "traps."

I called Milo.

He picked up sounding sleepy.

I said, "Another Martini?"

"Wine at dinner. Rick cooked and he picked a really nice Rioja, how could I say no? What's up?"

I told him about Barker.

He said, "Nineteen years. Seventeen after Dottie, not exactly a pattern."

"True."

"But they did both go over cliffs."

"And Ellie didn't mention it."

"Maybe she wanted to concentrate on Mommy. Speaking of Mommy, Petra called right after I dropped you off. She did come through with something, God bless her. Not the case file, but better than nothing—listing of three D's who worked it."

"Together or in sequence?"

"Passed from one to the other, there was never a task force. The first guy was before my time, D III named Elwin McClatchy. He was on it for six years, retired, died soon after. I know all this because googling him brings up a big departmental funeral, apparently he'd done some heroics as a patrolman. After McClatchy, the case sat there for three years before going to a guy I do know from when he worked at Pacific briefly before retiring. Drone named P. J. Seeger, we talked about a gang case that leaked over to West L.A. and then he was gone."

"Any idea why the case got reactivated?"

"Not yet. This was before cold cases were a thing so it could've been routine housecleaning—new captain comes in, wants to clear the cobwebs. Or the department ran an audit and Hollywood wanted good stats."

"Or Seeger got curious."

"Maybe, but P.J. wasn't an inquisitive guy and the fact that it was given to him tells me it *wasn't* prioritized."

"No Sherlock."

"A dim bulb with low energy. Taaawked-liiike-thiiis, when I got off the phone with him I felt like shooting speed. He held on to Swoboda for five years before transferring so by the time he took his pension, the case was fourteen years old. I didn't expect much from talking to him but no stone and all that, so I dug up the last home number in his file and talked to his widow. Chatty lady lives in the same house in Granada Hills. Turns out P.J. celebrated his newfound freedom by buying a Harley that he crashed fatally a month later."

"She know anything about Swoboda?"

"Nope, Philly never brought his work home. Right after he transferred to Pacific, the case went to a name I don't know, D I named Dudley Gallway."

"Lower-grade detective," I said. "That mean anything?"

"Probably. Haven't found paper or internet info on Gallway yet but I don't feel like attacking the issue under the influence of Spanish wine. Tomorrow I'll ask Petra for some old-timer contacts, maybe take her to Musso as a gesture of gratitude. Speaking of which, lunch was pretty good, no?"

"Great," I said.

"My imagination or did the portions get smaller?"

CHAPTER

7

I heard from him at eleven thirty a.m. the following day.

"Petra got more info, the angel. I offered her a repast but she had a big breakfast, all she wants is ice cream. Hour and a half, McConnell's on the boulevard, if you can make it."

"It'll be nice to see her," I said.

"You bet, form and function. The PC squad comes knocking, I never said that."

The ice cream parlor sported white brick walls, golden hardwood floors, and a spotless freezer case. The ground floor was for ordering and take-out, the eat-in tables upstairs.

I'd taken a while to find parking, arrived to find D III Petra Connor spooning something from a cup as Milo, his back to me, assaulted an unseen target with rapid scooping motions. The only other patrons were a large group of Nordic tourists eating and talking gutturally and guffawing, all in slo-mo.

Petra's one of Hollywood Division's best homicide investigators, promoted via fast-track based on smarts, dependability, and an eye for detail honed during her civilian career as a commercial artist.

Her model-thin frame, ivory angular face, and gleaming black hair created an interesting, borderline-comical counterpoint to Milo's rumpled bulk and assorted convexities. She was dressed, as usual, in a tailored dark pantsuit, this one charcoal, mandarin-collared, buttoned to the neck. An oversized black knit leather bag rested in her lap. When there's a gun in your purse, you don't leave it dangling over your chair.

She saw me and finger-waved. Milo turned around for a moment, resumed eating. The object of his fury was a hot fudge sundae topped with pineapple, maraschino cherries, and sliced almonds.

I pulled up a chair. He said, "You didn't order?"

"I'm fine."

Petra said, "This is Turkish Coffee, Alex. Has a real coffee taste."

"Maybe also real caffeine," said Milo. "If you're flagging." He squinted at me.

"Wide awake. What's up?"

Milo said, "Ms. Ace came through with data."

"That makes it sound like more than it is," said Petra.

"It's a start, kid." He turned to me. "My guess about an audit was right. Found one bemoaned in the police union rag, just before Seeger got the case. And turns out Seeger is recalled by an old-timer."

Petra said, "I knew a guy, Maurice Jardine, went off the job fifteen years ago pushing seventy and is alive and well in Desert Hot Springs. I called him, he's got a sharp memory and his impression of Seeger fits Milo's. Slow-moving, slow-thinking, unlikely to solve anything but an obvious."

I said, "Does Jardine have any memory of Swoboda?"

"None," she said. "Seeger never mentioned the case and there were definitely no meetings on it."

Milo said, "Bureaucratic housecleaning leads to a low-priority bullshit-assignment." He wiped his lips and looked at Petra.

She said, "Jardine also remembered the next link in the chain, Dudley Gallway. Who *he* thought was Gall-*o*-way, but couldn't be sure."

Milo said, "Plenty of lousy spellers in the department so I checked both of them. Nada."

Petra said, "Guy's probably not worth talking to anyway, Jardine said he was a new transfer from somewhere, totally green, didn't stick around long."

"Are we sensing a pattern, Alex? Whatever was done is probably irrelevant. And no paper on Gall-whoever might mean he's also dead. I did look for a certificate and didn't find one but if he met his maker overseas there might not be."

Petra smiled and spooned ice cream. "Tell him your hypothesis."

"What—nah, what's the diff?"

She put her spoon down and turned to me. "I'll do my best to quote faithfully, Alex." She lowered her voice to basso. "'Guy probably bit it south of the border after years of tequila, vanilla, fiestas, and siestas.'"

I pretended to study the sundae. "Vanilla your thing? Looks like chocolate to me."

Milo said, "German chocolate with cookie bits, if you must know."

Petra said, "However . . ."

Milo groaned.

She said, "I learn so much from my superiors, Alex. The lieutenant informs me that in Spanish idiom, *vanilla* can also mean 'sex.'"

I said, "Really. Never knew fun on the beach was your fantasy."

Milo said, "I'm talking a theoretical individual, not personal *vida loca*."

We both looked at him.

He said, "Think what you like but I sack out too long on *la playa*, the Coast Guard gets called out on a beached whale."

"Aw," said Petra, touching the top of his hand. "Nothing fish-like about you. You're a man of earthy substance."

"Whales are mammals, kid, but I'm not gonna quibble seeing as I owe you for taking the time."

"Consider it an even trade."

"What'd you get out of it?"

"It's what I didn't get," she said. "Swoboda died on my patch, there but for the grace."

"Don't rub it in."

Another hand pat. "I commiserate, I really do. Being ordered around by brass monkeys isn't a—ahem—day at the beach."

Fighting back laughter, she ate a third of a spoonful of ice cream. "Though it might've been cool working with Ellie Barker. What's she like?"

Milo said, "Why?"

"You said she was the brains behind Beterkraft. I love their stuff, wear it when I run, Spin, hike, anything active. Super-comfortable, flattering, moisture-wicking."

"You sweat?"

"It's been known to happen."

"Well," he said, "if you feel like opening some serious pores, I can ask the brass monkeys to—"

"That's kind, sir, but no thanks. However, should additional questions regarding miscellaneous details arise in the future, feel free to have your people call my people. Assuming the proper forms have been filled out in triplicate."

Milo extended his arm in a flourish. "And that, ladies and gentlemen, is how she ended up a superstar."

When Petra was gone, his smile faded. "Good intentions but I thought she'd have more. Guess I will have to trek to the archive and waste a bunch of time. Unless you have other ideas."

I shook my head.

"Then mea culpa for bringing you out here. As compensation, let's go downstairs and you buy an ice cream on me, unlimited toppings."

"I'll bring some home to Robin."

"Get a quart—forget that, a gallon. *Ten* gallons, we'll pretend we're in Texas."

"A pint'll be fine."

"Discretion," he said, hitching his trousers. "One day I'll understand the concept."

Driving home, a pint of Turkish Coffee on the passenger seat, I found myself wondering about accidental death.

Nothing deductive or fact-based, just the kind of mental lint that settles in an unsatisfied brain.

Dorothy Swoboda's murder had been staged as a car-crash immolation.

Fourteen years later, a detective assigned to her case had perished on his motorcycle.

Three years after that, Swoboda's widower had tumbled off an isolated cliff.

With all that time separation, a pattern was far-fetched. But . . . how common were fatal accidents? When I got home I'd check.

I'd also try alternative spellings for Dudley Gallway/Galloway, a man Milo figured was deceased.

Wouldn't it be interesting if *he'd* died from something other than illness?

I popped back to Robin's studio and told her about the ice cream. She kissed me, said, "Something to look forward to, thanks," and returned to mandolin micro-surgery.

This time Blanche trailed me back to the house, pausing to take care of business near an azalea bush. One of her customary spots; the blooms were especially lush.

I said, "I thank you for the flowers," and continued to my office.

The previous year, 1,314,000 Americans had succumbed to the three most commonly lethal maladies: Heart disease had claimed 630,000 lives, cancer, a little over 600,000, diabetes, 84,000.

Deaths on motorcycles totaled 5,000. On the face of it, a substantial statistic, but when you did the math, less than a third of one percent of the disease total.

Falls while hiking were so rare they barely registered: 35.

A freak event had taken the life of a man who posed outdoors in a suit.

◆

I began searching for the vanished Dudley Gallway/Galloway, adding *lapd detective* to the subject box and coming up empty. Tacking on *retired* didn't help. Neither did spelling out *los angeles police department*, appending Dorothy Swoboda's name, or repeating the entire process using *dudley galway.*

But *dudley galoway* popped up in three paragraphs retrieved by Nexis.

Ten-year-old article from a weekly called *The Piro Clarion.* Bookmarking, I looked up the town. Fifteen miles north of Simi Valley, population 2,340. Once agricultural, now a golf community.

A decade ago, the descendants of a farming family who'd homesteaded thirty acres of citrus on the outskirts of Piro back in the late 1800s had applied for a zoning variance in order to build "mixed-income housing." Public opinion had immediately massed against the idea with the exception of a city council member named Dara Guzman, who bemoaned "NIMBY small-mindedness. The workers who service our town deserve decent housing."

The other members of the council had squashed the proposal, including Councilman Dudley W. Galoway.

Armed with the proper spelling, I returned to Google.

Nothing.

I texted Milo anyway.

He called back instantaneously. "He worked Swoboda then went into politics. Figures."

"How so?"

"He acquired a taste for accomplishing nothing. Nothing else on him, huh?"

"Not that I could find."

"So he probably is dead. Okay, thanks for taking the time."

"At least you can look up his service records."

"If nothing else comes up, maybe—in the absence of fire, blow smoke. Speaking of which, Chief Martz just called me at home wanting to know how the meeting with Barker went, did I get hold of the file yet, what was my 'proactive progress status.' This from a pencil-jockey who's never investigated a jaywalking. She called Barker 'the client' like this is a private gig. Apparently, I'm supposed to report regularly to 'the client.' Robin dig the ice cream?"

"She's saving it for when she's finished working."

"Delay of gratification, a clear sign of maturity. Or so they say."

I looked up the current Piro city council. Five new names, one of them designated mayor for the year. The *Clarion* had closed down six years ago and no paper or website had taken its place. Coverage of the town was scant—a few brief pieces in the *Ventura County Star* and the *Simi Valley Acorn*—most of it along the lines of "Little Guy, Huge Heart" about a nine-year-old who'd raised money for typhoon victims in Indonesia. What wasn't happy news was straight reporting of bake sales and charity golf tournaments.

"Yum." Robin stood in the doorway, taking her time with a spoonful of Turkish Coffee. Blanche hurried over to her, sat, looked up and smiled.

"Sorry, girlfriend—okay, fine, just a finger-lick."

I said, "She deserves a bit of spoiling. The azalea looks amazing."

"Must be the nitrates." She bent and ruffled the folds of Blanche's neck, then crossed the room and sat down on my battered leather couch. "So what'd you do today?"

I told her, asked if she had any suggestions.

"Why would I have any?"

Last year she'd provided vital info on the limo massacre. I reminded her.

"That was luck," she said. Two nibbles later: "The accident thing is interesting but I see what you mean about all those years in between. Still, first the victim, then a cop looking into it, then the husband, and you think another cop who worked on it could also be dead. Maybe someone doesn't want this raked up."

My phone rang.

Milo said, "Guess who's alive and well and willing to help any way he can."

"Dudley Galoway."

"He goes by 'Du.' As in 'I Du.' Har har."

"How'd you find him?"

"Used the right spelling and got hold of his pension records, which list a cellphone. He retired at forty-five, is only sixty-four now."

"Soon after he picked up Swoboda."

"He said it was an in-and-out. Maybe that's why he sounds hale and hearty. I doubt he can tell me anything, but he was okay schmoozing so tomorrow at two."

"Is he still out in Piro?"

"Ojai. I offered to go there, he said he'd rather drive in to La-La Land and give the old Jag a workout. He's vegan, said anywhere with a salad. Given that, no reason I should trust him but beggars-choosers-losers and all that. I found a place near the station, here's the address."

I clicked off and summed up for Robin. "One less link in the accident chain."

"Well, that's good, something not to worry about, and maybe this guy will have something of value." She smiled. "A preference for plant-based notwithstanding."

9

The unfortunately named Outer House was a couple of miles from the station, on Montana west of Barrington. Inside was a counter staffed by a young woman with a retro blond bob and enough piercings to drive a magnet mad. Dining took place at two rough wooden cable spools turned on their side.

I found Milo glaring at a jam jar filled with liquid the color of a silty river.

"Apple juice," he said, without looking up. "Unfiltered and augmented with ground-up stems and peel. Apparently that's where the vitamins are."

I said, "Fiber."

"Something's gotta give."

Next to us, a white-garbed Sikh couple shared something massive that looked like a burrito. They smiled and I returned the gesture.

Milo said, "You order over there."

"I'm fine."

"What's that, your restaurant mantra? Fine, this time I'm not gonna argue." He tasted the juice. "What it lacks in taste it makes up in grit." He looked at his watch. "Hope the Jag didn't break down."

Only two minutes past the appointed time but antsy. I sat as he checked his email, did a lot of grimly enthusiastic deleting, put the phone down, and pinged the juice jar. "Eight bucks. I'm billing the department."

I said, "They'll probably approve."

"Of what?"

"Taking the healthy approach."

He shuddered. Turned to the front door as it opened.

The man who walked in managed to be thickly built and trim. Six feet tall, a muscular two hundred, great posture, broad-shouldered, with oversized hands and baseball-catcher thighs that filled dark-blue stretch jeans.

He saw us, grinned, and gave a thumbs-up. "Milo? Du Galoway. Hey!"

Galoway's stride was long and confident, his complexion ruddy and smooth for sixty-four. Bright-blue eyes nested in thatches of laugh lines. His hair was thick, coarse, colored an unlikely black. A white collarless peasant shirt billowed over the jeans. The big hands ended in glossy, manicured nails. Sandals revealed equally impressive toenails. He could easily pass for ten years younger. Walking ad for healthy living.

Milo introduced me.

Galoway said, "Psychologist? That's a new one. My day all the psychologists did was try to drum out maladjusts."

Handshakes all around. His palms were soft and dry, his grip cautious, suggesting awareness of latent power. A glance at Milo's juice. "Looks yum. Apple?"

Milo repeated the details.

"That's true, peel's full of good stuff." Galoway patted a flat abdomen. "Our phase of life you need to keep the shipping routes open, right?"

"For sure," said Milo, not coming close to credibility. "You order there. On me, Du."

Galoway strode to the counter, returned with a glass filled with chartreuse fluid.

"Did your apple, added broccoli plus cumin and cardamom and turmeric and just a hint of chili powder. Reasonable, only ten bucks."

Milo fished out a bill.

Galoway sat down. "Not going to happen, pal. I know it's going to come out of your pocket not the department's."

"Either way, I insist, Du."

"Uh-uh, not necessary, you did me a favor." Perfect, blinding white smile.

"What favor is that?"

"Getting me out of the house. I'm not going to lie, life is overall good. But sometimes the days kind of drag. Even after I take my walk and do my biking and three times a week the lifting, then the gardening and the cleanup. Even with twice-a-week yoga there's still a whole bunch of time to fill. I tried taking piano lessons but that didn't work, far from it."

He flexed his fingers. "Tone-deaf and clumsy. Can't draw a straight line so art's out. I thought of bonsai—those little Japanese trees? There's a class near where I live. But it didn't grab me. I even thought of writing a novel but that would take actual talent, right?"

"Happy to fill your day, Du."

Galoway drank and exhaled with pleasure. The ten remained on the table. "C'mon, really, friend."

"I insist."

"Okay, don't want to insult you." Tweezing the bill between thumb and forefinger, Galoway slid it into a jean pocket. "So you're reopening Swoboda. Man, that's a blast from the past, took a sec to figure out the name. What got that going, some cold-case campaign?"

"Swoboda's daughter is mega-rich and she pulled strings."

"The daughter," said Galoway. "One of the things I did when I got the case was try to talk to her, she was some sort of student. But her father didn't want to give me her number, said she had nothing to add. He wasn't cooperative, period. So what, she remembers something after all these years? One of those recuperating memory deals?"

"She knows nothing," said Milo. "That's why she pulled strings."

"Strings. Huh." Galoway finished half his juice, produced another gust of air rife with pleasure. "*Dee*-li-cious. How'd she make her dough?"

"Gym ware."

"Wow," said Galoway. "Go know. So heavy-duty strings."

Milo nodded. "Bridge cables. I was contacted by a deputy chief and ordered to prioritize."

"Same old story, huh? Money talks, cow-slop walks. I had kind of the same feeling when they handed it to me."

"What feeling is that?"

"Strings," said Galoway. "Not that I ever found out for sure."

I said, "Why'd you suspect outside influence?"

"Because it didn't make sense, by then the case was—let me think— fourteen years cold. Don't know how much you know about the particulars, Doc, but I was the third guy assigned to work it. They hand me this skimpy murder book and say go."

"How skimpy?"

"Skimpiest I've ever seen." Galoway measured a quarter of an inch between thumb and forefinger. "Basically just a general description— the one you just gave me, Milo. Plus some illegible notes and the coroner's summary. There wasn't even an address where it went down, just the approximate site. The first guy picked it up when it happened, forget his name. Worked it, got nothing, retired. I tried to call him, too. After that, it sat for like . . . three, four years? Who remembers? The second guy had it for a while. Him I spoke to. His name was Seeger. Not too swift. He still around?"

Milo shook his head. "So neither of them had accomplished much."

"To be honest, neither did I. It was like trying to build a house without a foundation." Galoway frowned. "It felt as I was being set up to fail. I was barely a D I, had something like four months investigating financial crimes under my belt, zero experience with homicide. One day my captain calls me in and tells me I'm transferred to Homicide. I never even applied."

He pushed his glass to the side. "Milo, I'm sure you like what you do. And I've nothing but respect for what you do. But I never had any interest in bodies, my plan was to do financial for a few years, then go back to school for a CPA and get a fed job. Secret Service or the IRS. Or maybe go private and get into industrial security. Homicide? What's that going to do for me? I tried to beg off, it was like talking to a brick. So I must've pissed someone off. Why else would they assign me to a loser?"

Milo said, "Any idea who?"

"No, that's the thing. It was like that writer . . . the guy who turned into a bug?"

I said, "Kafka."

"Exactly, Kafka. It was like him, stuff starts happening and you have no idea. The only thing I could think of was working white collar I got too close to some moneybags. But none of my cases fit the bill, I was strictly small-time."

"Why bother reopening the case if the goal was to fail?"

"You tell me," said Galoway. "Here's the funny thing, rookie me might've actually solved it if I had some decent intel. You know what they say, it's always in the file. I went over that sucker a hundred times, at first it was like reading Chinese."

He jiggled an index finger. "Truth is, I've got a pretty good feeling for who did it. But good luck proving it."

Milo's bulk edged forward. "You developed a lead?"

"No, no, just what I said, a feeling, that's all."

"About what?"

"Well," said Galoway, "I don't want to make more of this than it is but something Seeger wrote down got me going. Though he didn't realize it. His handwriting sucked, you could barely make it out, but once I did I got curious. I played with it for a while, went to my new captain and told him I was making progress. He gives me a look like I just pulled my dick out and wanted to rub it on his face. A few days later, I'm back on financial. After that, I had enough with the job. Department was incentivizing early retirement so I left with my pension and got my real estate license and worked for a brokerage. The plan was to make enough to go back to school but all of a sudden I'm making serious dough selling property so I decided to stick with that a bit longer. Then I get bigger listings and serious commissions. *Then* I start using my earnings to flip houses."

He lifted his juice. "Here's to good luck."

Milo pulled out his pad. "What did Seeger write down?"

Galoway looked uneasy. "Like I said, it was based on a feeling, not evidence. Plus all these years later, it's like I'm handing you a glass of spoiled milk."

"I'll take what I can get, Du."

Galoway looked back at the counter. "Hold on, let me get myself one of those muffins."

10

Fortified by two large bites of a fist-sized, rust-colored concoction laced with pumpkin seeds, Galoway wiped his lips and sat up straight, as if called upon to recite in class.

"You mind if I back up a bit? To make things clear for you."

"Sure," said Milo.

"How much do you know about her? Dorothy."

"She was shot in the head in her car somewhere on the L.A. side of Mulholland, the car was pushed over the side then torched to look like an accident."

Galoway stared at him. "That's it?"

"We just started, Du."

"Wow. Okay. First, I'm going to give you what I see as the psychology—her psychological state, you can appreciate that, Doctor." He cleared his throat. "To me it was obvious she was unhappy with her marriage. She'd left him—what was his name . . . Seymour . . . *Stanley.* Right?"

"Stanley Barker."

"An eye doctor. Right?"

"Right."

Galoway grinned. "Nice to know the memory's got some battery power left. Anyway, Stanley's living up north but Dorothy dies down here. Obviously, that's a red flag. I called him. He didn't sound thrilled to hear from me, I'm thinking this is probably the guy. 'Cause that's what they teach us, right? Start from the inside and work your way out. I figured he'd clam up but he answered my questions, just not with enthusiasm. He admitted they weren't getting along, she'd left him six months before she was killed. No warning. He comes home, there's a note on the bed and the kid's at the next-door neighbor's. Which tells you she had to be pretty miserable. I ask a few more questions—confirming the basics—and we finish. After that, Stanley's not so great about getting back to me. So he stays on top of my list."

I said, "Did you ever meet him face-to-face?"

"That would've required a plane ticket and a hotel, Doc. Milo, tell him the way it is when you're soloing on a loser and ask for dough."

"Got it," I said.

"I'd have loved to sit down with the guy," said Galoway. "You going to?"

Milo said, "He died nineteen years ago."

"Oh. So like . . . two years after I talked to him. Who picked the case up after me?"

"No one."

"All these years?" said Galoway. "Bummer. Anyway, no way was I going to dip into my own pocket. So I'm ready to fold my tents, figuring Stanley got away with it. Then something else Seeger wrote down—this smudged-pencil writing in the corner of a page, you could barely make it out—attracted my attention. The car wasn't hers, it was registered to a company. Precision machining outfit, forget the name."

He tapped his forehead, wrinkled it, tapped again. "Nope, gone, time for some new double A's. Anyway, they made surgical knives, stuff like that. No indication Dorothy's got those types of skills, I'm figuring if she had a job there, she was a secretary, something along those lines. But then I read the file for the zillionth time and the car she was in gets to me. Not a cheapo, we're talking a one-year-old Cadillac Eldorado. Are you getting the same feeling I did, Milo?"

"Young woman, rich guy."

"Bingo," said Galoway, giving a thumbs-up. "Good-looking chick comes to town with no job experience, what's she going to do? Use what God gave her."

"Who owned the car?"

"Exactly, the obvious question. The first guy didn't ask, or if he did, he didn't record it. Same for Seeger. But I sniffed around. Unfortunately, the company wasn't listed locally, so I backtracked with some business directories at the public library and then I went to the newspaper morgue. All of which takes time, by then there's a little internet going on but the department's not using computers except to teach clerks word processing. So we're talking prying open Tut's Tomb with my fingernails. Anyway the owner of the company is a guy named Dee-*barze.* Spelled D-E-S separate word B-A-R-R-E-S, probably a French dude. Anton Des Barres. I check the backwards directory for an address and get nothing, makes sense, rich guys keep it private. So I go to the assessor and Des Barres had a house in L.A. but the last property tax payment was four years ago. I'm thinking shit, he split to France or wherever. But then I wonder if he's dead so I check and sure enough, he kicked the bucket a year before that."

I said, "Cause of death?"

He gave me a pitying smile. "Was he murdered, Doc? That would be juicy but nope, some disease, forget which. But here's something that is juicy: The house was right on Mulholland, maybe two miles east of where they estimate Dorothy was found in that torched Caddy. I say estimate because if the site was recorded, it's lost."

Milo said, "Interesting."

"*I* thought so," said Galoway. "A picture's forming, right? Good-looking chick leaves her old man, comes down here, gets with a rich older guy who gives her a Caddy to tool around in. Then things go bad. I mean they had to, right, for a car like that to get sacrificed? That tells me getting rid of her was a priority. Now I'm feeling some energy. I put it all together and tell my new captain and he gives me that dick-on-the-face look, says you have any actual evidence? I say not yet. A few days later, I'm re-transferred."

"What was your captain's name?"

"Alomar. Gregory Alomar, real bastard. Probably also dead, he smoked like a stack, ate crap, had a gut out to there. Even if he is alive, it's not like he's going to admit being in someone's pocket. But sure, go for it, I'd be interested in what he has to say."

Galoway finished the muffin. "Yum. I may get some takeout, bring it back home for my after-golf snack tomorrow. You play?"

Milo shook his head. "Not enough patience."

"Exactly why you should try it, Milo. Good training for the soul. You, Doc?"

"Nope."

"I thought docs spent their Wednesdays on the course." To Milo. "So did I help?"

"Big-time," said Milo.

"Really?" said Galoway. "That's terrific. Maybe I could've been a homicide D." He laughed. "God forbid."

"Do you have time to show us the spot where she died, Du?"

"Now?"

"If possible."

"Hmm. Sure why not, might as well spend some time in Los Angle-eeze. As Mayor Yorty used to say. Remember him? Sam the Man? My dad loved him—I grew up in Highland Park, this whole thing is bringing back La-La memories. I'll go home to Ojai thanking my lucky stars."

◆

We waited as Galoway bought a bagful of herbaceous goods at the counter. He swung it as we walked him half a block to his car.

The "old Jag" was a red F-type convertible new enough to sport a paper plate.

Milo said, "Pretty wheels."

"A boy needs a hobby. Got room to take one of you."

"How about meeting us in front of the station, we'll get our drive and follow you."

"Your choice," said Galoway. "We've got three routes. Closest east-west-wise is Beverly Glen but it lets you off north of Mulholland so I don't see the point. Closest to the site is Laurel but that means hassling city traffic to get there. So I say let's split the difference and take Cold-water. That work for you?"

"Sounds good, Du."

"Excellent." Galoway clapped Milo's back. "This is kind of fun for an old failure like me. Hope you've got something with an engine. You don't want to be eating my dust."

He tailed us to the station, idled noisily at the curb until we exited the staff lot in Milo's Impala.

"That's it, huh? The big V-8, should be fine." Swinging a U-turn, he sped north to Santa Monica Boulevard and turned right.

Milo said, "Ebullient fellow," and pressed down on the throttle.

I said, "Maybe it's golf."

Galoway's route was Santa Monica Boulevard east through Beverly Hills, then a left on Walden Drive where he crossed Sunset. A right onto Lexington took us into the shade of fifty-foot Canary Island pines that should never have succeeded in L.A. and the massive estates they sentried. Galoway's approach to motoring emphasized advanced tail-gating techniques and speed limits as suggestions. Amber lights meant acceleration. Same for the onset of red lights.

Milo bore down hard as the red Jaguar headed north on Beverly Drive, soon transformed to Coldwater Canyon. Just past a small park to the left, a sightseeing bus blocked the street, a driver on speaker lying to wide-eyed tourists about celebrity addresses.

Galoway passed on the left, narrowly missing a head-on with a southbound gardener's truck.

Milo braked hard and cursed, nudged forward, finally managed his own loop around the bus. The Jaguar was a faint red speck in the distance, rocketing through the high-end suburbia that was Beverly Hills POB.

A five-car queue at the light south of the Mulholland East junction allowed us to catch up.

Milo wiped sweat from his face. "Amazing he made it to his sixties."

Green-lit, the four cars in front of Galoway continued on Coldwater toward Studio City as he swung a radical right onto Mulholland Drive.

The terrain changed immediately, luxury housing ceding to stretches of dry brush and drought-puckered hillside specked by the occasional stilt-propped box. I came to L.A. as a sixteen-year-old college freshman, wondered how hill-houses on chopsticks stayed up. Then storms and quakes came and they didn't. In SoCal, optimism's the fossil fuel.

As we traveled east, straightaways shriveled and the road became a succession of S-curves that ribboned through wilderness. Guardrails girded some sections of pavement but plenty of stretches were unprotected.

Where the road wasn't bordered by trees and scrub and rocks, it offered eye-blink views of steep gorges slaloming down to the city-sized table that had become the San Fernando Valley. At its highest, the sky was unruffled blue. Below that, a mucoid gray cloud hovered.

Galoway picked up speed, brake-tapping at the apex of hairpins then immediately speeding up on the exit swoop.

I said, "Looks like he took high-performance driving."

"Or he's just nuts."

Two more miles of white-knuckle road-churning took us to the Laurel Canyon junction where another red light forced the Jag to snort and wait. When released, the red car bulleted up a sharp rise east of Laurel and raced past a small enclave of ranch houses that looked as if they'd been dropped in place simultaneously. Then, more uninhabited land, broken only by *Fire Hazard* warning signs and reduced speed limits.

About a mile in, Galoway swung an abrupt left across the road and screeched to a stop inches from a particularly battered section of guardrail. By the time we pulled up next to him, he was out of the Jaguar beaming, sunglasses hanging from a neck chain.

"Man, that was the most fun I've had since I took the Skip Barber course at Laguna Seca. You get to strip brakes, end up doing two hours around the track in a Formula Four. I was the oldest guy there but they loved me."

Milo said, "This is the place?"

His failure to chitchat demolished Galoway's smile. He put his shades on. Mirrored lenses. The mouth below them was a hyphen. "It's an estimate. And logical. Take a look around, my friend. You see any addresses? Only thing I had to go on was Seeger's notes. He put down something like one point three miles past Laurel. Am I remembering it wrong after twenty years? Can't promise no, so give or take."

He turned his back, folded his arms across his chest.

Milo walked to the edge of the cliff and stood next to him. "Thanks for taking the time, Du."

"Sure," said Galoway, grudgingly. "What the diff, anyway? It's not like after all this time you're going to get DNA in the brush down there. You saw what it was like coming up here. No people. Anywhere near here would be easy to pull off a car-dump at night."

He ticked a finger. "No streetlights, it's late enough, only thing you're going to encounter are owls and deer and cah-yotes."

Milo got on one knee and craned downward.

Galoway said, "Now you're going to ask me where she landed and I'm going to tell you not a clue." He kicked the guardrail. "Was this here back then? No idea. But there's plenty of places still not railed. Wherever it went down, it's got to be a dead drop for, what, at least five hundred feet? Light it up, push it over, business taken care of."

He rubbed his palms together.

I said, "Who discovered the car?"

Galoway snorted. "You'd think someone would write that down in the book but you'd be wrong."

Milo said, "Any idea where the book got filed?"

Galoway swiveled and faced him. "I wish. It was a loser when I got it and I went nowhere fast. Which was the plan, Alomar didn't want me there. When I quit I handed all my paperwork over to some clerk."

He turned toward the view. "All that crud over the Valley." Down came the shades. The eyes behind them were weary. "Don't mean to be touchy, I guess this brings back bad memories. Working my ass off and accomplishing nothing—you want to see Des Barres's place?"

"If you don't mind."

"Nah," said Galoway. "We're here already."

He led us another 1.9 miles past a spot where another group of houses appeared. Not the homogeneous development just past Laurel. The more typical L.A. random toss of bungalows and mansions and everything in between.

Again, without warning, the Jag made a sudden stop in front of a property on the south side of Mulholland.

Du Galoway got out, expressionless, and pointed to arched iron gates. Returning to the Jag, he flashed a brief smile. "Anything else?"

Milo said, "Can't think of anything."

"Good luck, then." Hooking an oblivious U-ey, Galoway rumbled back toward Laurel.

Milo put on the hand brake and said, "Making friends and losing them."

The property Galoway had indicated was on the corner of Mulholland and Marilyn Drive, hedged by twelve feet of dense, emerald-green ficus. The hedge ran along both streets, far enough on either arm to suggest a huge spread.

We walked to the gates. Two feet lower than the hedge, beefy iron pickets fashioned decades ago and updated by mint-green paint and gilded spearhead finials. A gently curving cobbled road climbed past an alternating array of Mexican fan palms, sagos, and Italian cypresses. At the top of the drive, the barest hint of white wall and red-tiled roof.

Milo said, "This was never anything but serious real estate. Time to learn more about Mr. Des Barres."

11

Sunset Boulevard was relatively fluid, so Milo took Laurel Canyon down to the Strip.

We cruised past dormant nightclubs, hair and nail salons, strip joints, skin palaces, sex shops, and cannabis cafés. Everything topped by gigantic recording- and movie-biz billboards. Some of the boards were electronic and kinetic. More movement up there than among loitering addicts, shuffling homeless, misdirected foreign tourists, and the occasional hooker hungry enough to venture out during daylight.

At San Vicente, Milo said, "On paper, Galoway sounded like the least likely source of info. Go know. What do you think of his conspiracy theory?"

"He was set up to fail? Maybe."

"It happens. But then why open it up at all?"

I said, "We could be talking departmental politics. A token attempt to appease someone, nothing happens, the nets get hauled."

"Who would the brass want to appease? Don't see an optometrist from up north having much pull down here."

"A guy like Des Barres might. So contrary to Galoway's suspicions, he could be a would-be hero not a suspect. Dorothy was his love inter-est, he wanted to know what had happened to her and why."

"Galoway got the case fourteen years after it happened, Alex. Long time to get all sentimental."

I thought about that. "Des Barres died soon after Galoway took over, from some sort of disease. Terminal illness can change your per-spective."

"I guess. Either way, time to learn more about him. Another long-dead person."

"Want me to call Maxine and see if he has an interesting past she knows about?"

Maxine Driver was a history prof at the U., the daughter of Korean immigrants who'd disappointed her parents by rejecting med school to become an expert on L.A. gangsters. In the past, she'd traded informa-tion for early access to closed-case files. Her work product: academic papers, book chapters, presentations at conferences.

Milo said, "Des Barres was a tycoon who hung with sketchy types?"

"A tycoon who shacked up with a much younger woman and gave her a Caddy."

"Good point—sure, ask her. Meanwhile, I'll buy a dust mask and see if I can find the book."

"Galoway said it didn't amount to much."

"Anything's better than nada."

He shifted forward in the driver's seat, jaw jutting, eyes narrow.

Work-mode.

Hooked.

No answer at Maxine's campus office. I was leaving a message on her cell when she broke in.

"Just saw it was you. What's up, Alex?"

"Looking for anything you have on a guy named Anton Des Barres." I went through the same spelling recitation Galoway had given.

She said, "French guy or a guy with a French name?"

"Don't know."

"Doesn't ring a bell, Alex. He a small-timer?"

"Not a hood," I said. "A rich guy who owned a company that made surgical equipment. But there are hints of playboy so I thought he might've hung with some of your people."

"My people." She laughed. "Now you sound like my dad. You could be right, swinging types have always been drawn to the demimonde. Surgical equipment as in scalpels?"

"I believe so."

"This some sort of Ripper deal?"

"A shooting thirty-six years ago." I gave her the basics on Dorothy Swoboda.

"Des Barres was her boyfriend and hence a suspect?"

"It's not at that level, yet."

"What got this going after all this time?"

"She had one child, a three-year-old daughter. She's pushing forty, retired, rich, and curious."

"Retired from what?"

"Gym wear. Company called Beterkraft. She started it and sold it."

"That's hers? Love their stuff. Use it all the time."

"Happy to pass that along, Maxine."

"Like she'd ever care about a starving academic struggling to avoid the assault of time. So in terms of Des Barres, we're talking big money, hence big influence, hence trying to dig up dirt."

"Exactly."

"Why not?" she said. "I'm getting a little bored with Bugsy and Mickey and their ilk, this could lead me in an interesting direction. Notorious unsolveds. Enriched, of course, by a whole bunch of scholarly theory. And we have worked well together, Alex."

"That we have."

"So tit for tat?" she said. "Same as before."

"No problem."

"You're authorized by Milo to deal."

"Can't imagine he'd object."

"I sure hope not. The last one, I got three peer-reviews plus coverage on the U.'s website. Insulated me from having to take over as department head when the rotation reached me."

"No interest in bossing people around?"

"On the contrary, I *love* bossing people around, ask my husband. Problem is nowadays leadership means contending with Orwellian word-warp, chronically whining students, and terminally *mewling* faculty members. Utter the wrong syllable, you face a tribunal. You haven't encountered that at the old-school med school?"

"I'm not important enough," I said.

"You're a full prof, no?"

"Still have the title but I don't get paid and the last time I lectured was a year ago. Third-year pediatric residents. Too exhausted to protest anything."

"Ha. Maybe my parents were right. Wrong field. Let me think about that for a sec . . . nah. All right, I'll see what I can find about Monsieur Des Barres. What was the name of his company?"

"Don't know."

"What do you know?"

"He was in his sixties twenty years ago, had a big place on Mulholland."

"That's it?"

"Unfortunately."

"Hmm . . . you do understand that his not being a gangster lowers the chance of him cropping up in my database. Unless he was a thinly *veiled* bad guy with a respectable front who appears in a footnote or a side reference. And those guys usually ran restaurants and clubs, they didn't get into surgical steel."

"Understood. But like you said, maybe a hanger-on."

"Just so you don't get your hopes up," she said.

"I will be appropriately pseudo-pessimistic."

"And Milo?"

"He'll be genuine pessimistic and I'll give him emotional support."

"Ha. Okay, soon as I get back, I'll start digging."

"Where are you?"

"One guess."

"A convention."

"What tipped you off?" she said. "The despair in my voice?"

"Where's the idea-fest?"

"New Haven, talk about rarefied hot air."

"Groupthink."

"Oh, yeah," she said. "And the group's an idiot."

I ran my own search for Anton Des Barres. Got immediate gratification in the latest quarterly report of a corporation called ADB-Tec and Research.

The company's "mission" was "ultra-precision manufacture of high-grade scalpels, clamps, cannulas, stylets, trocars, endoscopes, elastomeric balloons, catheters, and arthroscopes."

Now a subsidiary of a Taiwan-based conglomerate called Healing Hands, Ltd., ADB operated satellite facilities in Singapore, Stockholm, and, most recently, Dubrovnik, Croatia.

Des Barres's name came up in a two-paragraph *Company History* exposition.

ADB, founded in 1962 by **Dr. Anton Venable Des Barres,** a California Institute of Technology–trained mechanical engineer, achieved rapid renown by dependably supplying the U.S. military with the highest-quality surgical instruments available anywhere in the world. So admired were ADB's field kits during the Vietnam War that the company was entrusted with writing "Mil-

Specs"—military specifications—for a variety of surgical imple-
ments, an honor that persisted for decades.

Dr. Des Barres's motto, *Puritas, Salus, Virtus*—Latin for "Pu-
rity, Safety, and Efficacy"—has remained the company's operating principle. Originally situated in Los Angeles, the company
moved to Franklin Park, Illinois, where manufacturing operations have since ceased but administrative offices remain: Accounting, Marketing, Sales Supervision, and Human Resources.
Specific purchase orders are handled by each manufacturing facil-
ity, however inquiries regarding corporate liaisons and promo-
tions should be directed to Franklin Park . . .

Between the paragraphs was a color headshot of a man with a long,
seamed face thatched by a head of full white hair. Black suit, white
shirt, black tie, a taut smoothness to the face that said professional re-
touching. Anton Des Barres's eyes were pale and sharply focused, his
nose an off-kilter beak that shadowed a dark pencil mustache.

Below the photo were the bracketed dates of the founder's birth
and death. Des Barres had passed away nineteen years ago at the age of
sixty-two.

The scenario I'd suggested didn't seem unlikely: a dying man reaching out for answers.

If that was true, a living relative might have something to say. I ran
a search using Des Barres's surname alone and came up with three
likelies.

Anthony Des Barres, M.D., practiced vascular surgery in Win-
netka, Illinois. William Des Barres, Esq., practiced estate and trusts law
in Highland Park, Illinois. Both towns were affluent suburbs of Chicago a brief drive from ADB Corporate Headquarters in Franklin Park.

Promo photos showed two beefy men in their mid- to late fifties. A
strong resemblance and logic made brotherhood a cinch. So did an
overall similarity to Anton Des Barres's facial structure when you ac-

counted for the extra flesh common on adults of the postwar, ample-food era.

Excellent candidates for contact, but Valerie Des Barres of Los Angeles, California, no neighborhood or photo provided, was a more geographically convenient target.

Her name brought up the IMDb database, where she was listed as executive producer of three animated TV movies shown on a family-friendly channel.

Muffy Comes Home.

Muffy Finds a Friend.

Lionel Roars but No One Hears.

The next reference linked me to an author's website.

Valerie Des Barres was a narrow-shouldered, dark-haired woman with a pinched but pretty face and a hesitant smile. Younger than Anthony and William—midforties.

She described herself as "an artist and activist passionate about children's growth and development" whose interests had led her to write eleven books for preschoolers in as many years. All had been released by Muffy Press. I found no other authors on the company's list, suggesting self-publication.

Six Muffy books starred a streetwise squirrel, three featured Lionel Van Noise, a cheeky, high-volume raven, and the most recent two, released three years ago, described the adventures of Lady Hildegard, a once-pampered Maltese separated from her family by a yacht wreck and forced to make her way through an urban jungle closely resembling Lower Manhattan.

For each column, Valerie Des Barres was listed as both author and illustrator. Samples of her artwork revealed vibrant, eye-catching watercolors. Serious talent, well beyond a vanity project.

The bottom of the *Books* page posted sales links and the assurance that proceeds were "donated wholly to charity." The final line was a small-print list of "suggested nonprofits recommended by Muffy, Lionel and Lady H. But the choice is yours."

I returned to IMDB and found the name of the production company that had put the trio of films together. Muff-Li Ltd. Likely another self-fund.

The books had garnered a scatter of online reviews, most praising the gentleness of the story lines. One anonymous rater panned *Lionel Puffs Up His Treasure Chest* for the bird's "classical male abrasiveness."

Pushing away from the computer, I poured coffee in the kitchen and carried it back to my office, wondering if Valerie Des Barres's interest in child welfare had ever led her to one of L.A.'s most deserving nonprofits: the children's hospital where I'd trained then worked for a decade.

I spent the next hour talking to doctors, nurses, child activity specialists, and social workers at Western Pediatric Medical Center, made a last stab at the Development Office. No one had heard of Valerie Des Barres.

Not a total surprise; there are rich neighborhoods throughout L.A. but the concentration of wealth is highest on the Westside and the hospital's scruffy East Hollywood location sometimes puts Westsiders off.

Years ago, while I was working in Hematology-Oncology, my boss had ordered me to train a group of "highly motivated" Junior Leaguers from Pasadena to serve as volunteers. I'd spent a month with what seemed to be an enthusiastic bunch of young matrons only to have the project fall apart because the women decided the half-hour drive was "too intense."

I shifted west and tried contacts at the U. med center in Westwood. Same result.

Logging back onto Valerie Des Barres's website, I scrolled down to the organizations "recommended" by her characters.

Aprendemos, a group in Modesto that provided after-school tutoring to the children of migrant workers.

The supplies funds of five PTAs in South Central and East L.A.

The Comfort Zone, a San Francisco group providing "toys, recreational opportunities, and emotional support to bereaved youngsters."

That made me wonder. Ellie Barker had talked to a woman, a San Francisco fundraiser for children whose parents had died, before Andrea Bauer had taken over. I didn't have Ellie's number but I did have Bauer's.

Her voicemail said, "Traveling somewhere." Her Facebook page said Asia.

I looked up time differences between L.A. and the Far East. China, Hong Kong, and Singapore were fifteen hours later, Japan, sixteen.

Four p.m. here meant seven to eight a.m. in what used to be called the Orient. If Bauer wasn't an early riser, she could learn to be flexible.

She answered her cell sounding cloudy. "Who?"

"Alex Delaware. We met on the—"

"Oh. The psychologist." Yawn. "Why would you be calling me at this hour?"

"I figured by seven you might be up."

"It's six. I'm in Saigon."

"Sorry."

Another yawn. "I'll cope. I assume this is about that girl—Ellie whatever?"

"Barker."

"So Milo did get assigned." She chuckled. "How'd he take that?"

"He's a pro."

"Meaning he's ticked off. But so goes reality. Any progress to report?"

"He just started."

"Meaning no," she said. "So what do you imagine I can do for you?"

"Ellie Barker described meeting another woman at the Comfort Zone fundraiser—"

"And?"

"What's her name?"

"Why don't you ask her?"

"Don't have her number."

"What's this about?"

"Can't get into that, yet."

"But you can call me at six?"

"Given your initiative in getting the process going, I thought you'd be pleased to help."

"You . . . are something. Okay, fine, I did get the ball rolling, can't complain about it bouncing back. Her first name was Val, never met her before, don't know her surname. She was some kind of movie person, was sitting between me and that poor girl. We traded places because I said I might be able to help. I'm a people-pleaser and I always follow through."

I said, "A movie person."

"I knew she wasn't an actress," said Bauer, "because she didn't have that actress thing going on and I never heard of her. I asked her what aspect—this was after the whole murder discussion, we were having dessert—and she said she wrote and produced. That could mean anything, right? More often than not it's rich kids dabbling and she has money from somewhere. Donated twenty thousand at the luncheon. I'd tell you what I gave but it's none of your business."

"I'm sure you were generous. Thanks. Bye."

"Wham bam?" she said.

"Unless you've got something to add."

"I do not. And no need to contact me again unless you've got a progress report. I don't know either of them from Adam, did a good deed and am not committed *nor* involved in their issues. Know the difference? With a ham-and-eggs breakfast, the chicken's involved but the pig's committed."

With a trip to the archive scheduled tomorrow and total autonomy, I figured Milo would avoid his office. But he didn't answer his cell so I tried his desk and got him.

"Had to clear paper, just about to leave."

I said, "Stay in your seat," and told him about Valerie Des Barres.

He said, "The guy's daughter . . . ol' Du might actually be *onto* something? Except if she thought Daddy was involved in murder, why would she encourage Ellie to dig?"

"Maybe it's been an issue for her, too. She's a few years older than Ellie, would've been around eight or nine at the time Swoboda went over the cliff. Easily old enough to have seen something and hold on to the memory. What if she's been carrying around disturbing memories from her childhood? All of a sudden, Ellie's sitting next to her at a fundraiser and telling her a story that shocks her. It would've seemed like massive karma."

"She's one of those moral compass types, wants the truth at all costs?"

"She seems to devote herself to good works. I don't want to demean altruism but it can be a form of atonement."

"Any idea where she lives?"

"Her website says L.A."

"Let's find out where she pays property tax."

I sat through a couple minutes of keyboard clicks.

He said, "Here we are, the Valerie Antonia Des Barres Trust . . . well, look at *this*. We've already been there. Today."

"The gated place on the corner of Marilyn."

"None other, according to the plat map. That's like . . . three and a quarter acres of ancestral soil. So whatever feelings she has for the old

man, she's okay with living in his manse. Ready for a drop-in tomorrow, say nine?"

"Instead of the archive?"

"Way instead, I'm allergic to dust."

"Since when?"

"Now."

12

Same trip as yesterday, different route.

Milo was racing the Impala's engine as I came down the stairs. Before I had my seatbelt on, he hurtled down the old bridle path leading to my gate and gunned toward the Glen.

I said, "Galoway's driving inspired you?"

He eased up on the gas, hooked a left. "So what approach do I take with Val?"

"Hard to say until we've met her."

"I thought about calling her first but with zero info beyond her DMV data—forty-six, brown, blue, wears glasses—I couldn't come up with anything. So no sense losing the surprise factor. And if she's not in, maybe I can impress a servant to get past the gates and give the place a once-over."

A mile later: "Ellie texted me as I drove over. Wishing me luck, happy face emojis for good measure. Think she's really that nice?"

"Why wouldn't she be?"

"'Cause I'm a cynical bastard. I didn't get back to her. The way things are looking, no sense getting too cozy."

◆

We reached the green gates of the Des Barres estate thirty-five minutes later. Milo maneuvered close to a left-hand call box and jabbed a button.

Dial tone on speaker, five rings before a female voice said, "Yes?"

"Ms. Des Barres?"

"Who's this?"

"Lieutenant Milo Sturgis, Los Angeles Police."

"Oh. About those robberies. Thanks, one sec, please."

Movement several feet above the box to the right caught my eye. An eyeball lens partially concealed by the hedge rotated silently.

I mouthed, *Camera.* Milo fished in his pocket.

The voice said, "Lieutenant, just to be careful could you please show your credentials to the camera above the box? It's a round white dealie on the right but you can probably just stick your hand out and rotate it a smidge. See it?"

"I do, ma'am."

Flash of shield. The gates swung open.

Midway up the cobbled drive, a short, thin, dark-haired woman appeared, walking a black and tan hound on a loose leash. Valerie Des Barres wore a shapeless brown and rust-splotched batik dress and white sneakers. Brown hair was streaked with gray and cut in a jaw-length pageboy. She waved at us merrily. The dog's tongue lolled and its tail wagged.

"Good start," said Milo. "For the nanoseconds it's gonna last."

He inched the car up and stopped next to her. Up close, her skin was smooth and soft-looking, almost juvenile, the blue of her eyes deep and languid.

"Thanks for coming, Lieutenant. I forgot to send in the neighborhood watch card, it's good you used the list."

Milo smiled. "Want a ride?"

Valerie Des Barres said, "Tempting but I need the exercise. Keep going, I'll catch up."

Woman and dog watched as the Impala resumed climbing. Another wave, another wag. Milo's lips worked ferociously, growling something that ended with "Right?"

I said, "Didn't hear the rest of it."

"Another nice one. Cop's curse."

The road's final curve was the sharpest, turning the appearance of the house into a visual surprise. Two generous stories topped by a bell tower rose above a gazania lawn planted with sycamores, scarlet-blossoming crepe myrtles, and Aleppo pines. A flagstoned parking area could accommodate twenty more vehicles than the three in sight: dusty, long-bed pickup with a lawnmower in the back, Mazda SUV, Toyota Corolla.

Four men in khakis and pith helmets snipped and raked and swept. The mansion's front door was wide open, enlarged visually by the short stature of the sixtyish Hispanic man standing in the opening.

White shirt, dark slacks, waving at us. When we reached him, he said, "Welcome," as if he meant it. Behind him, a stocky, kerchiefed woman in her forties mopped the green onyx floor of an entry hall the size of a starter apartment. A deco ebony table in the center of the onyx sported a vase full of crepe myrtle branches. Earbuds played something that pleased the maid and made her head bob, but she paused long enough to smile.

The small man pointed to a great room on the left, said, "Make yourselves comfortable," and left.

Milo muttered, "Freaky-happy."

No rental furniture, here. The mammoth space was set up with more period deco: velvet-and-rosewood sling chairs, macassar occasional tables, geometrically patterned couches, plus the mirrored pieces from the forties decorators call Hollywood Regency.

I knew that because a house I'd visited while working a custody evaluation last year had been furnished with tons of the stuff, the father, a manic, spike-haired film producer, interrupting a tirade against his actress soon-to-be ex to educate me about his exquisite taste. Then back on track, ranting. ("She's got no clue about synchrony or glamour. I like the way the Brits spell it, with a *u*.")

That prince had bought everything as a package at the behest of his "noted designer, she's been in *Architectural Digest* twice." These pieces looked original to the Des Barres mansion.

For all the difference in scale, another Spanish with the same layout as Ellie Barker's rental, the entry leading to a staircase. These steps were padded by a Persian runner moored by brass rods and railed in sinuous, hand-carved ebony.

Scaled for an embassy, some notable making a dramatic entrance.

The small man returned with two tall glasses. Ice water, lime slices floating on top. A bow and he was gone.

It took a while before Valerie Des Barres entered the house, flushed and mouth-breathing in time with the hound's panting. The dog strained at the leash. The man in the white shirt materialized and took it.

"Thanks, Sabino. One second, guys, let me throw some water on my face."

She scooted across the onyx.

I said, "Nice place."

Milo said, "If you like cozy."

The great room was fifty by thirty with a double-height vaulted ceiling. Crossbeams were painted with floral loops of pale blue and pink. Quarter-sawn oak floors had been foot-polished to a patina you couldn't fake. The fireplace was large enough for Milo to step into.

California impressionist paintings in period frames adorned the walls; hillsides vibrant with poppies and lupine, oak groves, rocky coasts, harbor scenes of burly fishermen hauling in catch.

Mr. Exquisite Taste had peppered his place with unframed canvases of "cutting-edge thought-through-woke conceptual imagery," which translated to rectangles in various tones of sludge.

We'd finished our water when Val Des Barres reappeared, drinking from a can of Diet Coke. "I figured water was safe but if you want one of these?"

Milo said, "We're fine, thanks."

"Thank *you* for taking the time. I would've come to the meeting but I had to be out of town."

Milo said, "Actually, ma'am, we're not here about neighborhood watch."

"Oh? Please don't tell me something even more serious has happened. The burglaries were scary enough."

Milo crossed his legs. "We're here about a homicide that took place thirty-six years ago."

Val Des Barres's blue eyes popped. "Thirty-six? That's kind of weird . . . but I'm sure it's nothing."

"What is, ma'am?"

"A few weeks ago I heard about a thirty-six-year-old murder. A person I met at a charity benefit in San Francisco. She'd lost her mom when she was a child and did mention that it happened on Mulholland. That sure caught my ear, so we started chatting." She frowned. "You *can't* be talking about the same person?"

"Ellie Barker," said Milo.

"Ellie. I never got her last name. Oh, my, it *is* her." Her face puckered like that of a kid eyeing a too-pricey toy in a window. "It was a brief conversation. Another person at her table said she had influence and could help, so we exchanged seats. Unbelievable."

She put down her can. "I still don't get why you're *here*."

Milo sighed.

Val Des Barres said, "I don't like the sound of *that*."

"Ma'am, we've received information that Ellie Barker's mother may have lived here."

Val Des Barres rose an inch off her seat, buttocks suspended briefly in midair before lowering. "Here? What makes you say that?"

"Sorry, I can't get into details." He gave an uneasy smile and braced himself for outrage: hands on knees, neck taut. One of those tough-part-of-the-job days.

Val Des Barres said, "Huh. Was she an attractive woman?"

"Reasonably."

"I suppose she could've been one of them."

"One of who?"

"Father's collection," she said. "At least that's how I thought of it. I collected leaves, rocks, and flowers, Dad had pretty women. My brothers had another word for it: harem. It *really* bothered them. It began shortly after my mother died. The changes in Father. But he continued to be a good dad to me, so I wanted him to be happy."

Milo said, "May I ask when your mom passed?"

"I'm almost forty-seven and I was ten, so thirty-seven years ago. It wasn't a sudden thing, just kind of . . . evolved."

Milo looked at me. I said, "How so?"

"For the first year or so, Father didn't date. Or go out much at all. I'd hear him crying in his bedroom, he lost weight. Eventually he started."

"Going out."

"And dating," she said. "He'd bring some of them home. Younger women, pretty, he liked blondes. Mother had been a blonde. In the beginning they'd just spend some time here with him—have a drink or a snack. Then I guess he got more comfortable and you'd see them at breakfast. Then it began to stretch. Weeks at a time. More than one woman."

I said, "Big change for you."

"It would have to be, I suppose. But honestly, I don't remember it bothering me. Maybe I'm in denial, but what I recall is feeling relieved because Father was happier. My brothers didn't like it, that's for sure.

But they were away—Bill was in prep school, Tony was in college. Dad doted on me, and some of them—his women—were lovely to me."

"Some."

"Different personalities," she said. "Some more child-oriented than others, I suppose. None of them were mean to me. Father wouldn't have tolerated that."

"You adapted."

"I honestly don't recall it as a huge adjustment. The big trauma was not having Mother. I suppose having Father functional made that easier."

Milo said, "The woman in question was named Dorothy Swoboda."

"None of their names have stuck with me, Lieutenant. I didn't get up close and personal with them." She managed a smile. "I guess I regarded them as recreational for Father. Like golf clubs or sports cars— I know that sounds terrible but my focus was on getting through life with one parent."

I said, "Of course."

Milo showed her the snapshot in the forest.

Val Des Barres studied it and shook her heard. "Sorry, can't say I remember her. But I don't *not* remember her, either. It's certainly possible. She's the type Dad went for."

"How so?"

"Young, pretty—she's not blond but that could be fixed pretty easily . . . I always thought the main thing was finding women *unlike* Mother. She was British, trained as a physician though she never practiced. Beautiful but she played herself down. Who's the man? Ellie's father?"

"Yes, ma'am."

"He's considerably older than her, same thing as with Father. I suppose it's trying to deny mortality."

She returned the photo. "Sorry I can't be more helpful. It really *is* bizarre that Ellie and I happened to find ourselves at the same table. On the other hand, the spiritual world can be like that and I do like to think of myself as spiritual. Not in a crazy way. But haven't you seen it in the course of your work? Karma, fate, whatever you want to call it? Sometimes the planets just align."

Milo said, "Sure." No giveaway in his tone. All these years and sometimes I still can't tell when he's lying.

Val Des Barres said, "I have to tell you, this is a lot to take in." Hefting the soda can. "I need something stronger."

She left and came back with a tumbler half filled with something amber, sat back down and took a long sip. Eyes clear and searching above the rim of the glass. "Ah, that's better. I'd offer you guys some but I know on duty you can't."

"Appreciate the intention," said Milo.

Val Des Barres grinned. "I'll cope for all of us."

She drained the glass. Placed it on a gilded-mirror coffee table. "I'm still a little shaky. The more I think about this, the weirder it gets. But I don't want you to think I'm a lush, so that will have to do."

Milo said, "Whatever you need, ma'am. Frankly, love to join you."

"You're not saying the death occurred here."

"No, ma'am. Up the road."

"How far?"

"Two miles or so."

"Mulholland's a long road," she said. "It can get pretty dark up here, that's why the neighborhood got so concerned about the break-ins."

"You were ten," I said, "but never heard anything about it."

"I was a highly sheltered ten. And ten back then wasn't like ten today. Kids have the internet, they're slammed with all sorts of bad news constantly. It's way tougher being a child nowadays. That's why I write books for children. Do you guys have any kids?"

Dual head shakes.

She said, "Me neither. Married young but it didn't work out. The books don't make any money but I do get to hear nice things from parents and sometimes the kids themselves. It helps me deal with my guilt."

"About what?"

"This," she said, sweeping an arm in a circle. "Living the way I do without earning it."

"Your father left you the house."

"He left it to all three of us but my brothers are dolls and they let me live here. They're back east, one's an attorney, one's a surgeon. I was planning to be a psychologist, got a B.A. in psych. But when it comes to math I've got some learning disabilities and when I found out all the statistics I'd have to take I said forget it. I was always pretty good with writing and drawing. So." Shrug. "I've made a couple of movies, too. From my books."

Milo said, "Writing and drawing. You illustrate everything?"

"I do."

"Impressive."

"It would be more impressive if I didn't fund everything."

"Still sounds major to me."

"Kind of you to say so," said Val Des Barres. "All one can do is try. Two miles up, huh?"

"We're not sure of the exact spot and probably won't be."

"Either way," she said, "anytime I go into town I pass right by. Sad. Ellie told me she was a little girl, has no memory of her mother. I was fortunate, have lovely memories."

She stood and fluffed her hair. "I've got so much to be thankful for. Going to get some writing done, no need for more of this."

Pinging the tumbler with a fingernail. The sound resonated in the cavernous space.

13

Milo took out his pad. "We'd like to talk to your brothers. Could you give me their numbers?"

Val Des Barres said, "Sure," and recited clearly. "Just spoke to Tony. His birthday. I sang him 'Happy Birthday.' Say hi to both of them."

We got up. Before Milo took a step, she'd taken his hand in both of hers. "Good luck helping Ellie. She seemed so wounded."

Dropping the hand, she headed for the stairs. As if beckoned, Sabino appeared. He opened the door, walked us out and to the Impala. The unmarked's data screen seemed to fascinate him.

"Very nice computer."

"Does the trick," said Milo. "Been working here long?"

"Twenty-four years."

"Nice place."

Sabino's hand rose to his heart and stayed there. "Lucky."

We rolled down the cobbled drive, passing the team of gardeners, now paused for food and drink beneath one of the pines.

Milo said, "Think Miss Val could have alcohol issues?"

I said, "If she does she's not hiding it. Why?"

"She gets stressed, heads straight for the bourbon. She seems too good to be true. Painting a rosy picture of Daddy but it couldn't have been easy losing Mommy and then he goes all Sultan on her."

"She admitted she might be in denial."

"So?"

"There are no ironclad rules but I've found it's the tightly buttoned-up ones who have the most issues."

"You liked her."

"Nothing unlikable about her, so far. The main thing is she gave off no tells I picked up. Including when she said she didn't recognize Dorothy. Did you catch something I didn't?"

"Nah. So some people are just well adjusted even when shit happens."

I smiled. "Most people are. The planet keeps spinning."

A few moments later he said, "What about the way she reacted to our coming in under false pretenses? Wouldn't most people get at least a little peeved? Couldn't everything we just saw be an act?"

"Like I said, no rules. But I'm not ready to establish a surtax on nice."

"Nice makes me fidget. What's that say about me?"

"Nice guy with a tough job."

"Ha."

I said, "Maybe it's your year for nice. First Ellie, then Val."

"Wonderful," he said. "Who did I piss off?"

He drove until he reached the place Du Galoway had guessed to be near the death-spot. Pulled over sharply and stared out at the haze and returned to the road.

I said, "Lonely place to end up."

"Poor Dottie," he said, shifting into gear. "Val didn't recognize her but she didn't say impossible. So what Galoway figured from the Caddy makes sense. Good-looking woman escapes a bad marriage, comes to L.A., hooks up with Professor Scalpel and joins his fan club. Whatever his daughter's level of insight, I'm not buying her image of Daddy as a great guy who just *happens* to collect women like stamps. To me that says Des Barres had no problem depersonalizing women. And we know where that can lead."

"Something began at the house and finished on the road."

"The only other thing that comes to mind is Stan Barker stalked her to L.A., found out how she was living, and got enraged. But then why would she end up in Des Barres's car? If, on the other hand, Des Barres was involved, it makes sense. Do her in the house, store the body until it's safe and drive her away. Or it did happen on the road: Invite her for a late-night drive, pull over, shoot her, reposition her behind the wheel. Release the hand brake, torch the car, and you're done. No big deal walking back to the house in the dark. And a guy that rich, sacrificing a Caddy wouldn't be a big deal."

I said, "If he had good insurance, there'd be no loss at all."

"There you go. The house is huge, Alex. All sorts of places to get away with stuff. Maybe there's a basement with thick walls. Plus those outbuildings. Toss in all that acreage and you've got plenty of kill-spots and hidey-holes. A gun goes off far from the action, who's gonna know?"

"And with the women coming in and out, one of them not returning wouldn't be an issue."

"So you're with me on this. Good. I don't like when you get that skeptical look on your face."

I said, "When's the last time that happened?"

"No idea, I've repressed the memory."

He glanced at his Timex. "Let's get back and see what the Des Barres's sons have to say about life back in the good old days."

He set up in my kitchen, fortified by leftover Genoa salami, pepperoncini, tomato slices, and onions, all on slabs of sourdough he'd sawed off savagely.

"Man, your leavings are better than most people's meals."

Robin and I do try to eat well but a while back we realized we'd begun to buy groceries with him in mind.

He chewed as he tried Dr. Anthony Des Barres's phone. Listened and shook his head.

"*If I do not answer I'm likely in surgery, if it's an emergency dial 911.*' Let's try Brother Lawyer."

A hearty, melodious voice picked up at the other end of William Des Barres's cell. "This is Bill. My sister said you'd be calling."

"Did she tell you what it was about?"

"Something about one of Dad's harem gals disappearing years ago."

"Her name was Dorothy Swoboda."

"Means nothing to me, Lieutenant. When that period of Dad's life was in full gear, I was at Phillips Andover. It's a prep school in Massachusetts."

"All the way across the country."

"I was an idiot jock, sir. Hockey, ice and field. Water polo, soccer, lacrosse. Opportunities in L.A. were lacking. Also, I didn't approve of what was happening to Dad. Before Val's mother died, he'd been pretty much a regular dad."

Milo said, "Val's mother, not yours?"

"Correct. Arlette was Dad's second wife," said Bill Des Barres. "My mom—and my brother's—was Helen. She died when we were young, and Dad married Arlette pretty soon after and had Val. None of that evil-stepmom business, Arlette was great to us, *became* our functional mom. She was British and refined and soft-spoken."

He cleared his throat. "When she died it meant we'd been orphaned twice. We weren't little kids, I was fifteen, Tony was nineteen, but still."

"And then your dad changed."

"Took him a while, but yes. I rarely came home, ended up at Yale, then U. of Chicago Law because my brother was in med school there. Both of us stayed in Illinois. The only thing we regretted was being so far from Val, she was a cute kid. But she claimed Dad was taking great care of her, said she was fine."

"Did you have your doubts?"

A beat.

"How should I put this?" said Bill Des Barres. "Dad basically *was* a good guy. Like most fathers back then, he worked all the time. But after Arlette's passing he started taking more time for himself. Brought *them* in, first for overnights, then days, then some were sticking around longer. Using the pool, sunning themselves. I wondered about the effect on Val but to be truthful, I didn't lose sleep over it. I was a self-centered adolescent. And like I said, Val never complained, she always seemed happy."

"Still does."

"What can I say, Lieutenant. My sister's got one of those inherently sunny dispositions. She could've turned out to be a total spoiled brat but she didn't because materialism was never her thing. Give her paper and pencil and she's humming along. She's super-talented, writes and illustrates books, did a couple of animation movies—anyway, in terms of this Dorothy whatever, can't help you."

"Could I email you a picture of her?"

"It's not going to change anything," said Des Barres.

"Would you mind, anyway?"

"Why not, go for it."

"Really appreciate it, sir. Thanks for your time, sir."

"Got plenty of it, Lieutenant. Kids are married and moved out, wife's off on a bird-watching tour of Central America, dog's ancient, sleeps and farts all day."

Milo emailed the forest shot. Seconds later, his phone played Handel.

Bill Des Barres said, "I guess I spoke too soon, I actually do recognize her. Minus the hair, she was blond, they all were. What I remember is she tended to . . . how shall I say this . . . use various body parts to be noticed."

"Seductive."

"Not specifically with me, just an overall manner. A lot of them were like that but she stood out because she seemed to be taking it seriously—no smiles, no flirtatiousness. Like wiggling around was her assignment."

"Aimed at your father."

"No one else to target," said Bill Des Barres. "He was sowing a whole lot of wild oats. Kind of a delayed reaction, I guess."

"To what?"

"Getting married young, working like a dog since he was a kid, putting himself through school all the way to Ph.D. I guess he had a right to kick loose."

"Any idea where he met all these women?"

"Not a clue. Maybe cocktail lounges in fancy hotels? It's not like you could log on and click a picture—look, I don't want you to get the wrong idea about Dad. He never did anything inappropriate in front of us. Not once. It was just a party scene and it was his time and money to spend. Did it bug me? Sure. The changes in Dad were a little unsettling. But that's not really why I left. I just wanted to do my own thing."

He chuckled. "If anything, the girls would've been an incentive to stick around, right? All those bathing suits by the pool, who needs *Playboy*?"

Milo put down his phone. "Am I the only one hearing ambivalence?"

I said, "Complicated childhoods for both of them. So now you know Dorothy was definitely there. Small steps."

Chomp chomp. "Bathing suits by the pool, place like that there's got to be a pool house or cabanas. Got your phone handy?"

As he consumed, I google-earthed an aerial view of the property, studied the image, and showed it to him.

He pointed to an aqua-colored rectangle. "Big pool. And yeah, this block has to be ye olde changing rooms . . . and this one, further back . . . servants' quarters?"

"Or a guesthouse."

His finger traveled. "Here's the tennis court . . . the building behind that is probably a garage . . . and all the way back here looks like a belt of trees. *Plenty* of places to get the job done."

He returned the phone, got up and paced. Sat back down. "Any suggestions?"

I said, "Just to be thorough. I'd like to know how Des Barres's wives died."

14

Milo's detective I.D. turbocharged a county records search, but it still took time. By the time the coffee I'd brewed was ready, he'd copied the info in his pad.

Helen Archer Des Barres had died fifty-one years ago at Hollywood Presbyterian Hospital. Age, forty-two. Epithelial carcinoma of the ovaries.

Arlette Melville Des Barres had died thirty-seven years ago in Angeles Crest National Forest.

Age, thirty-five.

Accident, unspecified.

I said, "Interesting."

He said, "I call your interesting and raise."

Obtaining the details was an ordeal. Starting with the coroner's office, he endured voicemail at the extension of his favorite pathologist, Dr. Basia Lopatinski, then tried the main desk at the crypt. That left him alternating between being put on hold and talking to people unable or unwilling to help him.

"Damn turnover," he said. "Everyone I used to work with has re-tired. *Except* Basia."

I thought, *The price of enduring.*

He tried Basia a second time. She picked up, characteristically buoyant, listened to his request.

"That long ago? Best I can do is probably just a summary like on the Swoboda woman."

"I'll take what I can get, Basia."

"Are the cases related?"

"She's the wife of a guy Swoboda was living with. Died a year be-fore Swoboda."

"Hold on . . . okay, here it is," she said. "Fatal equine accident, multiple skull fractures, brain bleed. Sounds like she fell off a horse in Angeles Crest."

"Where specifically in Angeles Crest?"

"Doesn't say. I know bad guys like to dump bodies out there but isn't that usually biker-types and gangsters? Did she associate with ei-ther?"

"Don't know much about her, Basia, but unlikely. Anything suspi-cious about the death?"

"If there was it wouldn't have been signed off as accidental."

"How many fatal horse falls have you seen?"

"Since I'm in the States?" she said. "None. When I was in medical school in Poland, a drunk stole a wagon that was hitched to a beautiful Sztumski—a big dray horse—and crashed it into a wall. Fortunately the horse was unharmed. People do fall off but it's generally not fatal, especially now with helmets. More often than not when there's an ac-cident it has to do with racing and the horse is the victim."

"So we're talking a rare occurrence," he said.

"Ah, I see where you're going. Swoboda—there's a nice Slavic name—was made to look like an accident and so poor Ms. Arlette is gnawing at you."

"You should be a shrink, Basia."

"Too frightening a thought, Milo. Being bombarded with all that insight. Besides, you've got Alex for that."

I said, "Hi, Basia."

"Hello. I figured you'd be there."

"Why's that?"

"Milo's gnawing."

While the two of them talked, I worked my phone. I was still clicking when Milo signed off.

He said, "What?"

"Trying to find out how many lethal horse falls occur per year. There's no precise number, best guess is around a hundred. Back when Arlette died, the country's population was significantly smaller so the number would probably be smaller unless a behavioral change—helmets, like Basia said—lowered the risk. Hold on . . . looks like helmets became popular right around the time Arlette had her fall."

"Either way," he said, "it didn't help *her*. Dorothy, Stan Barker, now Arlette. People who associate with Dr. Des Barres tend to lose out to gravity."

I said, "Getting rid of a wife in order to start a harem I can see. I can even see paring down the harem if a member grew troublesome—demanding more than a casual relationship. But why, years after Dorothy left Barker, would he be targeted?"

He checked his notes. "Seventeen years. Good point. Fine, let's put ol' Stan aside—though as you pointed out, he didn't look like the outdoors-type and fatal hiking falls are super-rare. We've still got two dead women who lived with Des Barres kicking it prematurely a year apart and one's a verified homicide. Galoway said Des Barres didn't shuffle off the coil until nearly twenty years ago from a disease. Guy outlives his victims and dies in bed. Reassuring, Alex."

I said, "What is?"

"Validation of my credo."

"Life's not fair."

He bared his teeth. "How'd you guess?"

He searched for accounts of Arlette Des Barres's death, found only a paragraph in the *Pasadena Star-News*.

Hollywood Woman Suffers Fatal Fall from a Horse

A woman riding alone at the western edge of Angeles Crest National Forest plunged to her death after falling or being thrown from her own horse. The body of Arlette Des Barres, 35, was found by park rangers after she failed to return from a ride last Sunday.

The horse, housed at Agua Fria Stables in Pasadena, was found a half mile east of the body. Purchased a year ago by Mrs. Des Barres, it was described by stable owner Winifred Gaines as "young but well-behaved." Mrs. Des Barres was described as an experienced rider. She leaves behind a husband and three children.

I said, "Three children, two of whom remember their father fondly."

Milo said, "Maybe Dr. Tony doesn't? I'll try him again." Another call. Same message.

He looked up Agua Fria Stables. No current listing. "Same old story. Okay, tomorrow the archive. I find anything, you'll be the first to know."

His phone played something I didn't recognize. He checked the screen and ignored the call.

I said, "Who was that?"

He said, "Ellie Barker. She'll be the second to know."

◆

I heard nothing the following day. At eight p.m. on the second day, he phoned. "Any chance I can pop by, toss some stuff around?"

"When?"

"Now-ish, I'm a hundred feet from your ranchero."

I was waiting on the terrace with Robin and Blanche as he drove up in his personal ride, a white Porsche 928 he and Rick have shared for years. Un-Porsche-like with its front engine but with its own sense of style and freakishly reliable. Like me, the two of them appreciate loyalty.

We were outside relaxing, Blanche chewing a jerky stick with Gallic flair, Robin and I sharing a bottle of Israeli Cab-Merlot a wine-auctioneer friend had gifted us for Christmas. In my free hand was a glass for Milo.

He made his way to the top of the stairs and took it. "What's the occasion?"

Robin said, "Another day aboveground."

"Your age, you're thinking like that?"

"Have been since I turned ten, Big Guy."

"What happened when you were ten?"

"I grew up. Taste, it's great. From a forty-year-old vineyard where they found a two-thousand-year-old wine press."

"France?"

"A hill near Jerusalem."

He swirled and sipped. "*Very* nice." He gazed off into the trees that curtain the front of our property. "You know, I think I'll finish and be on my way."

I said, "Thought there was something to toss around."

"It'll keep, don't want to ruin the festive mood."

Robin took his arm. "C'mon, we've got some leftover rib-eye."

"Oh, ye Jezebel," he said. "Will temptation never cease to plague me?"

◆

Eating and drinking in the kitchen loosened him up. He removed his jacket and slung it over a chair, smiled as Blanche toddled over and settled at his feet, and dropped her a small piece of meat.

I said, "What's up?"

"Nothing. Literally."

"Dead end at the archives?"

Blanche was on her hind paws, panting with lust. "Okay to give her another?"

Robin said, "We get to be the bad parents? Just a smidge and make her sit."

Blanche obeyed the command before Milo had a chance to instruct her. He laughed and his arm lowered and the wet sound of ecstatic, slobbering bulldog jaws filtered up.

Then, cat-purrs.

I said, "The archive."

"Better organized than I expected. Lev always impressed me as kind of a stoner but apparently before he went back to Harvard, he whipped everything into chronological order and the new guy hasn't had time to screw it up. So finding the book shoulda been easy. But nothing there. Lev's system cataloged chronologically from the time each case opened officially. Sometimes the 911 call, sometimes when the detective logged it. Ten hours before Dorothy's coroner's summary, a stabbing went down in Watts, and five hours after there was a fatal downtown liquor store 211. In between? Air. Just to make sure, I spent the entire damn day looking over every case five *years* before and after. Then I expanded to twenty years either way. Zilch. It ain't there."

Robin said, "Someone took the file and didn't return it. Do people often get careless?"

"Sure," he said. "But there's no record of anyone checking that particular file out, so for all I know it was never cataloged in the first place."

She said, "Because a rich guy was involved?"

"Shocking as it may be, darling, cases involving the high and mighty do have a way of veering out of lane. Take O.J. His Defense made a big deal about how he was mistreated by a racist department. Truth is, he was coddled initially because celebrity trumps race and cops are the biggest star-fuckers of all. If Des Barres had enough pull, sweeping up a bread-crumb trail wouldn't be tough." To me: "Anything on him from Maxine?"

"Not yet."

"She's usually quick, bad sign." He played with his empty wine-glass.

I said, "Be interesting to see if Arlette Des Barres's file is there. If it's also missing, you've got capital *I* interesting."

"Problem is, Arlette's file wouldn't end up there under any circumstance. Angeles Crest jurisdiction is split between the forest service and the Sheriff's. I have no idea where they keep their relics or if they hold on to stuff, period. Top of that, she was tagged accidental from the get-go so there'd be no real investigation."

He tilted the glass toward the bottle. "Maybe a half pour."

Robin obliged. "More steak, as well?"

He smiled and pecked her cheek. "No thanks, Jez."

"Then how about we open another bottle and take it out back? Nice warm night, we can watch the fish."

Milo looked at me. "You got yourself a girl with good values."

We were sipping silently by the pond's rock edge when his phone interrupted. This time I recognized the ringtone. The first four notes of Debussy's "Clair de Lune," over and over. Some sort of rotating classical algorithm cooked up in a Silicon Valley lab full of tone-deaf geniuses.

Robin covered one ear. "Sacrilegious, slicing it up like that."

He said, "Sorry. Lemme snuff it." Quick look at the screen. "Petra. Gotta take it."

Hoisting himself from the pond bench, he walked a few feet away. Did a lot of listening and returned looking shaken.

"She just picked up a shooting on Franklin. Ellie's boyfriend."

I said, "Offender or victim?"

"Victim. Serious condition, in surgery at Hollywood Pres. Gotta go."

Robin said, "Both of you?"

I said, "Don't see what I can add."

"The poor girl. First her mom, now her boyfriend? If anyone can use emotional support, it's going to be her." She squeezed my arm. "I release you for the public good. With enough wine in me, I'm ready to make the sacrifice."

As we headed down the stairs, Milo said, "How much have you imbibed?"

"Glass and a half."

"Three for me." He cleared his throat. "I also had a beer before I got here. Mind driving? Time it'll take to get there, I can clear my head."

CHAPTER

15

The drive to Hollywood Presbyterian Medical Center is one I can pull off in my sleep. It's a venerable institution planted at Vermont and Fountain. Around the corner from the Western Peds campus on Sunset, where, as a newly licensed psychologist, I'd spent long days on the cancer ward.

I drove to the parking valet where Milo police-tagged my dashboard and told the attendant, "Leave it here, worth your while."

He badged us through the lobby and we headed for the ICU. The waiting room was full of miserable-looking people, as ICU waiting rooms always are. A nurse at the desk was prepared for Milo's badge.

"Second room to your right."

"How's Mr. Twohy doing?"

"You'd have to ask the doctor that."

Second room to the right was windowless, off-white, and sterile, set up with scarred furniture. A space accustomed to bad news.

The look on Ellie Barker's face said she'd heard plenty. She sat on a hard-pack, fake-leather sofa between Petra and Petra's partner, Raul Biro.

Brown sweats, maybe of her own design, bagged on her. Her complexion was one shade grayer than the room, her hair tied back carelessly with a red rubber band.

She saw us but didn't move or speak. Both detectives nodded.

Petra was her usual tailored self, this suit, black crepe. I've never seen Raul when his dense black hair isn't brushed back and sprayed perfectly in place and his suit's not a masterpiece of tailoring. Despite the blood and gore he encounters routinely, he favors light shades of featherweight twill and remains spookily stain-resistant. Tonight's one-button was cream-colored gabardine over a starched white shirt and a massively knotted raw-silk tie the color of Japanese eggplant.

Milo and I pulled up two facing chairs.

Ellie said, "Thanks for coming."

Milo said, "Of course."

She shifted to me. "You probably think I need help."

Just like the first time we'd met, cool to my presence. She'd spoken of being a difficult teen and I wondered if Stan Barker's attempts to deal with the issue before sending her away had led her to some bad therapeutic attempts.

Milo said, "We here to support you, Ellie."

"Thanks. Sorry, don't mean to be snippy." She lowered her eyes to her hands.

Petra said, "Let's step outside, guys." Unspoken signal to Raul.

He said, "I'll be here with you, Ms. Barker. Anything you need, let me know."

Ellie said, "I'm okay, really." Then she burst into tears.

Raul had a tissue already in hand. A good detective prepares.

The three of us walked up the nearest hallway, passed nurses and doctors hurrying by, finally found a quiet stretch.

Petra said, "Looks like I couldn't avoid your case."

Milo said, "You think this is related to Swoboda?"

"It's not an attempted robbery and given what you've told me about the file going missing, I can't exclude it. Maybe someone really doesn't want this dug up."

"How did it go down?"

Petra said, "Twohy got shot coming back from a run. He's a serious runner, has been working on speed goals for next year's marathon."

I said, "When we met him he was aiming for eight fast miles."

"According to Ellie he reached that goal yesterday and decided to dive right in for nine. When I ran seriously I always heard it was important to rest, but maybe he's at a different level."

"More like driven," I said.

Milo said, "More like a bad decision. What was his route?"

Petra said, "Out of his neighborhood, turn east on Los Feliz Boulevard, past the park, into Atwater and beyond. He got nailed four blocks from home. Before they prepped him for surgery he was conscious and in a lot of pain, staff didn't want me around. I got them to allow me a minute. Nothing substantive."

I said, "Fatigued and probably dehydrated. Easy target."

"Easy and unobservant. I asked if he saw anyone or anything. Negative. He got shot from behind, single entry wound in his lower back, exit right below his rib cage, probably small caliber."

Milo said, "Who called it in?"

"A neighbor heard the gunshot and came out with his own firearm. He's a vet, knows the diff between a weapon and a car backfiring. Fortunately for Twohy, he also knows first aid and stanched the wound while he 911'd."

"Hero of the story."

"Ninety-four-year-old hero, we're talking World War Two." She checked her own notes. "Herman Lieber, retired accountant."

Milo copied.

Petra said, "Feel free to talk to him but I doubt he'll have anything to add. We're still not sure where the shooter was stationed, there's mature foliage and trees all over, plenty of places to use as a blind. Just got a call from the scene, so far no casing, so maybe a revolver or we just haven't found it yet. That's it so far. Someone lay in wait, popped out and popped Twohy. What does that sound like to you?"

Milo said, "Personal."

I said, "Was it up close and personal?"

"Not so much," she said. "No scorch marks. CSI's best guess is ten, fifteen feet away."

I said, "Lucky shot in the dark."

"I thought so, too, Alex. It is pretty dark, nearest streetlight is up a ways."

"If it was an execution, why only one in the back? Once Twohy was down, a headshot would've sealed the deal."

Petra said, "Maybe Mr. Lieber opening the door scared the bad guy away."

I said, "Maybe."

Both of them looked at me.

"This is a reach but what if it didn't matter if Twohy died?"

"He may very well end up dying," she said. "What are you getting at?"

"If the goal was to scare Ellie off, a serious wounding might be enough."

Petra considered that.

Milo's frown said he didn't want to. "Or," he said, "this has zero to do with Ellie and everything to do with Twohy."

Petra said, "Ellie doesn't know anyone who'd hate him."

"That may or may not be relevant, kiddo. They haven't been going together that long, come from different circles."

"Twohy has a secret life? I guess anything's possible, obviously I need to learn more about my vic. But what Alex is saying about wounding could be right." She grinned. "He often is right, no?"

"So I've been told."

She said, "Let's go with the warning thing, just for argument's sake. Who knows about your investigation?"

"Bunch of politicians including the mayor, Martz and her boss, and the third D to try to solve it. I'm voting for Martz."

"Wouldn't that be nice. Seriously."

"Don't know if Ellie told anyone but from our perspective, all that's left is a rich lady from Montecito who we know from another case. She's the one who revved up the politicos. Plus two of Des Barres's heirs that we know about: daughter and son. There's another son but we haven't talked to him yet."

Petra said, "Dredging up Dorothy threatens them?"

Milo frowned. "At this point, that's a giant leap. The daughter was actually at the fundraiser where Ellie made contact with Bauer. When we spoke to her a couple days ago, she was open, didn't seem bugged by our questions. Same for the brother we spoke to right after."

"I'm sure you're right," she said. "Still, we're talking two days later and Twohy gets ambushed. Plenty of time to put something together." Her turn to jot. "Names?"

"Valerie Des Barres, William Des Barres. The one we haven't contacted is Anthony. She lives here, the sons are in Illinois. William's a lawyer, Anthony's a doctor."

"Where's here?"

"Daddy's former mansion," he said. "Where Dorothy also lived."

"Whoa," said Petra. "Contracting a shooter from Illinois is feasible, but keeping it local sounds a lot easier. What if the daughter faked being chill? What else do you know about her?"

"Writes and illustrates kiddie books, comes across like a female Mr. Rogers."

I said, "How would she know where to find Twohy?"

"Did she and Ellie exchange addresses at the fundraiser?"

Milo said, "I doubt it, don't want to bring it up now. Could get Ellie needlessly freaked out."

Petra tapped her pad against her thigh. "Kiddie books. She make money at it?"

"Probably not. She self-publishes."

"Not Dr. Seuss but lives in a big house," she said, "so we're likely in trust-fund territory. The world finding out Daddy was a homicidal letch could threaten her on multiple levels. I have to say, guys, she doesn't *dis*interest me. I have your okay to contact her?"

"If you don't mind, hold off," he said. "For your sake and mine."

"What's my sake?"

"If she is dirty, no sense alerting her. For now, I'd rather do a loose surveillance on her place, see if anyone interesting goes in and out. You know how contract kills usually go. No slick movie hit man, some loser who needs dough. It's a huge property, we saw a gardening crew and a butler-type houseman but there could be more guys in and out."

"Who do you see surveilling, you or me?"

"I can do it."

"Hoped you'd say that. Are we talking live-in staff?"

"Probably not the gardeners but maybe the butler. I've only got a first name—Sabino—but I can try to cross-ref with the address. If he turns out to have a record, it gets kicked up several notches."

Petra copied the name. "Wouldn't that be something? The butler did it? Heck, if I get lucky my next call-out will be on a dark and stormy night."

I cleared my throat.

Milo said, "Unless you're coming down with a cold, I don't like the sound of that."

"Here's the thing," I said, "everyone who knows about the Swoboda investigation—from Martz to Galoway—helped it along. Even Val Des Barres, by switching seats with Ellie so she could talk to Bauer. I think her openness was real and I didn't pick up any sense of threat on her part. Also, with social media, a whole lot of people could know Ellie's personal info, especially if she posted about her mother. And I'll bet

Twohy's got a serious online presence, maybe to the point of charting his runs."

Petra whipped out her phone. "The Web Deities. Why didn't I think of that?"

Milo said, "Job stress. Clogs the neurons."

16

We hovered around Petra's phone.

Ellie Barker's cyber-engagement was minimal. No photos, nothing about the search for her mother's killer. Maybe leaving the world of e-trade made the computer a reminder of work that she wanted to escape. Or she just liked her privacy.

Brannon Twohy, on the other hand, had no concept of privacy.

Scores of photos of him. Scuba diving, skiing, paragliding, ziplining, usually bare-chested.

His main thing, though, was trumpeting his running triumphs down to the second. Every race for the past two years memorialized, complete with dates, places, stats, and photographs.

The most recent data dump had been posted at six p.m. today, reporting on his nine-mile speed goal, which he intended to expand regularly as a pathway to making the top twenty in next year's L.A. Marathon.

Included was a map of tonight's run, complete with a red line tracing the route from the house he shared with Ellie to a destination 0.6 miles past Atwater Village.

"the magic 4.5 each way, let's go for warpspeed!"

Milo said, "Jesus, he might as well have put a target on his back."

I said, "He didn't feel threatened. Tonight was a first attempt."

Petra said, "Use a gun, all it takes is one. What a mess. So what, we're back on Twohy being the target not as a surrogate for Ellie?"

Milo said, "Who the hell knows?"

She nodded. "I'm thrashed and I still need to revisit the scene. You sticking around?"

"Just to say goodbye."

"To your client," she said. "And my interested party."

When we got back to the room, a surgeon in scrubs was leaving.

R. Chopra, M.D.'s shoulders were stooped. Dark crescents tugged his eyes downward.

Hard to gauge anything from his expression.

Petra introduced herself and asked Twohy's status.

He said, "No major organ damage, the big risk at this point is infection."

"He'll survive."

"Probably."

Milo said, "Lucky man."

Chopra said, "If you don't include getting shot. The bullet nicked his dorsal ribs, bounced around, and exited here." He fingered a spot well to the right of his own navel. "Missed the diaphragm by a millimeter, tore up a bunch of fascia and muscle. Very lean guy, if he was fat, he could've had a bit of liposuction."

Eyeing Milo, then yawning.

Milo said, "A little flab coulda cushioned him, huh? So much for my gym membership."

Chopra's mouth opened and closed. "Gotta go, Officers."

Petra said, "Any guesses about the bullet, Doctor?"

"Not a pathologist," said Chopra. "You didn't find it?"

"Not yet. When we see bouncing around, it's usually small caliber."

"If you know, why ask me." He hurried off.

Milo patted his own midriff. "Guess the charm offensive didn't work."

Petra said, "Including mine." She opened the door to the waiting room.

Ellie Barker's posture hadn't changed. Raul was in the same spot, working his phone. I caught brief images of his children before he clicked off and looked at Petra. "Good news from the surgeon."

"We just spoke to him."

No reaction from Ellie.

Milo approached her and stood in front of her until she raised her eyes. Tear tracks striped her face.

He said, "Terrible thing but it coulda been a lot worse."

Reluctant nod. Near-whisper afterthought: "Thank God."

Milo turned to Raul, who stood and gave him the seat. The couch shifted like a lagoon accommodating an ocean liner. Ellie played with her hands.

He said, "So no idea who'd want to hurt Brannon."

"I can't imagine anyone would, Lieutenant."

Petra said, "Did he ever have problems with other runners?"

Ellie looked up again. "Why would he?"

"When was his most recent race?"

"I'd have to say . . . a month ago? Nothing important, just a 10K for an animal shelter."

"Where?"

"Palm Springs. It was super-hot, a lot of people dropped out."

I said, "Not Brannon."

"He never quits, he's got a great constitution." Her voice caught. "Did."

Petra said, "I'm sure he'll heal up and be right back on track. So nothing happened at the 10K."

"It was a good race," said Ellie. "Brannon came in second."

"No problems related to that."

"I'm not sure what you're getting at, Detective."

"With intense competition, sometimes people get a little out of hand."

"No, no, no, there was nothing remotely like that." Ellie's hands stilled. "Why would you think this is related to running?"

"We're a long ways from any sort of theory," said Petra. "The thing is, Brannon put his routes on his Facebook and Instagram pages. Including tonight's practice run."

"He does that to keep himself disciplined. Once he schedules, he's obligated to keep his— Oh. I see what you're getting at. Someone stalked him? Honestly, I can't see that. Brannon has no enemies. Unless some street criminal from Hollywood reads his posts—like what you told me the first time, Lieutenant. There's a lot of crime nearby."

Milo said, "Brannon wasn't robbed."

"Maybe someone tried but lost his nerve? I don't know, the whole thing's—" She breathed in deeply. "Okay. I might as well say this. I can't help feeling guilty."

"About what?"

"Could it be related to *me*? What you're helping me with, Lieutenant."

"How so?"

"I move here, you start investigating, and Brannon gets shot? What if someone doesn't want the truth to come out? But then I thought, it was so long ago, who'd even know what you were doing? So I'm probably being paranoid."

Milo said, "Have you talked about the investigation to anyone we don't know about?"

"No one. Just you and Dr. Bauer and the other woman I met in San Francisco—Valerie."

"Know her last name?"

"Sorry, no."

"What about Brannon? Did he tell his friends?"

"He doesn't really have friends, his life is work and running and he's not working down here, so it's all running."

"How much detail did you go into with Dr. Bauer and this Valerie person?"

"You think—"

"Not at all," said Milo. "What Detective Connor said is true. We have no theories, but we do need to ask questions to be thorough. So if you can recall your conversations with each of them, we'd appreciate it."

"All right. Let me think back . . . Valerie was sitting next to me. We introduced ourselves to be polite, the way you do when you're seated next to someone you don't know. We made some small talk. She's a writer, I told her I admired that, asked her what she wrote. She said children's books. I said how interesting. She said, I guess I do it because I'm trying to get back in touch with my own childhood. I asked her what she meant. She told me she'd lost her mom when she was young. That's what got me telling her my story. Dr. Bauer must've been listening because she joined the conversation. Basically took charge."

Petra said, "Took charge how?"

"Talking past Valerie to me. Telling me not to accept failure, it was all about perseverance. And contacts. Which she had."

I said, "So you and Valerie switched seats."

"Yes. I really can't see either of them wanting to do Brannon—or me—any harm. Dr. Bauer was a bit pushy but she followed through and Val seemed to empathize. I came home from the event feeling more buoyed up than I've been in . . . more hopeful than *ever*."

She threw up her hands. Cried some more. Again, Raul was ready.

Petra said, "We'll do our best to figure out what happened. Meanwhile, you might want to examine your home security. I work Hollywood and there are some tough areas not far from you."

Ellie's eyes rounded. "You think they could try again?"

"There's no reason to think that," said Petra. "But it pays to be careful. In any neighborhood. Does the house have an alarm system?"

"Yes."

"Switch it on even when you're home. How about security cameras?"

"No. You're kind of scaring me, Detective."

"Don't mean to," said Petra. "But I'd be remiss if I didn't tell you all this."

Milo said, "If she didn't, I would."

"We're not talking extreme measures, just normal caution," said Petra. "The bad guys have learned to use social media. We advise people to never announce a vacation, it's like sending the villains an e-vite."

"Makes sense," said Ellie Barker. Her chest heaved. "About the only thing that does, tonight."

17

Raul stayed in the room and the three of us left and reconvened in another quiet spot near the elevators.

Milo said, "I just keep thinking about Twohy laying out his route. What a genius."

Petra said, "I'll see if he's a genius with a past."

"You've got the crime scene to deal with, I don't mind."

"Sure, thanks."

He turned to me. "What do you think of Ellie and the whole guilt thing?"

"Does she know more than she's letting on? I didn't pick anything up. What does make me wonder is if Bauer hadn't butted in, her contact with Val would have ended as a casual conversation."

Petra said, "Val realizes Ellie could be talking about her dad? Feels like throwing up in her mouth but figures it'll go nowhere. Then Bauer takes over and it gets *bad*."

Milo said, "If so, she coulda been ready for us, what we saw was well rehearsed. Next step call one or both of her big brothers. Raking up the past could pose the same risk for them. Or she handles it herself."

I said, "After you sent Dorothy's photo to Bill, he could've said he had no idea. Instead he said he didn't know her but he did recognize her as a harem member."

"Strategy," said Petra. "Guy's a lawyer, used to scheming. We see that in suspects who are smart or think they are, right? Be semi-cooperative and you come across innocent. And sometimes it works. Besides, there's no evidence. What would Dorothy's presence in the house thirty-plus years ago prove? So it pays to play along, maybe learn details of the investigation."

I said, "But then why shoot Twohy?"

Both of them frowned.

Milo said, "Maybe that wasn't Bill's decision."

Petra said, "Kiddie-Book arranged a hit on her own?"

"Or she talked to Dr. Tony, her other brother, and he was more action-oriented. I've tried the guy three times and he still hasn't called me back. It's too late in Illinois but I'll give it another go tomorrow."

Petra said, "I'm going to synchronize with Raul then head over to the scene."

"See you, kid."

She yawned. "Wish I felt like a kid."

The Seville was where we'd left it. Milo handed the valet a bill that evoked joy, got into the passenger seat, and removed the placard from my dash.

I drove toward the Vermont exit.

He said, "Good thinking on my part, having you drive."

"Still feeling the wine?"

"Not a whit. Time to work. Onward, coachman."

Vermont Avenue is one of L.A.'s longest streets, stretching twenty-three miles from Los Feliz down to the Wilmington Harbor. There's nothing pretty about most of it but darkness has a way of concealing defect, and being able to glide through a dim, latent Vermont as Milo made notes in his pad was strangely soothing.

That lasted half a block until I turned west on Sunset, a street that never calms down.

Hospital Row dominates huge swaths of Sunset real estate, with all the ambulance din and peripheral anxiety that entails. Next come the Scientologists massing in and around their cathedral, a former hospital now painted cobalt blue and topped by a massive sign and a crucifix.

L. Ron Hubbardsville eventually gave way to grim blocks of dope fiends buying, selling, and bartering, wild-eyed unfortunates lost in various states of fantasy, homeless encampments you can smell from the curb, and, farther west, the liveliest stretch of all, the Strip, which mixes all of the previous with hipsters and party creatures and adolescents out way too late.

None of that stopped Milo's pencil. When he stopped writing and began thinking, I said, "You okay with some music?"

"Why not?"

I switched on my favorite Stan Getz tape.

He said, "*Definitely* why not."

As I continued west, he swapped the pad for his phone and began logging onto one database after another, cursing silently when Bluetooth went out, muttering, "Finally," when connection resumed. "Nothing . . . nothing . . . et cetera . . ."

I'd just passed the Roxy, now sadly dark, and pulled to a stop at the Sunset–Doheny light when he shouted, "Finally!" and held out the tiny screen.

Small print. Before I had a chance to decipher, the light turned green. I drove on.

"As the TV bobbleheads say, here's the recap: A Sabino Eduardo Chavez is listed on Val Des Barres's IMDb page as the caterer on her second animation. Not exactly a tough gig, feeding toons. So she met him dishing out grub and hired him. But the main thing is NCIC knows him, too. Convictions for larceny and theft, jail time in River-side . . . twenty-six and . . . twenty-eight years ago. Yeah, I know, ancient history, he's totally repentant and completely rehabilitated. On the other hand, Alex, he coulda just gotten better at avoiding arrest. Whatever the case, he's no virgin and parts of Riverside are serious gang territory. You want a shooter, you could do worse. Speaking of which, let's see about our shooting *victim*."

Two blocks into Beverly Hills: "Well, look at this. Mr. Twohy *out-did* Mr. Chavez and was busted *four* times . . . little run of naughtiness three to six years ago. One marijuana possession and three booze DUIs. Only one conviction, for the third deuce. He pled to misdemeanor, paid a fine. Maybe ol' Sabino shoulda used *his* lawyer."

"A substance history could explain Twohy's approach to running."

"Trading one addiction for another? Eight miles today, nine miles tomorrow, ten, eleven, blah blah blah? And by the way, here's my route, look at me, everyone, I'm sober."

"What I meant was he might be trying to stay healthy and structuring his life so he doesn't relapse."

"Oh," he said. "Maybe that, too."

No further conversation or revelations until I pulled past my gate and parked alongside the Impala.

He said, "Thanks for the best Uber in town. Val's estate isn't easy to watch but I'll figure out something. I get lucky, Mr. Chavez goes somewhere interesting. That doesn't happen, there's all that panoramic view."

He stretched. "You know, it's kinda nice making my own schedule. What's on your agenda?"

"Busy all day," I said.

"With?"

"New patients."

"Custody messes?"

"Two of those plus a trauma case."

He winced. "A kid got hurt? Badly?"

"Car crash, no physical injuries but plenty of emotional issues."

"Oh, man," he said. "Glad he has you to talk to."

"Eighteen months old," I said. "Doesn't talk much."

"A baby? So what the hell do you do?"

"Observe, build trust, try some play therapy, then some incompatible response training."

"Which is?"

"Teaching new ways to process what scares you."

"A baby can do that?"

"Quite well," I said. "Anger and fear don't usually coexist in kids. If you can teach them to get mad at what frightens them, it can drive out anxiety."

"Ah," he said. "Maybe that's why I'm never anxious, didn't grow up. You work with the little ones a lot?"

"More often than most psychologists."

"Because . . ."

"I don't mind not talking."

"Huh. That a hint?"

I laughed. "No."

"The technique," he said. "You invented it?"

"The research was in place. I put stuff together."

"Eighteen months old. Phew."

He got out of the car. "Thanks for your time, amigo. Let me ask you. When I call do you sometimes think it's pain-in-the-ass complicated?"

"Never."

He looked at me.

I said, "Not once."

CHAPTER

18

I spent the next two days with children under stress. The custody cases weren't the worst I'd seen but neither were they ideal. Nice, well-balanced kids; I'd work hard to keep it that way.

The eighteen-month-old trauma victim was a chubby, black-eyed girl named Amelia with a surprisingly quick smile. Good temperament; a plus. When her mother, a five-eight, hundred-pound graphic designer named Lara, warily introduced me as a doctor, she said, "Da-ka."

The collision had sprained Lara's shoulder and ankle. The latter was swaddled by an elastic bandage, and every step was clearly painful. As was the session we'd had last week when I'd taken a history.

This morning, she said, "She keeps waking up. This has been hell."

I said, "Sorry for what you've been through."

"Not sorrier than me." She began playing with her phone, leaving Amelia to toddle around the office.

I keep toys to a minimum, using the few that play a role in therapy. For a child this age, the playhouse would do. I'd positioned it in the center of the floor, and it didn't take long for Amelia to get to it.

Cheerful and relaxed as she sat down and began exploring. Good sign.

Then she spotted the miniature cars in the garage, shrank back and hugged herself. A run to her mother ended with a swing up to the maternal lap.

"See what I mean? She freaks out. Just getting here in the loaner was an ordeal."

I picked up the cars. "It's understandable."

"You really think you can help her?"

"I do."

"Hard to believe," she said. "But my lawyer said try. He also said you'll document everything for the case."

Amelia looked at her.

I said, "Bad cars," and tossed them onto the floor.

Amelia's gaze switched back to me.

"Bad," I said, louder. Extending a foot and kicking the vehicles.

"Bah," she said. Looking to her mother for guidance.

Lara folded her arms across her chest. "What would you like her to do, now?"

I picked up the cars and tossed them again. Amelia scampered off the sofa and did the same.

Her mother said, "Really? Again?"

I said, "Bad bad cars. You can throw them again."

I pantomimed a toss.

Another glance at her mother.

Lara rolled her eyes. "If he says so."

Amelia turned to me, turned doubtful by her mother's tone. I retrieved the toys and threw them nearly to the far wall. "Bad cars!"

Inhaling and squeezing her hands into tiny fists, Amelia ran over and aped my motions. Picked the cars up. "Bah bah bah."

She began breathing hard.

"That's okay? The way she's panting."

I nodded.

"If you say so."

We watched as Amelia went through car-assault eight more times. I use hard-plastic miniatures able to take the abuse. Sometimes I spackle and repaint the wall.

By the time Amelia left the office, insistent upon walking unaided, one of the cars was clutched in her tiny hand.

Her mother said, "That's the doctor's."

I said, "That's okay, now it's Amelia's."

Swinging the vehicle overhead, the child trotted away, laughing. Her mother muttered, "Go know."

I walked them out of the house and down to a Mercedes of Beverly Hills loaner SUV.

Amelia's mother opened a rear passenger door and said, "Okay."

Amelia hesitated for a second, then climbed in and allowed herself to be buckled in. All the while passing the toy from hand to hand.

"Ooom, bah bah bah."

I said, "Oom va-roooom."

She tittered then broke into a giggle fit.

Lara smiled despite herself. Before she got behind the wheel, she faced me, biting her lip.

I said, "A question?"

"So that's it?"

"No, we'll need more sessions. In the meantime, don't do anything different. But if she does want to get mad at the cars, don't stop her."

Amelia began humming.

"Okay . . . maybe this will actually be useful. I guess."

Amelia said, "Vuhooom!"

Lara said, "Um, do you do eating disorders?"

19

At eight p.m., Milo called my private line and asked if I was still "healing miniature psyches."

"Free now but tied up until noon tomorrow. Progress?"

"Nah, I've just got something I want you to hear."

"I'm listening."

"Hear as in verbal exchange, then we discuss. Not over the phone."

I was tired, had planned to finish my paperwork then unwind with Chivas and my guitar gently weeping. But he sounded needy and Robin had returned to her shop and would be working late tweezing minuscule inlay onto the mandolin's sound-hole rosette.

Her guess: back by nine. Eleven was more likely.

I said, "I'll leave the door open."

I was at my keyboard when he tapped on the doorframe. The playhouse was still in the center of the room.

"That for me?"

"If you can handle deep psychic exploration."

"Sounds like my nightly sleep pattern."

He plopped onto the battered leather couch, leaned forward, and began examining the house. "Kinda Beaver Cleaverville. Do I get to pick a favorite room? And don't say the kitchen."

"What, then?"

"Bypass the process and head straight for the outcome. The dining room."

He removed a steak the size of a toenail. "For plastic, this stuff looks pretty good, but the portions? Tsk . . . is this broccoli or cauli-flower . . . or a lawn cutting from Dad's mower?"

I saved the file I was working on, double-checked, and logged off just as he was plucking a Mom-doll out of the house. "Apron *and* bouf-fant hair?"

I said, "I bought it when I started in practice."

"Maybe you should update. Mama with skinny jeans and a coupla tattoos?" He rotated the doll. "Is her name Susan or Mary Jane? Is she still true to her sorority?"

"Sorry," I said, "patient confidentiality. How's Twohy?"

"Still in the hospital, nothing new to say. In terms of the crime scene, Petra doesn't know for sure where the shooter hid but she's got a good guess. Indentation in some brush twenty feet from where Twohy fell. Unfortunately, no footprints. Or casing, maybe it *was* a revolver."

He held up the doll. "Back to Formica and TV dinners for you, Suzy."

I said, "Did you have time to watch the mansion?"

"Briefly, still can't figure a good way to do it, road's too open, traf-fic's too thin. I used the Porsche to blend in, did some drive-bys seven to ten a.m. and four to seven p.m., figuring those were the likely times Sabino or some other employee would be coming or going. No one came or went except for FedEx delivering what looked like boxes of books. Top of that, Martz called me yesterday emphasizing I was to report to her and no one else. Meaning I can't request backup from Moe or Sean or Alicia. Now the topic for discussion."

He triggered his phone. Two beeps were followed by a deep male voice.

"This is Dr. Des Barres."

"Doctor, Lieutenant Sturgis."

"You, again? I got your messages and ignored them because I'm busy and have nothing to say to you."

"If you could just—"

"You misled my service, saying it was an urgent call."

"It kind of is, Doctor."

"It kind of *isn't*," said Anthony Des Barres. "False premises. Not right, Lieutenant. Goodbye."

"Sorry, sir, no harm intended but if you could give me just a second? Your brother and sister did."

"A second to do what?" said Anthony Des Barres. "What in the world do you think I can tell you?"

"Did they fill you in?"

"I haven't talked to my brother. My sister said something about a woman who lived with our father umpteen years ago."

"And was murdered during that time."

"That's supposed to concern me because . . ."

"It may not concern you at all, Doctor. The case has been reopened and I'm trying to gather background information."

"By operating scattershot? If I went about my job that way I'd never get any work done."

"You're a surgeon?"

"*Vascular* surgeon," said Anthony Des Barres. "I take apart blood vessels and put them back together again. I *don't* ask my patients about their childhoods or their ears or their rectums. Now, if you'll excuse me, I've got reality to attend to."

"The woman in question was named Dorothy Swoboda."

"That means nothing to me."

"I sent your brother a photo and he thought he recognized her. Could I do the same with you?"

"You're serious," said Des Barres.

"It won't take long, sir."

"Then can we put this to bed? I don't like talking about them."

"Who?"

"My father's houris. It wasn't a great time for us, seeing him change after my mother died."

"Running a harem."

"I said 'houris,' didn't I? I believe it's the root of 'whore.' "

"Not a classy bunch."

"Hah. Cheap types traipsing in and out of the house. A flesh parade. I was in college but my sister was a little kid. What kind of environment do you think that was for her? If I could've taken her with me I would've, but a dorm isn't exactly the right place for a ten-year-old."

"The home environment affected your sister?"

"I'm not a psychiatrist." A beat. "I'm not saying Valerie needs one, she's doing fine. Goodbye."

"That photo?"

"Email it."

"Where, please?"

Des Barres rattled off a Gmail address. "Do *not* send it to my office. If you do, I'll lodge a complaint. I *cannot* have my staff distracted."

Click.

I said, "Angry man."

Milo shook his head. "You'd think people would learn what hostility sets off in detectives. Now listen to this."

He pushed a button. New connection.

"Sturgis."

"This is Dr. Des Barres. I remember her because she didn't even try."

"Try what?" said Milo.

"To ingratiate herself."

"The other women did."

"Not effectively, but they tried."

"In what way?"

"Fake smiles and unctuous voices for my sister, honey, this, sweetheart, that. For my brother and me—and for my father, of course—it was batting the lashes and shaking their you-know-whats. *Tacky*, the bunch of them."

Milo said, "Dorothy Swoboda didn't do any of that."

"That's the *only* reason I remember her. It was as if she felt confident in her situation."

"What situation was that?"

"I don't know—maybe thinking she was the Queen Bee houri."

I scrawled *entitled* on a Post-it and showed it to Milo.

He spoke the word.

Dr. Anthony Des Barres said, "Exactly. Entitled *and* arrogant."

Milo said, "That kind of attitude could cause resentment. Did she have any enemies?"

"How would I know, Lieutenant? I was barely around and when I was, my thoughts weren't on whatever drama my father had put himself in. I concentrated on spending the minimum amount of time there and then getting back to my studies."

"So no one you know of—"

"What do you want me to say? That I saw *her* and one of the other houris engage in a claws-out catfight? It's not beyond the realm of possibility, these were gold diggers not debutantes. Father probably would've liked that—being fought over. But I never witnessed anything remotely like that."

Milo said, "So Ms. Swoboda's goal was being your father's favorite."

"Don't put words in my mouth, Lieutenant. I don't know that, I'm inferring." Tony Des Barres let out a derisive laugh. "If they had brains they'd have realized he had no intention of developing a relationship with any of them."

"He told you that."

"Do you people get paid to be thick? No, he didn't *tell* me that. His actions made it *obvious*. If you want domesticity you don't assemble a bunch of sluts."

"Got it," said Milo. "So the other women jockeyed for position by sucking up to you and your sibs but Dorothy Swoboda didn't."

"She couldn't have cared less." Snide noise that might've been a chuckle. "There you go, you've solved it. Another houri bumped her off. Now if—"

"Your brother said she could get seductive with him."

"Bill thinks he's God's gift to women, he's been married four times. And in answer to your inevitable question, no she didn't do that with me. I'm the last person to think I'm God's gift to women. Would you like to know why?"

"Please."

"I'm gay," said Anthony Des Barres. "Does that shock you?"

"No, sir."

"I'll *bet*. You people aren't known for your tolerance."

Click.

Milo put the phone down, flexing his fingers as if letting go of a hot frying pan. "Sssss. What do you think?"

I said, "He just floated the other women as potential suspects, but if Dorothy did have a chance of being Des Barres's chosen one, she'd have been a bigger threat to the heirs."

"Follow the money."

"Val was a kid, Bill still a teenage preppie, but Tony was a legal adult most likely to appreciate the consequences."

"Dr. Genius just gave himself a motive."

I said, "And if he was still closeted, Dorothy could've posed a double threat—capturing Dad's heart and informing on Son Number

One." I smiled. "Of course, you intolerant law enforcement types wouldn't understand that."

He cracked up. "What was I gonna say? Feel your pain, sourpuss? Take a look at some internet photos I pulled up, medical galas and such."

I scrolled through four images, each featuring small clutches of partygoers. Two of the affairs were black-tie, the others, business attire.

Dr. Anthony Des Barres was a tall, broad, heavy-jawed man with a steel-colored crew cut and a pugnacious jaw. A hyphen of thin lips completed the disapproving-elder look. Beyond serious; grim. Hollywood would've cast him as a drill sergeant.

The exception to his crankiness was one shot where he stood next to a slender, younger Asian man identified as Richard Hu, M.D. The two of them pressed close together, Hu beaming boyishly as Tony Des Barres managed a pained semi-smile.

Milo said, "Like he was weaned on vinegar. Look at his size, gotta be in my league."

I said, "Young adult thirty-six years ago and easily able to overpower a woman."

"Plus he'd have access to Daddy's car. And remember: Dottie was killed in July."

"Summer vacation," I said. "He could've been home from college."

"He gets back to the manse, doesn't like what he sees, has words with the Queen Gold Digger and it goes far, far south. I ran a search on him, hoping for anything anger-related, but no dice. No priors, period, not a single complaint to the medical board or any online griping. Which nowadays qualifies you for sainthood. Just the opposite, his patients love him. Apparently when it comes to varicose veins, he's a miracle worker. With an *excellent* bedside manner."

I said, "Maybe he knows how to compartmentalize."

"Dr. Nice at work, something else when you get his goat?"

Or, I thought, bringing up his childhood had simply been a trigger for bad memories, nothing more. But no sense getting any more analytic; at this point it led nowhere.

I nodded and left it at that.

Milo pocketed his phone. "What do you think about the brothers living near each other but not talking much? Tony's dig about Bill *thinking* he's God's gift to women."

I said, "Could you use Bill to learn more about Tony? At this point, I wouldn't risk it. The same goes for giving Valerie another try. They could still be a cohesive trio, in which case everything will blow up in your face."

He gave a resigned shrug. "I was hoping you'd contradict what I already figured. Any other ideas?"

"You could search for someone outside the family who remembers the harem days. Maybe a friend of Des Barres's wives."

He drummed his knees with his fingers. "Helen died of natural causes but with the pattern of accidents, concentrate on Arlette the Horsewoman, maybe one of her gal-pals had suspicions."

He left the office, came back chomping on an apple, sat on the battered leather couch. "I was also thinking it's time to have a sit-down with Ellie."

"Reassuring her?"

"More like seeing if there's more she remembers. I had it set up for ten tomorrow but you're busy till noon. If I move it, can you make it?"

Out came the phone.

Before "Sure" had left my mouth, he punched a preset. "Ellie? Need to move it to two thirty."

20

At two the following day, he picked me up in the Impala, newly redolent of refried beans and hot sauce, and drove to Los Feliz. A couple of blocks into the leafy enclave where Ellie Barker had chosen to rent, he pulled to the curb.

"Here's the place."

We got out and looked. A man had been shot here three days ago but you'd never know it.

Nice houses, well-tended lawns, not a speck of blood on the sidewalk. Time alone didn't explain that. No rain had fallen, neither cops nor techs do cleanup. I'd been to scenes where body fluids had lingered for weeks.

Peering closely revealed some lightening of the concrete. Scour marks, a citizen effort.

Milo said, "Like it never happened."

I said, "Pride of ownership."

"Leads to janitorial inequality." He examined a screen shot Petra had sent him and continued to a ten-foot mock orange fronting a neat white colonial. No obvious entry from the street, but parting the bush's branches revealed a cave-like space.

We stepped in. Roundish, four feet square, only a foot higher so we both needed to hunch.

Natural hollow created by the mock orange seeking sunlight. Tough posture for the long run but someone able to sit or squat comfortably would've been fine. And once sequestered, a stalker would be safe from view and able to sight through the shrub's lacy growth.

Perfect hunter's blind.

The prey, easy; giving himself away with shuffling and hard breathing.

Milo and I inspected the cavity. Not a shred of evidence left behind. Someone taking the time to clean up faultlessly.

We returned to the car and drove on.

Nothing different at Ellie's residence until Milo pushed the bell and the door opened on a black man the size of a defensive tackle wearing a blue blazer and gray slacks. *Iconic Security* embroidered in gold above the breast pocket. The jacket had been left open, advertising the chunky handle of a black plastic automatic in a black mesh shoulder holster.

The guard's eyes scanned us rapidly. Inspection over, he smiled but didn't move or speak.

Milo said, "Lieutenant Sturgis."

"Expecting you, sir. You don't mind showing some I.D."

Statement of fact, not a request.

Out came the badge.

"Nice. I got to sergeant." He turned to me. "You're the doctor?"

"Alex Delaware."

"Sorry for the inconvenience but you don't mind showing some I.D."

Quick read of my driver's license. "Thanks again and excuse the formality but regs are regs."

Milo said, "Understood. Glad you're here, friend. Name?"

"Melvin Boudreaux."

"Louisiana?"

"Born in Baton Rouge," said Boudreaux, "but moved to SoCal as a kid, worked El Monte PD eleven years. C'mon in, there's a pitcher of iced tea. Had some, it's good."

Boudreaux held the door as we entered the house and crossed to the living room. Before closing the door, he checked out the street, then stationed himself in the entry hall.

Ellie was seated in the same chair. The coffee table was set with a pitcher of amber liquid, plastic glasses, napkins, a paper plate of cookies.

Since I'd seen her in the hospital, she'd lost skin tone and color. Maybe some weight, as well, though a baggy dress clouded that assessment. The dress was dust-colored printed with pale-pink flowers. On her feet were brown rubber bath sandals. No sign of the serpentine necklace. No adornment at all, not even a watch.

We sat on the couch. Milo said, "How's Brannon doing?"

"Better?" she said, turning it into a question. "So far no infection, which was the main danger. I'm hoping to get him home in a couple of days. He's miserable about not running."

"Tough when you're active."

Biting her lip, she glanced at Mel Boudreaux. "I'm okay, Mr. B. Have some lunch, there's that pasta and pizza in the fridge."

Boudreaux said, "Yes, ma'am," and left for the kitchen.

Milo said, "Good step, hiring him."

Ellie said, "I had to, the first day—alone here—was terrifying. I didn't eat or sleep. So there was no choice. He seems very competent. Do you know the company? I guess I should've asked you before?"

"I don't but that doesn't mean anything. Private security isn't part of my world."

"Yes, I'd imagine," she said. "The people you deal with *weren't* careful. Not that there was any reason for Brannon to be careful. Who'd imagine?" She placed her hands in her lap. Sat there, like a kid waiting for a reprimand. When none came, she said, "Have you given more thought to whether it's related to my mother?"

Milo shook his head. "Whatever the reason, protecting yourself is a good idea."

"I got the referral from the firm we use at our factories—the firm I *used* to use when I ran the company. I took your advice and told them it needed to be local and they said Iconic's got a branch office right here in Hollywood, they do a lot of entertainment security. I also checked out references. Real ones, not online blurbs that can be faked Then I made calls to some CEOs I know. They come highly recommended . . . I still can't believe it happened. It feels weirder *now* than right after. Is that normal, Dr. Delaware?"

"Absolutely."

"Good . . . not that it matters. I suppose. Being normal. You feel what you feel and have no control. Right now I'm feeling pretty power-less. So what kind of feedback do you have for me, Lieutenant—and yes, I remember you said it was limited." An almost-smile stretched and made the grade. "Don't worry, my expectations are realistic."

Despite the claim, her shoulders bunched as she scooted forward.

Milo said, "Before we get into that, is there anything else you've remembered since we last spoke?"

"Like what?"

"Anything, Ellie. Even if you think it's too trivial to mention— maybe a remark your dad made before he passed? About your mom, their relationship, why she left?"

She edged back. "No, he never said much of anything, just that she'd left us behind."

That sounded like blame. I said, "Did he have any resentment about that?"

"None at all," she said, too quickly. Then she colored. "Okay, I'm lying. But only partially. For the most part, he really wasn't emotional about it. But there was one time—only one time, so I'm not sure how relevant it is."

Her spine was pressing against the chair-back. Full retreat but nowhere else to go. She looked from side to side, then down at her lap. "It was my fault, I was badgering him."

"About your mom?"

"No, about something stupid—who remembers? This was back when I was in my rebel-without-a-cause stage, determined to torment him every way I could think of."

The corners of her eyes filled with moisture. She used a napkin to dry them. "I really put him through it."

I said, "How old were you?"

"Fourteen, fifteen—even part of thirteen got messed up. I think of those years as the hurricane season, they must've been hellish for him." Deep sigh. "I didn't say anything about this when we first met because I didn't want to make *her* sound bad. But . . ."

We waited. She poured tea. Didn't drink it. Pincer-grasped a cookie between thumb and forefinger, examined it, rotated it, put it down. "Oh, what the hey, might as well give you all the gory details. Back then, I wasn't just truant, I was a major pain-in-the-ass stoner, hanging with other stoners, basically toking up all day." Looking to the side. "Sometimes using more than weed."

Waiting for a reaction. We gave her none. She shook her head. "Also . . . I was having sex with boys. Bad boys. Stupid boys. Doing everything I could to mess up my life."

I said, "But your grades stayed good."

She'd told us that but the memory seemed to jar her. "How do you know that?"

"You said so."

"I did? My brain must be rotting—well, that's true, I did everything wrong but still got all A's. I attribute it to school being mostly a waste of time. I could read fast, had a good attention span, and *those* days I had an *excellent* memory. And even when I was slutting it up, I kept college tucked in a corner of my brain. Like, one day this is going to end and I'll make something of myself. Anyway, I was rarely in class but ended up scoring in the school's top three achievement test scores. *That* really ticked off the administration."

I said, "Confronting them with their essential uselessness."

She burst into laughter. Looked at me in a new way. *Maybe this guy isn't out to drill my skull.*

"Ha ha, probably. Meanwhile, Dad's at his wit's end, no matter how many times he tried to explain things rationally and patiently, I did what he *didn't* want. One day, he just lost it and started screaming at me. I was wasting my life, being an idiot, behaving like a strumpet—he actually used that word, strumpet. I thought it was hilarious, like something out of Monty Python. I laughed in his face and *that* did it. He turned purple—I mean literally, not just flushed, *purple*. And all dark around the eyes. It was bizarre. Like seeing a new creature morph."

She laughed again. Softly. Sadly. "Of course being grokked out of my head didn't help my perception. There I was, barely able to maintain and he's *purple*. He started coming at me, like this." Shoving her face forward and balling her fists.

The memory leached color from an already pallid face. "I was terrified. He'd never hit me, not even close, but this was different, I'm thinking you've lit a match, stupid, now you're going to get burned. I backed away but he kept coming and now his lips are shaking and his eyes are bulging and I'm freaking one hundred percent out but I can't move any farther because I'm up against the kitchen wall. So I screamed. This insane, banshee shriek, I couldn't believe it came out of me. And he stopped. As if he knew a bad thing was on the verge of happening—something that couldn't be reversed."

Twisting in her chair, she began to cry, used the napkin, crumpled it, hung her head. "He had this look on his face, like I was disgusting. I'd stopped screaming but inside I was still freaking out. Then this creepy grin crept onto his face. His teeth weren't great, he grew up poor. I remember thinking how brown and crooked they looked at that moment. Feral, you know? Then, as if someone had twisted a dial, he shrugged and said, 'Like mother, like daughter,' turned his back on me, and left. The next day when I got home I found his bedroom door locked and a note on my bed saying he'd registered me at Milrock, I could either go or find somewhere else to live."

"Tough love," said Milo.

"I deserved it. Sorry for not telling you the first time."

I said, "You didn't want to cast a bad light on either of them."

"Especially Dad. He was the only parent I ever knew, never pressured me or made demands until I acted like a complete moron. Which even at the time I knew I was doing, but I wouldn't—couldn't relent." Head shake. "Disruption for its own sake."

Milo said, "Like mother like daughter."

"After calling me a strumpet. The implication was clear. And it makes sense. What kind of mother leaves her biological child with a man she wasn't even married to? For all she knew he could've given me up and I'd end up in foster care. So maybe she *was* loose. And egocentric. And whatever else—maybe I shouldn't waste your time and mine. But I feel driven to—it's like a hole that needs to be filled. If I don't try, I'll never feel resolved."

She breathed in and out, ran her fingers through her hair, rubbed her eyes. "So what did you want to tell me?"

"We've verified your mother coming down to L.A. and living with a wealthy man."

"Who? Someone famous?"

"Just rich," said Milo. "At this stage, it's best not to get into details."

"Oh, c'mon, Lieutenant. Why can't I know? Did what I just tell you cast aspersions on my sanity?"

"Not at all."

"Then what? Do you think I'll misuse the information?"

"It may not be relevant information."

"So?"

"If you really want a thorough investigation, we can't afford any sort of snafu."

"Meaning what?"

"You confront someone, they complain to the cops, I'm pulled off the case."

Masterful improv.

Ellie Barker said, "So we're talking someone with clout."

Milo smiled.

"Fine, be enigmatic—I have to tell you, your reasoning is kind of paternalistic. Hysterical woman bound to confront."

"Not at all, Ellie."

"Then what?"

"A hole that needs to be filled can fuel all sorts of things."

"I am *not* going to—fine, I'll back off, you barely know me, why should you trust me? But you'll see, I *can* be trusted. And at some point, when you do have good information, I *deserve* to be informed."

"You will be," said Milo. "Just bear with it."

"Oh, Lord—I've lasted this long, suppose I can endure. Are we talking someone in the movie business? Not famous like an actor, maybe behind the scenes?"

"Why would you think that?"

"She came to Hollywood. And in that picture I gave you, she looks pretty theatrical, don't you think? Standing in some forest and she's dolled up like for a party?"

I said, "Neither of them look like outdoorsy types. Your dad's wearing a suit."

"You're right about that. I don't think he owned a pair of sneakers."

I glanced at Milo.

All these years, we're attuned to cuing and receiving.

He said, "That's kind of interesting. We looked into his death and he—"

"Went hiking and fell off a cliff," she said. "I also thought about telling you but couldn't see that it mattered. But yes, it is weird."

"That park," he said. "Did you know him to frequent it?"

"Never. But by then I was out of the house, for all I knew he was trying to get in shape—late-in-life exercise or something. For all I know he was interested in a new woman and that's why. Though I doubt that. Dad just wasn't like that. Or so I'd like to think."

I said, "Like what?"

"Superficial, out for appearances. Unlike her. Maybe."

Flash of heat in the gray eyes. "She walks out on us and goes to live with a rich guy in Hollywood? It's pathetic, no? A cliché."

Her lips moved. A single muttered word. If I hadn't just heard it recently, I might not have deciphered.

Strumpet.

21

As Ellie walked us to the door, Melvin Boudreaux appeared. Before Ellie got there he was in front of her, cracking the oak six inches and peering outside. Satisfied, he opened all the way and stationed himself in the center of the inner courtyard.

Ellie looked startled at being cut off.

Boudreaux said, "Part of the job, ma'am."

"Ma'am, again. Do they teach you guys that in police school?"

Milo said, "We pride ourselves on being gentlemen."

"Ah," said Ellie Barker. "I suppose I could get used to it."

As we drove away, I said, "Artful dodge."

"What was?"

"You told her nothing but left her satisfied."

"Couldn't have her confronting Val and screwing things up."

"Double bonus, she gave you new info."

"Stanley hated Dorothy."

"And Stanley could have a temper when pushed hard enough."

He reached Los Feliz Boulevard, waited to make the illegal left.

"Turning purple. Think I pay a little more attention to Barker. What we said before: He finds her and waylays her."

"In a shiny new Caddy," I said. "Maybe that was symbolic: You left me for someone richer, look what good it did you."

"The mansion, the car, yeah, I can see that bringing on some serious magenta."

Five-second traffic gap. He swung across the boulevard. "Problem is, I can't see any avenue to Stan. For Tony—or the other Des Barres kids, for that matter—I can at least look for someone who knew the not-so-merry wives of Mulholland."

"Maybe there's someone around who recalls Stan and Dorothy as a couple."

"Thirty-six years ago and five hundred miles away? You come up with something, let me know. Meanwhile, I'm gonna see what I can dig up about Helen and Arlette."

I said, "Here's a possible arrow to Arlette. In the article about her accident, the owner of the stables is mentioned."

"Remember her name?"

"Nope."

"Me, neither." He handed me his notepad.

As he headed south, I made my way through two pages of his back-hand scrawl before I found it.

Agua Fria Stables. Pasadena. Winifred Gaines.

I searched. "No current listing for the business. Hold on . . . nothing online about her, personally."

He pulled to the curb on Western just past Franklin. "You drive and I'll play with the databases."

For years, he'd been violating protocol by conducting police business in the Seville, but never had he relinquished the wheel of an official vehicle.

I said, "You're off the grid so it's legit?"

"Can't imagine it would be," he said. "You can move the seat."

Property tax rolls showed Winifred Gaines divvying to the county for a single-family residence on Los Robles Avenue in San Marino. A DMV check revealed an eighty-eight-year-old with an active driver's license and a fifteen-year-old Mercedes 500 living at the address.

I said, "Not far from the stables in Pasadena."

He scrolled through a map. "Not far from Huntington Gardens plus a nice car. Maybe another one with a butler."

The reverse directory kicked up Winifred Gaines's landline.

I said, "One advantage of dealing with mature folk."

"Always looking on the bright side, huh?" Five rings sounded before a strong female voice said, "Hello?"

"Ms. Gaines?"

"Who's this?"

"Lieutenant Sturgis of the Los Angeles Police Department."

"This better not be one of those scams."

"It's about Arlette Des Barres, ma'am. If you remember—"

"I remember just fine. If you're some kind of reporter doing one of those retrospectives, forget it."

"I'm not, ma'am. Feel free to check me out. Lieutenant Milo B. Sturgis—"

"One of my nephews is a deputy police chief in Philadelphia, he's always ma'am this, ma'am that. The only other people who ma'am that much are Filipino caregivers. Sir, this, ma'am, that. Nice people, well trained and well bred. A couple of them took care of my mother and she lasted to a hundred and four. What do you want to know about that poor woman? The fools who investigated the first time certainly weren't interested in what I had to say."

"Forest rangers?"

"You bet," said Winifred Gaines. "Bermuda shorts and funny hats."

"Well, I certainly *am* interested."

"You've got something on him posthumously?"

"Who?"

"That dissolute husband of hers."

"Not exactly."

"Then why bother?"

"Is there any way we can meet to discuss it, ma'am?"

"Forget that."

"Just briefly?"

"You *are* persistent—you'd *better* not be a reporter."

"Feel free to call West L.A. Division and—"

"And be put on hold? I don't think so, sir."

"Ma'am—"

"Can't stand to hear a grown man cry, tell you what," said Winifred Gaines. "I was planning to have a nice quiet *alone* dinner at four thirty. If you can make it by then, fine."

Hour and twenty minutes' grace time.

Milo said, "Four thirty it is. Where?"

"San Marino Fish Market on Huntington Drive. You show up with a badge that didn't come out of the Cracker Jack box, I'll talk to you. And it's not Ms., it's Mrs."

Click.

Milo said, "Her mother made a hundred and four. Maybe what my aunt Agnes called 'too mean to die.'" He looked up the restaurant. "Looks pretty good."

"Want the reins back?"

"Nah, you're doing great with the oversteer. Drop yourself at home, plenty of time for me to make it back on time."

I said, "You're kidding."

"About what?"

"I miss the charm-fest and suffer informatus interruptus?"

"That's a thing?"

"It should be."

He got back behind the wheel, pulled a three-pointer on Western, and returned to Los Feliz Boulevard. Two miles past the turnoff to Ellie Barker's house was an on-ramp to the I-5, a bipolar highway. This afternoon, the phase was acute depression: miles of vehicles bunched up due to a capsized produce truck. Severe dent in the city's cabbage supply.

That finally surrendered to eight miles of overcompensating speed on the 134 E followed by a commuter clot on the 210.

Freeways. I thought of something an econ prof had said back in college. No such thing as free.

When we landed on the elegant streets of San Marino, an hour and ten minutes had passed.

Milo said, "Time to spare," but broke some speed limits anyway. Drumming the wheel, then the dash, then back to the wheel. The edginess that comes when he tries to convince himself something's going to break.

22

San Marino Fish Market was a sparkling storefront on a busy intersection. The city's genteel with an older demographic, and that shaped the driving. Steady but civilized traffic created a constant low thunder.

Plenty of free parking was available near the entrance. Milo slid in next to a chocolate-brown Mercedes 500 with a miniature horseshoe hanging from the rearview mirror. Chocolate-colored cowgirl hat on the backseat. He rubbed his face, like washing without water. Edginess kicked up several notches.

Inside the restaurant were four round tables covered in white butcher paper and backed by a small refrigerated case featuring treasures from the briny. On the wall was what you'd expect in an old-school seafood joint: coiled ropes and nets, wood-and-brass captain's wheels, a deep-sea diver mask, an illustrated chart featuring sketches of finned and shelled creatures.

Three tables were occupied by groups of white-haired people. The one closest to the door was set with three chairs, one of them filled amply by a large, poodle-coiffed woman wearing a blue denim, pearl-snap western shirt. Diet Coke and a basket of sourdough in front of her. Jaws working on the bread.

Milo said, "Mrs. Gaines?"

She chewed some more then swallowed, all the while studying us. "Brilliant deduction, you must be a detective. Who's this?"

"Alex Delaware."

"My son's named Alex. He's an actuary. I ordered for myself, it's probably too early for you."

"We're fine." He began to sit down.

"Uh-uh, at the counter," said Winifred Gaines, pointing. "You pick out your victim, they cook it and bring it to you."

"The fish are live?"

"No, dead. Like your victims."

When we got back to the table, Winifred Gaines said, "What did you order?"

Milo said, "Shrimp-crab combo with fries, grilled halibut and fries for him."

"Grilled. That's why he's skinny and we're not. I got the same as you. Don't read too much into it."

A young, smiling waitress brought Milo's iced coffee and my water and said, "More Diet Coke, Mrs. Gaines?"

"Sure." Glancing at me. "Water? Tasteless. Way too much virtue, Slim. So what do you want to know about poor Arlette and why after all these years?"

"We're looking into a thirty-six-year-old murder that may or may not be related to her."

"That's around the same time as Arlette."

"One year after."

"Someone else was taken in by his charms?"

"Dr. Des Barres?"

"That's who we're talking about, right?"

"You didn't like him."

"I judge people by how they treat animals. When he thought no one was watching, he kicked his mounts way too hard. One day, Robert the Bruce—my biggest, strongest stallion—got fed up and gave him a good rock and roll, nearly threw him. Tony was lucky he didn't get brained."

"He called himself Tony."

"Everyone did."

"He's got a son named Tony."

"That one was called Junior. Handsome kid, very bright. They both were, there were two sons. The little girl was much younger. Quiet. They all deserved better than Tony."

"Not a great dad."

Winifred Gaines snorted. Hard not to hear it as equine.

I said, "Sounds like you knew the family pretty well."

"Just from a business perspective. Arlette was British. She grew up with horses, learned to use the Western saddle, really got into our way of life. She got two beauties from me and boarded them with me. Sometimes she'd ride with Junior or the other one—forget his name. She wasn't the boys' real mother, you know. *He* was a widow when they met but she raised those kids as if they were hers. The baby *was* hers. That one didn't ride, rarely came to the stables. When she did, she sat in the office and drew pictures."

"The boys and Tony rode."

"More the boys, once in a while him. When Arlette brought the kids, she'd ride Butter, a lovely pinto, and Junior would ride Bramble, the other one I sold her, a black beauty. The younger boy—Bill, that's what it was—would take a rental. When it was just two of them, both their mounts got ridden. The time he almost got thrown, he showed up late and Junior was already on Bramble."

Her eyes flashed. "Not only did he kick too hard, he'd dig his heels into their flanks and grind." Scowling, she twisted a fist to demonstrate.

"He had these fancy cowboy boots with big heels he bought in Beverly Hills of all places. Rodeo Drive—did you know they named it that because in the old days you could ride horses up and down? Now it's traffic and tourists."

Another snort. "World's going this way fast." She aimed a fist downward and let it plummet.

Milo said, "The day Arlette died—"

"She was riding Bramble because I thought Butter had a touch of white line disease. Turned out it was just some superficial gunk, but I needed the vet to see her. Either way, it made no sense, her being thrown. Both horses were gentle and Arlette knew how to ride."

I said, "Could Bramble have gotten spooked by a forest animal?"

"Could the sky fall? Anything's possible, there's cah-yotes out there, high-strung deer, even a bear or a puma once in a blue. But if it was a puma, believe me, it would've taken advantage, they wouldn't have found Arlette intact. And Bramble wouldn't be standing a few yards away whimpering. Besides, they were followed."

Milo and I sat forward.

Winifred Gaines's smile was smug—an oracle entrusted with a sacred truth. "You didn't know, huh?"

"No, ma'am."

"Figures," she said. "I told those clowns, they couldn't care less."

"Tell us," said Milo.

The smile turned wicked. "Guess I will if you behave yourselves— here's our dinner."

When Milo's anxious and is presented with food, he either gorges or abstains. This time he just watched in admiration as Winifred Gaines began a frontal assault on her food.

Four thirty was early. I had no appetite, either.

Two chew-and-swallows, a breather, one more mouthful, then: "What's your problem? Can't handle fish before dark?"

He picked up his fork and knife, excised a tiny piece of shrimp.

"Hmph. What about you, Slim?"

I ingested a french fry.

She shook her head. Loss of faith in humanity.

A minute or so later, she put down her utensils and grinned. "Keeping you in suspense? Yeah, I'm a coldhearted biddy. Learned about delay of gratification from being married."

I said, "Your delay or your husband's?"

She glowered at me, then her lips worked as she fought laughter. Finally, losing the battle, she let out a belch of guffaw. Her chest heaved. A pearl snap came loose. "Slim's a comedian. Well, I'm taking the Fifth on that."

She swigged Diet Coke and sat back.

"Okay, I won't torture you anymore. Strictly speaking, Arlette wasn't followed. But someone rode into the forest soon after her."

Milo said, "How soon?"

"A few minutes—three, four, five. I didn't think much of it until I heard what happened to her."

Milo said, "Who'd you see?"

"Can't swear to it but my impression was a woman, from the size and the way she moved in the saddle. Women have wider pelvises, sometimes they shift around a bit until they get a firm grip. That's what this one was doing."

I said, "Maybe someone without much experience?"

"You and your maybes. Yeah, could be that, but even experienced females sometimes jiggle around. My daughter was a dressage champ and when she'd first get on, she'd be this and that and back to this before she settled down."

Milo said, "What did this person look like?"

"No idea, it was far away, a hundred yards give or take. *Maybe* it was like you said, Slim. A rookie rider, female or some small guy. All I can tell you is the horse was brown and not one of mine. There were two other rental ranches near me, one north, one south. Clip joints, anyone could waltz in and pay for an hour ride. Their animals were old and tired, more chance dropping on the trail than going wild and throwing anyone. I told the rangers all this. They looked at me like I was nuts."

"Are either of the other ranches still in business?" said Milo.

"Nah, it's all strip malls and apartments. You obviously haven't taken the time to look."

"You're our first stop, ma'am."

"Am I supposed to be flattered?" Her fist did another swan dive. "Strip malls."

I said, "Did you see the person who followed Arlette emerge from the forest?"

"Nope," she said. "But I wouldn't have, by then a ranger had found the body, it was a hubbub, all sorts of official vehicles. So I was pretty distracted."

Milo said, "So someone could have come out without being noticed."

"Absolutely," said Winifred Gaines, "and there are also other trails that would lead you north or south of where Arlette started."

Milo pulled out his pad. "Just to be thorough, what were the names of the other ranches?"

"Clip Joint One was Open Trails, Clip Joint Two was River Ridge, which made no sense 'cause there's no river anywhere nearby."

"Do you happen to recall who ran them?"

She put down her fork. "Open Trails were some Armenians from Glendale, River Ridge was this woman from Tujunga, real scatterbrain, had no clue. Neither of them lasted—maybe a year after Arlette died. That's when the Armenians started selling off land and the whole development thing started. Now you answer my question: Why so gung ho after all this time?"

"Just what I told you, ma'am. We're looking into a thirty—"

"Six-year-old murder. You're thinking he did it to Arlette and then to someone else?"

"I can't really get into—"

"Ha. Your eyes just got shifty, there's my answer. Well, makes sense. Do you have any idea what he got up to after Arlette died?"

"We've been told he had women living with him at his house."

"Bimbos coming in and out," said Winifred Gaines. "Like he was that *Playboy* character . . . Hefner. It was common knowledge. Not a wholesome environment for the kids, especially the little one. He even changed the way he looked."

"How so?"

"Before then he was this engineer-businessman type. Suits, ties, little Walter Pidgeon mustache." She wiggled a finger under her nose. "Coke-bottle eyeglasses, the whole Mr. Wizard thing. Next time I saw him—we ran into each other at Huntington Gardens—he was with the little girl, had a total switcheroo."

Another sub-nose wiggle was followed by a four-finger fan under her chin. "Now he had one of those goatee beards. Dyed it black, as believable as a campaign promise. And he was wearing those *bell*-bottoms. And one of those *shirts*."

She stuck out her tongue, retrieved her fork, ate four shrimp.

I said, "Tasteless shirt?"

"Shiny silk," she said, as if that settled it. "Shiny fake-diamond buttons, puffy sleeves—sissy sleeves. *Paisley* in crazy colors. Probably got it along with the boots on Rodeo *Drive*. I heard he went there for entertainment, too."

"What kind of entertainment?"

"Some tacky nightclub. My husband told me. Jack was a lawyer with Skinner Thorndike downtown, avoided the Westside like a plague but had to take a deposition in Beverly Hills. Some movie producer who'd cheated someone, big surprise. The crook kept Jack waiting, he got stuck there until evening. He was walking to his car and guess who he spotted going into some club on Rodeo."

"The new Dr. Des Barres."

"New and *not* improved," said Winifred Gaines. "When Jack came home he was laughing. 'Honey, you'll never guess who turned all hippie-dippie.'"

Milo said, "Did Jack tell you the name of the club?"

"I didn't ask, he didn't tell. Like I said, he steered clear of anything west of Spring Street."

"Was Dr. Des Barres with anyone?"

"Jack didn't say, so he probably wasn't. I'm sure all the company he needed was inside." She snorted. "Beverly *Hills.* Place hasn't been classy for a long time. Last year my granddaughter insisted we go there, there's a store she likes on Beverly Drive, it was her birthday. You should've seen it. *Hordes* of Orientals, they're dying their hair blue and yellow and whatnot, you'd think you were in Tokyo."

Milo said, "So Dr. Des Barres made a lifestyle change. Anything else you can tell us about him or his family?"

"We didn't socialize, they were just clients—Arlette was."

I said, "What kind of person was she?"

"Sweet, soft-spoken, nice British accent. When we chitchatted it was about the horses. She knew her stuff. That's why I can't see her taking a tumble from a sweet thing like Bramble. So you suspect Tony of being a really bad guy. Even so, why bother? He's dead, it's all ancient history."

Milo said, "Doing my job, ma'am. Trying to do it well."

Her lips pursed and her brows arced.

"Well," she said, "guess you can't ask more than that from anyone." New voice. Soft, unguarded. "Don't mean to give you grief, you're just catching me at a bad time. Yesterday was the anniversary of Jack's death."

"Sorry about that, ma'am."

"Yeah, it's been a laugh a minute."

He said, "How long has he been gone?"

I figured that might elicit a sharp retort. Winifred Gaines sighed.

"Four years. Year after that, Alex moved away, six months later, Melinda. Can't blame them, they've got great jobs, I'm grateful they're not wastrels. When the area turned into a construction zone, the riding business dried up. I finally sold everything at auction. Except the horses, those I personally made sure were adopted by good people."

She shook her head. "Now it's just me and the house, which is too darn big. But I can't bring myself to sell it. Bridget?"

The waitress came over. "What can I get you, Mrs. Gaines?"

"A beer. I know I said I was watching the calories but to heck with that."

"Sure, Mrs. Gaines. Sam Adams like always?"

"Anything as long as it's not some poor-excuse *light*. I want to feel *full*." She looked at our plates. "Obviously you don't. Bridget, set them up with to-go bags."

Milo said, "That's okay."

"Waste," said Winifred Gaines, "is not okay. You don't want it, I'll take it."

Milo and I drank good robusto coffee as she nursed a tall glass of lager. When she'd emptied it, she called for the check.

He said, "On us, ma'am."

"No chance. I pay my own way."

But when Bridget came over and he was ready with enough cash to evoke a grinning "*Thank* you, sir!" Winifred Gaines made no attempt to stop the transaction.

The three of us got up from the table and she picked up the to-go bag containing our uneaten food. Her walk aimed for confidence but there was slight unsteadiness in her step.

I held the door open for her. "Thanks, Slim."

She made her way to the brown Mercedes. She'd left the car unlocked, opened the rear door and placed the bag on the seat.

Milo said, "Anything else you want to tell us, ma'am?"

"Just thanks for dinner. I noticed you paid with legal tender. Maybe there's hope."

We stood by as Winifred Gaines backed heedlessly into traffic, setting off tire squeals but no honks or road rage. She sped off, gray smoke belching from the Mercedes's rear exhaust.

Milo said, "No one flipped her off. Place is a bastion of etiquette."

I said, "Unlike that nest of barbarians, Beverly *Hills*."

He laughed, studied the sky, turned serious. "The club she was talking about is probably The Azalea, only place I know of on Rodeo. Foil paper walls, disco ball, drinks with parasols, bad Chinese food. And perfect for a guy like Tony Des Barres two point oh."

"Older guys and younger girls?"

"Members-only if you were male. The girls were a perk."

"Where'd they come from?"

"Who knows?"

We got in the unmarked.

I said, "Sounds like you were inside. When was it active?"

"Before my time but not before Dr. Silverman's."

Rick was four years older than us. I did the math. It didn't add up.

Splotches of pink had formed beneath his ears. I decided to let it ride.

He inserted the key but didn't turn it. "Strictly speaking, also before Rick's time. He wasn't legal to drink—barely seventeen, junior at Harvard-Westlake, but even then he had the mustache. He got taken there by a school benefactor—some finance honcho who'd seen Rick play varsity b-ball and wanted to 'counsel' him about a scholarship to an Ivy. Rick was figuring a steak dinner, instead they end up walking through an unmarked door and into all that merriment."

I said, "Older guys and younger girls? How'd taking Rick there figure in?"

"There was also a room *upstairs* where the perks *weren't* girls." Deep breath. "*Lavender* foil, fake-fur seating, Aubrey Beardsley prints. Subtle, huh? When the letch went to the john, Rick got the hell out of there and took a cab home. No further communication from the guy and no more scholarship talk. His parents couldn't afford the Ivies so he went to the U., undergrad and med school. You know the rest—chief resident, the job at Cedars. When he gets home tonight, I'll ask him what else he remembers about the place. If no one died in the E.R. and his mood's okay."

He waited for a lull in the traffic and backed out more smoothly than usual. As if compensating for Winifred Gaines's heedless shotgun entry.

At the first opportunity, he swung a U on Huntington. "Any thoughts about what we just heard?"

I said, "Someone riding into the forest a few minutes after Arlette doesn't mean much by itself. But with one staged accident we know about and two others that could also be setups, it is interesting."

"Hate that word," he said. "Let's hope it doesn't get *fascinating*."

Two options for getting back to the Westside: Arroyo Seco Parkway to the Pasadena Freeway and through the downtown interchange, or reversing our trip on the 210. Both featured sections of red on Waze, creating online peppermint sticks. The 210 would deposit us closer to Beverly Glen.

At this hour, the on-ramp was metered and we idled in a queue of commuters, mostly people driving alone.

Milo said, "For argument's sake, let's say ol' Winnie was right about a woman following Arlette and that it actually means something. That take you anywhere?"

I said, "A love rival."

"That's where *my* head went. Arlette died a year before Dorothy showed up. What if Des Barres started playing around while he was still married? Before he went all harem. He hooks up with a young lovely, she gets Dollar Sign Fever and sets her sights on being Wife Number Three. Only problem is, Number Two's alive and kicking, so Dreaming Girl decides to clear the deck."

"If so, it didn't work. Des Barres never married again. But maybe she settled for a position in the harem, figuring it was temporary. Especially if it was a prime slot."

"Meaning?"

"Top girl. What Tony Junior felt Dorothy was aiming for."

He smiled sourly. "A pecking order."

"There always is," I said.

"Among women?"

"Among people."

"Ah. Don't tell the internet I just asked that."

"I don't know, man, you're making me feel kind of uncomfortable."

I flashed jazz hands. He flashed a new flavor of smile. Weak around the edges—preoccupied.

A few minutes later, he said, "Arlette's in the way of Dreamy's aspirations so she saddles up and takes action. Ride in, act nonchalant, strike up a conversation, and shove or yank Arlette off. She's waiting for the marriage proposal but ol' Tony Senior goes in a whole new directions and now there's serious competition in the form of Dorothy. One fake accident worked, why not another. Now all I have to do is I.D. Ms. Maleficent."

The auto queue opened suddenly and stayed that way. Muttering, "The Red Sea parts," he eased onto the freeway and merged.

I said, "The scenario fits Dorothy's murder but I can't see any tie-in to P. J. Seeger's motorcycle crash or Stan Barker's tumble."

"Why not? The same thing we've suggested all along. They both got too close to the truth."

"Femme fatale clearing the decks years later? And years apart? As far as we know neither Barker or Seeger—anyone for that matter—made a connection to a woman living in the mansion. Du Galoway came the closest, and he didn't suspect anyone but Des Barres."

"Which, now that you mentioned it, could be righteous, Alex."

"Des Barres collaborated on both murders."

"Guy had enough charisma and dough to corral a harem. So what the hell do I do now?"

"More archaeology."

As we passed into Glendale, he said, "All the time it's taking, maybe we shoulda eaten."

Before I could answer, his phone tooted horrific abuse of Handel's *Messiah*. He glanced at the screen. "Martz. She's been bugging me for a progress report. You'd think my ignoring her would be enough."

Placing the phone between us on the bench seat, he speed-dialed and switched to speaker.

A male voice said, "Deputy Chief Martz's office."

"Lieutenant Sturgis returning her call."

Throat clear. "*Three* calls according to my records, Lieutenant."

"And you are?"

"Sergeant Schifter."

"Glad you keep good records. She in?"

"Not at this moment."

"Tell her I called with a regress report."

"Pardon?"

"Regress, Sergeant. It's the opposite of progress."

Click. Wolf-grin.

I said, "You must've been fun to teach in grade school."

"Actually, I was the soul of obedience and conformity."

I laughed.

"No, really. By grade four I knew I was different but didn't really understand it and figured I should keep my mouth shut. I was so quiet the teachers told my parents I needed to be 'brought out.' How's that for irony? What about you? Model kid?"

"I liked school."

"Big shock. Straight A's, why not."

"More than that," I said. "It was safe. Then I'd go home."

23

We rolled up to my house eighty-eight tedious minutes later. Nearly an hour and a half of stop-and-go to cover twenty miles.

Milo turned off the car. "You mind making some coffee? I'm gonna be up for a while trying to figure things out."

"No prob."

We trudged up the stairs to the terrace and I unlocked the door.

Robin was in the living room reading *Acoustic Guitar*. She'd changed out of her work clothes into a black cowl-necked sweater, charcoal tights, and red flats. A collection of bangle bracelets decorated one wrist, the watch I'd given her last Christmas banded the other.

She sprang up and hugged me, gave Milo a cheek peck.

I said, "You look gorgeous. Where're we going?"

Milo straightened from petting Blanche. "Have fun, kids." He turned to leave.

Robin held him back by his arm. "You look worn out. You both do. I was thinking something simple, burgers, sushi, whatever. Join us, Big Guy."

"You're an angel but I've got something protruding here." He reached around to the small of his back. "Oh, yeah, it's a fifth wheel."

"Poor baby. C'mon, let's get nutrition."

I said, "Heed her wise counsel."

Robin said, "Exactly. He does and look how well he's weathered the onslaught of time."

I drove the three of us to a place at the top of the Glen. Japanese fused with Italian, which translated to crudo coexisting with sashimi, pizza dating teppanyaki, and what seemed like random pairings labeled "what the chef's into tonight."

The waiter said, "Hey, guys, I'm Jaron and I'll be your server. I advise the eel. She won *Chopped* with it."

Milo said, "Let's start with a beer."

"No worries. We've got a great selection of imported—"

"Miller's fine."

"Um . . . I think we have that. You, ma'am?"

Robin said, "Knob Creek Old Fashioned."

I said, "Oban 14, neat, ice on the side."

"That's . . ."

"Single-malt scotch."

The waiter said, "Wow, you guys know your bevs." He read back the order, corrected the errors. Out came a handheld device. "Okay, guys. Eel will go great with all those drinks."

Milo said, "Bumper crop on slithery things, huh?"

Robin said, "Poor little orphan elvers."

Jaron said, "Pardon?"

Her smile, beautiful and wide, dismissed him.

The drinks were followed by a torrent of small plates, the quantity dictated by Milo, back in fine form. He tucked in immediately as Robin looked on like an approving mother.

I fiddled with my chopsticks.

She said, "You okay, honey?"

"Thinking."

Milo said, "About what?"

The honest answer was too many suspects and no real progress.

I said, "Another scotch."

Dessert was a pair of scorched cedar shingles each containing three scoops of ice cream decorated with a juniper sprig. On one slab, chewy Japanese mochi: green tea, red bean, sesame. The other featured gelato "infused" with "organic Buddha's fingers citron, winter melon, and a breeze of chianti."

More geographic meld; world peace should be so easy.

I said, "Nicely curated."

Milo said, "What the hell does that mean?"

"Absolutely nothing."

He used a tiny shovel-shaped spoon to slice off some red bean. Tasted. Considered. "Different texture. Pretty good. Actually, good."

Robin said, "They make ice cream out of everything in Japan. Including raw horsemeat."

"C'mon."

"Really."

"Jesus. Where'd you pick up that nugget?"

I said, "I'm guessing Misota Metaru."

She gave me a thumbs-up.

Milo said, "Who's that?"

I said, "Mister Metal, big-time guitar god in Tokyo. She works on his gear."

"Guy comes all the way here to get his stuff fixed?"

Robin said, "He lives in Thousand Oaks. His real name is Mitchell Mandelbaum."

"Huh. I'm visualizing black ninja p.j.'s on stage."

"It varies. Last time was a set of antique Japanese armor. He looked like Darth Vader."

"All that metal," he said. "I'd worry about electrocution."

"I've mentioned it to him," she said. She crossed her fingers.

He said, "You lead a different life, kiddo."

"Only vicariously. Mostly I'm in a room all day sawing and gluing."

He regarded the spoon, mumbled "too damn small" and put it down. "Raw horsemeat." He looked at me. "Must be our day for quadrupeds."

I drummed a horse-hoof clop on the table.

Robin said, "What does that mean?"

I explained.

She said, "Maybe another fake accident? Interesting."

Milo clutched his head. "That word again."

Robin looked at me.

I said, "He's developed an allergy to 'interesting.'"

"Ah. I think you can get shots for that."

He laughed, fiddled with the sprig, licked his lips. "No aftertaste of Trigger, so far, so good." Eyeing what was left of the ice cream. "You guys full?"

Robin said, "All yours."

"Why not?" he said. "All in the name of recycling."

When he'd finished every dollop, she said, "I don't want to give you a migraine but can I ask a question?"

"Sure."

"You always say you start with the victim. Since the case started I've heard a lot about suspects but not much about her."

"That's 'cause there's not much to know, kiddo, can't even get biographical basics."

"Mystery woman," she said. "Hiding something?"

"She ended up in California, which is where everyone comes to reinvent, so good chance. Does it tie in to her murder? Who the hell knows? All I can work with is facts on the ground. They keep piling up but nothing's really clarifying."

I said, "Making it worse, Ellie has no early memories. She was a baby when the relationship with her stepdad began and a toddler when Dorothy walked out."

Robin said, "Leaving a little kid behind to hook up with a rich guy? Not exactly a world-class woman." Metal in her voice. Her relationship with her own mother had always been a challenge.

I said, "The older Des Barres brother said other women in the mansion tried to ingratiate themselves with him and his sibs. Dorothy didn't bother. Just the opposite, she was aloof."

"She sounds pretty unlikable."

Milo said, "Worst type of victim."

"Why?"

"Too many potential enemies."

"Do you think she just landed in L.A. and started hunting for a sugar daddy? Or had she been involved with Des Barres before?"

"Good question," said Milo. "*They* keep popping up, too."

He drained his beer.

Robin said, "One more thing?"

"Hit me."

"Ellie's boyfriend getting shot. If the goal was to dissuade her, why not simply target her? And if there really was a woman on horseback bumping off the competition, she'd have to be, what—late fifties minimum, more likely sixties by now. It's hard to see someone like that lurking in the bushes. How, for that matter, would she even know about the investigation?"

"The Des Barres sibs know about it, thanks to me, and rich folk are used to delegating. Val Des Barres's butler has a bit of a record, so I watched him for a couple of days. So far the worst thing he's done is glide through a boulevard stop."

He caught the waiter's eye and mouthed, *Check.*

This time I got there first with a credit card.

"Aw c'mon."

"Nope."

"At least let me do the tip." He began to reach for his wallet.

Robin placed her hand on his. "We're your support group. Accept the love."

The following morning at ten, I got a text from Maxine Driver.

Found something but probably not useful.

Open to anything. Can you send?

Not great condition, might be better to hand over in person.

Name the time and place.

An hour, the pizza place?

Perfect. Thanks, Maxine.

You'll find a way to pay me back.

The "pizza place" was Gipetto's, a student hangout on Westwood Boulevard, two blocks south of campus. Questionable beer by the pitcher was the star, everything else, the supporting cast.

I'd have sprung for somewhere nicer but Maxine has a thing for pizza. The basic American pie, nothing designer. Her Korean-immigrant parents forbade it when she was small.

I'd asked what they were worried about.

"Anything new."

I arrived first. At eleven in the morning the place was nearly empty, a few groggy-looking sophomores praying to their phones.

A waitress who was probably their peer came over. "Oven just got to the right temp, orders won't be ready for fifteen minutes, maybe twenty."

"No problem. Large mushroom whenever."

"Cool attitude," she said. "Are you a prof? I'm looking for a comfortable elective."

"At the med school across town."

Shrug. "That doesn't help me."

At ten after, Maxine strode in carrying an oversized tan leather bag and wearing a black wrap dress swirled with purple and a string of pearls too large to be real.

She's a tall, slim woman just turned forty but looking younger, pretty without the self-consciousness of someone who's traded on her looks. She wears her hair in a flapper-type bob that fits her fascination with the past.

L.A.'s criminal past, in particular, a topic that stymied the History Department because she refused to infuse her conclusions with "analyses of contemporary hot-button topics." Instead, she plugged away like a true scholar, piling up more awards and peer-review publications than could be ignored, making tenure unavoidable.

Her life's work also baffled her parents. ("Bad people should be forgotten.") Another insult added to the familial injury Maxine had inflicted by forsaking premed. Marrying a physician had blunted the issue but hadn't erased it. ("I'm sure they're convinced David will leave me for someone younger and appropriately obedient, I'll be poor and be unable to take care of them.")

She waved as she approached. "Did you order?"

"The usual."

"Excellent." We shook hands and she sat. "How's it going on the case?"

"It's not."

"Sorry. Like I said, this is unlikely to change that."

Out of the bag came a brown, marbleized folder. Out of the folder came a page-sized color photo that she slid across the table.

Back in the pre-digital days, photographs could be stunningly sharp when developed by pros in darkrooms, clouded and blurry when amateurs clicked their Brownies and Polaroids or pretended to comprehend their Nikons. Acid-laced paper, ultraviolet rays, and the passage of time didn't help.

This was clearly an amateur effort, deteriorating to white space at the edges and blunted further by enlargement. A few pinpoints of missing pigment freckled sections of the subjects.

Four subjects, seated at a bright-red table loaded with massive cocktails in tulip glasses, the liquids within garishly tinted. The wall behind the quartet was silver foil patterned with flowers. Crude, unidentifiable, blue and mustard-colored blossoms.

Older man, one younger woman to his right, two others to his left.

His face was the least damaged. Ironic because time had done just fine on its own.

Hatchet face covered by coarse, slack, too-tan skin. Marsupial pouches tugged at bleary, heavily lidded eyes. Thinning hair was brushed back Dracula-style and tinted the same unlikely matte black as a pointy goatee. A chunky gold link chain hung across the hairless triangle created by three undone buttons of a pink-and-orange paisley shirt.

Huge change from Dr. Anton Des Barres's corporate photo.

Maxine said, "Your guy." A statement, not a question.

I nodded. "Where'd you find this?"

"A book on L.A. called *Be-Inns*. Two *n*'s, as in hostelries. Self-published deal on SoCal nightlife during the period you're interested in. I'd exhausted all the criminal leads on Des Barres. As far as I can tell, he never hung out with hoods, nor was he implicated in high crimes and misdemeanors. So I did what I always do: fan out and try subsidiary sources. Starting with acquainting myself with the company headshot you sent me, memorizing the layout of his features and seeing if I could spot it somewhere else. Usually it leads nowhere, this time it didn't. The book was in pretty bad shape, self-published, cheaply made, literally falling apart. I tried phone-shooting this image, wasn't happy with the result, and did a few runs on the department Xerox machine. This is the best I came up with."

"Appreciate the effort, Maxine. Who's the author?"

"Alastair Stash, obviously a pseudonym. I wouldn't bother looking for another copy, Alex. I tried and it's not on the Web, any academic library or vintage dealer. I got my copy years ago when Acres of Books went out of business and I drove down to Long Beach and scrounged through their discount pile. Marginal junk that I boxed up and stored in my garage. I kept telling myself I'd go through it but never did."

"Amazing."

"What is?"

"That you connected the headshot to this."

"Really? To me it was kind of obvious. Cosmetics change but basic dimensions stay the same. I'm flipping through pages and he jumped out at me. He looks sauced, no? Deliciously dissolute. What's his story?"

"Probably a midlife crisis fueled by big bucks."

The pizza arrived. Maxine nibbled. "So you can't tell me anything, yet?"

I said, "There's not much to tell you beyond a possible location. B.H. club called The Azalea."

She lifted the photo and showed me the back.

Single line in black marker, Maxine's assertive block lettering:

PROB. AZALEA CLUB, RODEO DRIVE 35–40 YRS AGO.

"How'd you figure it out?"

"The book identified it as being on Rodeo and the only place that fit was The Azalea. Just to make sure, I looked at some shots from an old design mag in the research library. Same wallpaper in what they called The Chic Room. Subtle, huh? Unfortunately I haven't turned up any serious criminal activity at the place. Just a reputation for cheesy disco music, major-league boozing, and minor-league doping. The clientele was rich guys hanging with younger chickadees. Which fits your guy."

I flipped the photo and studied the three women with Des Barres. Trio of blurry faces under long, straight platinum-blond hair. Strapless dresses: black, red, yellow.

Poor resolution wasn't enough to hide the truth.

I'd never seen the two faces to Des Barres's left but Black Dress to the right was Dorothy Swoboda.

I squinted and searched for nuance through the freckling.

The other two women beamed drunkenly but Dorothy's expression was the same borderline grim as in the forest shot with Stanley Barker.

I'd assumed that was due to tension between her and Barker. Maybe it was just her emotional default.

At first glance, not a fun gal—the contrast to the smiling duo was stark. That hadn't stopped Anton Des Barres from recruiting her to his harem. Puzzling, because what older men usually like in younger women is nonstop cheer and worship, genuine or not.

Just as with the Des Barres kids, Dorothy Swoboda was making no effort.

I examined the entire photo again. Red and Yellow wore gems too huge to be real at their ears and suspended from gold chains. Dorothy wore a single necklace.

Question marks filled my head. I felt my face tighten up.

Maxine said, "What?"

I pointed. "This is our victim."

"You're kidding. Amazing. Let me look at her."

She fiddled in her bag for a pair of reading glasses, studied as if examining a relic. "Kind of a sourpuss. She must've been a sexual genius."

"I was wondering what her secret was."

"That's what comes to my mind, Alex. Of course, vaginal virtuosity only goes so far, because men live for constant novelty. And with his setup, Des Barres would have plenty of that. Maybe he got tired of her and she didn't take well to rejection—somehow threatened him—so he got rid of her."

She shifted to Des Barres's face. "He doesn't look like a guy burdened by inhibition . . . notice the exact same hairdo on all of three of them. Obviously, wigs. Obviously, at his behest. It's like they're blow-up dolls. He's into control."

She chuckled. "Pardon my veering into your territory."

"Veer away, Maxine. You're making sense."

"Oh, good. Historians are known for being self-appointed experts on everything . . . so he decides to dump her permanently. Shoot her, burn the car, push it off a cliff. Not a pretty ending. Guy like him probably collected insurance."

She returned the photo and I studied Dorothy's face some more, came up with nothing, and turned to the smiling blondes. Dorothy looked early to midtwenties. The others were younger, maybe even late adolescents.

Assuming the woman on the horse meant anything, could either of them have served as a calculating assassin?

Immature, impressionable, bowled over by wealth and possibility? Absolutely.

But no sign of hostility in this shot. No sideward, hostile glance at Dorothy, just glossy, intoxicated glee. The same went for Anton Des Barres, dull-eyed and slack-lipped.

Dorothy's cool sobriety stood out. A party she'd opted out of.

I placed the photo in the leather briefcase I take to court, thought about what I hadn't told Maxine, fought the urge to make up an excuse and leave. Instead, I listened as she griped enthusiastically about the pathetic emotional stamina of the undergrads foisted upon her.

She'd said the same thing last year.

I said, "It's gotten worse?"

"It's nonstop devolution, Alex. The batch I got this semester is allergic to facts and feels entitled to unearned adoration. We're talking the emotional musculature of blind cave worms."

I laughed. "Are the grad students any better?"

"Worse. They think they're Nobel winners who accidentally missed the flight to Sweden. And in answer to your next question, don't get me started on my colleagues. When utterly compelled to, I go to faculty meetings and listen to incessant bitching about times never being more dire. Apparently we're nudging Armageddon. Which is absurd for people supposedly knowledgeable about the past. The Dark Ages, anyone? Plagues and despots and life expectancies in the thirties? The problem is academics are students afraid to graduate, so their grasp on reality is for shit. On top of that, my so-called peers haven't a clue what it's like to live under Orwellian nightmare communism like my dad did before he deserted his post and sneaked across the DMZ to the South."

"Didn't know that about him. Heroic."

"More like desperation," she said. "Unfortunately, it only reinforced his lifelong sense of caution. And now I've run up a serious therapy bill with you."

"Professional courtesy."

"Thanks. But there's still tit for tat, info-wise."

"You bet."

I watched her nibble. Just when I figured I could leave gracefully, she said, "One promising phenomenon is that comedians are getting roundly ticked off about being told what to think and say. Spread enough ridicule out there, I suppose norms could eventually change. Meanwhile, I soldier on. How about you? Any effect on your work? Not the Milo cases, the clinical stuff."

"Kids under stress aren't concerned with pseudo-suffering."

"Pseudo-suffering. I like that. Maybe I'll find a way to work it into something. Want credit?"

"Take it all."

"Believe me, I will, Alex. And you will let me know once the case resolves?"

"Love your optimism, Maxine."

Something Milo had said to me countless times.

Maxine said, "What else is there?"

The moment I was back in the Seville, I phoned Milo's cell. "Where are you?"

"The office. What's up?"

"I'm looking at a photo of Des Barres with Dorothy at The Azalea. She's wearing the serpentine necklace. Barker told Ellie she left it behind when she left. This shows she had it in L.A. so either Barker lied and he took it from her, maybe when he killed her. Or she traveled between Danville and here at least once."

"When was the photo taken?"

"It's undated."

"How'd you come up with it?"

"Maxine did." I filled him in.

He said, "God bless Maxine. Two other women, huh? Either of them shooting daggers at Dorothy?"

"The equestrian assassin? No, it's a friendly, boozy scene. Except for Dorothy. She looks fetching but serious and sober."

"Nonconformist," he said. "That can get you in trouble."

"Maxine suggested her sexual skills outweighed a failure to worship Des Barres. If that's true, it could've worn thin."

"What'd Maxine think about the necklace?"

"I didn't tell her."

"Why not?"

"Trying to keep the information flow minimal."

A beat. "Good idea. I want to see the photo. Where are you?"

"Ten minutes from you if you arrange parking."

"You will be cheerfully and promptly VIP'd."

24

Pooh-bah parking translated to Milo waiting by the gate to the staff lot and inserting his card as I drove up.

He bowed and scraped. "Second aisle, midway down. Sir. Better yet, I'll accompany you, how's that for service?"

He opened the passenger door and got in.

I said, "Babysitting for a few yards?"

"Got the photo in your briefcase? You can have cookies and milk."

We walked through the lot, crossed Butler Avenue, and entered the station.

I gave him the photo as we climbed the stairs.

"Yeah, Dottie does look serious. Sexual acrobatics, huh?"

"That was Maxine's theory," I said. "Or maybe the others tried too hard and she stood out by playing hard to get."

"Trying to make herself the goal," he said. "Instead, she became prime prey."

"On the way over, I thought of something. Stan Barker, then Des

Barres, both older men, one prosperous, one rich. If she made repeated trips down here, there could be others."

"What we wondered about in the beginning—some L.A. boy-friend. Popular in life, nightmare victim in death."

His office door was wide open. Slouching the one step it took to get to his desk, he collapsed onto a groaning swivel chair. Piles of paper crowded the computer, neatly stacked but higher than usual.

Using the solo assignment to ignore bureaucratic torture.

He swept the highest pile into the trash with clear pleasure. Took the photo, was gone for a few minutes, came back with the original and a copy, both of which went into a blue folder. Unlabeled but the same covers as a standard murder book. Old habits.

"If I don't look daisy-fresh," he said, "it's because I spent a whole bunch of the evening and night watching Sabino Chavez. He left the house once at eight p.m., bought a bag of something at a liquor store on Sunset, returned and never reappeared. From what I've seen so far, Val never leaves. Thrilling bunch, huh?"

His desk phone rang. "Sturgis . . . oh, hi . . . go ahead, at this point I'll believe anything, kiddo."

He listened for a long while, body stiffening and leaning forward, as if torturously winched.

"That *is* nuts. Okay, thanks for filling me in. She know? You want to tell her or should I? No prob. Good work. Onward."

He hung up, shaking his head.

"That was Petra. She just made an arrest in Brannon Twohy's shooting. Turns out, nothing to do with Ellie. A psycho runner signed up for the same race."

"You're kidding."

"Sounds so stupid, I wish I was. Seems there was another shooting yesterday evening, one of the top-rated entrants, Ethiopian, long history of marathon victories. Poor guy was doing his thing near the Observatory in Griffith Park and got nailed in the thigh. Through-and-through, missed the femoral artery, but I don't imagine he'll be competing this year."

"Just like Twohy."

"*Unlike* Twohy, this time there were onlookers who'd come to watch the Ethiopian, including a bunch of firefighters and off-duty cops. The shooter was behind some trees but had to show himself as he ran away. He got chased and tackled and cuffed. Another Hollywood D caught the case, talk about a gimme. Petra heard about it, put it together, and got to co-interview the suspect who crumpled like wet toilet paper. Weapon was an old revolver, Russian manufacture, the idiot's daddy's Vietnam souvenir."

"How old's the idiot?"

"Twenty-nine. And listen to this: grad student at the U. on leave for personal problems."

I muttered, "Blind cave worms."

"What?"

"Professional jealousy gone to the extreme."

"Except the fool's never been close to Twohy's league, even farther from the Ethiopian's. Blames it on a shin splint, if I ran I'd care about what the hell that is. So getting rid of a coupla top seeds would do nothing for him. Petra kept working that, finally got his motive. Quote unquote: fighting athletic inequality."

"Oh, God."

"Trust me, amigo, God is also baffled. Anyway, it boils down to the usual: pathetic loser with a firearm. His public defender's already talking about a mental health plea." He laughed. "Want me to recommend you as a consultant?"

"Not if the PD wants confirmation."

"Wouldn't that be a hoot? You get paid to evaluate the asshole then send in a report that demolishes their strategy? Anyway, I'm gonna let Ellie know."

He dialed, got voicemail, left a message. "Maybe she's over at the hospital, I'll try later."

Seconds later, his phone rang. "Here she is."

"Hi, there, kid— Oh, hey, Mel, you've got her phone? That so? Any idea why? Hmm. I just got some news on him . . . you think she's okay for that? Okay, we'll give it a try."

I said, "Boudreaux answers her phone?"

"Apparently he does when she's up in her bedroom crying."

Melvin Boudreaux answered the door looking less cop-like and more concerned friend.

As he closed the door behind us, he said, "What's the news on the boyfriend?"

Milo summed up the arrest.

Boudreaux said, "Nutcases everywhere. One thing less to worry about, this might be the end of the gig." Eyeing the stairs.

Milo said, "What's going on with her?"

"It started after she went to see him in the hospital. I'm waiting in the hall, there, she comes out looking upset but not like she wants to talk about it. It stayed like that during the ride home, moment we get here, she starts bawling and runs up the stairs. I go up and ask her if everything's okay. Which, looking back, was a dumb-ass question. She says, 'I'll be fine, don't worry,' through the closed door. So I head downstairs and hear her letting out the sobs."

Boudreaux shook his head. "She took the time to reassure me. Say one thing, this gig is different."

Milo said, "How so?"

"I'm with rich people constantly. They're like anyone else, some are nice, some are obnoxious. But I never met anyone as nice as her."

I said, "Is it possible Twohy took a turn for the worse?"

"That was my first thought, Doc. But then she would've stuck around and talked to a doctor, right? She was only in his room for a few minutes, so I'm figuring something more . . . I don't know, interpersonal?"

Milo said, "No sense guessing."

We left Boudreaux downstairs and climbed the steps. A round landing led to two open doors and one that was closed. Milo knocked softly, got no reply, turned a white porcelain doorknob that gave.

Cracking the door, he peeked in, curled his finger in a signal to follow, and stepped in.

Big bedroom, maybe twenty feet square, with high, hand-plastered ceilings, broad-plank oak floors, and vintage moldings. An open doorway to the left fed to an anteroom and a walk-in closet. A half-open door revealed a white-tiled bathroom.

Avocado-colored, gold-tasseled drapes were drawn over the windows. An off-kilter plastic lamp sat on one of two Ikea nightstands, oozing sickly chartreuse light. Next to the lamp sat a tissue box, a noise machine switched off, and several wads of used paper.

Enough space to house a king bed. Or two. Ellie had rented a queen with a cheap-looking slatted headboard, had added no other furniture.

The bedcovers were thin gray chenille that revealed the tight nautilus curl of her body. She'd wrapped herself in the flimsy cloth and drawn the covers over half her head.

A few strawberry strands laced the pillow. Medium-sized woman but the position made her look small, childlike.

Childhood is the essence of powerlessness. Yet for some reason, when we feel helpless, we try to time-travel in reverse.

Milo stepped close. "Ellie?"

Nothing. Then a sniffle followed by a nearly inaudible moan.

"It's Milo, Ellie. I'm here with Dr. Alex."

Prolonged silence. The hiss of a long sigh. Another moan as she labored to shift from her side to her back. Giving us a full view of her face but no emotional entrée: Her eyes remained clamped tight.

"Take your time, Ellie."

As if rebelling, she puffed her lips, propped herself up, opened her eyes and studied the bedcovers. Her face looked eroded as if scrubbed by an overly zealous char. Strangely pretty in a waifish way.

Her lips worked a few seconds before producing sound. "Sorry."

Milo said, "For what?"

She sat up higher, dared eye contact. "For being a baby."

"How so, Ellie?"

"Mel didn't tell you?"

"He said the visit to the hospital made you upset but he has no idea why."

She shifted some more, finally attained a full sit, bracing herself against the too-low headboard. No upper back or neck support. She scooted forward. The covers fell to her waist.

She wore street clothes, a black knit top with white trim around the neckline. Part of a leg protruded. Jeans.

No energy to change when she got home. Collapsing the moment she had privacy and hoping for gray chenille sanctuary. Red-rimmed eyes said that hadn't happened.

Milo perched on the edge of the bed.

Ellie said, "Mel asked but I didn't answer him. Rude. Sorry about that, too."

"Can't see anything you need to be sorry for."

Quivery smile. "According to *him* I have *lots* to be sorry for."

"Brannon?"

She reached for the tissue box, snagged a chunk, and covered her eyes.

I'd been trained in strategic silence. So had Milo. The same goal: getting people to talk.

It didn't work. Ellie Barker said nothing.

Milo smiled down at her. Every inch, the benevolent uncle.

I smiled, too. Ellie kept her eyes on Milo, never looked my way.

"Do I have to spell it out?" she said. "He dumped me. Right there in the hospital."

"Sorry," said Milo.

"So was I. So there it is, I'm pathetic. Yet *another* character flaw, apparently I have *many.*"

"He told you that?"

She folded her arms across her chest.

Milo said, "He suffered a serious injury, maybe he's not thinking straight."

"He got shot in his back, not his brain, Lieutenant. Oh, he meant it, Brannon always says what he means. I'm stupid for being taken by surprise. Since we moved down here he's been different."

"How so?"

"All the usual warning signs that I of course ignored. Distant, restless, distracted—not *there.* When he told me today, I asked him if there was someone else. He laughed and said how could there be, he was too busy running. That was his real love. His damn *marathons.*"

"Huh."

"Huh, indeed—what an *asshole!*"

Her right hand flew to her lips and covered them. She let it drop. "I can't believe I just said that. I told myself not to sink to a low level."

I said, "I'm pretty sure you can be pardoned."

Her head swung toward me. "Can I? I suppose I can. But I don't like myself when I'm angry."

Back to Milo. "Do you know what he said about what you're doing? That I was obsessed and had no mental *space* for him. That it stressed *him* out. This from someone who's gone all day churning his legs. I said, Bran, you're never here. He said, That's not the point. When I am here I need *you* to be and not running off on a wild-goose chase."

Milo said, "Sounds kinda narcissistic."

"You think? Someone who obsesses on his body twenty-four seven? Stretching, running, push-ups, sit-ups, pull-ups? Drinking smoothies that smell like pond water? Then he said I shouldn't even be interested in my mother. She abandoned me, I needed to move on."

"Narcissistic *and* sensitive."

"So what does that make me? A gullible idiot."

I said, "It makes you someone in a relationship."

She swiveled toward me again. Held her gaze. Hard eyes and mouth. Back to the same distrust I'd seen all along. Oh, well.

"Doctor," she said, as if reminding herself why she resented me. Suddenly, her features softened and she threw up her hands. "I'm sure you've noticed I haven't been super-warm to you. Sorry about that, too. If Lieutenant Sturgis thinks enough of you to work with you, I should go with the plan. It's just that my experiences with shrinks—'scuse me, therapists—haven't been so great."

I said, "Understandable."

She smiled. "That was eminently therapeutic—sorry, I know you're being kind. Anyway, in the back of my head I always knew he'd do this. He's got issues."

Milo said, "Drugs and alcohol."

"You know?"

"I research people related to cases."

"Does that include me?"

"You bet."

"What'd you learn?"

"Nothing you didn't tell us."

"I'm boring, huh?"

"I prefer non-criminal. So the Roadrunner blames you for looking into your mother's death?"

"The Roadrunner?"

"Meep meep."

She burst into laughter. Reached for a tissue and wiped her eyes.

"And of course, he blames me for his getting shot and he's probably right about that."

"Actually, he's pretty wrong, Ellie."

"Pardon?"

He told her about the arrest.

"A jealous psycho? How bizarre. Part of me wants to rush over right now and let him know. At least one thing you accused me of is pure *bull.*"

To me: "That would be pretty pathetic, huh? As if it would change anything."

I said, "Do you want anything to change?"

"Now that," she said, "was *eminently* therapeutic. Of course you're right, I've probably known all along it was wrong—he was wrong for me. Why I even started with him . . . I'm so confused."

Casting off the covers, she swung her feet over the mattress, inhaled, exhaled, and stood.

"I'm going to make some coffee."

Milo said, "Make some for us, too."

Mel Boudreaux was reading his phone in the entry hall. Sports scores. He clicked off.

Milo said, "You mind waiting in the kitchen, amigo?"

Boudreaux said, "Don't mind at all, ready for a snack."

He followed Ellie in but emerged a few moments later in the lead. Carrying coffee, cups, and accoutrements on a tray.

Long legs covered a lot of ground. She hurried to keep up. "You really don't have to, Mel."

"Need the exercise." Boudreaux placed the tray on the living room coffee table, saluted, and returned to the kitchen.

Ellie said, "I'll pour. Cream, sugar?"

Milo said, "Two blacks." He sipped. "Good stuff."

"Fazenda Santa Inês from Brazil." She flinched. "Brannon used to like it."

"Used to?"

"He got fanatical about training and gave up caffeine."

"Fun guy."

"He was," she said. "At the beginning." Her face began to crumple.

Milo reached for one of the clean hankies he keeps in his jacket pocket. But, again, she composed herself and put down her cup.

"That deputy chief—Martz—called me and asked if I was happy with your progress. Like she was checking up on you. I hope I didn't put you in a weird position."

"Nah, business as usual."

"I told her I was happy. But if you do have something new, I wouldn't mind hearing about it. Maybe a little more data than the last time?"

Milo placed his own cup near hers. "We've uncovered some minor question marks but nothing close to evidence. If you're up to it, I have more questions for you."

"Sure. What?"

"The necklace you showed us. Your father told you your mom left it behind?"

"No, what he told me was he bought it for her, I assumed she left it. How else would Dad have it?"

"Did she leave anything else behind?"

Her eyes slid to the right. "The dress. The one she wore with the necklace in that forest photo. I didn't mention it because I didn't think it was important. Also, I wear the necklace once in a while but never the dress. It's in a zip bag in a storage locker back home. Could it be relevant?"

Milo said, "In terms of the murder, highly unlikely. If at some point we get past that and want to learn more about your mom's background, a label in the dress could theoretically help."

"It does have a label and I was thinking the same thing so I tried to do some research on my own. The manufacturer was Jenny Leighton, Fort Lee, New Jersey. They were in business until twenty-four years ago. Even with my garment-biz connections, I couldn't find out if they sold locally or jobbed nationwide. That's the way it is with the rag trade. Here, today, gone . . ." She smiled. "If you want, I can fly up and bring the dress back."

"Not necessary."

"You think it'll be another dead end."

"I wouldn't call it high priority."

"Fair enough. So what are those minor question marks you mentioned?"

"We learned something curious about the necklace."

He withdrew a folded sheet of paper from his jacket.

The photo from The Azalea.

Reluctant to get into details with Ellie but willing to reveal her mother with Des Barres and two other women?

Then as he handed it past me I caught a glimpse. The copy he'd made in the station blanked out Des Barres and the other two blondes.

She studied the image. Her eyes got wet. Several tears got loose. "This is only the second photo I've seen of her. She's wearing a wig . . . where was it taken and how'd you get it?"

"A nightspot in L.A. It was in a pamphlet about L.A. nightlife but don't try to find another copy. I did and zilch."

A mix of truths and lies. He's good at that. So am I. Deceit in service of the greater good.

Ellie said, "A nightspot in Hollywood?"

"Don't know." What a tangled web we weave . . .

"The necklace," she said. "I get it. If she left it when she came to L.A., what's it doing in L.A.?"

"Exactly."

"So she came and went more than once."

"Only thing we can think of."

"Hmm," she said. "So maybe it wasn't a onetime thing. Maybe they had problems from the beginning. And maybe Dad didn't like her dangling him back and forth. So when she comes back the last time he said enough and took back the gift he gave her. The dress, too—maybe that was also a gift? Or she tossed it in his face." Sad smile. "It is a pretty ugly dress. Listen to me. Hypothesizing."

Milo said, "Join the club."

"A bad relationship," she said. "But he saved the necklace and the dress. Maybe he still missed her."

Maybe a trophy.

"The going back and forth—does it change anything?"

Unwilling to grasp the implications of Stan Barker's rage after repeated abandonment.

Milo said, "Not really, we're just trying to clarify details."

She reexamined the photo. "A party wig and a party dress but she doesn't exactly look festive . . . just the opposite. Same as in the forest shot. That always struck me. How serious she was."

That made me wonder about something. I filed it for later.

Ellie's eyes remained on the photo. "In the forest, I assumed they already weren't getting along. But here she is without Dad and she's got the same expression . . . unless, maybe he *was* here? In the club? Is that possible?"

Milo said, "Did he ever mention going to L.A. with her?"

"Never. But he didn't talk about those days. I mean it's possible he was there, right? They had a date. Trying to patch up—though I don't know why she'd wear a wig . . . whatever. He went to the bathroom or something when the photo was taken? Maybe by one of those table-hopping photographers who charged per shot?"

"Anything's possible, Ellie."

She tapped the photo. "This little number, bare shoulders and all that . . . she really was beautiful. Despite not having fun. The truth is, Daddy was a good man but he wasn't much fun."

She looked at Milo. "Sorry for running on with stuff that doesn't lead anywhere."

"Don't be," he said. "And thanks for being patient."

"Do I have a choice? Sorry, that was snippy. I should be thanking you for *your* patience. Grateful for whatever you find. Like this. Another view of her. May I keep it?"

"All yours."

We stood and she did the same. Circling the coffee table, she hurried to Milo, stood on her tiptoe, and kissed his cheek. A millimeter from his lips. He was caught off-guard but he smiled.

She turned to me, weighing etiquette equity—*Can I kiss one and not the other*—versus gut reluctance: *The cop's working for me. What's the shrink actually doing?*

I tried to get her off the hook by adding space between us and smiling.

She got it. Smiled back.

Then she danced over and kissed me, too.

As we drove away from the house, I said, "She's pretty enamored of you."

"Poor kid," he said.

He cruised past the spot where Twohy had been shot without giving it a glance, waited for the non-fatal left turn on Los Feliz.

"Probably best in the long run," he said. "Brannon bailing. Guy lacked substance, she's vulnerable, deserves better."

From angry conscript to protective uncle.

"I never saw much depth in him," I said. "You're right about vulnerability. She's in self-protective mode, doesn't see the possibility that Dorothy was with another man and Barker came to L.A. and killed her.

Something else: When she called it 'the forest photo,' I wondered if it was taken in the same park where Barker tumbled. Maybe a place he and Dorothy went repeatedly so he returned there to die."

"Suicide due to guilt?"

"That or his life just hadn't worked out. It makes more sense than some phantom killer chasing him down years after doing Dorothy. Who'd know about the place other than him?"

"How about her L.A. boyfriend—pillow talk and all that."

"Seventeen years later?" I said. "And what's the motive?"

"True," he said. "If Barker did kill her, he stayed mad rather than guilty? Exploding on Ellie and telling her Mom was a slut."

"A strumpet."

"'Scuse me. Am I making sense?"

"Rage can coexist with guilt. Or fluctuate depending on what else is going on in a person's life."

"Barker's life doesn't sound like a hoot," he said. "No other rela-tionships, Ellie gives him teenage shit and then leaves for college. So he goes back to the park and does a swan dive? Or maybe has one of the accidents you guys say really aren't—getting all emotional, distracting himself, stumbling and tumbling."

"It's a possibility."

"Great. Do I get my Ph.D.? Hey, look at the pace car."

Brief lapse in four lanes of two-way traffic. He made the left, barely avoiding a thundering Corvette.

"Goddamn hot dog. Guy obviously ran a light and jumped the gun." We coasted down the hill.

"If Barker's our bad guy," he said, "and inflicted capital punish-ment on himself, you see any link to Arlette? Or Seeger's motorcycle crash?"

I said, "Accidents do happen."

"Nothing with Freudian overtones?"

"If I come up with anything, you'll be the first to know."

We stopped at the light at Franklin, waiting behind a dozen other cars.

"A world of possibilities, no evidence," he said. "Translation: hell."

His pocket got musical, the cellphone beeping manically paced violin music.

He fished it out. "Sturgis."

"Lieutenant, it's Val Des Barres."

"Hi, what's up."

"I'm sure you're busy, don't want to bother you. But if you do get some time in the near future, perhaps we could chat?"

"About what, ma'am?"

"I'd rather discuss it in person."

"Okay. I can be there in twenty minutes or so."

"Right now?" she said.

"If it's not a problem."

"I guess. Sure, why not. But let's not do it at the house. I'd prefer to meet you down the road where it happened."

Milo said, "Like I told you, we're not sure where that is."

"The approximate spot, then. If that's not a problem."

"Not at all, we'll pick you up."

"No need," she said. "Call or text when you get there and I'll come down. What are you driving?"

"A green Chevy Impala."

"Okay, then. I hope I'm doing the right thing."

Click.

The light turned green. Milo said, "Can I dare to hope?"

"Maxine says without optimism, there's nothing."

"Maxine's a smart woman, so for the time being, I'll go with that."

"My optimism doesn't count?"

"You're biased," he said. "You care."

25

He took Franklin west to La Brea, continued on Hollywood Boulevard, passing the elegant, vintage apartment buildings and newer rectangles that made up the skimpy residential section of the boulevard.

A right onto Laurel rewarded us with congestion due to work crews that weren't working, followed by a crawl up to Mulholland and a right turn that granted us isolation and clarity.

He sped to the spot Du Galoway had guesstimated, pulled to the left and parked, and we got out of the car.

Interesting sky, the western half a lucid blue so saturated with pigment it bordered on lurid, the eastern section a mirage-like mass of smoke-colored clouds. Probably ocean currents doing half the job. The separation was almost artificial.

Below all that, the Valley was a vast circuit board, brown and white and beige, with dots of coral red where tile roofs sprouted like spores.

Milo phoned Val Des Barres.

She said, "On my way."

◆

Minutes later, a white Mazda CX SUV appeared from the east, rolling slowly. Val Des Barres stopped five yards from where we stood, stuck her hand out the driver's window to wave, and pulled over behind the unmarked.

Milo went to open her door. She got there first, smiled and said, "Thanks," paused for a moment before following us to the edge of the drop.

Sunglasses blocked her eyes. She wore another shapeless dress, no pattern, just green cotton, a dark shade just shy of black, with pockets below the waistline and frilly sleeves. The blue section of the sky was radiating sunlight and it highlighted gray strands in her dark hair, amplifying them, making them glow like electric filament.

She said, "So this is near where it happened."

"Best guess," said Milo.

"I've probably passed by here—what, ten thousand times? No idea something so horrid ever took place. We have had other incidents. Cars and motorbikes going over, mostly kids speeding in the dark. At night it's a tough road if you don't know where you're going. Did it happen at night?"

"Most likely."

"But you're saying this couldn't have been an accident."

"Definitely not. What's on your mind, Ms. Des Barres?"

"Your visit is," she said. "I can't seem to get it out of my head. The fact that something so terrible happened to a person who lived with us. The fact that it was Ellie Barker's mother of all people. She seemed such a sweet person. I can't help thinking Fate put us together."

She turned and faced us. In the process, shifting herself inches closer to the edge. Milo guided her away.

She said, "Oh, my—thanks." Off came the sunshades. Her eyes were soft, searching.

"Why did I call you? Because how can I ignore reality? How can I

ignore the fact that this person—Dorothy—may have known my father? When you showed up, I was numb. Then it turned seismic. Emotionally speaking."

She rubbed the side of her nose. Moved farther from the edge,
rubbed again, blinked, folded her lips inward. "I called you, Lieutenant, because I can't eliminate the possibility that my father was involved
in something terrible."

Milo's eyes sparked for a second before returning to detective-
impassive. During the moment of surprise, the blue half of the sky had
turned his green irises aqua.

He tapped his thigh and waited. Valerie Des Barres looked at me. I
played statue.

She said, "This is hard for me."

He said, "Take your time."

"Time won't help . . . it's too . . . I'm not saying I have any evidence, it's just a . . . it's more than a feeling." She licked her lips. "Can
we sit in my car? I'm feeling like my balance is slipping."

Milo sat in the front passenger seat, I took the back and scooted to the
right to see as much of Val's profile as possible.

Tight jaw, the lips folding and unfolding, again. Dainty hands
gripping the steering wheel.

She said, "All right, no sense putting it off. You remember what I
told you about Father changing after Mother died."

"Of course."

"Radical change," she said. "Looking back, I think he was depressed. I was ten, didn't think in those terms. I *did* know he'd changed.
Went to work, as usual, came home and did his best to be fatherly but
he really couldn't pull it off. He'd give me a token greeting, a hug, force
himself to chat, and then he'd escape to his bedroom or his study, close
the door and stay there. Bill and Tony were both away at school, so I

spent a lot of time alone. Sometimes I wondered if it was something I'd done. Strictly speaking, I wasn't neglected, he hired a couple of nannies to take care of me and they were okay."

I said, "Not much of an endorsement."

She swung around, surprised. As if she'd forgotten I was there.

"No, it's not, they were adequate. By the book. All that solitude worked out fine, that's when I really got into drawing. Sitting in my room all day—but this isn't about me. It's about Father. Basically, he left me."

She turned back to Milo.

"After a few months of that, the other change began. All of a sudden he began going out at night, and in the morning, at breakfast, more often than not, there'd be a woman at the table. Then women, plural. Two or three, sitting around nibbling toast. Blondes, he always liked blondes. My mom was a blonde. She was English, fair-skinned, blue-eyed. Bill and Tony's mother was American and also blond. So there we were in the morning, Father, blondes, and me."

Milo said, "That musta been jarring."

"At first. I got used to it." Pained smile. "I'm good at getting used to things. They were pretty nice to me, I got a lot of 'Oh, how adorable.' 'Isn't she the sweetest.' That kind of thing. My nannies didn't approve, they were old-school, one was French, the other was German. They'd whisk me away as soon as I finished my cereal. Sometimes Father would take the blondes with him, or he'd leave them behind and they'd be gone by the afternoon. Then *that* started to change and they'd be around for days. Then weeks."

She fiddled with her hair. "The biggest changes were the ones Father made to *himself.* He used to have this cute little mustache. Like David Niven—do you know David Niven."

Milo said, "*The Pink Panther.*"

"Sure, there's that. Also lovely, earlier films like *Bonjour Tristesse*— I'm a bit of an antiquarian. Anyway, Father's mustache always amused me. I'd tickle him under the nose and he'd be good-natured about it and pretend to sneeze and I'd just love that. Then all of a sudden he stopped shaving and got all grizzly and then one day he'd trimmed around all the hair and showed up with a rather satanic goatee. Black. Like his hair, he'd begun coloring everything. His attire changed, as well. He'd always been conservative. Suits to work, blazers on the weekend, dress shirt and tie for supper. Now he was wearing brightly colored—okay, garish—silk shirts with buccaneer sleeves, plus tight bell-bottom pants way too young for him and patent-leather shoes with big heels in crazy colors."

She shivered. "I thought it was ludicrous but of course I'd never say anything. I would catch the nannies raising their eyebrows but they knew better than to insult the boss. And the blondes were all over him. Tony this, Tony that, you're so cool and out of sight."

I said, "Trying to be young and hip."

"Trying far too hard. I found it sad. And confusing. Accepting a caricature of my father. But he must've liked the attention because he held on to that look for years. All through my adolescence, you're with something long enough, you get used to it and I did. The world seemed to be going casual, anyway, so it wasn't that. And eventually, he toned down—more tasteful casual clothes. But the hair and the beard stayed black."

Her knuckles blanched around the wheel. "I was a quiet, obedient kid but when I got older—twelve, thirteen—I found myself drawing secret caricatures of him and the blondes. Writing mean-spirited captions. Then I'd immediately shred them and toss them in the trash. That lasted until I was fourteen, fifteen. That's when his health began giving way. First there were heart issues, then arthritis, he got bowed over and moved more slowly. Basically the aging process, maybe accelerated by fast living. Then, when I was twenty-one—right after my twenty-first birthday, he got cancer. First prostate, which they said was curable, he had surgery and was supposedly cured. But he was never the same—listless, he gained weight. No more blondes, I'm assuming it affected his masculinity. Then, when I was twenty-three, came the stomach cancer, which wasn't curable. That's when things got horrific. The pain, wasting away."

I said, "You're a young woman and you're dealing with it."

"I'd just graduated college and was living at home." She fussed with her hair some more, twisting, tugging. "I never left, just turned inward, found my own space—internal space. That's when my stories and my art took off—not that I wouldn't have traded all of that for Father to get well. But he didn't. And it drove me creatively—I had to have some kind of escape."

"Of course."

"I really did," she said. "By the time I turned twenty-four, he was terminal— Would you mind if we go back outside? I'm feeling a little closed-in."

We left the Mazda and walked to the rear of the unmarked. Valerie Des Barres, paler by several shades, pretended to study the bifurcated sky. Milo and I studied her. He was back to drumming his thigh.

Her nostrils flared as she inhaled and blew air out audibly. The sound merged with the gentle prod of trees by a brief gust of warm breeze.

She said, "He was on his deathbed, doctors and nurses were coming in and giving him morphine. My brothers had flown in the previous week thinking this was the end. When it wasn't, they returned to Chicago. I remember thinking, Father disappointed them again."

I said, "Your brothers thought he'd let them down?"

"Oh, yes. The whole blonde thing offended them profoundly. Whatever respect they'd had for him was gone. Ironically, though, Bill began imitating Father. Or at least that's how it seems to me."

Milo said, "He had a harem of his own?"

"No, no." She laughed. "He just really got into chasing women. He's been married and divorced four times, I can't tell you how many girlfriends he's had. But that's neither here nor there. Yes, they resented Father but I didn't—I firmly believe I'm being honest when I say that."

Her hands folded across her chest. As if realizing the defensiveness that implied, she dropped them quickly, squared her shoulders and stood taller.

Martyr accepting sacrifice.

"So," she said. "Deathbed scene. It's a Sunday, the nannies are in church. No doctors around, just one of the nurses the hospice sends by but she's not there in his room, it's a huge house, who knows where she is? I'd been sleeping in the anteroom next to his bedroom, wanting to be close in case he needed me. I'd set up my drawing table, so it really wasn't an imposition. There was no point remaining at his bedside, for the most part he was in and out of consciousness. And when he came to consciousness he just moaned in pain. He was down to skin and bones . . . so . . . I just couldn't look at that all day. So there I am in the next room, sketching away, and I hear him croak my name and I rush in. He wasn't moaning but I could tell from his face that he was in great pain. I said, 'Let's get you some medicine.' He shook his head. Violently. I wasn't sure what that meant—some sort of higher-level agony throe or he didn't want any morphine? I was about to get the nurse when he let out this different— this hoarse noise, almost animalistic, and began waving a hand I thought had been too weak to even move. Beckoning me over. I sat on the edge of his bed and held his other hand. It was so frail and cold . . . he was breathing shallowly, I'm thinking this is it, I'm going to actually *see* it. *Terrifying.* Then all of a sudden he raises himself up and puts his lips close to my ear and frees his hand and *clamps* it around my arm."

She touched her right biceps. "I mean clamped. I was amazed at how strong his grip was, his nails were actually *biting* into my arm but of course I didn't say anything. He breathed a few times then, clear as day, he uttered the first words he'd spoken in a week."

She walked away from us, stopped perilously close to the edge, froze for a moment and returned.

"Here's what he said: 'Bring the devil into your home, you're the devil's disciple.'"

Milo scrawled in his pad.

Val Des Barres shook her head. "What do you say to that? I figured he was delirious but his eyes were suddenly clear and they seemed full of *intent*. Struggling to *communicate*. I said something meaningless and mumbly and that *really* upset him. He actually moved what was left of his body into a full, upright sit, kept squeezing my arm, and waved his other hand in the air. Then he repeated it. Louder. Almost like an evangelical preacher."

Milo read. "'Bring the devil into your home, you're the devil's disciple.'"

"Word for word, Lieutenant. It's not something you forget. I convinced myself it was delirium, shoved the whole incident to the back of my head, why wouldn't I? But now that you've told me about Ellie's mother, I can't help wondering. Was he talking about something that actually happened?"

Again, she turned her back on us. "Did he do something evil himself?"

Milo and I said nothing.

Val Des Barres said, "And then, at eleven thirty-four p.m., he died."

We let the quiet linger, broken by the breeze and a faint, miles-away traffic hum from the grid below.

"That's it," she said. "That's all of it."

Milo said, "We really appreciate your telling us something so difficult."

"Does it mean anything? Based upon what you know?"

"No, ma'am. And a man on his deathbed . . ."

"Who knows what the brain cells are doing, I get that. That's what I keep telling myself. I hope it's true."

She stepped up to Milo. "I needed to get it off my chest. You're so kind, Lieutenant." She took his hand, squeezed it briefly, let go with reluctance.

I wagered on his first comment when we were alone: *My week for Mr. Popular. If they only knew.*

He said, "We've got no evidence your dad did anything criminal but can you handle a tough question?"

"Sure."

"Did you ever witness your dad injure any of the blondes?"

"Never."

I said, "When the car went over the side of the road, you weren't aware of it."

"I wasn't."

Milo said, "No investigators ever showed up at your house."

"Not that I ever saw. And I'm sure if it did happen, the nannies would've shielded me from it."

She smiled. "That was my life, the helpless nerdy kid buffered from reality. I suppose that's why I've never left."

I said, "For the most part the blondes were nice to you."

"When there was contact," she said. "When they started hanging around for prolonged periods, walking to and from the pool and the tennis court in bikinis and skimpy outfits, it embarrassed me. Again, the nannies rushed me along but they didn't have to. I thought it was gross—all that jiggling. But the funny thing is, I was in so much denial I never consciously associated Father with it. As in, *This is what he wants.* Pretty stupid, huh? I guess I needed to see him in the best image possible. Even with that ridiculous beard and those clothes."

I said, "Were the nannies also tutors?"

"Was I homeschooled? Oh, no. I went to Evangeline—a girls' academy over the hill in Studio City. It's no longer there, got absorbed into Hollyhock and Bel Air Prep decades ago."

"So you wouldn't have been home for a good part of the day."

"Did I miss seeing something? It's certainly possible. All I can tell you is that I never witnessed anything violent or even conflictual. Just the opposite. Father seemed to be happier than he'd ever been, but it was an unsettling happiness for me. As if he was pushing himself too hard to be different. When I was older and learned what was going on in the world out there, I began wondering if that happiness had been helped along. If you know what I mean."

I said, "Drugs."

"Or alcohol. Or both. He could get spacy-looking and his smiles could get . . . the best word is flaky. Like he wasn't really there. I talked to my brothers about it and they laughed at me and said, 'What do you think? He's probably stoned out of his gourd.' But I saw no firsthand evidence of it. No joints or pills lying around and certainly no needles or anything truly gross. There was drinking. Beer, wine, cocktails. But everyone did that. Our home ec textbooks at Evangeline showed well-dressed families sitting around with the parents nursing from Martini glasses."

Milo said, "The clan that imbibes together, jibes together."

Val Des Barres, still standing close to him, took his hand again. "You're a witty man, Lieutenant Sturgis. You've made this experience tolerable."

Then she tiptoed, as if ready to kiss him, thought better of it and settled back on flat shoes.

Two people blushing.

I amended my bet. The initial comment would be *My week for Mr. Romeo. If they only knew.*

He let some time pass, asked if there was anything else she wanted to say.

"Just that I hope you find out what happened to Ellie's mother. No matter where that leads."

"You're a brave woman."

"That's kind but I don't think so," she said. "If I was brave, I'd get out more."

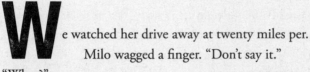e watched her drive away at twenty miles per.

Milo wagged a finger. "Don't say it."

"What?"

"My newfound animal magnetism."

I said, "If they only knew."

"Hey, don't dismiss it, either." He clapped me on the back. "Maybe all the time I've been hanging with you, something's rubbed off."

We got back in the car. He backed onto Mulholland and headed west. "Letting the devil in. Think he was talking about himself or one of his femmes getting fatale with Arlette and Dorothy?"

I said, "Arlette's death opened up a whole new world for Des Barres. He'd have no motive for thinning the harem but a jealous competitor would."

"Coupla blondes take a ride in the Caddy, one comes back."

"And even if Des Barres hadn't played a role in Dorothy's death, he might have figured it out. Or been told about it. Either way, it sat in his brain for decades. Then he got prostate cancer. If it impacted his sexual drive that might've seemed like rough justice. Soon after, his stomach went bad and he became terminally ill. On his deathbed, with the neurons scrambled, he blurted out a veiled confession."

"Makes sense. Now try to prove it."

As we reached Laurel Canyon, I said, "Someone like Femme, can't see her just walking away empty-handed."

"She blackmailed Des Barres?"

"Or just lifted trinkets from the mansion and split. It's an enormous place, with an owner not paying attention, it might not have been that hard."

"True," he said. "When I was starting out I had a burglary case. Holmby Hills, housekeeper gradually stole designer gowns and furs. Took the victim fifteen months to discover it, and by that time the maid was gone."

He phoned Petra, got voicemail, asked her to see if she could find any burglary complaints at the Des Barres residence between twenty-five and forty years ago. Clicking off, he sang the chorus from Tom Petty's "The Waiting" in a rumbly basso. His voice isn't bad when he pays attention.

I said, "Maybe there's a shortcut. Give me Val's number."

A male voice, soft, Latin-inflected, picked up. "Des Barres residence."

"Sabino? This is one of the men who just met with Ms. Des Barres. Can I talk to her for a sec."

"She's drawing, sir."

"Just for a moment."

"I dunno."

"It's important," I said. "Police business."

"Hold on. Sir."

Moments later, Val came on: "Hi, Lieutenant."

"This is Alex," I said. "He's driving without distraction."

"Oh, of course. What can I do for you?"

"We'd like to know if your house was ever burgled when your dad was alive."

Simple yes-or-no question.

She said, "I'm not sure."

"You were too young to remember?"

"No, I remember clearly. Father did think something had happened, he was pretty upset. But to my knowledge he never called the police and the issue faded away."

"When did this happen?"

"Not that long after your murder—maybe a month or so after? Possibly two, can't say for sure. I do know I was young."

"How long did it take for the issue to fade?"

"Just a day," she said. "One night, I heard him cursing, almost growling, went to his bedroom and saw him pawing through his drawers, tossing things all over the place. Not like him, he was extremely meticulous. I asked what was going on and he said someone had taken advantage of him. I asked how. He said, 'The Seventh Commandment, darling,' and then he gritted his teeth. I asked who but he just shook his head. The following morning, he told me he'd been wrong, just forget about it."

"What did he think was missing?"

"If he was rummaging in his drawers, it was probably his jewelry. He'd really gotten into chunky gold chains, had boxes of them from Beverly Hills boutiques. Rings, too—diamonds and ruby pinkie rings. After it happened, he eased off a bit on the gaudy stuff. But he never gave it up. Why's the lieutenant asking?"

Milo said, "Just trying to be thorough."

Another non-explanation.

Val Des Barres said, "Oh, hi. Of course, being thorough is the only way. By the way, our chat was helpful. For some reason I feel lighter."

"That's great," he said.

She and Milo exchanged goodbyes and I hung up.

He said, "The timing fits. Femme gets rid of Dorothy, sticks around, finally figures snagging the boss is a lost cause, and collects some combat pay."

"If Des Barres was implicated in Arlette's death, he couldn't very well report a burglary by his accomplice."

"Let the devil in . . ." He redialed Petra. "Forget the previous request, kid. If this all sounds weird, call me and I'll fill you in." To me: "Now what?"

I said, "Only thing I can think of is trying to identify and find Femme. Maybe starting with the two blondes in the Azalea photo and seeing where that leads."

"Put the shot on social media?"

"That or start old-school—find someone who remembers the club."

"Suggestions?"

"Sure," I said. "Keep it close to home."

He took Fountain to La Cienega, continued south to Third Street and the ever-growing megalith that is Cedars-Sinai hospital. Gliding easily, as if moving along a well-worn track, he continued to the emergency drop-off and parked in a No Parking zone. A valet came over.

"Keys are in the ignition, Armando."

"Hi, Lieutenant. Dr. Silverman is here."

"Great."

"Um, sorry, I have to ask you how long. They're kind of clamping down on non-essentials."

"This is essential, Armando. Homicide case." Milo slipped him a five.

"Oh," said the valet. "Sure, whatever you need, I'll take care of you."

The E.R. waiting room was the usual acrid mix of anxiety, resignation, and human secretions. Faces out of Dickens. No one waiting looked in imminent danger, but you never know.

The triage nurse said, "Hey, Milo. You're in luck, he just got out of surgery."

"Hope his patient's in luck."

She laughed. "She is. Stitched up like a football but nothing serious."

We kept going.

I said, "Everything's relative."

Rick was sitting on a rock-hard brown couch in the doctors' room, wearing fresh scrubs and a long white coat and drinking from a bottle of Fiji water. He's broad-shouldered and rock-jawed with huge, agile hands, a seamed, angular face, tightly curled gray hair, and a matching brush-mustache. The kind of hewn good looks that used to earn actors leading-man roles before the norms changed to juvenile and androgynous.

His default mood is somber. When he saw Milo, he raised his eyebrows in surprise, half smiled, and hugged him.

"Hi, Alex." Firm handshake for me. "It's business, huh? I'll take what I can get."

Milo said, "I came by to ask about dinner. Coq au vin or stale pizza?"

"Ha. What's up, Big Guy?"

"Remember that place you told me about, The Azalea?"

"Tacky-Mahal? Is this related to your impossible one?"

"Yup. Take a look at this, see if it rings any bells." Handing over the shot of Anton Des Barres and the blonde trio.

Rick said, "Older guy, bevy of cuties. Exactly what I saw when I was there . . . that wallpaper. Ugh. Looked even worse in real life . . . who are these people?"

"The one on the left is my victim and he's the rich guy she lived with. It's these two I'm interested in."

"They look kind of . . . generic. As I told you, I was whisked past all that." Another near-smile. "Did he tell you what they called the upstairs room, Alex? The Lavender Lair."

I said, "Subtle."

"The times weren't subtle." To Milo: "They're suspects?"

"More likely potential sources. Can you think of anyone who'd know the place well?"

"Just one."

"Who?"

"Mr. H."

"Him? Thought he was an upstairs guy."

"When we came in, everyone greeted him, so he probably circulated."

"He still around?"

"Don't know but haven't heard to the contrary."

"Think he'd cooperate?"

"That I can't say. But he did like attention so you could play off that."

"You haven't seen him since?"

"Actually," said Rick, "a couple of years back, his daughter brought him here with chest pains. Turned out to be indigestion. I didn't think he'd recognize me but he did."

"From high school senior to now?"

"You're saying I've changed? Yeah, it was surprising."

"Maybe he's been keeping tabs on you."

"I doubt it but whatever the reason, he was quite lovely about it. And more secure. He told me he came out a while back and his kids were supportive."

"And he supports them, in return?" Milo rubbed his thumb and forefinger together.

"Cynic. You may be right but the interaction I saw, the daughter adored him."

He pointed to one of several computers arrayed near the facing wall. "His records are in there. Maybe. He's got to be, what, mideighties."

He sprang up, crossed to a terminal, typed. "Still listed as an active patient, so if he died it didn't happen here. You can check with the coroner or I can just call him for you."

"The latter would be great, Richard."

Rick patted his cheek. "Great is what I aim for."

Harlow Hunter Hesse was alive and well and still living on the 900 block of North Roxbury Drive in Beverly Hills.

He picked up his own phone, barking "Yes?" loud enough for the sound to travel across the room. Rick introduced himself, then did a lot of listening. Churning the air with one hand as the monologue persisted. We were too far to hear the content but the pace and tone were turbocharged.

Finally, Rick broke in. "Nexium's an appropriate choice, Mr. H . . . he's a very qualified gastroenterologist . . . I do, we were actually in the same year at med school . . . that I can't tell you but he was certainly well thought of . . . there you go, Mr. H, you're in good hands. May I ask you a question? It's for a friend of mine . . . no, nothing to do with investment, he's trying to learn more about The Azalea . . . yes, we were there . . . yes, I know . . . is that so? Glad you got it at a good price . . . anyway, if—no, not a writer, he's a police detective."

Tensing up, as he said that. Then, one of the widest smiles I'd ever seen on Rick's face spread smoothly. "That's great, Mr. H. His name's Milo Sturgis. Lieutenant Sturgis. What's a good time for him to call . . . really? Hold on and I'll check."

Stretching the phone to arm's length, he whispered: "Could you go there now?"

Milo said, "What's the address?"

As we reached the door, I said, "Good price? Did he buy the building?"

Rick said, "Just the disco ball."

The address matched a fieldstone-and-stucco, multigabled traditional on a double-wide lot one block north of Sunset.

H. H. Hesse met us at the door, wearing a maroon velour jumpsuit and red loafers. Four black-and-lace-uniformed maids buzzed around him like bees turned frantic by pheromones.

Milo introduced himself.

"Lieutenant—and other cop—glad to meet you, I'm Heck."

Clear-eyed and gravel-voiced, looking every year of his eighty-seven, Heck Hesse was average height despite a bowed back, meaning he'd once been tall. Despite that, he came across gnome-like, with a smallish round face, impish and inescapably chimp-like under an arid thatch of ginger hair.

The four maids re-formed behind him in a line, a retinue waiting on nobility. As Milo and I entered, they curtsied.

Hesse said, "Make yourselves snacks, ladies. Have fun, life's short."

A collective, "Thank you, Heck," as they scattered.

"Come on in, gents."

He walked ahead of us, soles scuffing hardwood, maintaining a good pace despite the hunched spine and stiff legs. We passed several enormous, art-filled spaces, each of which could be a living room. It's like that in many of the big houses I see. Set up for large-scale entertainment flow rather than family life.

The library was at the rear, any outdoors view blocked by pink damask drapes. A crystal chandelier subbed for the sun.

A disco ball, three feet in diameter and encrusted with mirrored squares, sat floodlit on a custom-fitted Lucite stand.

Other than the garish sphere, the room was traditional. Spacious enough for three arrangements of tufted leather chairs. Four walls of pickled-pine cases were crammed with volumes. Not leather-bound showy stuff; the kinds of books people actually read.

H. H. Hesse chose the center-most seating area: two club chairs and a love seat arranged around a glass-topped table. On the table was a copper-colored plastic pitcher purloined from IHOP slumming alongside three gilt-edged porcelain cups on saucers.

He took the couch, lowering himself slowly, taking more time to cross his legs.

"Sorry for the creaking," he said. "Coffee?"

Milo said, "Thank you, sir."

"You pour, my shoulder hurts."

Milo semi-filled three cups. Hesse said, "You've got finesse for a husky fellow. Great to meet you. I'm sure Dr. Rick told you. My forte was finance but I did get behind some small-screen productions, including cop shows."

He rattled off several titles, most forgettable or forgotten, plus a long-running drama that could've earned him a few mansions.

"You look like the real deal, Lieutenant. You, on the other hand, are what casting directors like. The two of you would make a great pair. Either of you ever done any T.A.'ing?"

Milo said, "Teaching assistant?"

"Technical advising," said Hesse. "Terrific money, even with the tightening up. It's the kind of line item that makes its way through the budgetary process because compared with all the waste, it's penny ante."

"I'll bear that in mind, sir."

"I wouldn't advise either of you trying to break in solo, too much competition, too much hassle. But as a pairing, you've got something different. Synergy. They could tap into your repartee as well as your expertise. Who knows, you might score a reality show or something. Though you'd probably need to retire first. Want some phone numbers?"

"Sure, thanks," said Milo. "Before that, could we talk about why we're here?"

"Cut to the chase," said Heck Hesse. "I like your style. Go."

Milo handed the photo across the table. "We're trying to identify these people."

Hesse said, "I need my glasses—over there, near the art section." Pointing to a bookcase filled with oversized spines. From Renaissance to Basquiat.

Milo retrieved a pair of specs with lime-green frames and handed them over. Even assisted, Hesse squinted.

He began on the left side, the way most readers of English do. "This one"—tapping Dorothy's image—"I don't know her but I may have a vague memory of seeing her there, that doesn't help you . . . the guy I saw plenty of times. Some sort of scientist? Doctor?"

Milo said, "Engineer."

"So you know him," said Hesse. "So why come to me?"

"We don't know much about him."

"Neither do I, other than what I told you. Engineers are buttoned-up types, this one probably had a second adolescence, trying too hard to be a hippie. Silk shirts from Battaglia, good luck with that, the whole key to being a hippie was pretending to come off poor. My daughters tried it. Then they found out being poor was no picnic."

Hesse's eyes shifted to the right. "This one I don't know . . . this one, the chubby one. I'm pretty sure she's the one who went missing. Am I right? That what you're after?"

We got up and studied the photo.

The woman to Des Barres's immediate left had a narrow face and fashion-model cheekbones. The woman Hesse had labeled chubby was anything but overweight. Just a bit of extra padding on her cheeks.

More fresh-faced than exotic.

Everything's relative.

Milo said, "What else do you know about her?"

"So I'm right." Hesse slapped a knee. "Good to know the brain's still working. That said, don't ask me about names, haven't been able to hold on to names for longer than I'll admit. What I do remember is once I was there with a . . . friend. The manager comes upstairs looking upset and tells us there's a cop downstairs asking questions. Nothing that could involve us, a girl went missing, could we please go downstairs and talk to them. Naturally, I'm not tickled. Upstairs was a place to get privacy, good drinks, listen to that Indian Beatle music, jasmine or whatever in the air. Although by that time, it's losing business. But they lowered the membership, I love a bargain . . . anyway . . . I'm loosening up after a tough day, aluminum had just gone nuts, or maybe it was the raw ore . . . bauxite. I ended up making a killing but what a day, it damaged my arteries, heh. But I go downstairs because it's a cop, let's keep it simple. He shows me a picture of this one." Tapping. "I say no idea, he thanks me and leaves."

Hesse sat back. "The whole thing was two minutes, if that. But still not a pleasant experience. That's what we remember, right? The bad stuff and the good stuff, everything in between gets shoved in the mental dumpster. What was bad wasn't the cop, per se. It was any cop. My situation back then. You guys, even when you're not trying to, you get accusatory. I get it. You see the worst in everyone. But it doesn't make you fun to talk to."

He smiled. "Not you two. This *is* fun. Maybe nowadays they train you better in human relations, psychology, whatever."

Milo said, "We do have some top-notch psychologists."

"Well, that's good. Anyway, I'm sorry for her, she looks like a nice girl—corn-fed. As to why she'd be at The Azalea, I don't have to tell you."

"Please educate us, sir."

"Forget sir. *Heck.*" Velour legs crossed painfully slowly. "Think about it: What does L.A. mean to everyone in the outside world? New York, China, Russia, India, everywhere."

"The film business."

"Bingo. Like that movie, the Steve Martin one—guy's brilliant, plays the banjo. Cute blonde gets off the bus and says, 'Where do I go to become a star?' Hilarious but not far from the truth. A girl's got good looks, not too much in the brainpan, she comes here, ends up broke. Then what? You need me to spell it out."

"Prostitution."

"Literally or conceptually," said Hesse. "The premise is the same: I can sell my looks so why not? During The Azalea's heyday, it was free love, anyway, so you had social norms on your side. Even with that, females giving it away like crazy, there was a pecking order. You want a hippie chick with unshaved legs studying for a Ph.D., fine but that is not to everyone's taste. Hairy legs wouldn't make it through the door of The Azalea."

Hesse chuckled. "Unless you're a guy who likes guys and thinks the bear thing is *the* thing." Peering at Milo's trousers and winking. "So, sure, some of the poor dears ended up as call girls. Or just plain hooking on the street if they got addicted to hard drugs. But there were also plenty of ambiguous situations. Cutie goes home with a rich guy, spends a few days, he gives her cash, takes her shopping, she spends a few more nights, even weeks. Some of them even got married. Plenty of women who call themselves socialites started off that way."

He pointed to Des Barres's goatee. "He looks like some cartoon devil, no? No Adonis, that's for sure, but with three cuties hanging on to him, his money made him feel gorgeous. He do something to Corn-Fed?"

"No indication of that."

"Then what?"

"It's part of another case, Heck. Complicated. Sorry."

"Can't argue with complicated, complicated always wins." Hesse returned the photo. "That's all I can tell you, let me get you those phone numbers for T.A.'ing."

Milo said, "Do you recall if the detective who asked about her was L.A. or Beverly Hills?"

Head shake. "If he said, it didn't register. All I wanted was to get myself back upstairs. I *can* tell you what he looked like but all these years, that's not going to help you."

"Tell us anyway."

"The reason," said Hesse, "that I remember is a thing about me. Faces stay in here forever"—tapping his forehead. "One of my grand-daughters is studying psychology, she said I'm a super-recognizer."

Smiling proudly.

"Also, this face wasn't an average face. You remember *The Munsters?*"

"Sure."

"The guy who played Herman, Fred Gwynne. Before that, he was in *Car 54,* you're probably too young to recall that one. Take away the Frankenstein makeup from Herman Munster, and picture the face."

I said, "Long, narrow."

"With big lips, droopy eyes—like a tired horse. Which isn't to say Gwynne wasn't a great actor. And smart, a class act. I met him at a Harvard thing, he was Adams House, I was Cabot. He could sing, draw, very talented. Limited by his size and that face, but still, he delivered some great performances—anyway, the cop who showed up looked like Fred. Not as tall, Fred had to be six-five, six, this guy was probably six . . . two. But he could've been Gwynne's less impressive brother. Once you took away the mustache."

Ball-bearing-sized lumps rolled up and down Milo's jaw, tenting and releasing the skin. His hands had tightened.

Heck Hesse said, "Not the classiest thing, the mustache, but guys were doing that back then. Doing all sorts of tonsorial stuff—

muttonchops, *that* never helps anyone aesthetically. I saw this guy and was surprised the cops allowed it."

He traced a horizontal line over his upper lip, used both hands to drop at right angles down to his chin.

I said, "Fu Manchu."

"Nah, Fu was wispy—you see the movie? This thing was geometric. Like a croquet wicket. Dark brown wicket. That sums it up perfectly: Freddy Gwynne with a croquet wicket mustache. Only other thing I remember was he wore a cheap suit. Can't tell you what color 'cause it's not a face, only faces stay in here."

Milo said, "When did this happen?"

Hesse gave a start. His eyes fluttered. "Not so good with time . . . long time ago . . . thirty-five years? More?" He slumped.

I said, "With your visual recognition skills, you'd know if you saw the missing woman at the club."

He perked up. "I would indeed and I didn't. All I saw was a photo the cop showed me. Was she ever at The Azalea? The cop came around so I'm assuming yes. Or maybe he was just fishing around. You guys do that, I know from working with T.A.'s."

Quick sidelong glance at the disco ball. "You need to bear in mind that back then I was always upstairs, would go straight up like there was a lit fuse in my keister. Which is what I probably did when the cop asked someone else."

Louder chuckle. "That was me, back then. Hiding from reality. Nowadays, I'm comfortable. Unfortunately, I'm also ancient."

Milo thanked him, declined the offer of more coffee and "a little snack." But we stuck around for a few more minutes, serving as a patient audience for Heck Hesse's tour of the library and capsule descriptions of his favorite books. ("Oscar Wilde, and not because of that. Guy was a dynamite writer.") Then a detour into one of the other ambiguously functioned great rooms where he showed us three Emmys. All for forgettable shows.

When we left, the four maids had split into two pairs flanking the door. They stood by as Hesse took his time working the knob.

"I like to do as much for myself while I can," he said. "Who knows how long that'll last."

I said, "You look in great shape."

"Appearances are deceiving."

27

Hesse stood in the doorway as we walked to the unmarked. Before we reached the car, he shouted, "I bought plenty of those as props. Afterward we gave 'em to the stuntmen, they liked to hot-rod 'em."

We laughed. Hesse beamed.

Milo said, "Good deed for the day," as we got in.

The lumps in his jaw had receded but his shoulders were bunched and his hands were restless. He sped south toward Sunset.

I said, "You know the Missing Persons D."

Pulling over just short of the boulevard, he produced his phone, scrolled for a while, handed it over.

LAPD personnel headshot of a long-faced man with a gray, wicket-shaped mustache. The resemblance to Fred Gwynne more than passing.

Below the image: *P. J. Seeger, Detective II.*

I said, "Before Homicide, he worked Missing Persons."

"I'll take that bet. You thinking what I am?"

"Seeger worked the missing girl and connected her to Des Barres but couldn't take it further. Years later, he's in Homicide and gets handed Dorothy's murder as a low-priority cold case. He began the same way Galoway did, with the Cadillac, and connected it to Des Barres. Now he's wondering about multiple murders at the mansion but too much time has lapsed to make any progress."

"Exactly. Dorothy was handed to him as really warm beer, same as with Galoway. In Galoway's case because he was a rookie and his captain didn't like him. In Seeger's case maybe his rep as a drudge was the reason. Whatever the case, without results, the bosses wouldn't have allowed him much time to poke around."

I said, "What if both cases stuck with Seeger and after he retired, he began digging around on his own? Asked the wrong questions of the wrong people and ended up run off the road on his Harley. That could explain the time lag between working Dorothy and his death."

He took his time considering that. "Lemme have the phone back."

More scrolling, another preset, switch to speaker.

"Hi, Deirdre, it's Milo Sturgis again."

A woman said, "Oh, hi. What's up?"

"I know you said Phil didn't talk about his cases but did he ever happen to mention any missings from way back?"

"He had so many of those, Milo. Have you ever worked them?"

"Never."

"Phil hated missings," said Deirdre Seeger. "He said you put so much time into them and most of them resolve by themselves. He was happy to switch to Property Crimes and then when his application for Homicide finally got approved, he was jumping for joy."

"So no discussions about specific cases."

"No, Phil cherished our time together. Cherished me and kept me away from bad things. I mean, sometimes he'd say I've got a frustrating one, doll. But that's about it. How long ago is 'way back'?"

"Thirty-seven, -eight years, maybe forty. Give or take."

"That's right after he got out of uniform and started at Missings. All

I know from that time was he kept long hours and came home tired. But my cooking revived him. My desserts, especially."

"The missing in question is a young woman, Deirdre. Early twenties, hung out in Beverly Hills."

"That doesn't help," she said. "And Beverly Hills? Way outside of Phil's jurisdiction. What he would've called above my pay grade."

"Okay, thanks, and sorry for bothering you."

"Oh, it's no bother, Milo. I'm not exactly on a tight schedule."

The phone went back into his pocket.

I said, "Frustration can hang you up or push you forward."

"Seeger somehow got a fire in his belly?"

"Free to do what he wanted, no pressure from above? Maybe bored with retirement?"

"Hmm . . . never experienced pressure myself but that's because of my magnetism."

"No doubt."

As he reached for the shift lever, I said, "Maybe Galoway remembers something from Seeger's notes."

"Didn't sound that way when we talked to him but can't hurt to ask."

Du Galoway's hearty voice came on after two rings. "Milo. Hey, what's up? Progress, I hope? You got me thinking about the case."

"I wish, Du. I'm calling to ask you something."

"Sure, shoot."

"Was there any mention in Seeger's notes about a missing at Des Barres's place prior to Dorothy's murder?"

"Des Barres," said Galoway. "You're looking into the bastard. Great."

"Baby steps," said Milo.

"But sorry, nothing like that. You're thinking the bastard was a serial? Shit, wouldn't that be something."

"What caught my interest in the missing is Seeger worked it before he got to Homicide."

"You're kidding," said Galoway. "It's getting that smell, isn't it? Too bad I never got time to work it properly."

"Pressure from the boss."

"Nuclear pressure. I'm a greenhorn, getting nowhere, the fat slob's pissed in the first place that I applied to Homicide and got in—why'm I telling you this, you know what the job's like. So who was the missing?"

"All I know so far is she hung with Des Barres."

"At the house?"

"Maybe."

"Maybe," said Galoway. "Sorry for poking, I used to hate when I was working a tough one and someone did that to me."

"No prob, Du. If you remember anything about anything, let me know."

Galoway sighed. "Wish I could say that was going to happen. It's the failures that stick with us, right? Good luck."

Milo hung up but kept the phone in his hand. "Any other suggestions?"

I said, "Don't imagine Hollywood missings files were preserved better than homicides, but . . ."

"You're right, less than unlikely." But he phoned the archivist, got voicemail.

Just as he began to pull away from the curb, Petra called.

He explained about the burglary at Des Barres's house and how the decision not to file a report had mooted the issue.

She said, "He loses a bunch of bling but lets it ride? *That's* different. My experience is rich folks are the most aggressive when it comes to their stuff. You're thinking there was another reason Des Barres didn't want any poking around at the castle."

"Buried bodies," said Milo. "Literally or otherwise."

"Any way to get in there and poke around?"

"Not yet but there's a possible hook for the long run." He filled her in about the missing woman and P. J. Seeger's involvement.

She said, "Two women gone. I'm picturing an unofficial graveyard out back."

"Could be, it's a big place."

"Yuck. When did this other girl go missing?"

"Before Dorothy's death. Des Barres's second wife died a year before, maybe they're connected."

He told her about the woman Winifred Gaines had seen following Arlette Des Barres into the forest, our theory about an aspiring Queen Bee.

She said, "Money's always motive number one and there was plenty of it. A murder victim and a missing in the same photo. Sounds like joining the harem was a high-risk endeavor."

"Val Des Barres has that same feeling." He related our meeting.

She said, "Letting the devil in. Think she knows more than what she can admit right now?"

"Could be. She didn't have to step forward in the first place, so there'd be no reason to be evasive."

"Still, there could be something psychological—denial, whatever. Alex there?"

I said, "Here."

"That make sense to you? Whatever she suspects of her dad, he's still her dad, there's just so much she can handle?"

"Could be."

She laughed. "That's all I'm going to get?"

Milo said, "He's like that. But when he does consent to elaborate, it can get interesting."

"Still waters running deep," she said. "Yeah, I've seen him do that."

I said, "Ahem."

"C'mon, Alex, worship from afar is the best a consultant can hope for. Milo, what about the third girl in the photo? Could she be the bad girl?"

"Maybe, she's got great cheekbones," said Milo.

Winking at me. The same was true of Petra and she'd heard about it plenty.

She laughed. "Excellent structure is *not* a personality flaw."

"So you claim. Listen, kid, don't want to keep bugging you but Seeger *was* at your shop. Any chance there are prehistoric missing files lying around?"

"I doubt it. Since the remodel, anything that shows up is random. But I'll check."

"Appreciate it. Want me to email the photo?"

"Can't hurt. Unless those cheekbones are *too* impressive."

"I wouldn't worry."

"Aw, gee," she said. "All this workplace support."

Three days passed with as many letdowns.

Day One, Deirdre Seeger called to let Milo know she'd taken the time to go into her garage because it contained some of the "elements of Phil's life. Including his Harley manual and all sorts of spare parts, I have no clue what they are."

That memory choked her up. She went on to say that she'd found no old files, no case notes, just books and magazines. "All moldy and falling apart. Phil was a big reader. *American Rifleman, Shooting and Fishing, National Geographic,* some old *Life*s, a few of those gross detective rags, why Phil loved them I could never figure out. I guess I should do a thorough housecleaning but . . . what am I going to end up with? Blank space?"

"Thanks, Deirdre."

"Sorry I couldn't help."

Day Two, Du Galoway called to let Milo know he'd spent a long time thinking and meditating "because that sometimes feeds my memory. But in this case, nothing. I guess I told you everything I know the first time. Sorry."

"Thanks, Du."

Day Three, Petra called to let Milo know she'd assigned two police scouts to look into "every conceivable nook, cranny, drawer, and storage area. No missing files, period. Sorry."

"Thanks, kiddo."

We were returning to his office from a walk and some decent coffee when he said, "All those apologies and no one's running for office. And the one whose job it is to check, hasn't."

He phoned the archive. A slurred voice said, "Records."

"Officer Bardem, Lieutenant Sturgis."

"Oh. Had a cold, just got back but still feeling it, forgot to let you know."

"Let me know what?"

"Found you some missing females from that time."

"Great, email 'em."

"Sure." Sniffle. Click.

The file arrived seconds later. And kept arriving.

Page after page filled his screen. Milo saved and printed, groaned as the bin filled and overflowed.

When the printer stopped whining, the bin held a stack as thick as a phone book. He leafed through, cursed, and gave it to me.

Single-spaced list of alphabetized names.

Over a fifteen-year period, spanning twenty-five to forty years ago, 56,154 females had gone missing in L.A. County. Of those, 44,723 had been accounted for, leaving 11,431 still gone.

All those families in limbo.

Milo had no bandwidth left for empathy. "This is bullshit. By the time I get through it I'll be on a walker. Optimistically speaking."

Yanking open a bottom drawer, he stuffed the list atop a ream of blank paper. The drawer wouldn't close until he pounded the stack.

"Eleven thousand opens," he said. "City of the Lost."

I said, "You could put her face online and try missing persons databases, the department's social media pages. Or create your own website."

"All those sad stories, someone's going to happen to find me?"

"Magnetism."

He glared, dark brows knitting. Return of the jaw-cherries.

I said, "Son, we need to work on your confidence."

Green eyes ignited. Then he roared with laughter.

He called for a technical officer and a five-foot-tall woman built like a fireplug showed up half an hour later. During the wait, we'd both worked on inspecting missing persons sites.

No room for three of us, so he spoke to Officer Shirlee Best out in the hallway.

She said, "That's your office?"

"Rank has its privileges."

Best remained impassive.

"Thanks for coming, Officer."

"My job. What do you need?"

When he finished explaining, Best said, "A to B to C, you don't need me for that."

"Humor me."

"It'll slow you down, I can't get back here until tomorrow."

"I'm sure you're worth the wait."

"Yeah, right. Obviously, I can't modify the department site or anyone else's."

"Don't expect you to." He ducked into the office and returned with the photo. "The woman on the right is the subject."

She glanced at the image with no apparent interest. "Crap resolution, don't expect much by way of enhancement. Do you want something pretty?"

"Meaning?"

"Cool graphics, attention-grabbing font, animation."

"You can do that?"

"It's not a big deal," said Best. "I had one guy, Ruffalo in Auto Theft, out looking for a hot Mercedes, wanted me to splice in scenes from video games. I told him no dice unless he could show me the licensing fee had been paid. He found out what that cost and said forget it."

"Beyond the call," said Milo.

"Mercedes belonged to an actress, Ruffalo wouldn't say who, just leered a lot. Guy looks like a pot of porridge but maybe he figured he could score if he produced the wheels. Not motivated enough to pay for the licensing, though. So how fancy do you want to get?"

"Does fancy make a difference?"

"No idea," said Best. "In the meantime, do us both a favor and accomplish what you can by yourself."

By the following morning at nine, he was at my kitchen table slurping coffee and demolishing an omelet he'd fixed from a staggeringly dubious mix of leftovers. Mushrooms plus salami plus candied walnuts plus jicama Robin and I had forgotten about unearthed from the recesses of the vegetable bin.

I ate toast and marveled.

Six mouthfuls in, he took a breather. "Right after Best left, she emailed and informed me one day has now stretched to two. So I did do some DIY: narrowed the national sites to the top five and sent them each Corn-Fed's headshot. The department's page has no sexy graphics and doesn't seem to be attracting the public big-time. Who it did attract was someone in Martz's office. She called me at home at ten p.m. *demanding* to know why when I was assigned to Swoboda I was *veering off* onto another case. I told her the victims were potentially linked, which got her all inquisitorial. But being a pencil-pusher, when I started explaining she spaced out and said, Whatever. Then she asked if Ellie had *approved* the 'digression.' That made all sorts of very bad thoughts swirl through my brain but you and Orwell will be proud to know I reacted with discretion and finessed her with doublespeak. Then I called Ellie, because I knew Martz would."

"How'd she react?"

"Graciously, I'm the expert, whatever I choose to do is fine," he said. Three more hurried swallows and a coffee wash-down. "That was after she gasped at the notion of another potential victim and asked what you'd expect."

"Could it be a serial killer."

"Cliché of our century. I finessed her, too. Don't know how long I can keep doing it, though."

He drained his cup, refilled. "It was Mel Boudreaux who answered her cell. He said she was sleeping, had been doing a lot of that. When she phoned a few minutes later, she sounded pretty low. Probably the aftermath of being dumped by Runner Boy."

That and her own limbo. No sense reminding him.

I said, "Makes sense."

"Anyway, mood issues are your thing, not mine. Meanwhile, there's nothing to do but bide time on what I've inputted and hope Best comes by tomorrow and isn't just putting me off. How's your day shaping up?"

"Appointments from noon to four."

"Busy man," he said. "No digressions for you."

Two days later, he texted me.

Best finally showed up, here's the hoo-hah production.

Below that, a link. No cute graphics, bright colors, or animation. Just a young, smiling face, unintentionally soft-focus, bordered top and bottom by somber black print.

DO YOU KNOW THIS WOMAN?

She went missing in or near Los Angeles sometime during the eighties and has never been identified. Someone must care about her. If you do, please contact Lieutenant Milo Sturgis, LAPD, Westside Division, at 310 . . .

Another day passed, as the week slid into a warm, blue-sky Friday. Busier week than I'd anticipated, with two additional custody referrals from the court. One came with a personal email from a judge I respected.

Big bucks, small minds. Hope you don't end up putting my face on a dartboard.

I looked up the names on the order. Husband-and-wife tycoons, mutual accusations of neglect, cruelty, and child endangerment. One child, a toddler. Enough money to keep the battle going indefinitely.

I'd do my best and try to protect the poor kid's psyche. Protect *my* soul from erosion.

No word from Milo since he'd posted the missing woman's image. There had to be tips, there always are. The question was validity. I was writing clinical notes when he phoned at three.

"What's up?"

"You're probably in TGIF mode but if you want to see the war room, c'mon over."

"You managed to get some troops?"

"Begging has its virtues. Also, I had Ellie call Martz."

◆

I went out to Robin's studio. She was seated at her bench, gloved up and French-polishing a rosewood guitar back, using deft circular motions to massage her hand-blended shellac into the wood with a soft cotton pad.

A near-silent, old-school task that she said could be hypnotically calming. A serene face said today it was.

I hung back and Blanche trotted toward me. I embarked on my own massage, rubbing her knobby head, then behind her ears, eliciting cat-like mews.

Robin looked up. Her hand stilled. Delayed-reaction smile.

Off in her own world but willing to let me in.

I went over and looked down at the wood. Purplish chocolate with veins of cream, quarter-sawn, straight-grained, glistening with polish—an elixir secreted by a sap-intoxicated beetle from Southeast Asia. When Robin had gotten the slab, she'd showed it to me, tapping and producing a ringing tone.

What had once been a tree in Brazil, felled by a storm, hummed melodically, ready for its new life.

I said, "Really pretty."

"Going to be a winner." She leaned over for a kiss. "What's up?"

"Just got a call from Big Guy, asking me to look at his war room."

"Blue screens and encryption?"

"More likely piles of paper and bad language. What's your schedule?"

"Don't have one, darling. I was thinking dinner at sevenish but no big deal if it's later. I'm enjoying this and I've got enough juice to do the maple mandolin and the Macassar OM."

"Shouldn't take more than a couple of hours."

She pursed her lips and pushed words past them. "Then you can *come* up and *see* me. Again."

"Mae would be proud."

She laughed. "Who needs external validation?"

CHAPTER

28

The war room was an interview space on the second floor, down the hall from Milo's office. He'd set up two rolling whiteboards and a long folding table with five plug-in landlines. Four chairs along the length, one at the head. A smaller round table in the corner held a coffee urn, cups, and pink boxes from a bakery he passes driving from his house in West Hollywood to the station.

No crumbs. Everyone in work mode, reading and writing, the phones unused.

My friend's relative independence from departmental routine comes with hitches. One of them is that unlike other lieutenants, he has no one under his direct command and when the need for support comes up he's forced to petition his captain. What he calls "the bended knee routine."

Coming from a semi-freelance not on the department's books, any request on Swoboda would be deemed iffy. But helped along by Ellie's call, he'd done okay, scoring a team of three. Two faces I knew well, one I'd never seen before.

At the left end of the long table, Detective Moses Reed, muscle-bound, crew-cut, ruddy, and baby-faced, sifted through paper and made notes. He looked up for a sec and finger-waved. So did Detective I Alicia Bogomil, ponytailed, raptor-eyed, and clean-featured, positioned next to him.

To Alicia's right a uniformed officer kept squinting in concentration.

No sign of D II Sean Binchy, the usual third leg of the investigatory tripod.

Milo was on his feet, near one of the boards. He said, "Hey," and that drew the uniform away from her pen and pencil.

Young—early twenties—with big, black, startled eyes and French-braided hair the same color. *J. Arredondo.*

Milo settled next to her, which stretched her eyes wider. He indicated the chair at the head. "Doctor."

I said, "Position of honor?"

"Who better? Officer, this is Dr. Delaware, the psychologist I told you about."

Whatever he'd told J. Arredondo made her gnaw her lower lip and look at me with uncertainty.

I smiled and held out my hand. "Alex."

Her palm was moist. "Jen."

Milo said, "Sean's on vacation so patrol gave us this fine officer for a few days."

Arredondo's soft, rosy mouth allowed itself a tremulous smile.

I sat and read the boards. Both were filled with columns of hash marks labeled *P, N, F,* and *V?* Entire sections were slashed with diagonal lines.

I said, "Tips?"

Milo nodded and picked up a sheet. "Here's where we are, so far. The department missing site pulled up sixteen. A couple looked promising but didn't pan out."

Jen Arredondo's frown said she'd been assigned to that sift.

"The websites," he went on, "were the usual mixed blessing. From five of them, we got two hundred ninety responses. Those we divided into prankster, nutcase, flaky psychic, and potentially valid. Finished that tally yesterday and got it down to . . . a hundred and two possibles. Those people we've begun emailing, asking for phone numbers and recording each contact for follow-up. Responses are trickling in so we're repeating, sometimes three, four times. Of the people we actually spoke to, very little has turned out promising. Wrong time period, wrong age, physical stats not even close. Despite the dates I listed, some people were decades off."

I said, "Desperation distracts."

"Yeah, there's a whole lot of wishful thinking out there."

He put the paper down. "I pulled a few possibles for my own review. There are plenty of initials to go, and new tips may come in over time. If Officer Arredondo is still with us, she'll be handling them."

Arredondo said, "Yes, sir."

Alicia said, "Wishful thinking and sad endings, Doc. With death records so accessible, whoever runs the sites could've pared down."

Moe said, "The volume the sites deal with, they probably don't deal with that."

"Well, they should," she said. "Searching for the truth and going public means responsibility."

Milo said, "We must be talking about a different internet."

Moe smiled. Alicia shrugged and returned to work.

Arredondo had followed the interchange with fascination.

Milo said, "The deaths do create an issue. We have no obligation to inform family members but morally I think we need to. But my feeling is don't take the time now, wait and see what the final pile looks like."

I said, "Make sense."

He smiled at Arredondo: "I turn to him for occasional validation."

"Yes, sir."

"Whenever we do notify, Officer, you won't have to be part of it."

"I don't mind, sir."

"Appreciate the can-do attitude but it's the part of the job we hate and you don't need to put yourself through it."

"Okay, sir."

He turned to me. "Let's take a walk."

Out in the hallway, I said, "A real walk or just away from there?"

He crooked a thumb toward his office. When we got there, I squeezed into a corner and sat on an inhospitable plastic chair as he worked his bulk between me and his desk.

"Impressive phone bank," I said. "What disease are we combating?"

"How about chronic deceptivitis?"

"Good cause. I hear it's an epidemic."

"Goddamn pandemic. So why after that dog-and-pony no-show you just heard did I call you over? I want to show you a couple of possibles that slightly vibrate my antenna. One of mine, one Alicia pulled up."

"You didn't want the troops to know because . . ."

"Both will likely dud out and I don't want them to lose momentum."

He opened a desk drawer and drew out a sheet of yellow legal paper. In the center, his back-slanted cursive:

B. Owen???? N. Strattine???

Below that, two emails.

bjowen@mindbody.net had written:

Sir, this could just be my cousin named Victoria Barlow. She vanished without a trace around 1983, 84 when she was a young adult and I'm pretty sure she used to live in L.A. I have only one picture from when she was younger but I'm feeling it's her. Happy to share, appreciate hearing from you. Here's my number. Bella J. Owen.

A 310 prefix.

ncstrat@petalsworth.com had written:

Dear Lieutenant Milo Sturgis, I'm responding to the photo you posted on Missing Spirits. I can't be certain but it's possible the woman in question is my aunt, Benicia Cairn who disappeared, probably between 1983 and 1985, possibly in California. If you're interested in discussing, this is the best number to reach me at. I'm based in Tx, but just happen to be near you, in Carpenteria on business for a few days. Best, Nancy Strattine.

I said, "Both sound pretty reasoned."

"That's what impressed me. Cautious, no hyped-up, mouth-breathing crusade, and the timing's right."

"You've been getting a lot of over-exuberance."

"Oh, Lord. The Web is catnip for the loosely wired. I searched our files for both of them, came up empty and checked out the sources. Bella Owen's forty-three, single, works at a day spa in Brentwood. Bodywork, reflexology, yoga, skin care. Ergo the mind–body dominion in her address, which did make me wonder. But it belongs to her employer and there's nothing spacey on her social network. Friends, dogs, cats, outdoor sports, wine. Strattine's forty-five, married, kids, works as a sales rep for a big rose grower in Tyler, Texas. Apparently it's *the* place for bounteous blossoms. So you agree, worth looking into."

"I do."

"Owen's local so maybe I can get over to her today or tomorrow. Or, if Strattine's heading back soon, she'll be the priority. Want me to call you when I connect?"

"Definitely."

"Good. How about some grub?"

"Robin's planning on dinner around seven. I'll tell her for three."

"No, no, no, don't wanna wear out the welcome mat."

"You haven't seen what our new mat says."

"What's that?"

"Seekers of truth welcome, others tolerated."

He laughed hard enough to wheeze, loosened his tie, stretched arms and legs and neck, pulled out a panatela and passed it from hand to hand.

We stepped out into the corridor.

He said, "If I talk to Owen and Strattine and lose enthusiasm, I won't bother calling you. Now go home and get all romantic. The kids get piqued, I call out for pizza. Maybe calzones."

"Moe will want salad and lean protein."

"Whatever. Meanwhile, I will chase any damn truth I can find."

I got home by six fifteen, peered out the back door and saw lights on in Robin's studio. Pulling a couple of steelhead fillets from the freezer, I set them out to thaw. Leftover coleslaw that had somehow eluded Milo got tossed with carrot shreds, sesame oil, and glass noodles. I found some mushrooms and sautéed them, made a dry rub of chili powder, cumin, turmeric, coriander, salt, and pepper for the fish, fetched a tablecloth and set the table.

Two tall, beeswax tapers, long forgotten at the back of the linen closet, caught my eye, and I placed them in the center in glass stands. The fish had warmed minimally so I finished thawing with forty-five seconds in the microwave and began the rubdown.

That done, I called over to the studio. "Hi, baby. ETA?"

Robin said, "Another twenty, twenty-five, plus ten for me to clean up and we can go."

"Sure. Where?"

"You pick."

"Deal."

Eighteen minutes later, she and Blanche entered the kitchen. Lights off but for the candles, slaw in the fridge, steelhead crispy-skinned and sizzling.

Robin said, "Whoa. Milo had good news?"

"Not particularly."

"So what are we celebrating?"

"Who needs a reason?"

"So romantic." She kissed me.

No point telling her he'd given me the idea.

29

Type A parents don't mind weekend appointments and neither do I. So I worked on custody cases from eight to noon, celebrated a quiet house with coffee, then returned to my office to get organized. Thirty-five emails, mostly junk. One from Milo, at eleven fourteen.

> I texted and left a message. Appts with both Owen and
> Strattine.

I called his cell. He said, "Just about to give up on you and leave for a noon meeting with Owen. She sounds encouragingly not-crazy. You wanna meet me there?"

"Sure."

"Brentwood. She's working today, so close to her job, Hava-Java, San Vicente near Bundy."

"See you there."

"You already caffeinated? I am."

"Oh, yeah."

"So we'll go decaf."

Hava-Java was shoehorned into the northwest corner of a strip mall in the heart of Brentwood shopping. The parking lot was populated by electric cars, hybrids, scooters, and a few gas-eating SUVs for the atheists. A harried attendant stood guard at the entrance, dispensing time-stamped tickets and listless warnings not to park in handicapped slots.

I said, "How many spaces are still open?"

"Not many."

I circled twice without success, finally saw a rose-colored Tesla pulling out and zipped in. During the first circuit, I'd spotted Milo's Impala, which was good. I had no idea what Bella Owen looked like.

I found him alone at a table, checking his watch, then his phone.

Tall cup of something iced and foamy in front of him. He said, "She called fifteen minutes ago but didn't leave a message. Phoned her back, straight to voicemail, hope to hell she didn't cancel."

He pointed to his drink. "In answer to your next question, chai yogi something or other. Tastes like cloves and cotton candy—okay, this is probably her."

I turned to see a tall woman approaching and waving. She I.D.'d us immediately; we carried the only Y-chromosomes in the place.

Bella Owen was nice-looking, on the heavy side, with porcelain skin, bright-blue eyes, and pulled-back dark hair. A couple of curled tendrils hung intentionally loose. She wore a black tunic and pants. A yellow sunrise logo on the left breast sat above orange lettering. *Bodywise.*

Milo introduced me by name, not title.

She said, "Nice to meet you guys," sat and placed her hands on the table. Eight of ten fingers were banded by a ring. Reaching down, she produced her phone and placed it next to her right hand.

"Reason I called a few minutes ago is I might be getting another photo of Vicki. My aunt who lives in Downey said if she has one she'd email it. But she's old and not always with it so who knows? I figured if you could've made it a bit later, I'd wait to see if the jpeg came in, you might or might not want to meet. Then a client I don't like working with did a walk-in and I didn't want her to see me so I left."

Milo said, "No problem. Appreciate your getting in touch. Have you remembered anything more about your cousin?"

"No, sorry. She was quite a bit older than me, my mother was the baby of the family and Vicki's dad was the oldest. By the time I was born, she had to be eighteen, nineteen and not around much. Also, her family lived in Delano and we lived in Davis."

"The aunt in Downey is her mom?"

"No, Thelma's an aunt to both of us. She lives in care, can sometimes remember stuff or claim she does. But it comes and goes. I was surprised she had a picture. Her opinion of Vicki isn't exactly positive."

"How so?"

"Mind you, this is her speaking not me." She formed air-quotes with both hands. "Wild child, hung with hooligans, never learned anything at school, thought her looks could get her everything. But Thelma's a bitter person. Her own daughter committed suicide years ago. What'd you think of the photo I showed you of Vicki and some other cousins? She was just a kid, but maybe?"

Milo said, "The coloring's right."

Bella Owen slumped. "But the faces are teensy, I know. I'm feeling a little foolish about all of this, Lieutenant. You must be so busy."

"Never too busy to check out leads, ma'am. No matter how yours turns out, we appreciate your taking the initiative."

"Well," she said, "I figured it was the least I could do, my mom said Vicki's vanishing basically killed Vicki's parents. The stress of not knowing. Both of them did get cancer and what I know about holistic medicine tells me stress is a giant factor in that. What struck me was the time period in your post and the fact that we're talking L.A. According to my mom, Vicki definitely came here. Her parents heard from her a few times, then nothing."

I said, "Do you have any idea what led her to L.A.?"

"My guess would be excitement. Delano was pretty much grapes and screw-top wine. Vicki's mom and dad both worked for Gallo. I suppose she didn't want to slip into that."

She smiled. "Or as Thelma put it, 'The girl was old enough to vote but all she wanted to do was have fun.'"

"Vicki was twenty-one."

"Just."

"Does your mom remember anything else?"

"Wish I could ask her, she's gone, too," said Owen. "Those quotes are just stuff that came up. Everyone's gone except Thelma. Sometimes I think she's just too ornery to stop breathing."

She shrugged. "I guess if I could clear up what happened to Vicki, I'd feel a little bit heroic."

Milo and I nodded.

"Also," she said, "all that's left of the family besides Thelma—and she won't last long—is me and my daughter. The bad part of being the only child of the youngest child."

I said, "What was Vicki's family like?"

"Conventional, religious, no one before had just upped and left."

"But she did stay in contact."

"In the beginning. Thelma claims Vicki sent her a couple of post-cards. 'Dashed' them off. Hollywood cards—the sign, Grauman's Chinese."

I said, "Proof of sinfulness to Thelma?"

Bella Owen laughed. "You got it. She was always fire and brimstone but Suzette's suicide made it worse."

Milo said, "We've tried to find information on Vicki and haven't been successful. What I can tell you is she has no criminal record."

Bella Owen's hands relaxed. "That's good to hear. I like to think the best of everyone so I'd like her to be just a bored girl looking for some fun—is that the Chai Zen Frothy you're drinking? Mind if I get some? I've worked on some pretty tight backs all morning and it totally dehydrated me."

Milo said, "On me," and got to his feet.

"Oh, I couldn't do that."

Before the sentence was complete, he was at the counter ordering and paying.

Bella Owen looked at me. "Is that typical?"

"He's a generous person."

"Well, that's a nice quality in a guy. And pretty darn rare, especially the young ones who always seem to leave their wallets home by accident. I keep telling my daughter to be pickier. Then again, she knows from her father that I'm no expert."

Milo returned with the drink. Taller glass than his.

She said, "Oh, my, you got me the Molto, I'll never finish it."

"Give it the old college try."

Giggling, she sipped through a paper straw, following the gradual drop in fluid level with vivid blue eyes that seemed to gain wattage with each millimeter.

When the glass was down by a quarter, she removed the straw, now bent and soggy. "I know it's a good cause but these things are totally useless."

Her phone buzzed on the table.

She snatched it up. "Hi, Auntie . . . you have? That's amazing . . . yes, of course I believed you. Did you have trouble sending it . . . no, of course not, it was super-fast, sorry. That's great, Auntie, thanks so much . . . I'm not saying I approve of everything anyone does including her, but . . . sure, I'll tell them. Thanks again, Auntie, enjoy your snack."

Once the connection was cut, she puffed her lips in exhalation. "Apparently the picture is proof that Victoria was 'wanton and wild.' She wants you to know the family did not approve . . . let's take a look . . . okay, here it is."

Bigger frown. Long sigh. "Sorry. Vicki's not your girl."

Milo said, "Let's have a look anyway."

Owen handed him the phone. On the screen was a color shot of a blonde in a minimal white bikini posed on an unidentifiable empty beach. Careful positioning, sharp contours, and dramatic use of light suggested a professional job.

The woman leaned on her elbows in a way that thrust her chest upward. Sleek tan skin sheathed a slim but curvy body and a quartet of coltish limbs.

Pinpoints of condensed moisture topped smooth shoulders. The illusion of passion sweat courtesy a spritz from a water bottle? Or she really had been perspiring.

If so, it wasn't due to tension. Languid posture, clear confident eyes, and slightly parted lips revealing a hint of white teeth said this was someone who loved the camera.

Bella Owen said, "It actually is pretty racy. I can't believe she sent this to Thelma."

I said, "Maybe she was asserting herself to Thelma."

"Hmm, yes, you could be right. Standing up for herself. I like that. But Thelma held on to it."

"Maybe there's more to Thelma than you know."

"Hah. Anyway."

Milo held on to the phone. Staring, processing. The moment I'd seen the model's face my gut had tightened and from the way his jaw was working, so had his.

Not the woman we were seeking, but a familiar face.

The cheekbones.

◆

Bella Owen drank a bit more before pushing her cup away. Glanced at her phone. "Need to get back, guys. Sorry it didn't work out. Would've been nice."

I said, "If you don't mind, could you call your aunt and ask if anything's written on the back of the photo?"

"Why? She's not your girl."

"She's missing and who knows, something could come up during the investigation."

Milo's eyes had slid toward me. Owen didn't notice.

"Oh. Okay, I'll try her now." Rapid number punches. "Auntie, sorry to bother you again . . . that's why I said I'm sorry, Auntie . . . I understand, nutrition's important, but so is learning about Vicki so if you still have the picture, could you see if anything's written on the back? Yes, at their request. No problem, I'll wait . . . yes, I know it's my choice."

Sighing and rolling her eyes, she switched to speaker.

Milo whispered, "You deserve combat pay."

"Ain't that the truth."

A minute passed before a constricted voice said, "Only going to say this once so pay attention, Marabella. Sterling Lawrence Studio Nine Fifty-Three Gower Street Hollywood big C small A."

Click.

Milo had been scrawling rapidly. "Got it."

"A professional studio," said Bella Owen. "Vicki was a model. Or hoping to be one. Or maybe an actress." Her eyes misted. "All that dreaming and look what happened. She's dead, isn't she, Lieutenant?"

"No way to know."

"All these years?"

Milo said, "It's not looking great but we do get surprised."

Bella Owen said, "Appreciate your honesty. I never really knew Vicki, I just . . . I need to forget about it and go back to living life."

Quick hand squeeze for each of us before she walked away.

30

Milo said, "Oh, *do* we get surprised. Let's walk a bit."

We strode the strip-mall walkway, passing all kinds of opportunities to ingest calories and a gym where you could burn them off. Spandex and unspoken intensity abounded. People trying *so* hard to defy the passage of time.

He said, "Well, *that* was a game changer." Out came the Azalea Club photo from his case. "Three blondes, probably all murdered, and the Sultan dies in his bed confessing. You ever actually see that in psychopaths? Sudden burst of guilt?"

"So far not the ones who premeditate murder. But like I said, terminal illness can mess with the nervous system."

"Biology, not morality?"

"I wouldn't count on morality."

"Hunh. Sometimes I think you're more cynical than I am. Anyway, the creepiness level has just ratcheted higher and who knows where it'll end. Maybe I will ask Val for permission to bring in the radar."

"Think she'd agree?"

"She came to us about the confession."

"True but she's ambivalent, and too much disruption could tip her over. Also, the house isn't only hers, her brothers are co-owners. If she felt the need to call them, it could go bad pretty fast."

"What, then?"

"When's your appointment with Nancy Strattine?"

"Hour and a half, Oxnard."

"I'd wait to hear what she has to say. Meanwhile we can try to learn about the photo studio and Vicki Barlow. Sterling Lawrence and others like him could be where Des Barres sourced his women."

"Fine art covering for pimping."

"Lawrence could've had a steady supply, Des Barres and men like him provided the demand."

"What's that called, symbiosis?"

"If you're being charitable."

"If not?"

"Flesh peddling."

"Okay, let's get back to my wheels and see if ol' Sterling has a past."

He used the computer in the Impala and confirmed that the photography studio no longer existed. The 900 block of Gower was residential. The exact address was a big-box apartment complex that looked to be around ten years old.

NCIC had nothing criminal on Lawrence. A Find A Grave search pulled up a headstone for Sterling Adrian Lawrence at Hollywood Memorial. Smallish and simple, black granite. An old-fashioned camera with bellows engraved at the top.

The photographer had died fourteen years ago, age seventy-eight. That made finding a record at the coroner's office a decent shot.

He found it. Like Swoboda, just a summary: heart attack.

He said, "So much for that. Now what?"

"You could try Harlow Hesse."

"Why?"

"He's old, likes to talk, seems to know everyone."

"Fun times. Why not."

A woman, probably one of the maid-quartet, answered. "Hesse residence, who may I ask is calling?"

"Lieutenant Sturgis. We met with Mr. Hesse a few days ago and have a question."

"Oh," she said. "He went down for a nap but let me see."

Moments later, a familiar bellow shot through the tiny speaker: "Didn't you see me in the kitchen, Sheila? Of course I'm up . . . hello, Lieu*ten*ant, auld lang syne, how can I help you."

"A name came up during the investigation, sir. A photographer named Sterling—"

"Lawrence. Great guy, hope you're not going to tell me he did something nasty."

"Not at all."

"What, then?"

"We found a portrait he took of our missing girl and wondered what you could tell us about him."

"First off," said Hesse, "he's dead, so forget talking *to* him. Chainsmoker, loved steak, no surprise. I tried to tell him to moderate at least the cigs but he was puffing away since the army. So was the picture classy? I'm betting yes because Ster was a classy guy, extremely artistic, took his time with the lighting. A real artist, none of that cheesecake crap, none of those phony shutterbug clubs attracting perverts. He had a classy setup, worked out of this big Craftsman he owned in Hollywood. Great place, the neighborhood got a little iffy but Ster stayed . . . Sycamore Avenue maybe? Cherokee?"

"Gower."

"That's it, Gower. Don't know who owns it now." A beat. "Ster had no heirs."

"The building's long gone," said Milo.

"What's there now?"

"Big apartment complex."

"All the class of a shipping carton?"

"Something like that."

"Figures," said Hesse. "Like Joni used to say—she's got a great place in Bel Air, by the way—they paved paradise and discombobulated everything classy."

"The photo we have was shot on a beach."

"So?"

"So I guess Sterling traveled away from his studio."

"Same question. What's the diff?"

"Good point," said Milo. "What else can you tell us about him?"

A beat. Throat clearing. "You know, Lieutenant, I enjoyed talking to you, you seem like a really dedicated guy. You and the shrink, both of you seemed like good people. And I'm a civic-minded citizen so obviously I want to do anything I can to help with whatever it is you think you need help with. But if you're barking up Ster Lawrence's tree, don't. Great guy, had a tough life. Military brat, crazy-strict religious parents. Knew who he was but they didn't approve so he did his own thing and used his talent to make a life for himself. It wasn't easy. Are you catching my drift?"

Milo said, "Yes, sir."

"Trust me," said Hesse. "He was upright and ethical and a very, very, very talented guy."

His voice broke.

Milo waited.

Harlow Hesse said, "I'm not going to get into details but let's just say Ster was known to frequent the same place I went with your Dr. Silverman. Both floors."

"Got it."

"I'd hope so. Given who *you* are."

Click.

I said, "Upstairs/downstairs at The Azalea. Maybe there was more interplay than was obvious."

"Lawrence and Des Barres ran into each other and figured out the supply–demand thing?"

"Des Barres and others like him. Lawrence could've gotten kickbacks or Hesse is right and there was nothing sleazy going on, just some informal matchmaking. In any event, we've got a good theory of how three women ended up in the harem."

"But no clue what happened to them. And maybe others." He rubbed his face. "This is the point where I'd suggest nutrition but I'm supposed to meet Nancy Strattine for lunch. You have Saturday plans?"

"No, I'll come, once I figure out where to put my car."

"Let's see to that."

No letup in the strip-mall traffic. The attendant looked even more harried.

Milo said, "Hi."

Waving hands, scowling face. "One sec one sec hold on."

A flash of the badge drew the attendant's eyes. "Police? Okay, no problem." He let in a pink VW Bug. "*What?*"

"We came in with two cars, the Impala and a classic Seville."

"The green one, yeah, nice."

"Very nice and it's going to be here for a while."

"How long is a while?"

"Hours."

"I can't do that."

A twenty pressed into the man's palm. Milo folded his fingers over the bill.

"Got it, sir."

"Knew you would."

◆

Eighty minutes to get to Oxnard was close to a sure bet, even with a mishap or two on the 101. Today there were none and we sailed through the Valley into 805 territory, passed Camarillo and into its northern neighbor.

Once a high-crime scar on the pretty face of Ventura County, Oxnard had finally realized it was a beach town and matured accordingly. A few gang neighborhoods survived but between a well-designed harbor, surf-side resorts and condos to the west, and lush plantings of berries, artichokes, and leafy things to the east, once you got off the freeway, the drive was a pretty one.

We exited at Rice Avenue, continued a few miles, and turned right into a high-end industrial park. Wide, mostly empty streets crisscrossed multi-acre lots on which white and off-white buildings sat behind knolls of barbered grass. Some of the structures housed the headquarters of agribusiness firms and the companies that serve them—truckers, shippers, packers. Others with black glass windows sported the names of corporations—names that explained nothing and could have sprung from the feverish mind of a conspiracy theorist.

One of the few buildings that's not white is painted brick and cream and contains a large winery with a tasting room at the front and restaurant at the back consistently rated the best in the county. I'd discovered it years ago, interviewing a witness in a previous case, had turned Milo and Rick on to it because they're always looking for cuisine. They'd become fans, stopping on the way to rare weekends in Santa Barbara for Cabernet and prime rib.

Any eatery Milo frequents benefits from his habitual overtipping. It's a cop thing he takes even further. The result is usually a hero's welcome and today was no exception.

We arrived eighteen minutes before the appointment with Nancy Strattine, were immediately seated at a private corner table and comped with a charcuterie plate generous enough to nourish all three bears.

Milo said, "Aw, not necessary."

The waiter said, "Enjoy."

Milo said, "Sage advice," and reached for his fork.

Several bison sausages, strips of venison jerky, and chunks of veal pâté later, he took a breather, wiped his forehead, swigged ice water, and looked around. Seconds after he'd returned to the food, I noticed a blond woman enter, confer with the host, and head our way.

"Here she is, Big Guy. On the dot."

He wiped his face hurriedly, stood to greet her.

"Ms. Strattine. Thanks for coming."

"Nancy's fine."

Fine came out *"Fahn."*

He gave her the same name-only intro for me that he'd offered Bella Owen. She smiled, said, "Hi, Alex," and sat.

Nancy Strattine was five-three and trim, wearing full makeup that included exuberant false eyelashes and bright-red lipstick. The blond hair was an ash-colored, meringue-like cloud. Her eyes were dark, her chin firm and pointy. A slightly oversized nose aimed for the sky.

She carried a navy Gucci bag, wore yellow spike-heeled shoes and an olive-green pantsuit. The suit's neckline framed a vee of freckled chest and an inch of cleavage. On her left lapel was a gold brooch shaped like a rose. Three-inch gold hoop earrings, a fire-opal pendant on a chunky gold chain, a two-carat diamond ring paired with a wedding band crusted with pavé diamonds, and an Apple Watch with an orange leather band completed the ensemble.

She said, "Never get this far south. What's good?"

Milo said, "Everything, ma'am," and nudged the charcuterie toward her.

She inspected the plate, tweezed jerky between manicured fingers, and nibbled. "Yums."

"Glad you like it, ma'am."

"Ma'am? That sounds like where I'm from."

"No geographic boundaries when it comes to manners. Ma'am."

Nancy Strattine let out a throaty laugh. Then her face changed, as if suddenly warned to avoid merriment. "I shouldn't be frivolous, it's a sad situation with Benicia. Either way."

The waiter reappeared. Milo and I had turned down wine but he asked Nancy Strattine if she wanted some.

She looked at us. "Against your rules?"

"Unfortunately."

"Well . . . not against mine. I'll have a glass of Pinot."

"Coming up."

"Any questions or are you folks ready?"

Nancy Strattine speed-scanned the menu. "I am. Chicken sandwich."

Milo ordered the deluxe burger and I asked for a seven-ounce fillet.

The waiter said, "No worries," and left.

Nancy Strattine said, "Why do they say that? What would I be worried about unless he knows something I don't."

I said, "Generational anxiety."

"Ha—and he *didn't* say ma'am. In Texas even the kids are polite. So. When you emailed me I got charged up and called the only member of my family who was alive back when Benni—that's what we called her, two *n*'s, one *i*—when Benni disappeared. That's my uncle Nat, he's retired police in Austin. He was the baby, born after Benni and my mom. He said he didn't have anything but then he found what I'm going to show you and sent it. She's still a kid and her figure was different, but who knows, maybe you can draw a conclusion."

Out of the blue bag came an Apple 10 XR in a pink snakeskin case. An image already loaded.

Outdoor shot, clumped greenery backing a chubby girl sixteen to eighteen, wearing a yellow print dress with puffed sleeves.

None of the open glee of the smooth-faced blonde in the Azalea shot. This subject was barely able to meet the camera head-on. Long brown hair hung lank. Too-short bangs did nothing for a full face that was lightly spotted with acne.

Milo loaded the Azalea shot with everyone but the fresh-faced blonde blocked out and we did a side-by-side comparison.

Puberty, plastic surgery, and long-term aging can alter appearances radically but a handful of unmanipulated years, particularly during youth, don't have much impact on facial proportions.

He looked at me. I nodded.

He said, "Unless Benni had a twin, it's a match." He offered Strattine the comparison.

She said, "My oh my . . . so Benni did end up in L.A. That's what people said. But she sure looks different . . . but yes, it's her."

"Which people?"

"Let me rephrase. That's what my mom said. She used Benni as a bad example whenever she wanted me to toe the line. Her claim was Benni had slipped out through a bedroom window late at night and it was obvious where she went because she'd talked about being a Hollywood movie star. Which Mama said was stupid because Benni never acted a whit in school. Didn't do much of anything in school."

I said, "Not a student."

"Not according to Mama," said Strattine. "Stay in school, Nancy, don't drop out like stupid Benni. Use your time wisely, Nancy, don't sit around letting your rear get as wide a barn door like fat Benni. Get a respectable job, not like lazy Benni who ended up spreading manure at one of the rose growers. Watch your figure—I know, brutal. I suppose that's why I went searching for what happened to Benni. Kind of like saving a poor soul."

"She and Benni were first cousins?"

"Yes, sir."

"Any reason for the animosity?"

"My theory," said Strattine, "is it was really between *their* mothers. Mawmaw—my grandma—was religious, a total puritan. Benni's mom, Great-Aunt Sadie, was anything but. But again, that's just what I've been told. I asked Uncle Nat about it and he had no idea, said he'd never heard about the actress thing, either. The story his dad—Great-Uncle Nathaniel, Sr.—told him was totally different. Benni fell in with a criminal female and likely met a bad end because of it."

I said, "Either way, Benni was the bad example."

"Exactly."

Milo said, "Did the criminal have a name?"

"Not that Nat knows. What Senior said was she was an ex-con, got released and hired to work with the roses. Busy season, the growers brought on all sorts of temporaries. I suppose Benni could've met her while spreading manure. But if she made it to L.A., Nat was probably wrong and it was Hollywood she was after. Can I see that photo again, please?"

Milo handed her his phone.

"She looks so pretty," said Strattine. "She improved herself. All by herself." Fist-pump.

An exuberant voice said, "Here we go, folks." Three plates were set down silently.

Nancy Strattine tasted her sandwich. "Yums." Then her wine. "Yums, again." She put her glass down. "It's sad to think of Benni out there with no family. I suppose after all this time there's not much hope."

"No matter how it turns out, you did the right thing, ma'am."

"Thank you for saying that, Lieutenant. Mama would disagree."

"Why's that?"

"The road to hell's paved with good intentions, Nancy. Deal in facts, Nancy, not far-fetched ideas."

"Whew," said Milo. "She does sound tough."

"Let me tell you, there are times . . ." Head shake. "That attitude's part of what makes me want to do right by Benni."

Sudden flash of anger. Then a nibble of her sandwich. "This *is* good."

As the three of us ate, Milo and I rephrased questions we'd already asked. Nancy Strattine didn't resist but she had nothing to add.

Then I said, "Did Benni ride horses?"

"As a sport? No. Did she ever get on a horse? Probably, it's Texas. Tyler's a city but there's ranchland not too far, that's where I used to ride with my dad. So maybe Benni did, too. Though I never saw it personally. And her dad—Uncle Loudon—died when she was little."

"It was just her and her mother?"

"And her mother drank. A lot. So did Loudon, that's what killed him, driving drunk into a cottonwood. They were looked down upon by the rest of the family."

The check came. Nancy Strattine reached for it.

Milo snatched it up and carried it to the host station.

When he returned, she grinned. "I can't get into trouble for bribing a peace officer?"

"Nope, you're safe."

"Can I at least do the tip?"

"Taken care of, ma'am."

"Bummer—okay, can you at least call me Nancy? That way I can pretend this is a social thing and next time it'll be my turn."

"Sure, Nancy."

"You're an easygoing man. Texas would like you." She reached out to touch his hand, thought better of it.

The three of us stood and headed out of the restaurant.

Milo said, "If there's anything else you can recall or learn about Benni, let us know."

"Promise," said Nancy Strattine. "I'm really a source, huh? My husband and kids are going to get a huge kick out of that."

She drove away in a rental Explorer.

I said, "Two positive I.D.'s in one day."

"Unbelievable," he said. "Must be sunspots or something."

"Benni hanging with a bad girl could fit our Queen Bee guess. A tough, more streetwise girl brought her to L.A. and got her into the scene."

He nodded. "That's why you asked about horseback riding. Which she didn't rule out. Okay, let's check in with the kids." He phoned Moe Reed and gave him the news.

Reed said, "Funny you should say that, L.T. Alicia and I got nearly identical tips from two sources about a girl named Benni. Mine described her as intellectually challenged."

"Where are the tipsters from?"

"Dallas and Boston. Both said they grew up in East Texas, that's where they knew her."

"They have anything else to say?"

"Just that they thought they recognized her."

"How much info is left to go through?"

"At least a day's worth," said Reed. "Maybe some spillover tomorrow."

"You need a break from weekend work?"

"Nope, Alicia and I are charged up. The rookie's kind of bummed because none of her stuff has panned out but that's good training, right, L.T.? Getting used to failure."

31

We left the winery and headed east toward the Del Norte on-ramp to the 101. Milo maintained an easy seventy-eight mph all the way to Thousand Oaks, where his phone rang with a text.

He handed it to me. "See if it's anything."

"Detective Sherry Mulhern, Valley Division. Call when you have a chance, no reason given."

He said, "Keeping it brief, sounds like something active. Do me a favor and speaker it, then hold it close enough for me to talk."

I put the phone on my left leg, maxed the volume, called the number.

A tobacco voice said, "Mulhern."

"Sturgis."

"Thanks for getting back so quick. I'm Valley Burglary, caught one in Granada Hills. Complainant is extremely freaked out, which is understandable. What's different is she claims it could be related to some sort of contact with you but she won't say what. Older woman, she seems okay mentally, but I'm no doctor. Deirdre Seeger, did you have dealings with her?"

"Couple of phone conversations," said Milo. "Are you at the scene now?"

"For a while, the techies are doing their thing," said Sherry Mulhern. "So she's mentally stable?"

"Far as I know."

"It's probably shock, then. Can't blame her, every room was basically trashed, going to take time to get prints and whatever else."

"What's the address?"

"You're coming over?"

"Might as well, I'm in Thousand Oaks, can make it in twenty-five."

"Okay," said Mulhern, sounding amused. She read off an address on Southland Street. "That level of speed, watch out for the Chippies, they don't give us any breaks."

Thirty-one miles to the base of the Santa Susana Mountains, two more miles to reach the crime scene. One CHP car spotted, already ticketing a trucker.

Twenty-seven minutes.

The house was a low-slung, white midcentury with a sea-green door on a street lined with mature trees. One of the holdouts; most of neighbors had McMansionized. A venerable lemon tree spread across the left side of a fading lawn, evoking Granada Hills's orchard origins. Same for the navel orange on the right. Other than the trees, just grass split by a cement walkway. Entry blocked by yellow tape.

Milo pulled behind a navy-blue Crown Victoria sedan with a sagging rear end and cop plates. Ford had stopped making the big sedans in 2011 but they endured as the go-to unmarked for situations where you didn't need to be unmarked.

Behind the Crown Vic was a white Scientific Division van. The scenes I'm called to feature at least two vans. One for the technicians, one for the crypt drivers. Plus the compacts the coroner's investigators take when they're dispatched to go through dead people's pockets.

The absence of all that did nothing to mollify the woman on the sidewalk weeping into a handkerchief. Small, thin, bespectacled, mid- to late seventies. She wore a stiff, dark-brown bouffant, a blue sweatshirt with the U.'s insignia, white sweatpants, white flats.

At her side was a gray-haired woman in her midforties no taller but thirty pounds heavier. Cropped, frizzy, utilitarian hair topped sharp eyes, a nub nose, and an assertive chin. Detective badge clipped to the breast pocket of her black blazer. The blazer hung open, revealing a holstered semi-auto.

Stocky woman but not fat; broad and solid, the kind of body designed for long-term plodding not showy sprints.

She nodded at us, looked over at the crying woman, flashed a *goes with the territory* frown, and shifted a couple of feet away.

Milo recited his name and mine. Sherry Mulhern did the same. No time for handshakes. The older woman had let out a sheep-like mewl and Mulhern rushed back to her.

"So sorry for your losses, Mrs. Seeger."

"Sorry for being a crybaby," said Deirdre Seeger. "I know it's just things, not a person. But they're my things and I could've been here except for the grace of God."

Mulhern said, "Chances are if you were here, ma'am, they wouldn't have dared."

Deirdre Seeger looked up at Milo for confirmation.

He said, "Detective Mulhern's right. Most burglars are cowards who avoid confrontation."

Mulhern smiled, grateful for the support. "Anyway, I brought the lieutenant to you like you requested."

Deirdre Seeger said, "What about those home invaders? They just break in, don't care if you're home."

Mulhern said, "I won't tell you it doesn't happen. But not here, this is a really safe neighborhood."

As if realizing how lame that sounded, she exhaled and turned to the side.

Milo said, "What was taken, Deirdre?"

"My jewelry, my cash—I don't leave a lot around, maybe a hundred dollars for odds and ends. Then"—she began ticking her fingers— "there's my flat screen. I just got it for myself last Christmas. Then there's my iPad—it's been broken for a while so tough luck for them. Then there's my wine, four bottles, it's good wine, I got it on sale at Trader Joe's."

Mulhern turned to us. "The typical stuff."

Deirdre Seeger huffed. "It doesn't feel typical to me, Detective. It feels like a violation."

"Of course, ma'am. It's a terrible violation. As I told you, we're searching aggressively for fingerprints and any other physical evidence."

"What about other burglaries around here?" said Seeger. "Wouldn't that give you a lead?"

"It would, ma'am, but there haven't been any."

Seeger's eyes bulged. "See! I was singled out! It's me they wanted to violate!"

"Why would that be, ma'am?"

Seeger shook her head. Gave Milo a quick peek. Grim, conspiratorial. She folded her arms across her chest.

Sherry Mulhern's mouth got tight. "Mrs. Seeger, if you'd rather talk to them alone, that's fine. I've got a few things to do inside investigating *your* burglary."

"Go," said Deirdre Seeger. As if realizing how harsh that sounded, she followed up with, "Thank you, Miss Mulhern. Appreciate your service. Like I told you, I know about detection."

"It appears that you do, ma'am." Mulhern traded cards with Milo and ducked under the tape.

Deirdre Seeger said, "No sense involving her, I didn't want to get in the way of your investigation. Police work is specialized, Phil taught me that."

"You think this could be related to our conversations about Phil's last case?"

"You just heard what she said. This is a safe neighborhood, I was targeted. I mean, how long ago were we talking—few days and then this happens."

A tech exited the house with a hard-shell equipment case. "Stomping all over my home." More tears. "Sorry, I'm such a baby."

"Seems like a reasonable reaction to me, Deirdre."

"Phil and I bought it for thirty-one thousand dollars. They say it's worth seven hundred thousand but I don't care. Where am I going to go, to some rest home where they don't pay attention and you die in a corner?"

Biting her lip. "I loved my home. Want to love it again but . . . like I told her, it's only for the grace of God that I wasn't here and who knows what would've happened to me."

"Where were you?"

"Newhall, I've got a friend there, we play canasta twice a week, have a group, we rotate. The game was Friday night, Ada served snacks and prosecco, really delicious, I overindulged and knew enough not to drive. I was going to try one of those Ubers. Never did it before but what the hey, there's a first time for everything. Ada said she wouldn't hear of it, the spare bedroom was already made up, she keeps it that way for when her kids come home and they rarely do now, they all moved out of state, the taxes. So I slept over and then I got the call. From Mulhern."

"Any idea when the break-in occurred?"

"She thinks at night because no neighbors she talked to saw or heard anything. She said it was a real burglary not a staging because in staging the drawers are pulled out but not everything's removed and at least some valuables are left behind. But what do you think?"

"That sounds logical, Deirdre."

"Well, maybe. But the main thing is where am I going to stay? Even if they cleaned up, which they're not going to do, I'm not staying here by myself. Not until my mind settles and who knows how long that'll take? If Phil and I had children it would be a different story but God didn't shine that light on us." Brief glance at the sidewalk. "I have nowhere to go!"

Milo said, "I'll make a call, Deirdre."

"To who?"

"Someone who might be able to put you up temporarily."

"I can't afford to pay one of those Air-Bee-Bees."

"I know that. Gimme a sec to take a look inside and then I'll see what I can arrange."

He loped to the house, emerged a few minutes later, during which Deirdre Seeger clenched and unclenched her hands and fought back tears.

"He seems like a good man. I've got a nose for that. Phil was a good man. He always tried his best."

I said, "Last time you spoke to Lieutenant Sturgis, you mentioned Phil's books and magazines. Were any of those taken?"

"That junk, why would they be? Besides, they're out in the garage, which I keep bolted." Her lips trembled. "I keep the house locked, too, but they just ripped the rear door off its hinges. Phil put a good bolt on the garage because he kept his bikes there plus parts. People tell me it's worth a lot, one day I'll sell them but not now, that's for sure. I can't have bikers or who-knows-who coming by. Sir, I don't know if I'll ever feel safe *again*!"

"You will."

"How do you know?"

"Experience."

"Have you ever felt alone and scared?"

It's called being the child of a raging alcoholic.

I said, "I have."

"Really?"

I touched her arm. "Absolutely."

"Well . . . maybe."

When she'd remained silent for a while, I said, "Would it be possible for me to get into the garage?"

"You might be interested in the parts?"

"I'd like to take a look around."

"Is this something that could help catch the bad guys?"

"It could be, Mrs. Seeger. Every little bit helps."

"Hmm. Okay, you also seem like a nice guy. Nice goes with nice, Phil and I were like that. Everyone said it. He's nice, she's nice, adds up to a nice couple." Sniff. "We were happy together."

Milo joined us. "All arranged if you're agreeable, Deirdre."

"What is?"

"A comfortable bedroom in a nice big house in Los Feliz, totally free."

"Big empty house? Uh-uh, no way, too spooky."

"No, there's a woman living there and she's got a full-time guard looking after the premises."

"Why? Why does she need a full-time guard?"

He explained.

Deirdre Seeger said, "Oh . . . so her mother's the one Phil tried so hard to figure out? I don't know . . . oh, shoot, why not? If Phil cared, that means she was worth caring about and like I just told this other detective, nice goes with nice so the daughter's probably also a good person." A beat. "Is she?"

"Lovely person," said Milo. "She didn't hesitate to say yes."

"Los Feliz. I don't even know how to get there."

"You have GPS?"

"Hate computers."

"How about this, then: I'll drive you and have an officer bring your car."

"Hmm. Okay, it's a deal." As if doing Milo a favor. "Now go talk to Miss Mulhern so she'll let pack some of my stuff, it's already a mess on the floor, I'll just toss it into a suitcase. And I'll also get the key to the garage for your nice partner."

Milo looked at me.

I said, "Thought I'd check out Phil's books and such."

That answered nothing but he said, "Ah," and walked Deirdre into the house.

They returned ten minutes later, Milo toting two large suitcases, Deirdre Seeger lacing a bony arm around his sleeve. He loaded the luggage in the trunk of the unmarked after removing a shotgun to make space and placing it in the clamp at the front of the car. Deirdre was guided to a rear passenger seat and left there with the door open.

He jogged back to me.

I said, "What's it like inside?"

"Like Mulhern said, total trash job, valuables taken, does look real. She's gonna do the usual: neighborhood canvass, see who has cameras, ask about vehicles that don't belong, check if there has been anything similar in the Valley."

He held out a ring of keys, removed one. "That's her wheels over there, I called Moe and he's sending Arredondo over."

Pointing to a silver Honda Civic parked a few yards up. "This one, the Medeco does the garage. Better lock than on the damn house but the back door's a piece of crap, nothing woulda helped. Now tell me why you want to get in there."

"Long shot," I said. "Quick thinking, asking Ellie. Are you hoping for more than good-deed credits?"

"Such as?"

"Ellie and Deirdre get to know each other, Deirdre remembers something."

"Wish I was that smart but nah, just doing the bleeding-heart thing. Deirdre gets a safe place, Ellie gets some company, maybe it'll draw her out of her mood."

I said, "Emotionally smart. Wish I'd thought of it myself."

"Give yourself good-influence credits."

No sense wasting time debating but I knew he was wrong. He didn't need me or anyone else to do the right thing.

He said, "So why the *garage*?"

Ducking under the tape, keys in hand, with Milo following, I passed through an open wooden gate to the left of the house. The backyard was a meager square that mirrored the front lawn: grass, lemon tree, orange. Boxed by smog-pocked block walls that reduced it even further. A tech kneeled on the rear stoop, dusting the splintered remains of a sixty-year-old service door.

The garage was a single, taking up the left-hand corner of the property. The lock was gamy but I managed to key it open.

Manual door. The hinges groaned. I made sure it was stable in the open position before entering.

In front of me was a three-foot ribbon of empty space backed by clutter. Nothing messy or soiled, just too much stuff in too little space.

A good deal of the area was taken up by hacked-up sections of three Harleys that brought to mind butchered carcasses. The rest consisted of cartons, piles of them, sealed and neatly labeled in black marker. *Saddlebags, lids, fenders, fire ext., clutches, brk levers, tappets.*

The right-hand wall was lined with bolt-together steel shelves filled with smaller boxes. *Screws, bolts, nuts, nails, hand tools.*

For all of his rep as a sloppy detective, Phil Seeger had kept it organized at home.

A section of shelves in the far corner was my goal. It took some time clearing a path to reach it.

Floor-to-ceiling magazines that reminded me of my mother's collection. The way she sat pretending to read when I tried to escape my father's wrath.

I pushed that lovely memory aside and examined the periodicals. *National Geographic, Life, Look, Saturday Evening Post, Reader's Digest.*

What I was after was stacked at the bottom, which took more clearance time and some cramp-inducing kneeling that felt oddly prayerful.

Fifty or so luridly covered magazines, pulpy covers falling apart.

The front pages of a type: screaming headlines and paintings of minimally clad, voluptuous women on the verge of victimhood.

The titles were an exercise in adjective manipulation: *True Detective, Shocking Detective Stories, Ace Detective, Amateur Detective, Official Police Detective.*

I was prepared to remove the entire stack but Phil Seeger had made my life easy. A small yellow triangle extended from the third magazine from the top.

Corner of a yellow Post-it, *!!!* written on it in the same black marker.

Third from the top was where you'd stick something you wanted to shield from casual eyes but didn't want to waste time searching for.

I pulled out the issue, careful but unable to prevent a dandruff puff of acid-ruined paper dust.

Dark Detective, June 1976.

Turning to the tabbed page induced another dirt-fall but the interior of the magazine, shielded from the weather, was in surprisingly good shape, print and images still clear.

Bloody Trail of the Lolita Murderess! The Shocking Tale of an Orgy of Forbidden Love and Violence!

In the right-hand margin, Phil Seeger had written: *HER!!!*

◆

A brief scan gave me the basics of the story.

Martha Maude Hopple, a fifteen-year-old girl from the rural southern tip of Illinois, had teamed up with a thirty-four-year-old ex-con named Langdon "Mike" Leigh and embarked on a four-month, multi-state crime rampage. Eight people wounded, including a seven-year-old, plus six fatalities.

Plenty of black-and-white photos to go with the overheated prose.

Mike Leigh glared at the camera, scrawny, jug-eared, and with the flat eyes of a shark and a barely visible wisp of mustache trailing the top of a sneering mouth.

Martha Maude Hopple was equally hostile to the camera, managing to harden an adolescent face still larded with baby fat.

Compressed eyes, flaring nostrils, the barest upturn of lip.

Pretty girl once you got past the anger and the mannish, chopped haircut Mike Leigh had given her as a disguise.

A caption below his arrest photo proclaimed the habitual felon's intention to "take the rap, she didn't do nothing."

A caption below Martha Maude's portrait quoted her proclamation of innocence and the fact that "he forced me."

The twitchy partial smile—enjoying a private joke—suggested otherwise.

HER!!!

I didn't need Seeger to educate me.

Puberty, plastic surgery, and long-term aging can alter appearances radically, but short of that, facial proportions don't change.

I said, "Look."

Milo said, "Oh, shit."

Both of us staring into the smug, psychopathic, teenage face of the woman who'd called herself Dorothy Swoboda.

◆

I'd half expected, half hoped, but my heart rate had kicked up anyway. Milo was breathing fast. I heard his teeth grind.

He took the magazine, examined the title, the photos, the first paragraph of text. A droplet of sweat formed on his brow and rolled down to the magazine, forming a little gray dot on the browning paper. He wiped his face angrily with his hand.

"How the hell did you connect to *this*?"

"Small steps, nothing dramatic," I said.

"Screw the modesty. *Tell* me."

"When Strattine told us about an older bad girl Benni had fallen in with before she left town I flashed on the Azalea shot and Dorothy being a few years older than the other two women. Then I started thinking about the photo, itself."

I brought up the image on my phone. "She's apart from the other two. Not just physically, but emotionally. Apart from Des Barres, too."

"Everyone's having a good time except her."

"Grim," I said. "Same expression as in the forest shot with Stan Barker." I tapped the article. "Same as this, back when she was fifteen and committing violent crimes."

He studied all the screens. "Oh, man, once you point it out it's obvious . . . I'm seeing more than grim. That's perp anger—those eyes. Still, how'd you figure to find the story here?"

"Like I said, a long shot. You know I've been wondering on and off about all the accidents. Including Phil Seeger dying on his bike shortly after he retired. What if he'd learned something as a private citizen and died because of it? Then Deirdre mentioned he'd collected detective pulps. Why would a cop read about crime? So maybe he went digging into the past and discovered something. The final straw was the break-in. Maybe just a burglary, but what if it wasn't? Long as we were here, I figured couldn't hurt to look."

"How your mind works . . . so our gal is Martha Maude. Who the hell's Dorothy Swoboda?"

"Most likely the usual," I said. "Name on a gravestone. When the investigation started, I looked her up and the only thing I found was a woman who'd died in the 1800s."

"Me, too," he said. "Didn't figure it was worth mentioning." He swabbed his face again. "It's like a sauna in here, let's get the hell out."

The temperature felt fine to me. I said, "Sure. Want the magazine?"

"You carry it, I might drop it."

32

D eirdre Seeger was slumped in the backseat of the Impala, head down, mouth open, snoring.

People under stress do that, the body trying to recoup energy. Victims *and* suspects. Experienced detectives know that the guiltier the suspect, the easier the slumber.

Milo retrieved his attaché case from the front passenger seat. Moving the shotgun gingerly, even though the safety was on. Good habits pay off.

Popping the case, he took the magazine from me and laid it atop the blue file folder, shut the case, and placed it horizontally on the front seat. Leaving the door open, he motioned me away from the car, strode to the taped walkway, and crooked a thumb at the house.

"Looks like a bona fide burglary but maybe not if they were looking for Seeger's source material."

"That would be my bet."

"Who would know I talked to Deirdre about Seeger? No one I can think of. Or am I missing something? I could understand if I'd said something to Val Des Barres. She phones her brothers, they dispatch someone. Or she handles it herself via Sabino, guy's got a record, busting a door and rooting around wouldn't be a leap."

I said, "Actually, you did talk to one person about Seeger and a missing woman from the mansion. Someone with police experience who'd know to make a break-in look real."

"Who—" He went pale. "Galoway? That was . . . four, five days ago."

"Four."

"Plenty of time to plan. *Shit.*"

He stomped away, paced, returned, mopping his face repeatedly. "Bad-guy detective? That's a nightmare scenario . . . goddammit. Anyone else I blabbed to and forgot about?"

"Nope."

"Galoway," he said. "Mr. Helpful."

I said, "Pseudo-helpful. He's the one who directed us to Des Barres, which could've been a distraction from focusing on Dorothy Martha Maude, whoever."

"He knows her?"

"Be worth finding out. The timing works. Galoway caught the case shortly after Seeger retired, and we know they talked. He made sure to let us know Seeger was incompetent and had learned nothing. Another misdirection. Now we know Seeger had stayed curious and found the article. That was you, what would your next step be?"

"Call the new guy . . . the Harley . . . Jesus. So Dorothy's alive and well and evil?"

"Keep turning the prism," I said, "and there's no real evidence she died. Burnt-up body, no DNA back then, quick cremation. If so, who got immolated in the Cadillac? Likely another woman who lived at the mansion. We know of two others who went missing, but there could be more. And one more thing: Martha Maude grew up in a rural area, being comfortable on a horse doesn't seem a giant step."

"Mommy's a psychopath." His big chest heaved and swelled. "Just what Ellie needs to boost her mental health."

He walked away, paced past two houses and returned. "I need time to clear my head and make sense out of this, Alex. Meanwhile, let's get Deidre out of here and in a safe place."

He turned grim. "You think her being with Ellie is safe?"

I said, "What's the alternative? A random motel? Boudreaux seems to know what he's doing."

"Yeah, he's solid, I'll tell him what he needs to know." Wolfish, tooth-baring smile. "Guess the only alternative would be my place. Or yours, but who knows if she likes dogs?"

The shotgun and the attaché case rode in front. Deirdre Seeger and I shared the backseat.

I said, "Everything okay?"

Her look said, *What a stupid question.*

Milo drove more slowly than usual. No one spoke all the way to Hollywood.

When he drove north on Western, Deirdre said, "This is a lousy neighborhood."

Milo held up a *wait and see* finger and drove faster.

"Slow down. I get carsick."

"Yes. Ma'am."

Extruding the words like a machine. If she heard the tension, she didn't let on.

When he turned off Los Feliz into the luxury enclave, she said, "Big houses but surrounded by a lousy neighborhood. You're sure it's safe?"

"Movie stars live here."

"*They're* not exactly good citizens." A beat. "Which ones?"

"Not sure about now but back in the day Rudolph Valentino had a mansion not far from here. And Cecil B. DeMille built a bunch of houses."

"I liked *The Ten Commandments*." Folding her arms across her chest, she relapsed into silence.

When we were a block away, Milo texted Mel Boudreaux. We pulled up to find Boudreaux waiting in the doorway, filling most of the space. He wore a tight black T-shirt, black cargo pants, black sneakers, side-arm again displayed in a black mesh holster.

Deirdre Seeger said, "Him? He's . . . bl—big. That's a good thing. I guess."

"He's extremely well trained."

"If you say so."

Milo carried her bags and I followed with Deirdre. During the brief walk to the house, her elbow bumped my arm several times. Balance problems or one of those people with hazy concepts of personal space.

Boudreaux said, "Ma'am, welcome. We're going to take care of you."

"Hope so."

He stepped aside revealing Ellie standing behind him, wan and round-shouldered in a shapeless black dress. Something different: bright-red lipstick applied too generously. As if she'd felt faded and decided at the last minute to risk color.

Deirdre beelined to her, arms stretched wide for a hug. Ellie was surprised but she allowed herself to be clasped, finally laced a loose arm around Deirdre's back.

Satisfied by the reciprocation, Deirdre drew back, held on to Ellie's arms and studied her. "You *poor* thing. My late husband cared *so* much about your poor *mother*. He did *everything* in his power to solve what happened to her."

Ellie said, "Thank you, Mrs. Seeger."

"Call me Didi. And thank *you,* dear. For offering me the sanctuary of your lovely home." Edgy glance at Boudreaux. "And protection."

She turned back to Ellie. "I'm sure we'll have *lots* to talk about. Now where do I bunk?"

Boudreaux said, "Upstairs, ma'am, I'll show you."

Deirdre smiled at Ellie. "I'm not picky, anyplace to rest my weary head." Bending as if burdened, she followed Boudreaux up the stairs with surprising speed.

Ellie smiled feebly.

Milo said, "Thanks for doing this."

"Sure," she said, sounding anything but. "I didn't think to ask you about the break-in. Was that due to me?"

"No."

"No? Definitely not?"

"Ellie, even if it turns out to have something to do with the investigation, that's not your responsibility."

"Well," she said, "it kind of is. I'm the one who initiated the process."

"You did and it was your prerogative. But you did nothing other survivors haven't attempted."

"But you didn't want—"

Milo waved that off. "I want to *now.*"

"You're sure?"

"Couldn't be surer," he said. "My job boils down to chasing the truth. If that sounds corny and phony, can't help it."

She said nothing.

"Think of yourself as a flint in darkness, Ellie. You helped light a spark, it caught, and the fire's raging."

"So if I changed my mind—"

"Irrelevant. With or without you, I'm gonna take it as far as I can."

Tic of tension in his jaw. All the years we'd worked together, I got the implication.

Taking it places you don't want to go, kid.

She said, "That's reassuring. I guess."

Another flick of constricted muscle.

If you only knew.

Boudreaux's baritone floated down from the top of the landing. "You have bar soap? She doesn't do liquid."

Ellie Barker said, "Let me go up and check. If I don't, I'll get some. Whatever makes her comfortable."

She trudged up the stairs and Boudreaux descended. Milo motioned him into the living room. Boudreaux kept his mouth shut and his eyes clear, ready for input.

Milo said, "The break-in looks bona fide but something came up that's leaning me toward a staging. Not gonna get into details but an ex-D might be a bad guy and that's who you should prioritize when you're looking around. Don't ask why, too complicated."

"Don't like complicated," said Boudreaux.

Milo gave him Galoway's name and described Galoway's car.

"Red Jag," said Boudreaux.

"I know, conspicuous. So there could be another vehicle registered to him. Once I find out, I'll let you know. One more thing: Galoway might be operating in someone else's interests, not just his own." He cocked his chin toward the stairs. "This you absolutely keep to yourself."

Nod.

"Girlfriend, she'd be early sixties."

"Senior citizen," said Boudreaux.

"Don't let that comfort you, Mel. If it's true, her kind of bad doesn't fade with age."

"You're not saying . . ."

"I am saying." Milo lowered his voice to a near-whisper. "Mommy not-so-dearest."

Boudreaux blinked, then turned steely. "Interesting."

"You have a way with words, my friend."

"My philosophy," said Boudreaux. "Fewer the better."

At the Impala, Milo put the shotgun back in the trunk and his case on the backseat.

I said, "Wow, Dad, I get to go in front."

"Not for free. Start ideating."

"About what?"

"Who what where how then start over again. Any damn thing that floats into your cranium, let Boudreaux do the taciturn bit."

By the time he wended his way back to Los Feliz and made the iffy left turn, I hadn't spoken.

He said, "Ahem."

"Don't have much to add."

"Then add a little. For practice."

"You don't need me to tell you, you just told Boudreaux. Priority is learning what you can about Galoway."

He tapped the wheel impatiently, headed west on Franklin, barely acknowledged the next few stop signs. "Any suggestions?"

I said, "When I looked him up, I came across an article from a town where he served on the city council. Forget the town's name, it's in my notes back home. Some sort of controversy about zoning, there was one councilor on the other side. Nothing like political enemies."

"Excellent. See—once that massive brain of yours starts ticking it keeps going. Next."

"You're putting your order in, huh?"

"I am indeed. And throw in some bagels and a schmear."

I laughed. Thought for a while. Heard no ticking. "Okay, assuming Galoway's been lying about everything, the part about his captain forcing the case on him could be bullshit. Just the opposite could be the case, if we're right about him and Dorothy being together."

"Galoway volunteered."

"In order to find out what was known and then get rid of the files. Galoway said the captain was obese and a smoker but given his credibility, it's worth trying to locate him. That name I do remember: Gregory Alomar. Reminded me of the baseball player."

"Which one?"

"Robbie Alomar."

"You follow baseball?"

"Intermittently."

"I'm intermittent with football. Got my head knocked around plenty in high school, that's why I rely on *your* memory. Okay, let's start with Alomar. Call Petra and see if anyone at Hollywood remembers him."

I tried, got voicemail, left a message.

Milo said, "The nerve, working her own cases. Anything else?"

"Maybe carefully read the article on Martha and see if any details help."

"Let's both re-read. How's the rest of your day shaking out?"

"Open unless Robin needs me for something."

"I'll drop you at your car and meet you back at your place. Your kitchen has that big table for a work surface, the light, the peace and quiet."

Not to mention self-serve catering.

"Also," he said, "the cuisine. But not what you're thinking, we're getting deluxe takeout on my tab. Spago, Jean-Georges, you name it. We'll use Grubhub or something to deliver, throw in perks for the pooch. That work for you? If it doesn't, now's the time for stoic."

CHAPTER

33

When I got home, Milo was already there, parked in front. No surprise, the way he'd been driving.

As we climbed the stairs to the entry terrace, he said, "Found out a few more things about ol' Du, and yeah, he's been creative. He doesn't live in Ojai, never did from what I can tell, has a place in Tarzana mostly owned by the bank. If he's married or living with someone, they're not on the papers. The Jag's leased, from the amount still owed to the bank probably one of those minimal-down-payment deals."

"Possible money problems."

"At the very least, he's not as well heeled as he wanted us to think. The vehicle he does own outright is a ten-year-old Isuzu Trooper. Again, no one else on the papers, so if Dorothy-Martha is still kicking around, she's got her own wheels. I told Boudreaux to be ready for anything."

I said, "Think he's really vegan or into meat?"

He laughed. "I'm not even getting near that."

I unlocked the door and looked for Robin. Not in the house. No surprise, when she's fired up creatively, weekends get no respect.

Milo spread documents on the kitchen table.

I said, "Back in a sec."

No answer. He'd opened *Dark Detective,* was deep into the Lolita story.

I thought of Martha Hopple's eyes. So young and so hard. When they start that way, no telling what they're capable of.

As I passed through the garden to the studio, my phone chirped.

Petra said, "Got a missed call from you. What's up?"

"Quite a bit but best to hear it from Big Guy. He's in my kitchen right now."

"I know psychologists like to be enigmatic but give me a clue."

"Dorothy Swoboda might be alive and Du Galoway might be her boyfriend."

Silence.

"That's . . . a lot to take in, Alex. Okay, I'll get the details from the heights of Olympus. You want to hear about Captain Alomar or should I tell Milo?"

"He's alive?"

"And well. If Big Guy's in the kitchen, where are *you*? Foraging Bel Air for rare and exotic edibles?"

I laughed. "On the way to say hi to Robin."

"Such a good boyfriend," she said. "I give her a lot of credit."

I expected Robin to be working on the mandolin but she'd taken on the re-fret of a lovely, petite, hundred-year-old Martin guitar, the kind of comparatively simple job she sometimes tackles in spare moments.

She stopped cutting fret-wire and looked down, amused, as Blanche nuzzled my leg. "Not going to match her devotion to that extent but happy you're back. Any luck?"

"Total paradigm shift." I explained.

She said, "Lolita. Wonder what Nabokov would think. So what's next?"

"More research. Commencing in our kitchen as we speak. Milo insists on footing dinner—gourmet takeout."

"Not necessary, honey, we've got leftovers."

"He's thinking Spago or the like."

"Whoa," she said. "So you played a *major* role in the shift—no, no, don't aw shucks me."

Big smile, hard kiss; I let her work and returned to the house, wondering what it was like to make a living creating beauty.

Milo had covered half the table with paper.

"Found a Zillow shot of Galoway's house. Small, Spanish, corner lot. Can't find any records of him selling real estate but he said that was years ago and I don't know which companies he claimed to work for. Far as I can tell, he's got no current source of income. Ditto registered firearm or criminal record. If you could get me the name of that city councilor who went up against him, I'd appreciate it."

"Sure. Petra just called me. Alomar's still alive, here's his number."

He loaded his phone and called.

A deep, clipped voice said, "Pro shop."

"Is Mr. Alomar there?"

"Who's asking?"

"Lieutenant Milos Sturgis, LAPD—"

"What, they want to increase my pension?"

"Good luck on that," said Milo. "No, sir, I'm West L.A. Homicide and calling about a detective who worked for you years ago. Dudley Galoway."

"Worked?" said Greg Alomar. "According to who? Forget I said that—you're not taping this, are you?"

"No, sir."

"What's your Christian name?"

"Milo."

"Milo Sturgis . . . you the one who works with that shrink?"

"From time to time."

"Heard about it a few years before I retired," said Greg Alomar. "Got jealous. Hollywood, we had a whole different level of crazy than your civilized part of the city. We could've used some head-work."

"We get our share."

"What? Felonious anxiety when the Tesla won't charge? Listen, I'm willing to schmooze but I need to verify you are who you say you are and I don't truck with that FaceTime crap, anything on a phone or a computer can be faked. So if you want my side of the story, you're going to have to show yourself."

"No prob. Where are you?"

"Bel Air Ridge Country Club. I own the pro shop."

"Nice," said Milo. "How long have you been golfing?"

"Since never," said Alomar. "It's like being a specialist doc. You stay sharp and help people with an affliction."

Milo laughed. "Can we come by now?"

"We?"

"Dr. Delaware and myself."

"You've got the shrink with you? He works weekends?"

"When it's interesting."

"Psychology," said Alomar. "I took it in college. Except for statistics, which is just a way to say fancy lies, it was interesting."

The country club was a fifteen-minute ride from my house. I let Robin know I was leaving again and told her why.

"Your voice has that boyish lilt." Wink. "Like when you're interested."

"I'm always interested in you."

"Darling," she said, "your devotion isn't in question. But there's interested and there's *interested*. Go."

As in most cities, L.A.'s venerable country clubs were founded as citadels of us versus them. Wasn't success judged by who you rejected?

L.A. continues to be as exclusionary as ever—try parking within a mile of an Oscar after-party. But the people who run the city pretend to be tolerant so the old clubs are struggling.

Replacing them are a number of pay-to-play setups with the pay part steep enough to keep out all but the highly affluent. Bel Air Ridge Country Club was one of those.

Getting there took us north on the Glen and up to Mulholland but instead of heading east toward Hollywood and the Des Barres estate, we turned left and drove four miles past several luxury developments stacked with white, big-box contemporary houses before reaching a double-wide driveway railed with palm trees and blocked by a high iron gate.

Call-box chat, quick entry, then twenty additional yards of driving to a guard in a sentry box who didn't pretend to care. A hundred yards of gentle green climb brought us to the Big Daddy white box contemporary: two stories of white stucco with a band of black lava rock running along the bottom.

As if the clubhouse were a stud bull who'd spent a rollicking breeding season siring calves.

Just a sprinkle of cars in sight, all of them German, as well as several golf carts with yellow and white striped awnings. On the building's left end was a glass-faced store: *The Pro Shoppe,* as attested to by curvaceous gilt lettering. We pulled up in front and stepped in.

A door-triggered ding-a-ling introduced us to a cozy, softly lit space filled with the aroma of good leather and walled with mahogany cases. Callahan banner on one wall, Titleist on the other. Displays of bags, clubs, balls, and brightly colored clothing sat on waxed parquet floors.

No shoppers, just one man behind the counter, wearing a salmon-pink Bobby Jones polo and blue linen pants. Five-nine, deeply tan, trim and flat-bellied with razor-cut features topped by a thick, white brush cut.

Milo had accessed Gregory Alomar's retirement records, a sketchy endeavor but who was going to complain? The former captain would be seventy-seven next month but looked ten years younger.

"Milo and Dr. Delaware? Greg Alomar."

Confident, iron handshake. Alomar's eyes were olive-drab and watchful with smaller pupils than the lighting would suggest. An eagle appraising prey.

"Thanks for meeting with us, Captain."

"My pleasure, once you show me your I.D.'s."

The raptor eyes took their time examining Milo's card and my driver's license. Alomar read off my address. "Am I right and you live close to here, Doc?"

"A few miles down the Glen."

"Do you golf?"

"Sorry, no."

"Don't apologize. What exercise do you do?"

"Run."

"Ah. So your hips and knees still might go but at least your heart'll be okay. Let's go in back. Someone comes in, I'll need to interrupt but eventually we'll get the job done."

Alomar had been optimistic about our bona fides; he'd opened three black folding chairs in the center of a rear storage room and arranged them two facing one. Shelves of the same objects as in front took up the rest of the space. Everything neat, clean, organized.

He took the solo seat and we faced him.

"Dudley the Dud," he said. "Called himself Du. I used to think, preface that with 'Dog.'"

Milo said, "No love lost."

"He was foisted on me and I don't like foisting."

"By who?"

"Never found out," said Alomar. "I had an opening due to one of my senior D's retiring, had my eye on someone in Rampart. Female, smart, I asked for her, got him. No Homicide experience, the clown had done Traffic."

I said, "Connections."

"He sure had pull with someone. As to who that was, couldn't uncover it. What I do know is before Traffic, he drove an assistant chief around. Right out of the academy, got to go to celebrity parties, all that good stuff. So it was either that or he ate out some rich back-scratcher. However he pulled it off, I got stuck with him. He thought by being an A-plus ass-kisser he could get into my good graces. Sleazy. Did he finally turn criminal?"

Speaking evenly but no mistaking the anger.

Milo said, "Finally?"

"The guy had a truth problem. Lying for the heck of it, stupid stuff. Like saying he did something when he didn't, taking fake sick days, just a generally oily attitude. Like it was fun for him, piling on the bullshit. Not a big leap to criminal. You're Homicide. Did he actually kill someone?"

"Long story," said Milo.

"No one's rung the bell," said Alomar, crossing his legs.

"When he worked for you, he caught a case. Woman shot up on Mulholland."

"Dorothy something European," said Alomar. "I remember it because it never got closed. No surprise, it was stone-cold by the time he showed up and pushed himself into it."

"His story is that you pressured him to take on a loser."

"Is it? Like I said, the asshole lied when he breathed. No, just the opposite. Two D's had already taken it on for like, fourteen, fifteen years. There wasn't all the hoopla about cold cases you have today. It being a *thing*. All we had were winners and losers and in our shop this one was a loser. Meanwhile, we had no shortage of winners because of the idiot thing. You know what I'm talking about."

"Idiot One shoots Idiot Two in a bar and sticks around."

Alomar laughed. "Makes us look heroic. Dorothy . . . what was her name . . ."

"Swoboda."

"Swoboda . . . the likelihood of *her* being a winner was the same as me getting recruited by the Lakers to play center."

The olive eyes passed from Milo to me and back to Milo. "Are you saying something's changed? One of those DNA deals? That was a thing but I don't recall there being anything to test."

"There wasn't," said Milo. "I've been asked to look into it because of connections."

"What kind of connections?"

Milo said, "Ka-ching."

"Big bucks?" said Alomar. "Who?"

"A relative of Dorothy's."

"So what's Galoway's deal in all this?"

"I contacted him because he's the only living D. Turns out, he's been misdirecting us from the get-go. Can't say more yet."

Alomar digested that. "Understood. When you can say, will you?"

"You bet," said Milo. "If you didn't want him on the case, how'd he score it?"

"I didn't want him in my shop, period," said Alomar. "Initially figured the best way to make use of his limited talent was have him gofer for one of my seasoned D's. Scut work he couldn't screw up too badly. Problem is, no one wanted him because of his personality. Yessir yessir, accomplishing diddly-squat, always an excuse. What I wanted was him *out,* but given the way he came in, I needed to be careful. I was still figuring out what to do with him when he waltzes into my office with Swoboda's file, says he'd been looking through some old ones, figures he could accomplish something on this one. I said forget it, it's old and cold for a reason. He basically begged—I guess you'd call it wheedling. Please, sir, give me a chance, sir. Like that kid in the musical—Oliver Twist. Then I thought to myself, Why not, maybe this is a solution. Keep him out of everyone's hair, eventually I'll find a way to get rid of him. So I said sure. And guess what happened?"

"Nada," said Milo.

"Whole lot of nada, my friend. He spent a month or two on it, never filed any paper, quit and put in for disability retirement."

"What was the disability?"

"Some kind of back thing. You know, crap that can't be proven or disproven. I signed off, good riddance. I won't bug you for details but can you tell me if he had some personal involvement in the case? Because it never made sense, him being so industrious."

Milo thought about his answer.

The delay was sufficient for Alomar. "He did, huh? Evil bastard, I hope you nail him. God knows how much pension money he's been racking up."

"You really didn't like him."

"I *really* didn't." Alomar shifted in his chair. "Okay, full disclosure. One of my friends, worked Central, met Galoway at a cop bar on Main. Galoway's got no idea my friend is my friend. She's discreet, very good listener—like you seem to be, Doc. Anyway, he's trying to pick her up and starts bitching about work. About me. Tells her I'm a fat, chain-smoking fuck who wheezes when he walks."

He ran a hand across a flat, muscular chest. "Three years ago is when I stopped doing triathlons. Back then? I could climb walls."

We thanked Alomar and drove away from the country club.

Just outside the gate, Milo produced his wallet. "Let's go back to your place and find the name of that politician. Meanwhile, take out my Amex and order grub."

"From where?"

"Wherever you want."

I phoned Robin on speaker. She said, "Anything."

Milo said, "Long as it's gourmet."

"There's no need to make a production, Milo."

"Humor me."

"Okay, sushi from a place in Westwood, Alex knows it. Delivery in three hours."

"How about the pooch?"

"She likes fish and rice. Bye, boys."

I called and ordered enough for four.

Milo said, "That's enough?"

"It's not, we'll raid the fridge."

"Resourceful," he said. "Darwin would be proud."

34

Back at the house, he collected the papers from the kitchen table and we beelined to my office.

I said, "Alomar hit on what we've figured: Galoway took the case to kill it and get rid of any records. Just as he's about to leave the department, he gets a call from Seeger. Who's been snooping around old magazines and just learned about Martha Maude and tells him. Fatal error."

"Poor guy," he said. "Probably thought he'd get props for being a miracle man."

"Or he just wanted to solve the case."

"Hmm . . . yeah, that happens, too. Thirsty, gonna get some water."

I figured he wouldn't stop at tasteless, transparent fluid, picked up the pulp and began reading.

Mike Leigh had met Martha Maude Hopple when she rode her bike past a property he was clearing as a day laborer. He already had a long sheet, was less than a month out of prison for a theft charge. Five months later, the two of them were traveling together, hitchhiking and stealing cars and burglarizing houses in the Little Egypt section of Illinois, then Missouri, Arkansas, and Texas. One break-in involved the unexpected appearance of the homeowners, an elderly couple, the wife wheelchair-bound. Two corpses. Eighteen bucks taken.

According to the article's feverish prose, the double murder led to Leigh and his "Jailbait Juliet acquiring a taste for blood." By the time the duo was arrested for a reign of terror that included carjacking, armed robbery, kidnapping, assault, and murder, four more people had died.

Mike Leigh was executed in the electric chair ten months after his conviction.

Martha Hopple was been sentenced to a girl's reformatory in Jarvis, Texas. I did a map search. Fifty miles from Tyler.

Milo returned with cranberry juice and a half-eaten apple. I was at my keyboard running a search using Martha Hopple's name.

Nothing.

I told him about the reform school.

He said, "Longest she could be in there was till twenty-one, maybe even less. She gets out, finds a gig at a grower, meets Benni Cairn. So maybe Benni's the woman in the car."

"It fits," I said. "Martha—probably Dorothy by then, given the Lolita thing it would make sense for her to change her identity—is a few years older than Benni but a whole lot more experienced. And dominant. She tells Benni stories about Hollywood, Benni has nothing going for her in Tyler, the two of them cut town."

"Why would Dorothy want Benni along?"

"Someone to use."

"For what?"

"Gullible younger woman?" I said.

"She pimped her out?"

"Could be that or other scams. Maybe Dorothy gave her a make-over and she looked like she did in the photo. The two of them knock around for a while, make their way to L.A., end up at Des Barres's mansion. Benni's more attractive than she used to be but no smarter. Easy enough for Dorothy to get her in the Caddy. Let's go have some fun—oh, pull over for a second, I need my cigarettes."

"Then bang," he said. "Cold. What's the motive for killing her?"

"Dorothy wanted to disappear. Probably with a whole lot of Des Barres's bling."

"She was the aspiring Queen Bee."

"Or she just got bored with being a member of the pack and decided to bankroll another adventure. We're talking multiple murder by fifteen. Heavy-duty thrill factor. And think of those photos: She's not whooping it up. We know from the serpentine necklace that she was going back between L.A. and Stan Barker. Getting Barker to babysit and playing him. He wasn't as rich as Des Barres but he was comfortable enough and well heeled and had paternal instincts. An easy mark whom she eventually dropped."

"She'd just leave her baby?"

"A baby," I said. "What if it wasn't hers?"

"Benni's? She'd give it up."

"Young single mother, impressionable, overwhelmed. Dorothy convinces her it's in the child's best interest? It's just a theory at this point but Martha did have experience kidnapping."

"Oh, man . . . so why would she wait that long to ditch the kid?"

"Good prop," I said. "Coming across as a struggling mom for when she met Barker. It didn't take her long to walk out on both of them so we're not talking massive maternal instincts."

"Oh, God, poor Ellie . . . if we're talking that level of psychopath and Dorothy had been aiming for Queen, she could've also done Arlette."

I said, "Texas, horses? Nothing in her past says she'd give it a moment's hesitation."

He got up, retrieved the arrest photo from the pulp, and plopped down again. I settled next to him and we both studied the shot.

Fifteen-year-old girl in the grips of two fedora-wearing detectives. Uncowed—not even close. Defiant.

He sighed and put the magazine down. "How does Mr. Happy Vegan figure in?"

"Slick, shallow, lies when he breathes?"

"Psychopathy loves company."

"Good basis for a long-term relationship."

He frowned. "Find that councilperson?"

I shuffled through my notes, nailed it in seconds. "Dara Guzman, city of Piro, she got seriously outvoted. The second time I checked, Galoway was still on the council but she wasn't."

"Bitter ex-politician, even better." He got up and pointed to my keyboard. "You mind?"

I got up. "Go for it."

Settling in front of my monitor, he inputted his department access code.

Dara Guzman had turned fifty-three a couple of months ago. One registered vehicle, a twelve-year-old Corolla, home address an apartment in Venice. A few more keystrokes revealed a work address on the western edge of Pico, the tough part of Santa Monica. Guzman was the operations manager of a nonprofit called VistaVenture that aimed to support homeless adolescents.

Milo tried the number.

Seven rings. "Probably closed Saturday." He moved to click off.

"VeeVee."

"Could I please speak to Dara Guzman."

"You are."

"This is Lieutenant Milo Sturgis, LAPD Westside Division. Do you have a few minutes?"

"For what?"

"To talk about someone you knew in Piro. Dudley Galoway."

Silence. "And why would I want to do that?"

"His name has come up—"

"How did *my* name come up?"

"We were looking through some old references and found an article about—"

"Exactly," said Dara Guzman. "*Old.* How do I know you are who you say you are?"

Same reaction as Alomar's. Everyone ceded privacy to their online gizmos but embraced the pretense of pointless suspicion.

Or maybe Dara Guzman just didn't like cops.

Milo exhaled. "I'd be happy to give you my credentials and you can verify them."

"I need to go through a hassle so you can question me?"

"Of course not. If you'd rather—"

"Look," she said, "I'm not trying to be difficult but you're catching me at the tail end of a monstrously shitty day, okay? Two of our kids suicided. Together."

"I'm so sorry." Meaning it and sounding like he did.

"Not as sorry as we are. We try hard to focus on positivity, build on whatever they have going for them. In this case, I thought we'd pulled it off, they seemed . . . whatever. I'm not in the mood to rehash something a zillion years old."

"It needn't take long, ma'am. I'd be happy to come to you."

"Sorry, I'm going home."

"Tomorrow, then?"

Silence.

"Ms. Guzman?"

"What's really going on? Some sort of high-end real estate lawsuit crap, you represent a conglomerate, I'll get a subpoena in the mail and then get sued for slander after I testify?"

"This is a criminal case, nothing to do with real estate, ma'am."

"What crime?"

"Mr. Galoway's name came up in a homicide investigation."

"Shit. He actually killed someone?"

"It really would be helpful to have a brief chat, ma'am. If FaceTime or Skype are enough to assure you I'm who I say I am, I can log on at your convenience. If you'd rather we meet face-to-face, no problem, just name the place and time."

"If I'd *rather*," said Dara Guzman. "Giving me a limited choice so I start thinking one of my options is great? Nice tactic. Homicide, huh? Now I really don't want to get involved."

"I understand, ma'am. Sorry for bothering you and sorry about the suicides. I mean that."

"You know," she said, "you sound like you really do. Hold on, I'm going to subject you to my own brand of detection. What's your name? Or as you guys say, your alleged name."

Milo told her.

We sat there, listening to clicks on the other end.

Finally, Dara Guzman said, "You don't come up much but when you do it seems to be okay, no allegations of brutality . . . hold on . . . says here you work with a psychologist?"

"When it's called for."

"Does that include this homicide?"

"As a matter of fact it does."

"Tell you what," said Dara Guzman. "Bring him by and I'll check you both out. Maybe I can get him to volunteer, we need all the help we can get."

"Thank you, ma'am. Where—"

"Here. As close to now as possible. I'm beat. And beaten."

VistaVenture was a grubby gray building just east of Lincoln Boulevard. Spray stucco had fallen off in patches. On one side was a dealer in plumbing fixtures, on the other a school with minuscule signage surrounded by a high link fence that I knew specialized in the problem children of movie stars and other L.A. royalty.

Quick walk from the hundred-grand-a-year school to a place that aided teens living rough. Maybe not an inevitably big leap, when you thought about it. A banished scion or heiress fallen low and reaching out for warm soup, emotional comfort, and a housing chit for an SRO.

The front door was unlocked. Lights off, no one at the reception counter, the only person in sight a woman working her phone on a lint-colored sofa so vanquished its center section grazed the linoleum floor. Mental health and contagious disease posters filled the walls along with the Gestalt Prayer.

I do my thing and you do your thing.

If only it were that simple.

The woman had short, tightly curled gray hair, deep brown eyes, and a face riddled by worry lines. Road map to Sorry Town. She wore a black sweatshirt over jeans and cracked red patent slippers, barely looked up when Milo said, "Ms. Guzman?"

"Uh-huh . . ." She typed a bit more before her fingers stilled. Stood wearily, looked us over but with scant curiosity. "Lieutenant and therapist, interesting. If I was in a better state I'd have questions about that."

We followed her out of the front room and into a hallway lined with more posters. AIDS, other STDs, exhortations to get free flu shots, to reach out when emotional pain hit, to be proud of your gender.

Dara Guzman swung a left at the third door, continued to a windowless room with a brown metal desk and chair and three plastic chairs, and sat down behind the desk. Bare walls; maybe the lack of stimulation comforted her.

"Cop and shrink," she said. "Must be different."

Milo said, "It can be."

She turned to me. "You deal with teen suicides?"

"I have."

"Any words of wisdom?"

"I wish."

"Brutal," she said. "At least you're honest. The kids who died this morning jumped off a five-story building on Main Street. Fourteen and sixteen, horrible home lives, bad deal of cards for both of them. They were madly in love with each other. Also with heroin."

She threw up her hands.

I said, "Terrible."

Milo sighed.

Both of us hoping not to be pressed for wisdom we didn't have.

"Okay," said Dara Guzman, "might as well get on with your business."

Not asking for I.D. the way Greg Alomar had. We'd passed some kind of test.

Milo said, "Whatever you can tell us about Dudley Galoway would be helpful."

"How about he's a total asshole? What'd you find out about me and him? And where did you find out?"

"Newspaper clipping." He summed up the zoning dispute.

She said, "That says it all. Look, I'm not claiming he was the only reason I lost. I was young, stupid, had worked for the farmworkers out of college, went to law school but hated it and dropped out and moved out to the boonies with someone I thought I'd spend the rest of my life with."

She shrugged. "Not your problem. Anyway, Piro seemed like a sweet little town, I thought I'd grow vegetables and mellow out. No idea what it's like now but it was close to some serious real estate so for all I know it's like Calabasas."

I said, "Lots of golf courses there now."

"Figures. When I was on the council it was agricultural and depended on seasonal workers. Their living conditions were appalling. Falling-down shacks near the town garbage dump, no indoor plumbing, outhouses that overflowed, raw sewage, you get the picture."

Milo said, "Nasty picture."

She studied him, assessing sincerity. He sat there, calm.

Dara Guzman twiddled her fingers and continued. "The heirs to one of the old-time families tried to sell some land to a developer who wanted to build Section 8 housing. It sounds crazy, me siding with a developer, but given how the workers lived, lesser of two evils. The property was vacant, on the outskirts, being used for nothing. From all the uproar you'd think convicts were going to be bused in. I pushed for it, everyone piled up against me, I didn't stand a chance. But that's not what bothered me about Galoway and his wife. It was the way they went about it. Attacking me personally during council meetings. No raised voices, just sarcastic insinuations that I was a spy for some radical group, out to ruin the town. The other council members didn't agree with me but they were decent about it. The issue stayed civil until those two entered the picture. They actually got reprimanded by the other members of the council, but that didn't change the vote."

She opened a desk drawer, pulled out a box of staples, removed one and played with it. "I licked my wounds and tried to figure out my future. Then they killed my dog."

"Geez," said Milo.

"Geez Louise. Baxter was sixteen years old, big old husky with gorgeous blue eyes. Not doing great, he probably had a year or two. Despite all that coat, when he got old, he got cold. Liked to sit outside and snooze and sun himself. One evening, he's been out there enjoying himself for a few hours, I come out to take him for his wee-walk and find him on his back, stone-cold."

Her mouth twisted. A single tear ran down her right cheek. "I figured he's old, had a heart attack. Then I see white crusty stuff around his mouth and it kind of smells of almonds but it still didn't register. I bring Baxter to the vet for cremation and she smells it. Didn't say anything at the time but took it upon herself to do a necropsy gratis and found a big chunk of hamburger in Baxter's tummy, laced with what turned out to be cyanide. She asks me do I lay down rat poison, I say no way, I'm totally organic. She says do you have apricot trees, cherries, has he been known to chew a lot of pits. I say all I've got is one scraggly tangerine and Baxter didn't stray. She says, then I'm afraid someone killed your dog. I told the sheriffs, including who I suspected, lot of good that did. My property was unfenced, anyone could've walked in and fed the meat to Baxter. He loved his food. He had no protective instincts."

"You told them it was Galoway."

"Or her. Maybe only her, to my eye she was meaner than him. One of those hard-body types, the formfitting jeans, the cowgirl boots, big blond hair, full of herself. Never smiled. He did but it was sleazy. The two of them were a pair. Are they still in Piro?"

"No."

"Where, then?"

"The Valley."

"Big place," said Dara Guzman.

"It is."

"You're not going to be specific? Fine, I couldn't care less."

I said, "Did they own land in Piro?"

"They lived on a couple of acres, big old house, not much in the way of flowers or trees. Most of it was used for their horses."

"Ranch situation."

"More like a house with horses, four or five," said Guzman. "You'd see her prancing into town, tall in the saddle. Using a whip too much for my taste but what do I know? Never rode myself."

Milo showed her the Azalea photo with Dorothy/Martha's face isolated.

She said, "She was older when I knew her but could be . . . yeah, kick it up to probably. Notice the eyes? Mean. They really were a *pair*." To me: "There's probably a name for that. People building on each other's meanness."

I said, "Hooking up with the wrong people."

She laughed, looked at Milo.

He said, "Should've warned you. He hates jargon."

"Well," she said, "that's a plus. You interested in volunteering from time to time, Dr. Delaware?"

"It's possible."

"Noncommittal? He says you're only part-time with him. What else do you do?"

"Private practice and teaching."

"So you make good money, why not give back? We could use some teaching, here. In-service seminars for staff, maybe counsel some of the kids."

"Let's trade cards." I handed her mine and she scrounged in her desk before coming up with a fuzzy-edged rectangle of cheap paper.

"Got your number, Doc."

I said, "What name did she go by?"

"Hmm. Don't know if I ever knew it. He was on the council, she just hung around. I always thought of her as The Bitch."

Milo smiled, "Anything else you can tell us?"

"Nah," said Dara Guzman. "I do hope you pin something on them. Tonight I'm going to be thinking about Baxter."

35

Red everywhere on Waze, as if the city were bleeding. Time to settle back for the ride and pretend it was leisurely by choice.

Milo said, "Nasty woman, rides horses, maybe poisons a dog just for the fun of it. Add whoever was in the Caddy, the bodies she piled up with Leigh, and possibly Seeger, and she's a one-woman crime wave."

He shook his head. "Despite what we said about psychopaths, people like that aren't good at relationships, right? How'd she and Galoway manage to stick together all these years?"

I said, "Two hammers looking for nails."

He hooked north on Veteran Avenue, driving through a maze of residential streets that traced the U.'s western periphery. More foot traffic than usual for L.A. as skinny-jeaned, backpacked adolescents darted across the street, plugged in and unfocused.

Denying the concept of danger except when it came to ideas.

I thought of Martha Maude Hopple, fifteen and focused. On all the wrong things.

A lifetime of deception and cruelty. Making a career out of it.

When we pulled up in front of my house, Milo said, "*When's* that sushi coming?"

An hour to go, Robin still out in the studio.

Milo comforted himself with an orange and a banana, tossed the peel and the rind, drank water from the kitchen tap and sat down at the table. Using the time for what a corporate-type would call networking.

First, he cross-referenced police records with Dudley Galoway's Tarzana address but found no incidents. Then he called a detective he knew in Valley Division just to be sure. No idea who Galoway was.

Muttering, "Weekend, she won't be in," he tried his captain.

Ann-Margaret Meecham was a recent transfer from Central admin, not at West L.A. long enough for Milo to complain about her.

She answered her own phone after one ring. "Meecham."

"Milo Sturgis, ma'am."

"Lieutenant." As if she found the fact amusing and possibly short of credible.

"Long day, ma'am?"

"Obviously for you, as well. What do you need?"

"The people I asked you for, if I could have them a bit longer."

"Reed, Bogomil, and that rookie."

"Arredondo," said Milo. "Good group. Coherent and—"

"You need them because . . ."

"There's been a break in the case." Keeping it as spare and clear as possible, he explained about Galoway.

"Ex-D," said Meecham.

"I know, ma'am, it's tricky."

"Understatement. More like messy. More like a pigsty that hasn't been cleaned in weeks."

"Exactly," said Milo. "That's why I need to take special care. Starting with surveillance. His residence doesn't make it easy."

"Give me details."

When he was finished, Meecham said, "All I'm hearing is theory."

"I know it sounds that way—"

"Your instincts, I get it. Your stats do help you in that regard. What won't help you is what happens if a bunch of 211s break while you've got your little repertory going and Bancroft and Mendoza or whoever's on shift need personnel for real-time investigations?"

"I understand that," said Milo.

"Do you, Milo?" Slipping into first-name basis. A good sign? If so, Milo's face wasn't reflecting it.

"They can always be pulled off, ma'am."

"Not the same as being there on the ground," said Meecham. "Speaking of your little covert deal, I got a call from downtown."

"Did you."

"Martz," said Meecham. Not using the deputy chief's title. Definitely a good sign. Milo perked up.

He said, "About the case in question?"

"In a manner of speaking. She and I were in the same class at the academy."

"Old friends, huh?"

"Not a foregone conclusion," said Meecham. "She wants me to keep an eye on you. I don't operate that way with my people but I told her I would. Have I ever done that? Intruded?"

"No, ma'am."

"Meg is my preferred term of address from anyone above sergeant."

"You haven't intruded, Meg."

"Glad you appreciate it. Does Veronique know about this new development?"

"No."

"Let's keep it that way," said Meecham. "Something actually happens it's going to be a West L.A. deal, not some downtown dog-and-pony with her taking credit."

"Got it. So I can—"

"Unless an exigent situation evolves. You really need the rookie?"

"Given what I'm planning—"

"You take care of her. You make that a priority. The slightest sign she's not cut out for the job, you let her go."

"I will. Meg."

"You learn fast. Good."

"One more thing?" said Milo.

"Isn't there always," said Meecham.

"Detective Binchy's due back from vacation in two days. If he's not needed elsewhere—"

"Don't get pushy," said Meecham. "I'm going to start doubting your cognitive skills."

Click.

I said, "Tough but fair, huh?"

"I'm sure she likes to think of herself that way." He texted Moe and Bogomil and asked them to show up tomorrow morning at ten if they didn't have weekend plans. Added a request for Alicia to contact Jen Arredondo with the same instruction.

Two rapid replies:

Got it. Moe.
Had plans but boring. Will do. A.B.

I said, "It's so nice when the kids behave themselves."

Milo looked at his watch and got another orange.

CHAPTER

36

Sunday. Same war room, same whiteboards, same coffee and tea and pastries in pink boxes augmented by a heap of plastic-wrapped, handmade deli sandwiches financed by Milo's cash.

No writing on the boards; instead, Dudley Galoway's enlarged DMV photo, enlargements of a modest-looking single-story Spanish house taken from Zillow plus several aerial shots of the property. No vehicles in any of the images.

Milo explained the situation.

Moe Reed and Alicia Bogomil listened impassively. Jen Arredondo's eyes widened with each fact. She wore loose hair, a red tee, black jeggings, red Vans, looked like a high school senior.

When Milo finished, Alicia said, "This woman—if she is alive—is something else."

Milo walked to the board and pointed to one of the aerials. A wide view that covered two blocks. "Everyone's got a double-width driveway and a garage, not much parking on the street. So we can't just sit there, anything unusual's going to be spotted, especially by an ex-D like

Galoway. But even by an unsuspecting neighbor. We can't afford to have Valley patrol show itself."

Moe Reed said, "Not safe informing them?"

"Don't know if Galoway still has police contacts, so no. The best alternative I can come up with is pulling off a little theater. Meaning you guys play roles. I'd be part of the repertory but Galoway knows me."

Using Meg Meecham's word. Arredondo looked baffled and Milo noticed.

"There'll be some acting," he told her.

Alicia said, "All right, ready for my close-up, Mr. DeMille."

Moe and Arredondo squinted at her.

"It's a movie, guys. *Sunset Boulevard*?"

No response.

Alicia said, "Before my time, too, but my mom watches it all the time." Small smile. "On her VCR."

Milo said, "No close-ups. Let me emphasize, we're not trying to get cozy with the suspects, need to assume Galoway's gonna be more vigilant than a civilian and the same goes for Dorothy or whatever she's calling herself."

Reed said, "What is the goal?"

"I'd be happy with finding out who lives there. It may turn out to be simple. We know both of Galoway's vehicles but have no idea what she's driving. We spot a third vehicle and trace the tag to a female, big step. We don't, I'd settle for some inkling of her presence or absence."

Alicia said, "When's garbage day? We can go back at night, empty the cans, see if there's female stuff in there or who mail is addressed to."

"Too risky, kid."

She shrugged.

Milo turned to Reed. "For you, I'm figuring a delivery guy. There are three vans in the impound lot scheduled for the auction next month.

No logo or signage on any of them, we'll get stick-on vinyls that fit with whatever you're delivering. Any preferences?"

Alicia patted Reed's colossal biceps. "How about iron anvils?"

Reed smiled. "Whatever you choose, L.T. So I'm just driving by, not making a delivery."

"Correct," said Milo.

"Then I can alternate—plumbing, then electrical, whatever."

"That's fine if you can disguise yourself sufficiently so Galoway doesn't see the same face in different sets of wheels."

Jen Arredondo made a soft, mouse-like noise.

Milo looked at her.

She said, "I do makeup. Did. In high school, for drama."

"Excellent, what can you do with Detective Reed?"

Arredondo blushed. "Um, there's beards, mustaches. Wigs. If you want to go to the next level, there's putty you can add to the nose or the chin. We did that on *Les Miz*."

Alicia grinned. "You can turn him into Quasimodo?"

"There was no one like that . . ."

Milo said, "Hunchback of Notre Dame."

Alicia said, "Oops."

Arredondo said, "I mean I'm not like a professional but I could change him."

Milo said, "Give me a list of what you need."

"Is it okay if I contact my drama teacher? He knows where to get everything."

"Long as he's not a felon with a big mouth."

"I don't think so . . ."

"Tell him you're working on the department Christmas show."

"You have one of those?" said Arredondo.

Milo smiled. "This works out, we just might. Okay, kids, let's plan on starting tomorrow. I'll set up the vehicles, tell you where to pick them up."

Arredondo said, "Um, sir? What will I be delivering?"

"Not sure, yet. Let's see what Detectives Reed and Bogomil come up with first."

"I could do one of those magazine subscription deals? Ring the bell, someone answers I give a speech about bargains?"

"Too close for comfort, Officer."

"I'll be fine, sir," said Arredondo, not sounding convinced.

"Did you act in the school play or just do makeup?"

"Makeup, sir. But I did magazine subscriptions for real. Two summers, between my junior and senior years. I sold quite a few."

"Hmm, let me think about it. One more thing: If at any point Galoway shows himself and anyone can follow safely, do it. Any questions? Okay, then—"

"Actually, sir," said Arredondo, fidgeting.

All eyes on her.

"Yes, Officer."

"It's not a question, sir, it's something that maybe is relevant?"

Out of her pocket came a folded sheet of paper. "I've been looking at the sites with all the missings on them whenever I have a chance and a couple of hours ago something came up. While I was eating breakfast."

Alicia said, "Working meal? Dedicated."

More blush. "I had nothing else to do."

"That's good, Jen. Really."

Arredondo shrugged.

Milo took the paper and read. "Great work, Officer. *Unbelievably* great work."

For the first time since I'd met her, Jen Arredondo smiled.

Below the photo of Benicia Cairn was a new string of comments.

I'm not sure if I want to get involved but looking at this picture
really threw me because I knew this woman. It was a long time

ago and it was actually someone else I was looking for but
then I saw her and it really threw me. The thing is I don't know
anything that could help the police find her and I'm not sure I
want to get involved. I could use some advice from those of
you who come here frequently. Do you think there's a moral
obligation even though I can see nothing I have will help? V.Q.

That sparked six responses, one of which said a response wasn't
necessary "if you really have nothing new," and five that offered counsel
similar to that of Bonnie from Tulsa:

see your conflict V but I'd say contact the cops anyway because you never know they could be holding something back
they do that to confuse the criminal so you might have something that fits that.

Milo looked at me.

I said, "V."

Jen Arredondo said, "It could be something?"

"We know of another woman who associated with Benni Cairns
and Dorothy named Victoria Barlow. You all know how we feel about
coincidences. So let me try to sort this out. We'll still keep tomorrow in
mind but there might be a delay."

Alicia leaned over and slapped Arredondo's back lightly. "Let's hear
it for breakfast."

Milo pointed to the sandwiches. "Next we'll hear it for lunch. Officer Arredondo, you pick first."

37

Back in his office, he looked at the Azalea photo. "V. Gotta be."

I said, "One less corpse, it would be nice."

"Any reason I shouldn't try to contact her?"

"Not that I can see."

"How hard do I beg?"

I said, "Time to dig out the magnetism."

Dear V, this is Lt. Milo Sturgis the lead investigator on Benicia Cairn's disappearance. I'd greatly appreciate if you did get in touch. No problem keeping you anonymous. Email me as above or phone this number at the desk of the Los Angeles Police Department Westside Division.

He re-read and sent. Sat back and pulled out a panatela and passed it between his hands. "Now I wait. You know what's gonna happen."

I said, "A bit of slag then hopefully gold."

"A bit? I should be so lucky."

◆

During the next hour, twelve responses popped up under Benni Cairn's photo. Inquiries about other L.A. missings plus bellicose gripes about the department's insensitivity and incompetence.

Nothing initially from V.

I'd used the time to rewrite some preliminary custody findings, finding the claustrophobic space surprisingly good for concentration.

Shortly after one p.m., he said, "You finished?"

"You've been waiting?"

"Just for a few, you were looking professorial. Hungry? Even if you aren't, let's go."

We left and walked toward the war room.

I said, "Leftover sandwiches?"

"You kidding? Rank has its privileges."

The weather had turned encouraging. Cloudless blue sky, seventy-two degrees, dry but not Saharan.

"This," he said, "is why we live here. You up for a walk—scratch that, stupid question."

We headed north to Santa Monica Boulevard, crossed, continued several blocks to Wilshire, walked west and covered an additional half mile. Moving briskly, my runner's lungs and his long stride a good partnership.

The place he chose was Italian. Pleasant and clean but nothing out of the ordinary and no shortage of Italian close to the station. I figured he needed to stretch physically and mentally.

We ordered spaghetti carbonara and iced tea and took a cop's corner booth: facing the door with a clear view of anyone who entered but far enough to provide extra seconds for reacting to the unexpected. I've only seen him make use of that once: overpowering a ranting, knife-wielding psychotic who'd burst into his favorite Indian place. Milo had responded with astonishing swiftness, tackling, restraining, cuffing, calling for backup. Resuming his meal when the uniforms took the invader away as if nothing had happened.

He tucked a napkin under his collar. The Godfather look. "Anything you want to add to what I told the troops?"

"Nope."

"Way I see it, best case is Dorothy's living with Galoway. Second best is she isn't but he shows himself, Moe or Alicia can pull off a good tail and he leads us to her. The problem is, so what? No physical evidence or witnesses to justify a phone triangulation or a call subpoena, and these two don't sound like the confessing sort."

I thought about that. Was still considering when the food came.

Instead of picking up his fork, he stared at me.

I said, "The only thing I can think of is try to set them against each other."

"If they even talk to me."

"Galoway will. He's a show-off."

"All the years they've been together and he'll just fold?"

"Personality problems are on your side."

"Meaning?"

"Selfish, callous, cruel," I said. "Loyalty might not stand up to that."

We ate quickly and I had coffee while Milo demolished a square of spumoni. We were a block north of Santa Monica when his phone alerted.

He stopped, read, slapped a hand on his chest.

"You okay?"

"Having an arrhythmia of joy."

New email from Victoriaquandt@spacemail.com:

Lt. Sturgis, we can talk briefly. I live in Santa Monica Canyon but don't want to be public about it. I looked up your station and you're not that close and I don't want to be in a station anyway so can you think of a good alternative?

Dear Ms. Quandt, thanks so much for your quick response. Would somewhere in Pacific Palisades work for you? In the hills or on the beach? For the beach, not sure of Sunday parking but I can give you a police sticker that you can use. Best, Milo Sturgis, Lieutenant Detective.

Dear Lt. Detective Sturgis, I used to live in the Palisades but have been gone for many years so no one will remember me so fine. A block from my old house is Rambla Azul Terrace, you can GPS it. There's a roundabout kind of a little park. If no one's there we can use it. It'll take me thirty to forty-five minutes unless there's craziness on the road. Vicki.

Today?

Unless that's a problem. This will probably be a waste of time and I want to get it over with.

No problem at all. See you soon.

Racewalk back to the station. My runner's lungs, fine. His stride not long enough to prevent red-faced panting by the time we arrived. We walked straight to the parking lot and got into the Impala.

He said, "GPS the address, *por favor*," and sped toward the gate. Drumming the wheel, tapping the floor with his left foot. Barely containing himself as the yardarm lifted and he jetted through.

◆

Rambla Azul Terrace was a teardrop drooping from a narrow street at the north end of Temescal Canyon. The park Vicki Quandt had cited was a circle of grass maybe thirty feet in diameter. Four old sycamores at the periphery provided intermittent shade. No benches.

Pacific Palisades has its share of ocean-view estates. The surrounding houses here were pleasant and unremarkable and well maintained. Hard to pin down a style—maybe generic seventies. Somewhere else, a tract for junior managers. Here, four to five million a pop.

Like Du Galoway's block, unrestricted parking, a side benefit of obscurity.

One car was parked at the south end of the circle: newish silver Bentley Flying Spur sedan.

As we pulled up behind, a woman got out holding a rolled-up blanket. Fifties, tan and athletically built, showing off sinew and skin tone with a clinging turquoise tank top over clinging black yoga pants. Long, thick ash-blond hair, oversized white-framed sunglasses, grape-colored Gucci purse on a gold chain.

Even at a distance, the cheekbones.

She waved her fingers and walked to the circle of grass toting the blanket under one arm. Unfurling and spreading, she folded gracefully and sat.

Milo said, "Again, thanks, Ms. Quandt. This is Alex Delaware." We settled facing her.

"Vicki." With the oversized shades, no way to read her eyes. The rest of her face was immobile. "What would you like to know about Benicia?"

"How you met her, your relationship. Anything you think would be helpful."

"Helpful finding her? All this time you can't think she's just been hiding?"

"Whatever her status, it would help her family to know."

Off came the glasses. Large black eyes studied him. "At the station they said you were a homicide detective."

"I am."

"So maybe you should be upfront."

"Good point," said Milo. "Didn't mean to be evasive."

"Benicia's probably dead."

"We really don't know but that's a logical assumption."

"Who do you think killed her?"

"Again, ma'am, the facts aren't in place."

"But you suspect someone."

"Names have come up."

Vicki Quandt waited.

Milo said, "We've heard she lived at a mansion on Mulholland Drive and that another woman died there."

"The harem," she said. "I suppose now's when I'm supposed to expose my reckless youth."

"Whatever you're comfortable with, ma'am."

"Vicki. My housekeeper forgets not to call me ma'am. I find it irritating."

"Sorry—"

"Oh, stop apologizing, I'm just being difficult." Eye-dance to the right. "This is tough. Bringing up the bad old days."

She raised her arms, stretched, arced them from side to side, closed her eyes, opened them, put the shades back on.

"Okay, the short version. I grew up in Delano, boozehound parents, no future, hated my life and thought I was actress material because everyone told me I was. I ran away and bused to L.A., lived in a youth hostel with disgusting pigs, went looking for an acting school and found out what they cost. So I started saving by waiting tables at a pancake house during the day and cleaning offices at night, moved up to a rented room in an old lady's house that smelled of boiled chicken.

The offices were in bank buildings on Hollywood Boulevard. One night when I was leaving, a guy came up to me and said I was gorgeous, he wanted to photograph me, he'd pay me plus I'd get copies to keep. I figured it was sleazy and said no thanks. He said he could understand my reluctance, no pressure, here's my card. Then life started to drag. Working like a dog, dodging creeps, no serious money. So one day I walked by the address on the card and it was a private house, looked well kept. Which means nothing but I was desperate. So I called."

She'd promised the short version, had talked nonstop.

Most people have stories they want to tell.

"I got a phone message on his end which for some reason I interpreted as he was legit. So I left my name and number, he took a couple of days to call back, and we arranged a weekend session. Middle of the day, I was scared as hell but the future didn't look so bright. He answered the door, very nice, soft-spoken, obviously gay. Which was also encouraging, at least he wasn't going to grope me. Plus we weren't alone, he had a maid dusting and mopping, an old Chinese lady, she offered me tea." Crooked smile. "Green tea. Never had that before. So I had some and then we went into the studio and he took a bunch of headshots and close-ups and had me change into different dresses and casual wear. Everything by the book. Then he said if I wanted he could do a bikini shot but up to me. I said I've worn bikinis but no way is it going beyond that. He said he had no intention, my figure was perfect for a swimsuit, and we could go to a public beach to do the shoot."

She ran her hands over a flat abdomen, trailed them down to sleek thighs. "Genetic luck. My mother was a drunk but she never gained weight. Anyway, we did the bikini shots in Santa Monica and true to his word he sent me copies of every pose and they looked great. Artistic. Then he asked if he could submit them for print ads and if they ran, he'd pay me ten percent. I said sure and a month later I got a check for eighty bucks which was a lot more than I was getting from tips. And then a few weeks later, another check, hundred and three, then hundred and ten. So now I'm loving this guy, I was basically getting residuals. So a few weeks after that when he called and told me about a club where beautiful young girls got in free, my trust level was up. And he was upfront. Told me it was basically a singles bar for older rich men, they were the paying customers and girls got in free. I said, Sounds iffy. He said, Trust me, nothing freaky goes on, they just like having pretty things giving them aesthetic companionship. What today you'd call arm candy. Then came the topper, the club was in Beverly Hills on Rodeo Drive, which to me was like an invitation to fly to Paris. But I still said no."

Milo said, "The Azalea."

She gave him a sharp look. "You know about it?"

He reached into a side pocket and produced the photo of Des Barres and the three blondes.

Vicki Quandt's manicured hand flew to her mouth. "Omigod—so you already knew about *me*."

"No, ma'am. We knew about these three faces but not much *about* them." Smooth lie; emotional fly-casting: bob the lure while remaining out of view. "Now that we've met you, we know a bit more."

"Really? I've changed."

I said, "Not that much."

Off came the shades. Black eyes bored into mine. "Are you kissing up?"

"Nope, just telling the truth."

"Well," she said, flipping her hair, "I do try to be fit." She studied the photo. "Unbelievable. Where did you *get* this?"

"An old book," said Milo. "Out of print and no other copies that we've spotted."

"An old book . . . never knew you guys worked that hard. So you know that's Benicia."

"We also know the man is Anton Des Barres."

"Ah, Tony," she said. "Interesting piece of work."

More scrutiny of the image. "So how did I end up there after I turned Sterling—the photographer—down? Simple. Desperation. I was down and out, hadn't received a check in a while, and then I got hit with a disgusting flu that lasted three weeks and cost me both my jobs. So I called him and said I'd be willing to give it a try. He said he was going himself in a couple of days, would be happy to take me. He picked me up in this massive copper-colored Lincoln Continental—it had portholes, like a ship—and we *glided* to Beverly Hills. I was still feeling punk but did my darndest to look my best. Red dress I'd bought on sale, pink stilettos, my hair was up. I'm sure I looked horrid but Sterling told me I was ravishing. Then a few blocks from the place he told me he'd escort me in but he'd be going upstairs because that was a men's-only section. He looked embarrassed. Poor guy, he couldn't bring himself to say it."

I said, "He'd go upstairs and you'd be on your own."

"He didn't phrase it that way, he just told me to value myself and act accordingly. That night I met a lovely brain surgeon who'd just lost his wife to cancer and wanted to hold hands. Free dinner, free drinks, and when I got home—Sterling came downstairs and we left together— there were three hundred-dollar bills in my purse that I'd never spotted going in there."

Off went the glasses, again. "If that sounds like prostitution, it wasn't. He talked, I listened, he felt young and desirable again, and I guess with his surgeon's skills he was able to slip me those bills."

She laughed. "Thank God he wasn't an amateur pickpocket. Anyway, I went home to my pathetic little room feeling healthier and wealthier than I ever felt before. So the next week, when Sterling called, I said sure. And that's when I met Tony."

She poked the black dress. "Sterling bought this for me, said you can't go wrong with an LBD. He also gave me a wig. I was blond but apparently not blond enough and he wanted a certain style."

I said, "His preference or Tony's?"

"Obviously Tony's, because look at the three of us. It's basically a uniform."

"Did Sterling furnish their wigs?"

"I have no idea. They already knew Tony, were living in his house. Benicia called it a palace. Said he was a really nice guy, put girls up in luxury and didn't ask anything in return."

Third inspection of the photo. "Wow, this is a blast from the past. Do you know who the other girl is?"

"Dorothy Swoboda," said Milo. "She's who we're looking into."

"I knew her as Dot. Grumpy Dot . . . so why the interest in Benicia?"

"Cold case, we look for any connecting threads."

"You got the photo and went online and found her," said Victoria Quandt.

Not asking the obvious question: Is someone looking for me? But maybe not obvious; Bella Owen hadn't posted about a long-lost cousin, she'd responded to Milo's general description.

No reason to mention Owen. Time for focus.

He said, "That's exactly what happened, Vicki, and we got a response from a distant relative of hers. But they don't know much of anything. So when you got in touch, it was a big deal. Again, thanks."

Vicki Quandt recrossed her legs without the rest of her budging. "More connecting threads?"

Milo nodded.

"So you're assuming Dot was the murder victim."

"That was the official conclusion."

"Yes, it was," said Quandt. Shapely, glossed lips formed the knowing smile of an older, more sophisticated sibling. *Oh, you stupid kids.*

Milo said, "You had your doubts?"

"I got the heck out of that place two days after the car blew up. You do know about the car."

"Tony Des Barres's Cadillac."

"Big land yacht," she said. "With Dot inside. Allegedly, as you guys say on TV." She focused on Swoboda's face, frowned, returned the photo.

I said, "You've always had your doubts."

Victoria Quandt looked up at tree branches. Patches of sky glinted between the boughs like aquamarines. Her body tensed. She did some slow breathing but didn't look more relaxed.

"Okay, I'll tell you what I think if you swear to keep me out of it. If you come back and bug me, I'll shut you out completely."

"Fair enough," said Milo.

"Doesn't matter if it is or it isn't, that's the deal. You need to understand: I have an amazing life. Married to the same wonderful man for thirty-three years—and yes, I met him at The Azalea. Two kids, both married, one's a lawyer, the other's an entrepreneur. Two amazing grandkids, I want for nothing. So I probably shouldn't even have agreed to meet you. Why upset the apple cart?"

Milo and I stayed silent.

She tried more breathing. Shook her head. "I have more than doubts about the official version. I have logic. Because Dot had been mad at Benicia for weeks before it happened, don't ask me why, I have no idea. They seemed to be an item—not sexually—more like a package deal, showed up together, hung out together. But not as equal partners, Dot called the shots and Benicia obeyed like a slave. It wasn't hard to dominate Benni—that's what we called her. She was meek, submissive, and, trust me, *no* genius. Curvy, cute as a button, peaches-and-cream complexion, little Kewpie doll voice but dull as they come and not an inch of spine to her. Dot took advantage of it, boy did she. Basically she used Benicia as a handmaiden, and Benicia never complained, not a peep."

I said, "Did using her include anything sexual?"

"Not that I saw or heard," said Victoria Quandt.

"I was thinking between Benni and Des Barres."

"A threesome? Ha." Several beats. "Okay, you probably won't believe what I'm going to tell you but it's true. Nothing sexual went on in that place. *Nothing.* That was what was so weird about it. Here's Tony, richer than God, he's got an amazing place, tons of great-looking girls parading around in bikinis and skimpies and no one got touched. We all talked about it, traded notes, same story. All the poor guy wanted was to sit around and listen to classical music, read, work on his business books or whatever, while one of us kept him company and got him snacks and fixed him cocktails. *Lots* of cocktails, he was a Sazerac guy. It was this complicated deal—soaking sugar cubes with a special bitters and crushing it, three ounces of rye, then absinthe—which was illegal back then—rubbed into the glass and you'd pour it out. He could put away three, four, even five of those and by the end of a session, he'd be out. Maybe that's why he lost interest in doing the deed, too much alcohol. Whatever the reason, that's the way it was."

She laughed. "Like a convent but the nuns were hot."

I said, "Why do you think it wasn't Dot who perished in that car?"

"Because Benni disappeared the same time she did. Not hours later, the same time."

"They both left in the Caddy."

"Can't prove it but I'd bet on it. Like I said, they were a twosome. Pete and repeat. It's not like Benni could just wrap her stuff in a sheet and walk away. And no way Benni could've set something up like that. She didn't even know how to drive. Could barely read and write— really, guys, mentally challenged."

I said, "Dot, on the other hand."

"Cold bitch. But smart. Unfriendly to everyone except Tony. And Benni, when she needed something from her. But even then it was like she was playing at being nice. Not the sexy swagger she took with Tony—she *was* good looking, dynamite figure, I'll grant her that. Really knew how to use what she had."

"Coming across alluring even though Tony wasn't into sex."

"Who knows?" said Vicki Quandt. "Maybe with her he was. She did seem to be his favorite, he spent more time with her than anyone else."

Milo said, "Did that cause jealousy?"

"Are you kidding? We were thrilled. Getting dolled up in a blond wig to go into Tony's bedroom, mix Sazeracs, and listen to Beethoven or whatever wasn't scary but it sure was boring. And so was the rest of the day. Sitting around doing nothing? Some of the girls complained *they* weren't getting any you-know-what. That's why in general, they didn't stick around. I mean I was already climbing the walls and I'd only been there three weeks. You'd think you were entering the Garden of Eden, the place was gorgeous. But it ended up just what I said, a weird convent. Except with no vows and no obligations other than to be adorable."

I said, "Tony called it the harem?"

"No, we did. Tony was a decent guy, shy, we heard he'd lost two wives, was really broken up over the second, she fell off a horse."

"Did he talk about that?"

"Never. The extent of conversation with Tony was you'd come in, he'd be in a robe on his bed and say, 'You look lovely, my dear. Could you please lower the volume and fashion me a Sazerac.' *Fashion.* He was totally old school. Wore *ascots.*"

I said, "Did Dot and Benni ever talk about a baby?"

"Whose?"

"Either of theirs."

"There was one?" she said. "No, it was never mentioned. A baby, wow—obviously before they got there. You have no idea whose?"

Milo said, "We're far from knowing anything. So how long had Dot and Benni been there when you arrived?"

"No idea. Probably more than just a few weeks. They did seem comfortable. Especially Dot. She could act like she owned the place. And she'd taken the Caddy before. Several times."

"For what?"

"No idea," she said. "It wasn't like Tony's prized possession. He had a slew of other vehicles—this little James Bond Aston Martin, another English sports car, a . . . Bristol, I think. *Plus* another Caddy—an Eldorado convertible. *And* an old Chevy that the girls used when they wanted to go into town. Bumpy ride."

"But Dot got the Caddy."

"Hmm," she said. "Now that I think about, she was the only one. At least that I saw."

"It was common for the girls to drive back and forth."

"If they wanted to. It wasn't prison," said Vicki Quandt. "Till it started to feel like prison. Same old same old, you're constantly looking at yourself in the mirror to make sure you look your cutest. Not just for Tony, for the other girls. Maybe even more for them."

"Competitive atmosphere."

"Not out in the open. More of . . . that was just the way it felt. We were thrown together, a bunch of girls who happened to look good and couldn't figure out how they'd ended up there. You want to hear something strange? We started getting our periods at the same time."

Menstrual synchrony was a known fact, for animals as well as humans. I said, "Wow."

"Bizarre," she said. "Looking back, the whole experience was bizarre. One of those things you do when you're young then forget about and move on. I was fortunate to meet Sy a week after I left. And yes, I've told him everything. Because there's nothing to hide. Would you believe that when I met him I was a virgin?"

Milo and I nodded.

"You're bobbing like you do believe but you probably don't. Whatever you want to think, it's true. And that's all I have to say and that's the end of this, bye, guys."

Springing up quickly, she pointed to the blanket and, when we stood, rolled it up hastily and hurried to her Bentley.

The car started up with a purr but jerked and made an unpleasant noise as she fumbled with the transmission.

Then a smooth exit as two hundred grand of steel and chrome vanished.

W e shifted to a dim spot under the branches of the largest sycamore.

Milo said, "All Des Barres wanted was a little company. You believe her?"

"You think she was sanitizing her own role."

"Exactly, a nun, not a houri."

I said, "Bikini nun."

He laughed.

I said, "I do believe her. Why would she come forward in the first place? Only reason I can see is a moral compass. Benni's disappearance has been on her mind for thirty-six years. Enough for her to periodically check out the missing persons sites. Your post solidified her suspicions and activated her. And everything she told us—Sterling Lawrence, The Azalea, her own background—matches what we already know."

"Suspicions," he said.

"Same as ours. Dorothy shot Benni and passed herself off as the victim. Now the motive's solidified: just what we thought, wanting to make her escape."

"The aspiring Queen Bee looks for a new hive."

"Maybe because killing Arlette didn't have the desired results. Des Barres adored Arlette and unfortunately for Dorothy, he was also a passive alcoholic unwilling to take it to the next level. So she made her plan and lifted some goodies from his safe. Vicki just told us she'd been angry at Benni for a couple of weeks and Benni never fought back. She was used to being Dorothy's doormat since the two of them left Texas. Dorothy told her they were off on another adventure with an upgrade—the Caddy. A mile down Mulholland, middle of the night, Dorothy pulls over, shoots Benni without warning, and stages a fake accident. Clean break from Des Barres and Barker."

He said, "And Ellie. Can't wait to tell her about her heritage . . . it does firm up the picture. Unfortunately, it's not evidence."

"I've been thinking," I said.

"That can be scary or encouraging."

"Your plan to have the troops simulate tradespeople makes sense. But you could also try to talk to actual tradespeople: meter reader, postal carrier, maybe FedEx, UPS, any delivery service that comes by regularly. If Dorothy's living there, someone might've seen her, maybe knows what name she's using. The question is, could they be trusted to keep their mouths shut."

"My dominant personality wouldn't be enough to ensure that, huh?"

"Person-to-person, sure. Toss in the lure of the internet?" I shrugged.

He said, "Let me think about it," and drove away.

A block later: "Annoying."

"What is?"

"Why the hell didn't I think of it myself?"

39

I'd booked one of the new custody evaluations from nine a.m. to two p.m. on Monday, the second from three thirty to six thirty. In-person sessions with children and parents, phone contact with attorneys, schoolteachers, and, in one case, an ex-nanny. With appointments running flush, no time to check messages. I switched my phone off and stashed it in a desk drawer.

The upside of custody work is the chance to blunt the effects of divorce on kids. The downside is anyone who's not a kid is assumed to be lying. But the morning went well: children who'd entered the arena well adjusted, parents sincere about keeping that going. Not hard to see the connection. Most important, the lawyers each side had hired were retrievers not attack dogs.

Feeling energized, I broke for coffee and a sandwich at two fifteen, retrieved an earful of messages from my service, none from Milo. The last was a thinly veiled threat from a pit-bull lawyer representing the husband in the afternoon case. "Hope you're careful in your wording, Doctor. We examine everything with a *fine*-tooth comb."

Callbacks to the few people who merited a response and a chat with the judge in the afternoon case stretched the time to two forty-five.

Blanche woke from her nap, waddled in, and looked up at me with soft, beseeching eyes. I took her for an exploration out front, where a pine forest shades the property. Apart from the rare skittish raccoon or possum, a nice place for her to browse and snuffle and do her business. Back inside, I filled her water bowl, had just added some shredded mozzarella to her food when my cell chirped.

My designation *Big Guy* on the screen above Milo's private number. "What's up?"

"Any new thoughts?"

"Sorry, no."

"Shame," he said. "It's been the typical yawn fest, surveillance-wise. What we've learned so far is Galoway's a homebody. One sighting: Moe spotted him at eleven while doing a pass in a phony plumber truck. Asshole opened the door in his bathrobe, yawned, looked out, stretched, closed it. The only ride in his driveway is the Isuzu. Unless the Jag's in the shop, it's probably in his garage. Which is a double, so maybe her vehicle's also there. If she's got one. If she lives there. *If* she's real. I'm starting to think we're dealing with a phantom."

I said, "Galoway took the time and effort to misdirect us. That says there's someone worth protecting."

"There you go, restoring reality. Alicia's coming on in an hour, fixed her up with a van, cleaning service stick-on and dark windows. In the end, I decided not to take Arredondo up on her magazine ploy. Turns out she's three months out of the academy and her dad's a Rampart Division lieutenant. Instead, I've got her riding with Alicia. No postal carrier has showed up, yet, the plan is to chat if it can be done out of eyeshot of the house and the vibe feels right. I called FedEx and UPS and there's no regular driver who services the block. I asked about the delivery history and got the runaround—client privacy, get a subpoena. Which is pretty lame considering they leave packages out in the open."

"How're Ellie and Deirdre doing?"

"The odd couple? I just called Boudreaux and he's out with them at the zoo."

"That's some image," I said.

"Ain't it, though. How's your day going?"

"Great."

"Really? That happens?"

The afternoon evaluation was the other side of the coin. Not shocking considering the message from the husband's mouthpiece, whom the judge termed a "bottom-feeding asshole."

Adrenaline jet-fueled me and by the time I finished my notes it was seven fifteen and fatigue had finally made a welcome appearance.

Sounds from the kitchen half an hour ago meant Robin's workday had ended and she was fixing something. When I showed myself, she said, "Poor baby, dealing with jerks all day?"

"Half the day."

"Charge them extra—stress pay. Will this help?"

Pointing to a bowl of pasta with meat sauce. Noodles of all shapes and sizes, no reason to get fussy when you know how to cook.

I said, "Definitely. This too." Tapping the bottle of Sangiovese she'd uncorked.

We ate and drank.

I said, "You're the perfect woman."

She said, "Still hungry? I say you are."

By eight thirty, we were in bed, by nine thirty, in our robes, pondside, finishing off the wine. The water gurgled, the fish seltzered the surface, Blanche alternated between growly snores and high-pitched dog-dream bleats.

Robin said, "Dreaming. Wonder what she sees."

"Probably food."

"She and Milo could be roommates."

"He did okay sitting for her when we went to Denver."

"If you don't count the pound she gained." She rested her head on my shoulder. "We work too hard."

"Agreed."

"I keep adding obligations and so do you. It's not for the money, we don't overspend and last I checked we were doing fine. So how come?"

"Want me to answer like a shrink or a person?"

"Let's try person."

"Okay," I said. "I have no idea."

"Fine. Shrink."

"Not a clue."

Just before ten p.m., we returned to the bedroom, watched an episode of *Foyle's War*, and turned in, holding hands, playing footsie, slowing our breathing.

Robin said, "We really *should* try for more leisure, hon."

"Let's," I said. "We'll do some planning in the morning."

She kissed me. "'Night."

"'Night."

A minute later, the phone rang. I ignored it.

Silence, then a retry.

Robin said, "That sounds like it could be something."

"It'll keep."

"Maybe but you'll wonder and have trouble conking out."

"It's probably robotic junk, I'll be fine."

"If you say so."

Seconds later: another retry.

I got out of bed.

40

Milo's voice was tight. "Just about to give up on you. Something happened. No time to get into details, if you want to see it, come over."

"Where?"

"Hollywood. Not far from Ellie's."

"She okay?"

"Yeah—" Voices in the background. A siren. "Here's the address, gotta go."

At ten fifty I pulled to the curb and parked in a red zone on Western Avenue just north of Franklin. A uniform came forward shaking his head and looking pugnacious. I used my I.D. to get past him, did the same for an equally skeptical cop guarding a side street just below the climb to Los Feliz Boulevard.

The leafy lanes of Los Feliz were yards to the north. This bumpy strip was crowded with shabby apartments. Skimpy street lighting, like on a lot of L.A. streets where the residents lack political currency.

Most of the illumination came from four blinking cruisers, a crime scene van with its rear door ajar, and the portable streetlamps the techs position once they've scoped out a scene and established the angles.

One pole was still being adjusted. Several techs played with their phones. The numbered yellow plastic right-angles used to mark evidence dotted the asphalt like corn fallen off an oversized cob. Those, the cops on the scene can do. The highest number I spotted was *12*. Lots of bullets.

Beyond the white tech van sat a dark one, smaller. *Happy Maids Cleaning* vinyl on the side. Another set of wheels beyond that, impossible to identify because the van was taller and all I could see was the hazy outline of tires.

I continued slowly, inspecting the ground. To the left of the dark van were oily spots on the asphalt. Black where the light had missed, ruby where it hit.

Milo appeared from somewhere, unlit cigar in his mouth. He dropped it into a pocket of an exhausted tweed sport coat. His shirt was wrinkled, his tie loose.

"You decided to come. When you didn't answer, I figured you might be sleeping."

That hadn't stopped him from making three attempts.

I said, "What's going on?"

"Alicia and Arredondo decided to do a nighttime drive-by of Galoway's street. Up till then, he hadn't shown himself since the pajama thing. At nine fifteen he came out fully dressed, got in the Isuzu, and backed out. Alicia notified me and said she wanted to follow. She's good with tails so I okayed it but told her to be careful with the rookie. Galoway got on the 101, the same maniac driving style we saw. At the 5 South, he swung three lanes abruptly to transfer, got off at Los Feliz, which put Alicia on high alert."

"Ellie's house."

"That was her assumption. She'd been leaving four cars between her and Galoway, closed it to three, then two. Then the driver in front of her made a lane change and she was right behind. Not ideal, but why would he suspect anything?"

I said nothing.

He exhaled. "Exactly, best-laid plans. Alicia's expecting Galoway to turn into Ellie's neighborhood, instead, he keeps going and swings in here. Alicia played it by the book, making sure his taillights were a good block ahead before she followed. All of a sudden, Galoway's brake lights go on and he's *roaring* straight back at her, going thirty, forty per. Alicia thought she was gonna get pulverized, tries to back away, can't do it in time. Galoway's heading right at her but instead of crashing, he screeches to a stop, jumps out, and runs up to Alicia's window. Tinted glass, he can't see, that doesn't stop him from producing a gun and aiming it. We're talking seconds since they entered the street, Alicia goes for her sidearm but it's snapped into her holster, she keeps trying and ducks as low as she can, hoping to avoid a direct headshot."

He sucked in air, rubbed his face.

I said, "Trapped. Oh, God."

"Woulda been an oh God but the rookie jumped out on the passenger side with her service weapon and shot Galoway nine times."

"Oh, my."

"Didn't give the kid enough credit," he said. "Unfortunately, she's gonna find herself in an officer-involved situation."

"Sounds totally justified."

"Since when does truth have anything to do with it? I'm hoping her dad's well thought of. Anyway, Galoway's done for, crypt wagon just took him away. I had an ambulance cart Alicia and Arredondo to Hollywood Pres for evaluation. They claimed they were okay but I said observe them for shock. At the least, playing the sympathy card could help with the shooting board. You weren't involved I'd ask you to certify them traumatized."

Talking had shortened his breath. His eyes looked unfocused as his right hand rose to the left side of his chest and stayed there.

I said, "You okay?"

"Peachy. Funny thing is, I'd decided to take it easy tonight because Rick was off-shift. We made some spaghetti, had the wine uncorked, then I get the call."

I laughed.

He said, "What the hell is funny?"

"Synchronicity."

I explained about Robin and my dinner. Normally, he'd be amused by that kind of thing.

He said, "Weird . . . at least you got to eat . . . what I'm having trouble with is why would Galoway risk trying for Ellie? Unless you can see another reason he'd drive all the way here from the Valley with two guns—there was also a rifle with a nightscope on the backseat. And *then* after figuring out he was being tailed, he pulls that cowboy move on Alicia?"

I said, "No other reason. He was either after a kill or just planned to scare her off with some shooting. The motive's the same as when he bumped Phil Seeger off his bike."

"Clearing the deck."

"Hammer–nail."

"It's crazy-risky, Alex. And for what? Screwing up an investigation that as far as he knows is going nowhere?"

"Lying to you about everything is crazy-risky," I said. "We can't eliminate the possibility that Galoway got off on it. Or he looked up your solve rate and got nervous. Told Dorothy—imagine their pillow talk—and she dispensed him on an errand."

"Dispatched by the evil queen . . . if that's the case we could be talking kill your own daughter. Or not . . . okay, putting that aside, how did Galoway get Ellie's address? That I *know* I never told him." A beat. "You remember different?"

"You never mentioned it."

"Then how, Alex?"

I thought about that. He lit up his cigar, blew a single gelatinous smoke ring, and began tapping his foot.

I said, "If he was a real estate agent, he could have contacts with rental agencies."

"Real estate's cutthroat," he said. "The enemy calls you're gonna cough up client info?"

"With enough motivation, you are."

"A bribe."

"Something more subtle. Like telling the agency Ellie had contacted him wanting to rent a bigger, more expensive place, if they agreed to help terminate the lease, he'd split commission. He tosses out big dollars, the other agent says let's talk. Once it got to that point, it would've been easy enough get the address. He needed it for verification. Or better yet, he had another client for *that* property and they could pull off a two-fer."

"Devious," he said. "I'm always impressed by how quickly you don that hat."

"Nothing like a few years in academia," I said. "So what's next?"

"Besides handling this mess? Obviously the main thing is getting into Galoway's house but the one night-owl judge I can count on is on vacation. I'll start again in the morning, could have a warrant by noon."

I said, "How about a victim's warrant? Quicker."

"Too risky with an officer-involved and the possibility that Dorothy's in there. Once I get paper, I need to figure out the best approach. That I could use you for. C'mon, I'll walk you."

Cool night but he'd paled and began sweating.

At the Seville, he said, "Guess you really didn't need to come, apologize to Robin for me."

"Glad I'm here," I said.

"Why?"

"More time to think about tomorrow."

He craned his neck, as if working out a kink. Cherries in the jaw. Racing carotid pulse.

I said, "Take it easy, friend."

"What?"

"You look a little wound up."

"Par for the course. No prob, it always dissipates."

"Okay."

"I'll be *fine,* Alex. Know why?"

I shook my head.

"This feels like a turning point."

A white Benz coupe screeched to within inches of the Seville's rear bumper. The driver's door swung open, a woman got out, saw Milo, and stomped forward, arms swinging.

Forties, short blond hair, a chin that led the way.

She wore a knee-length plum-colored coat over a matching dress and shoes, pearls, heels, full makeup. None of that detracted from the image of an infantry soldier marching to battle.

She stopped within inches of Milo's face. All that was missing was the tire squeal.

"What happened?"

Milo said, "Dr. Delaware, this is Deputy Chief Martz."

Martz looked at me as if I was a flu-carrier who'd broken quarantine. Back to Milo. "What. Happened."

He told her.

She said, "When you decided to take the case on you were supposed to be careful."

"I decided?"

"Who else?" said Martz. "This is the era of modern policing. No one forces anything on anyone."

"Except for the criminals," said Milo. "Oh, yeah, not always that, either."

"Cut the humor, irrelevant," said Martz. "Any way you cut it, to-night's outing was at your behest. And now we've got a DB."

"Who was a prime suspect in multiple murders."

"So you say. I'm expecting backup and verification of any fact you purport to be in possession of. Understood?"

"And comprehended."

Martz said, "I'm not talking your usual level of data memorialization. Details."

"Got it."

She looked up the street. "What a disaster. Does Ernie Arredondo know about his daughter?"

"Not from me," said Milo.

"You didn't think to inform him?"

"My concern has been preserving the scene and making sure Officer Arredondo and Detective Bogomil are okay psychologically."

Martz turned to me. "You came here to certify their mental health?"

I said, "I'm sure Hollywood Pres will do a thorough job. I know the psych staff, if you'd like I can liaison."

"Why *are* you here, Doctor?"

"I've been consulted on the case."

"Have you . . . well, we'll go over all of this once the full data set is in place. In the meantime, Lieutenant, the officer-involved team will be assigned and you'll both be cooperating with them fully."

Milo said, "Dr. Delaware wasn't involved."

"Really?" said Martz. "He just said he's your consultant—uh-uh, no more debate." Martz looked at the dark van. "Nine shots? Really?"

"He was armed and dangerous. No sense taking chances."

"Of someone surviving."

"He was out to kill both of them."

"So you say."

"So I do," said Milo. "Far as I'm concerned she's a hero. Do you see it differently?"

Martz's chin edged farther into his personal space. "I'm not here to answer questions. I was at a bar association dinner, had to leave just before my husband's speech."

"So sorry."

No sarcasm in his tone; a feat of acting. Martz studied his face, anyway, hoping to pick out a shred of insolence. Failing, she settled for a withering glance.

Milo said, "What was the speech about?"

"Eminent domain, Ismail's a specialist in land-use law—what's the *difference*." Another glance at the scene. "Nine bullets."

"How many times have you had to actively fire your weapon, ma'am?"

Martz blinked hard, rocked back on her heels. "No times. Not that it's your concern but I view that as a testament to good judgment."

"I'm sure it is, ma'am, but it's tough to be in someone else's shoes unless . . ."

"So," she said, "when can we hope to wrap up your little adventure with Ms. Barker?"

"We're getting there."

"How much longer?"

"Hopefully a few days."

"Hopefully," said Martz. "Empty word."

She turned, sped back to her car, backed up, roared away.

Milo grinned. He'd stopped sweating. Inert jaw. The racing neck pulse was gone.

I said, "The power of fantasy."

"What does that mean?"

"You're thinking about all sorts of unpleasant ends for her and it's kicked in your parasympathetic nervous system and mellowed you out."

"*Moi?* Engaging in cruel and vindictive and bloodthirsty thoughts? Perish the notion." He chuckled. Welcome sound.

As I got in the Seville, he said, "Be nice, though, if some other perishing would go down."

41

Milo had expected a warrant by noon Tuesday but the day passed without my hearing from him. Probably tied up with the shooting board.

When radio silence stretched to Wednesday, I began to wonder if complications had set in. Bureaucracy's like untreated cancer: Once it takes hold, it ravages.

I searched for media coverage of Du Galoway's shooting, was surprised to find nothing but a page-32 squib in the *Times* about "the death of a gun-wielding felony suspect."

The department pulling up the drawbridge. That said nothing about how it would treat Jen Arredondo, Alicia, and Milo.

Wednesday at nine forty p.m., he finally called.

"I was starting to wonder."

"Yeah, it's been interesting. As in a pain. Fortunately, once we got through the bullshit, the people assigned to evaluate turned out to be sane and the kid's connections didn't hurt."

"Dad's well thought of."

"Big-time. Top of that, Mom's a dispatcher at Hollenbeck, there's a brother in Burbank PD, and an uncle is a robbery D in Saugus."

I said, "Police aristocracy."

He said, "Nothing like blue blood when you need a transfusion. What also helped was I told them about Galoway's lies, what he was suspected of. Nothing pisses off good cops more than bad cops. So no doubt about the kid being ruled justified. I managed to put in for the phone subpoena, no guarantee when the data dump will come in. In terms of the warrant for the house, you know how it is: time-limited so I waited until today to apply, just got it. Moe's been checking out Galoway's street, no movement, I'm starting to think she's somewhere else. The goal is to enter the house Friday morning, planning session's tomorrow. Nine work for you?"

"Tied up until ten, I can be there by twenty after."

"Then that's when we'll start."

The whiteboards were filled with the same shots of Galoway's street and house. Galoway's DMV photo had been removed.

In the first row was an empty chair for me, flanked by Milo, Reed, and Sean Binchy returned from vacation and sporting a sunburn.

A couple of years ago I'd saved Sean's life. Terrifying near-miss as a psychopath tried to toss him off a skyscraper. Tough thing to come to grips with but for the most part, we'd dealt. Still, sometimes he avoided eye contact.

This morning he waved and smiled. Let's hear it for sand and surf.

In the second row sat six uniformed officers from the SWAT team, the lieutenant a six-four, brush-cut, heavy-jawed stereotype named Mackleroy Bain.

Milo had prepped them. They stood, nodded, shook my hand.

Bain was the last to greet me, smiling warmly and offering just enough pressure in his grip to imply power. "*Really* great to meet you, Dr. Delaware. You taught my wife in grad school."

Soft, boyish voice.

I said, "Who's that?"

"Laurie Trabuco."

"Great student."

"She had wonderful things to say about your seminar," said Bain. "Got her Ph.D. last year, works for the V.A. Long Beach doing PTSD therapy."

"That's terrific. Give her my best."

"Will do, Doctor."

Milo said, "Good morning to all concerned," and people hustled to their seats. "Alex, let's start with your thoughts about approach."

I said, "Is your warrant no-knock?"

"Yup."

"Then I think you should take advantage. Go in with force and clear the place as quickly as possible."

Milo eyed Bain and the SWAT leader got up and pointed to an aerial of the house. "We lucked out on layout, not much square footage and only two doors, front and back. A fenced-in yard and a driveway gate means limited space for escape. I'm figuring an officer stationed outside on each door and four of us doing the entry in pairs."

Milo said, "You planning on getting all military?"

Bain smiled. "We'll bring the toys—gas, concussion grenades—but I really don't see using them unless you think she'll be waiting for us with a firearm."

Milo looked at me.

I said, "Suicide by cop? Nothing in her background suggests it but there are always surprises. She could be extremely edgy because Galoway left on Monday night and still hasn't returned. On top of that, there was a brief mention in yesterday's paper about an armed suspect going down and if she put it together, my guess would be she'd plan her escape rather than seek confrontation. But no guarantees."

Bain frowned. "Thought there was a media blackout."

Milo said, "So did I, amigo. I called Public Affairs and got a run-around. At least there were no details but sure, she could've figured it out."

Bain said, "What else can you say about her psychological makeup, Doctor?"

I said, "Criminally antisocial from a young age. At fifteen she hooked up with a felon in his thirties and they embarked on a multi-state crime spree. Burglary, robbery, kidnapping, several murders. He was executed, she got reform school, was released no later than at twenty-one. She changed her identity and nothing surfaces over the next few years other than a job in Texas. Which she left to come to L.A., traveling with and dominating a younger woman named Benicia Cairn. The working assumption is she stole money from the man they lived with and shot Cairn in order to fake her own death. At some point after that, she hooked up with Galoway and they've been to-gether since."

"Long-term relationship," said Bain. "She finds out he's dead at our hands, that's a big deal."

"It could be but she's emotionally shallow and self-serving to the point of abandoning a daughter she claimed as her own and as of Mon-day night, trying to have her murdered or at least terrorized. Also, other than murdering Cairn, she's been more director than actor. And the crimes we know about are well planned not impulsive. If I had to bet, I'd say trying to escape was more likely than confrontation. But if cor-nered, she could be volatile."

"The spree when she was a kid sounds pretty impulsive," said Bain.

"Fifteen isn't sixty. Her partner claimed it was all him, she was just along for the ride. But it was a long ride, so who knows?"

Milo said, "The fact that she hasn't been spotted over the last few days makes me wonder if she's already escaped."

"Even with you guys watching?"

Moe Reed said, "The layout made it too risky to do a sit-around, all we managed were intermittent drive-bys. Then, after the shooting, I had to go solo so she had plenty of opportunity to split."

Bain said, "Bottom line: mean but not stupid and crazy."

Milo said, "Mean as they come."

I said, "In any event, the psychology doesn't matter."

All eyes on me.

"Play it safe," I said. "Go in fast and with force."

42

Friday, four forty-five a.m. Inky morning, the chill blunted by the electrochemical heat of hearts racing in anticipation.

A black tactical van blocked the street, its arrival a near-silent coast. Moments later Bain and his crew had been egested, all six officers vanishing into the darkness.

Milo, Reed, Binchy, and I waited five houses south. Reed had brought Milo in his work-ride, a gray Dodge Charger; Binchy showed up seconds later in his, a maroon Chevy Caprice.

My orders were per usual: Don't get in the way. The Seville was parked well behind the police wheels.

Dark windows checkered Galoway's place and every other house on the block. If any of the neighbors had noticed the van, they weren't complaining.

Another ten minutes of nothing to make sure. Just as Bain was about to go in, headlights flashed a block north and swelled as they neared.

Bain and two of his officers ran toward the intrusion waving small-beam flashlights. The car stopped. Bain jogged to the driver's window and said something. The headlights died. Another officer got in the van and angled it so the car could pass.

Black Audi sedan, frightened-looking woman at the wheel. She drove for a block before switching her lights on.

Bain came over. "Poor thing, heading to LAX for a flight to Denver to see her daughter. Okay, no sense waiting for another disruption, we're a go."

Silent approach, dual entry punctuated by a single thump in front, followed by a second at the rear door, muted by distance.

Several more minutes of silence, then the front door opened and Mac Bain ambled out.

"All clear."

Milo said, "Shit, she's not there."

"I didn't say that."

The door opened to a small, neatly kept living room. The smell began at the mouth of a narrow hallway that paralleled the kitchen.

Bedroom to the left, another on the right, bathroom in between.

The smell became a stench that directed us to the left-hand bedroom. Another well-kept space if you didn't count what was on the bed.

What remained of a woman lay under heavy, deep-green covers. Odd color for a duvet; I'd seen it before on a string of beads. Maggots wriggled at the upper hem where cloth ended and flesh began.

Gray-brown flesh, matte finish. Sunken cheeks, sunken eyes, a tumble of red hair on the pillow. White at the roots where dye had dissipated.

Reed gagged and ran out. Binchy uttered a silent prayer and stayed.

Milo covered his nose and mouth with a fresh handkerchief. I used my sleeve. It didn't help much.

Everyone knew the rules: The scene belonged to the cops, the body to the coroner. No one would lift the covers and look for wounds—crimson parabolas and slits resulting from stabbing; the crushing and corrosion effected by blunt trauma; the obscenely precise mini-craters caused when bullets raped soft tissue.

What police euphemize as "defects."

Mackleroy Bain had already made the call to the crypt. A coroner's investigator would be here within half an hour to inspect and pronounce and identify.

No need for an official I.D. We knew who this was.

Pill bottles on her nightstand. Fighting back nausea, I got close enough to read.

Most recently, she'd called herself Martha Dee Ensler.

The prescribing physician was someone I knew. Edwin Rothsberger, a first-rate neurologist, practice in Encino. Years ago, Ed had rotated through Western Peds, one of the best interns from the med school where I taught. He'd been great with the kids and like a lot of sensitive trainees had decided to spend his career treating adults.

I examined the labels. Hyoscine hydrobromide for excess salivation, diazepam for anxiety, quinine bisulfate for cramps, dantrolene for muscle stiffness.

Symptomatic treatment, nothing curative. The palliative stage of a neuromuscular disease.

I took in the rest of the room. Stack of adult diapers in the corner, a hoist partially disassembled. Cartons of bottled water, bottles of liquid diet.

Whatever Du Galoway's sins, he'd taken good care of the woman he loved, had been tripped up by overstepping as he strove to cover up her sins.

I'm no pathologist but dull skin, and eyes depressed so deeply they resembled miniature lunar craters, said plenty and I was willing to bet on cause and manner of death.

Immobilized by disease, she'd spent four helpless days in bed without food, water, or attention.

Cause, dehydration.

Manner, accidental.

Milo said, "What the hell am I gonna tell Ellie?"

I said, "Nothing."

43

B asia Lopatinski worked heroically but it still took three weeks.

"And that," she informed us, "is a record."

During that time, Milo had paid a visit to Ellie and informed her that the case was going well but he had nothing definitive to report. Yet.

She didn't object but she did call him two days later wondering if anything had changed, and four days after that. He'd managed to put her off with ambiguous optimism and a request to be patient. She hung up sounding irritated. If she'd chosen at that point to complain to Martz or Andy Bauer or one of the political contacts, it could've gotten complicated.

She didn't.

No threats to Deirdre Seeger remained so she could've moved back to her house. But kept ignorant by Milo, she remained in Ellie Barker's rented house and the two of them, accompanied by an equally uninformed Mel Boudreaux, filled their days with outings.

Huntington Gardens, the Arboretum, Descanso Gardens, a three-day excursion to San Diego where they took in the wild animal park and SeaWorld. Then a detour on the trip back for a night at the Disneyland Hotel and an all-day pass at the park.

VIP pass, Ellie's money allowing them to jump lines. Deirdre revealed a lust for the Matterhorn and rode it three times.

Boudreaux: "Man, I felt like puking just watching her."

On the twenty-first day, at eleven a.m., everything was in place and Milo phoned Ellie.

Sounding subdued, she said, "We're at the art museum." She lowered her voice: "Special exhibit on contemporary German paintings. Deirdre says it's kindergarten garbage."

He laughed. "Everyone's a critic. When can we meet?"

"Meet as in . . ."

"Solving your case."

"Oh . . . can Deirdre be included?"

"Not a good idea."

"I'm kind of used to her and she's got nowhere to go."

"We could talk at the station," said Milo. "Whatever suits you."

"This really is it, Lieutenant?"

"It is."

"Am I going to be happy?"

"You'll know the facts."

"That sounds ominous."

"I wouldn't call it that."

"What would you call it?"

"Ellie, it's best we sit down and talk."

"Is it?" A beat. "Fine, let's do it at the house. I'll tell Mel to take Deirdre to lunch and I'll Uber back. If that's safe."

"It is."

"So this really is *it*."

◆

We were parked in front of the house on Curley Court when a dented white Celica in need of a muffler dropped Ellie off. VIP tickets for Deirdre, but no Uber Black for the woman with the credit card.

That fit with her understated approach to clothes and demeanor. Nothing wrong with that but I wondered if she held back due to feelings of unworthiness. I've seen that in patients with complicated childhoods. What I think of as Eternal Lent.

Sometimes they let you ease them out of it, sometimes not.

She said nothing to us and hurried to her front door. We caught up.

"Hi, Ellie."

She mumbled something well short of a greeting. Her hands shook hard enough to rattle her keys and she missed the keyhole a couple of times before unlocking the door. Deactivating the alarm, she stood in the entry hall with a frozen look on her face.

Milo guided her by the elbow to the same living room chair she'd occupied the first time we met. Her hands continued to vibrate. She rounded her back, laced her fingers, and pressed her knees together as if warding off assault.

Milo said, "It really *isn't* ominous, Ellie."

"Let's just get on with it, I'm ready to jump out of my skin."

Milo placed his attaché case on the sofa between us.

Ellie said, "What's in there, terrible police stuff?"

Milo ignored the question. "Okay, let's get into it. The woman you've believed was your mother, wasn't. DNA proves it. Her given name wasn't Dorothy Swoboda, it was Martha Maude Hopple. Swoboda was a stolen identity, one of several used by Martha Hopple. She was a career criminal."

Ellie's mouth dropped open. "Oh, God. So you have no idea who my mother was."

"We do. *Her* name was Benicia Cairn and she grew up near Tyler,

Texas, where she met Martha Hopple. She was barely twenty, Hopple was twenty-four. The two of them left town and traveled for a couple of years before they settled in L.A. You were born during that time and we figure Hopple convinced your mom she wasn't equipped to take care of a baby."

"You figure," she said.

"We can't know for sure, Ellie, but everything we know about Benicia tells us she was a caring person."

"Oh, *really*. A *caring* person just gives up her baby."

Not an unexpected question. Milo didn't need to cue me.

I said, "Martha Hopple was a manipulative psychopath and Benicia Cairn was young, impressionable, and, from what we've learned, extremely submissive."

"Submissive? So what? She just allows a criminal to take me and dump me on Dad? Are you going to tell me he was a criminal, too?"

"No, he was a victim. One of the many men Martha Hopple seduced and took money from."

And pushed off a cliff years later when she showed up unexpectedly and he wouldn't pony up more cash.

Ellie shuddered. "She sounds like a monster."

I said, "She was but your mother wasn't. From everything we've learned, she was kind."

"Not so kind she didn't abandon her baby."

"We believe she had regrets."

"You *believe*."

Milo said, "Her regrets may be the reason—and this is going to be another tough thing to hear, Ellie—Martha murdered her."

"Murdered . . . the body in the car?"

We nodded.

She clutched her belly. "God, I think I'm going to be sick . . . why would she *do* that? Kill a friend. What was the *point*?"

"Martha had just robbed the man she was living with and wanted to disappear and assume a new identity. She used Benicia to fake her own death."

"How can you know that?" she said. "And, wait a minute, how can you even *presume* to know this Benicia was my mother? You told me the body was burned up. And there was no DNA back then, anyway. You're just guessing, aren't you?"

"We're not," said Milo. "I matched your DNA to one of Benicia's relatives. She's your second cousin, her mom and Benicia were sisters. She still lives in Texas. You've got an extended family there."

"*My* DNA? I never gave you a sample!"

"Remember the time I came to see you a couple of weeks ago?"

"Yes, when you told me nothing." She set her lips grimly.

"True," said Milo. "I was putting you off until we had proof, not just theory. While you were in the bathroom, I went into the kitchen and swiped a juice glass you'd just used. We had your sample tested at the same time we express-shipped a DNA kit to your relative—her name is Nancy. She expressed it right back to us and we zipped everything to a private lab. The results came in yesterday and they're clear. Benicia Cairn was your mother."

She slumped. "This is insane . . . what about my *father*?"

"That's still unknown, Ellie. To us and to your Texas family. They were never aware Benni—that was her nickname—was pregnant. It may be the reason she left with Martha Hopple, or she could've met a man shortly after, we just don't know. In terms of paternity, there are ancestral geneticists who work with the big public DNA sites and sometimes they can get results. We figured this was enough information for you to take in."

"My Texas family . . . my real mom . . ." Bitter laugh. "Guess I'm no worse off, same story, murdered. Hello, world, I'm still an orphan."

She flashed a sick smile that crumpled. Let out a sob, beat her knees with her fists and wailed.

Out came Milo's fresh hankie.

Ellie Barker shook her head violently, then she snatched it and pressed it to her eyes. It took a while for her to catch her breath. "This is . . . I don't even know how to define it, my world is fucking *spinning*!"

"It's a lot to deal with," said Milo. "Wish there could've been a storybook ending. But your goal was to solve the mystery and that's been accomplished."

She lowered the handkerchief. Glared. "Congratulations on your big old detective *success*. For me it's not exactly a celebra . . . oh, crap, I'm taking my messed-up life out on you and all you've done is exactly what I asked. And frankly, what I thought was impossible. So you did an amazing job. Even though . . . I'm *sorry*, I should be *grateful*. But I'm feeling totally out of control. It's not like I had expectations of sugar plum fairies. You took on the challenge, came through, and I have no right to be anything but grateful. And I'll get there, I promise. It's just . . ."

"It's okay," I said. "How could you not be disoriented?"

She stared at me. Tottered to her feet, walked around the coffee table to Milo, bowed and kissed his cheek. Looking over at me, she laughed. "All this time, you haven't gotten half a gold star from me. Sorry for that, too. It's not your fault I had some crap shrinks."

Dry lips brushed my cheek lightly. She returned to her chair and sat with both feet on the floor. "Should I contact her—Nancy? Does she *want* me to contact her?"

I said, "She sure does. A lot of what we learned came from her responding to a post on a missing persons site. She and the rest of your family's wondered for decades what happened to Benni."

"My family," she said. "Alien concept." A hand poked her breast. "Hey, Lone Star folk, here's your mystery baby."

A few moments passed. "Benni. Cute name . . . you guys aren't lying to me, are you? About her being a good person."

"A good person and an innocent victim," I said.

"So the bitch *ruined* her," she said with sudden savagery. "You want to know something? This is starting to make me feel better. About *her*. How I've always felt about her in the back of my head and couldn't admit. That photo of her and Dad. The look on her face, so hard. Now I know it was worse than that, it was cruelty. It *always* bothered me. Feeling *off* about her. I figured it was resentment because she abandoned me. That's what the other shrinks said. Now I know I had an inner sense. That my judgment's not as messed up as I thought."

I nodded. "Good instincts, Ellie."

"We're not just talking cruel," she said. "We're talking evil. An evil, horrible, amoral slut just like Dad told me that time . . . okay, enough, I don't want to waste precious breath on her."

She stopped. "Oh, no. Is she alive?"

Milo said, "No, and she reached a very unpleasant end."

"Such as?"

"She was terminally ill and starved to death, alone and abandoned."

"Well that's pretty unpleasant," she said. "When and where?"

"No need to get into details, Ellie. Like you said, wasted breath."

I slid a sheet from the thin stack on the couch and handed it to her. The Azalea photo, everything cropped but an enlargement of Benni Cairn's smiling face.

"This is her?" she said, sniffing. "She's *pretty* . . . so young . . . kind of pure-looking . . . her eyes look soft. Yes, I can see the vulnerability . . . look at that smile. She thinks she's got a future."

Rush of tears. Another study of the image.

"I don't see a resemblance . . . maybe I look like my father. You think there's a good chance I can locate him?"

Milo said, "No way to know but if you're interested, it's worth a try."

"Why not, it's come this far," she said. "Okay, can you get me one of those ancestral geneticists? I don't want to make the wrong decision like I did with those slicksters who wasted my money."

I handed her another piece of paper. "This is a referral from a pathologist at the coroner's office who's been extremely helpful. She's worked with him before and says he's first-rate."

She said, "William Wendt, Ph.D., genetic counseling and forensic geneaology . . . impressive sounding . . . I guess I could learn something I didn't want to know but it's better than wondering. May I keep the photo?"

"Of course." I passed a third sheet over. "Here's the match between your DNA and Nancy's."

"Strattine . . . the link is maternal. What's my real name?"

"Holcroft."

"Eleanor Holcroft." She smiled. "Sounds like something out of Jane Austen . . . I think I'll stick with Barker, Dad was my everything . . . maybe I'll use Holcroft as my middle name."

She burst out laughing. "Maybe I'll dye my hair blond and start talking in a Texas accent and learn to ride horses and eat a lot of barbecued brisket."

I said, "A world of opportunities."

"Yeah, this could get interesting." Full smile. "Thanks *so* much. Both of you. As long as we're being earth-shattering is there *anything* else?"

Nothing you need to know.

Milo said, "Nope, that's it, Ellie. It's been good working on this."

"Really? Even though you were pushed into it?"

"Like the doctor just said, opportunities. I like learning and you've been a peach."

"What a *lovely* thing to say."

She stood, this time gracefully. Shook her hair loose and straightened her spine and held her head high. "You're a peach, too—both of you are."

She laughed. "We're a regular fruit basket. Let me see you out."

◆

At the door, Milo said, "Oh, yeah, Deirdre's safe returning to her house."

"I'll bear that in mind," said Ellie Barker. "Right now we've got some trips scheduled. Santa Barbara, tomorrow, then we'll keep going to San Simeon. With Mel. Even though we are safe, he's a great driver and he's got a beautiful singing voice."

"Sounds like a plan."

"A good plan," she said. "Places I wanted to see, anyway."

We hadn't told her about the box.

    Finding it hadn't resulted from ace detective work during the search of the house Du Galoway and Martha Dee Ensler had shared for twelve years. It filled the middle drawer of the nightstand where her medications sat.

Fifteen inches long, a foot wide, hardwood covered in genuine crocodile hide dyed green. A bilious shade slightly lighter than the bedcovers and the serpentine necklace.

Milo said, "Reptiles. No comment, too easy."

The interior of the box was lined in amber velvet. On the inside lid was the incised gold stamp of a luxury goods store in Brentwood, long defunct.

The contents, like the house, neat and organized.

Chronological order.

At the bottom was the Lolita article from *Dark Detective* protected by a plastic bag. On top of that, two similarly shielded articles from *The Jefferson Parish Times* in Metairie, Louisiana, and the *Houston Chronicle,* both brief accounts of homicides stingy on details.

Sharing space in that bag were a set of silver and turquoise cuff links and a half-used matchbook from The C'mon Inn, Bissonnet Street, Houston.

The victims were middle-aged men, a salesman and an accountant, found shot to death in their cars on the outskirts of town. The first crime had occurred when Martha Ensler was nineteen, the second two years later, making her release from the girl's reformatory at eighteen likely.

"Getting right back in practice," said Milo.

The next trophy was the *Pasadena Star-News* article on Arlette Des Barres's fatal horse tumble. Here, someone had annotated in the margin. A single word in red ink, the kind of ragged cursive that results from inadequate schooling.

Neeeiiigh!!!!

After that: the L.A. *Times* account of a dead woman burned in a car on Mulholland Drive.

Sizzle!!!!

Nothing for five years and three months, when the *San Francisco Chronicle* reported the shooting deaths of a well-to-do couple, both physicians, in the book-lined den of their Orinda, California, house. A trove of jewelry and art, taken along with cash and bearer bonds from a safe.

The victims had been last seen having cocktails in the company of another "well-dressed, middle-aged" couple, as yet unidentified.

Milo did follow up on that one. Still open.

Four years and eleven months after that was a clipping on a strikingly similar couple-slaughter in Portland, Oregon. This time the victims were two male antiques dealers who'd been together for twenty-eight years.

Unsolved.

Another stretch of quiet, then a plastic bag containing a key, later identified as operating Phil Seeger's motorcycle. No one at the scene of Seeger's "accident" had wondered about the lack of such.

A year after that: a hefty gold chain in a smaller bag. Engraved on the underside of the clasp: *Tony.*

Repeat burglary of Anton Des Barres's jewelry. Maybe an anniversary gift to herself, or she'd somehow learned he was terminally ill and vulnerable. She'd somehow gained entry to the mansion—my guess was an old key she'd taken during the first heist—and made a smooth exit.

Let the devil in . . .

Unlike the others, she'd left Des Barres alive. Maybe because he was ill and in pain and she enjoyed the notion of him suffering.

I wondered if she'd stood in the doorway to his bedroom and, despite that, considered it.

The final souvenir was the coverage of Dr. Stanley Barker's fatal tumble. Written in the margin: *Miser. Said no. Paid the ultimate price.*

Milo said, "Nothing about a poisoned dog."

I said, "A throwaway not worth commemorating."

"What a pair. I'll call Orinda and Portland, after all this time they probably won't be able to do anything about it but what the hell. The rest, no need to get into it. Right?"

I said, "Agreed but there are a few other calls that need to be made."

"To who?"

I told him.

He said, "You mind doing it? I gotta deal with Jen Arredondo. Got a call last night from her dad. He's concerned because she says she's fine, refused the department shrink, and he thinks better to pay up now and avoid PTSD. If we can convince her, can you hook her up with someone? Even you if you feel like it."

"I'm too involved, we'll go the referral route."

"Fair enough. So you'll do the other calls?"

"No prob."

"What a pal—scratch that, no wiseassery, you were the main deal on this one. I mean it. And don't say aw shucks."

I said, "Buy me lunch."

"Like I wouldn't if you didn't ask."

I reached Vicki Quandt at her home in Santa Monica Canyon and told her we'd located a relative who was looking for her.

She said, "I figured that might happen. Who?"

"A woman named Bella Owen. She's local and was your—"

"No need to get into it," said Quandt. "It was a long time ago and like I told you, I've got my life."

I said, "Just wanted you to know."

"And I appreciate that—tell you what, text me her information and I'll see how I feel."

Call Number Two: Val Des Barres.

She said, "All ears," when I told her I had new information. The same kind of quivery inflection we'd heard from Ellie at the onset of the sit-down.

When I finished, she said, "What an utter monster. Thank God she didn't hurt Father . . . is Ellie okay? Learning all this. Should I reach out to her?"

"At this point, it's probably best to let her work it out."

"I do hope she's okay."

"It's looking positive, Val."

"I hope so . . . Father was innocent."

"He was."

"Though a bit of a rogue." She laughed.

No sense telling her about Anton Des Barres's tastes in female companionship. Her laughter was genuine. Wanting to think of him as a guy with flair.

"That he was, Val."

"He *loved* me," she said. "Whatever made him happy."

I reached Maxine Driver at her campus office.

She said, "Giving or taking?"

I said, "The former."

"Goody. Juicy stuff?"

"Oh, yeah. There are things you won't be able to use but there's plenty you can. I'm figuring two, three papers, minimum, who knows how many symposia."

"Awesome," she said. "To paraphrase the tykes."

About the Author

JONATHAN KELLERMAN is the #1 *New York Times* bestselling author of more than forty crime novels, including the Alex Delaware series, *The Butcher's Theater, Billy Straight, The Conspiracy Club, Twisted, True Detectives,* and *The Murderer's Daughter.* With his wife, bestselling novelist Faye Kellerman, he co-authored *Double Homicide* and *Capital Crimes.* With his son, bestselling novelist Jesse Kellerman, he co-authored *Half Moon Bay, A Measure of Darkness, Crime Scene, The Golem of Hollywood,* and *The Golem of Paris.* He is also the author of two children's books and numerous nonfiction works, including *Savage Spawn: Reflections on Violent Children* and *With Strings Attached: The Art and Beauty of Vintage Guitars.* He has won the Goldwyn, Edgar, and Anthony awards and the Lifetime Achievement Award from the American Psychological Association, and has been nominated for a Shamus Award. Jonathan and Faye Kellerman live in California and New Mexico.

jonathankellerman.com
Facebook.com/JonathanKellerman

About the Type

This book was set in Garamond, a typeface originally designed by the Parisian type cutter Claude Garamond (c. 1500–61). This version of Garamond was modeled on a 1592 specimen sheet from the Egenolff-Berner foundry, which was produced from types assumed to have been brought to Frankfurt by the punch cutter Jacques Sabon (c. 1520–80).

Claude Garamond's distinguished romans and italics first appeared in *Opera Ciceronis* in 1543–44. The Garamond types are clear, open, and elegant.